Charlie Sm  Adventures in India

Book 2 of the Charlie Smithers Collection

C W Lovatt

A Wild Wolf Publication

Published by Wild Wolf Publishing in 2015

Copyright © 2015 C W Lovatt

ISBN: 978-1-907954-41-2

Also available in e-book

www.wildwolfpublishing.com

Further works by the author

The Adventures of Charlie Smithers (2013)

Wild Wolf's Twisted Tails (2013)

Josiah Stubb: The Siege of Louisbourg (2014)

For Amber, always…

Acknowledgements

Heartfelt thanks go out to a close circle of friends and family for their unfailing support, Wild Wolf Publishing for being Wild Wolf Publishing, and of course, to you, Treasured Reader.

As always, I save my greatest regard for my dear friend, Amber Clark, for being there to help iron out the wrinkles.

Table of Contents

Preface

One of the more difficult parts of writing this novel was deciding which should be the correct spelling for many of the places and titles on the Indian subcontinent, but specifically with regard to Bhutan (Bhotan, Bootan), and its people (Bhuteau, Butea, Bhuteax, Bhutanese). The same goes for their mountain passes, or duars (dooars, dhuors, doors) and the barons, or penlos, (pilos, penlows) who controlled them. I must say that it would have helped a great deal if the British at the time had any idea themselves, but I doubt that most even knew where Bhutan was, let alone how to spell it. So, in the end, via a complicated procedure (hammer, paper, scissors, if you must know), I chose whichever variation I felt most comfortable with...which turned out to be several *different* variations throughout the course of writing the first draft. With that in mind, I would like to give a big shout out to the good folks at Microsoft Word for their 'find and replace' option. It saved me countless hours of painstaking labour, going through the manuscript to check the spelling of dozens of terms, used dozens upon dozens of times. Some of them are similar to the modern spelling, but by no means all, and that I did on purpose, in an attempt to give a sense of antiquity to match all those volumes that I read during the course of my research (most written a century and a half ago).

As for the research itself, while a historian might fall down laughing if I claimed that it was extensive, all things being relative, I will state that claim nonetheless. Historical fiction is nothing more than make believe, but its background should be hard fact, whenever the writer has the opportunity to make it so. Many of the events actually took place exactly as described, and many of this story's characters actually existed on Ashley Eden's long trek to Poonakha (Punaka, Phonaqa, and so on). Their personalities, however, was my gift to them, or perhaps it was their gift to me, as always seems to be the case. For I believe that something of them still lives on in those dusty old tomes: an essence of who they were. Doubtless, many will disagree with my interpretation of some of those who were more famous. I can only reply that this was how they spoke to me while I poured over book after book, seeking out the heart of the story, by endeavouring to read between the lines.

CWL

Glossary

Anna: a coin of small denomination

Ayah: nursemaid

Badmashes: villains

Bahadur: hero or champion

Bhang: cannabis

Bhisti: water carrier

Chaggle: a container for carrying water

Chota-peg: a half-sized drink, mainly whiskey, or whiskey and soda

Dalit: an untouchable, the lowest of all in the Hindu caste system. Outcast.

Dewan: the first minister to a royal head of state, roughly equivalent to a prime minister.

Dhoti: a traditional garment for men, resembling a long skirt.

Duar: (Bhuteau) a mountain pass.

Durbhar: a governing body

Feringhee: European

GG: Governor General

Gho: (Bhuteau) traditional men's garment, roughly resembling a kimono

HMG: Her (or His) Majesty's Government

Havildar: a noncommissioned officer in the Indian army, equivalent in rank to sergeant.

Houri: a beautiful woman

Howdah: a seat for one or more people, usually fitted with a canopy and railing, placed on the back of an elephant or camel.

Huzoor: My lord

Indaba: business; area of concern

Jawan: a soldier of any rank below a commissioned officer

Jingal: an over-sized musket, requiring two men to operate

Jungpen: (Bhuteau) governor of a minor territory

Maidan: a plain, or parade ground

Mahout: an elephant driver or keeper

Moonshee: literary assistant

Nabob: a person of wealth

Naik: a native noncommissioned officer, equivalent to a corporal

11

Nieboo: (Bhuteau) a minor governor of a fort, subservient to a Jungpen.

Penlo: (Bhuteau) a powerful landowner governing a large territory, roughly the equivalent of a medieval baron.

Poshteen: sheepskin coat

Pugharee: turban

Rupee: Indian currency

Sahib: sir

Sahib-log: the British

Sal: a tall hardwood tree, native to the dryer, more temperate climes of the Indian subcontinent.

Sepoy: native soldier

Shabash: bravo

Sirdar: Commander in chief of the Egyptian Army

Sowars: native cavalry troopers

Subadar: foreman, leader

Surata: the act of lovemaking.

Suttee: the burning of a widow on her husband's funeral pyre

Syce: a native groom or stable attendant

Tantra: a form of meditation that seeks to transcend the barriers between the holy and unholy by embracing, rather than denying, temptation.

Thuggee: a sect devoted to the goddess, Kali, who practiced roadside murder as a form of worship.

Vaisya: the second lowest of Hindu castes

Wallah: a person associated with a specific duty

Zinkaff: (Bhuteau) messenger

Chapter One

The *howdahs* float like majestic ships upon the sea of tall, swaying grass. Overhead, the leaves of the mangroves marble everything below in shadow, creating the impression of movement where there is none. I found my eyes darting nervously, here and there, again and again, as they follow up every false lead. My rifle is at port arms across my breast, my finger tense against the trigger guard. This is the perfect place to conceal a tiger.

At my side, Lord Brampton slings his own rifle carelessly over his shoulder as he gazes out at the world through his monocle, much as God Himself must have done on the seventh day. The comparison ended there, however, as I knew that milord was in one of his more dyspeptic moods, the unfortunate legacy of having most of his innards shot away during the Charge at Balaclava. This in turn filled me with unease. Experience has proven that, during such episodes, my master seldom kept his irritation to himself.

Hard on that thought, he suddenly snapped at the *mahout*, his whiskers bristling with rage, "Confound it, man! Can't you make this beast move any faster?" Behind us, you'll note, the beaters were already jogging to keep up. "I don't want to be about this all day!"

The *mahout* turned from where he was perched on the back of the elephant's neck, and grinned ingratiatingly, obviously not understanding a word. He cried, "Han, sahib!" gave a little bow, and we continued on exactly as before.

Milord's complexion darkened noticeably.

"Nothing but idlers and scoundrels!" he growled under his breath. "The whole bloody lot of 'em!"

The elephant muttered disgruntledly, and I found myself quietly soothing her with a surreptitious pat over the side of the *howdah*, but dared nothing further. For my own opinion notwithstanding, I preferred to maintain a discrete silence. This not being the best of times for reason.

Perhaps a half-mile off, deeper in the forest, the rest of the beaters could be heard slowly closing in. From our position, the sound that they made was barely audible – yet too audible for milord.

"All those blasted rascals! How's a man supposed to think over such a din!" He chewed at his moustaches and growled, "Can't imagine why Jimmy insisted on having them along in the first place!"

My master was referring to James Bruce, the Lord Elgin and Governor General, who had indeed insisted that we take beaters along when Lord Brampton had stopped to pay his respects upon our arrival in Calcutta, and mentioned his keen interest in bagging a tiger. The words may have been Elgin's, but I fancy that they were brought about by your humble-obedient.

You see, in my time I'd been gored and chewed and clawed and run off towering cliffs, and whatnot else, more often than enough when in attendance on any one of my lord's hunting expeditions, and was doing my utmost to prevent history repeating itself here in India. So, unbeknownst to my master, I had taken the precaution of popping around Government House a day earlier, to see the Viceroy's man (a redoubtable old Sikh with splendid whiskers and a boozer's nose) to put a word in his ear with regard to milord's regrettable history with firearms. The inclusion of a bottle of hock during the conversation rendered the old geezer most amenable to my request, so he placed a word in *his* master's ear, with the desired result. I won't go so far as to think it was my own skin that drove Lord Elgin to make such an effort, but rather I suspect he realized that it would never do to have anything untoward happen to my lord's noble person while he remained under his domain. Therefore reasoning that there was safety in numbers, the beaters were insisted upon, much to my master's chagrin.

Then, too, my effort might not have had anything to do with it at all. It may have been a case of Lord Elgin having remembered an earlier hunting expedition with my master, while visiting Brampton Manor in his youth, and that he still carried some birdshot in his lower back from when milord's fowling piece had accidentally discharged. It's not for me to plumb the

14

depths of a gentleman's thoughts, but this alternate theory gained further credence when, asked to accompany us on this present expedition, Sir James (claiming urgency of work) had begged off with such speed that you could not help but admire his dedication.

Food for idle contemplation, you'll agree, but with one eye on the grass, and the other nervously on the muzzle of my master's rifle, as he twisted irritably back and forth, scanning the ground with careless diligence, there was precious little time for that. It was never wise to let my thoughts stray whenever he had a finger even remotely close to a trigger.

With one hand rubbing his belly, Lord Brampton called across to the other *howdah* some distance to our left, "Look here, Ram Singh, are you quite sure that the fellow knows his business? I can't see anything for the life of me." This was followed by an angry growl from what was left of his bowels, as if they, too, were perturbed (which, no doubt, they were).

Lord Elgin may have regarded his own life too precious to hazard on an outing with my master, but the situation had demanded that his hospitality not seem lacking, so honour was preserved by volunteering to have his man accompany us in his stead. The old fellow didn't seem to mind one bit. Ignorance of his peril may have had something to do with it, I suppose, but I rather think that the constant gurgling from his flask throughout the day had considerably more.

Finding himself addressed, Ram staggered to his feet, hinging at the waist in what I suppose he thought was a bow. A watchful hand from the *howdah*'s other occupant prevented him from toppling over the side.

"Most assuredly, sahib! There are few who know better!"

The 'fellow' milord was referring to was the village headman – a silver-bearded old sober-sides – partnering Ram on the other elephant. Still with his hand grasped in the silken depths of Ram's multi-flowered robe, he now proceeded to jabber something in his lingo, going on at great length.

"What's that?" Lord Brampton winced, continuing to massage his torso. His stomach gave an even greater rumble, "What's the man saying, confound it!"

15

"He says there are many tigers here, Lord Brampton, sahib! Oh yes, very many tigers indeed!"

The headman jabbered some more.

"Big ones, he says."

My master retorted, "Well I don't see a thing! Not even a blessed monkey!" Suddenly he convulsed, his stomach clamouring like a clogged drain, and I heard him mutter through his teeth, "Damn all curry!"

I could now no longer refrain from giving voice to my concern: "Milord, I fear you're not well…"

"Silence, Smithers!" As I feared, Lord Brampton rounded his fury on me, his voice quivering with rage, "Who the hell d'you think you are?"

It must have done the trick, for – not to put too delicate a point on the matter – at that very moment my lord broke wind.

In truth there is no adequate word to describe the sound. Thunderous? A gun report? The discharge of a cannon? A veritable *broadside* of cannon? All lack accuracy, although it might give you some idea. Now I'm not saying that this was the cause of what happened next, but I'm not saying that it wasn't neither. All I'm saying is that a sequence of events happened immediately thereafter, and so sudden, it was over before anyone could properly react.

First, an immense tiger startled out of the grass directly below me.

That was quite a shock, I can tell you. One moment there was nothing, the next there was a glimpse of fierce yellow eyes as big as pie plates, and a yawning cavern filled with long, cruel fangs. He vented his fury on the elephant, sinking his claws into her flank with a bellowed roar. Taken by surprise, the elephant squealed in pain, rearing high on her haunches, coming precariously close to unbalancing the *howdah*. Acting on instinct, with my master's welfare my only concern, I dove forward, seeking to come to his aid. In the split-second before I got there, however, Lord Brampton convulsed, and somehow discharged his weapon. There was a terrific flash, followed by a searing pain coursing across my forehead, and before I knew it I was reeling over the side.

16

I landed with a thud, hard enough to drive the air from my lungs, with my rifle lying inches from my hand. Unfortunately I had not lost consciousness, for there are some things to which no man should ever have to bear witness. I mean, there I was, flat on my back, unable to move (literally) to save my life, with one of God's most fearsome creatures turning the focus of his vengeance from the elephant to myself.

I had said that his eyes were large, and so they were: huge discs of angry gold, set in a head impossibly massive, with a snarling mouth to match, and they were looking at *me*! I'm here to tell you that they lacked even an ounce of pity for my plight, and for some ridiculous reason I found myself wondering how often those eyes had been the last thing seen on this earth by some unfortunate creature or other. I decided that the number must be high. In fact, I was sure of it.

The moment could only have been an instant, but it seemed like an eternity, as I lay there, transfixed by those eyes. Even if I hadn't been winded I still could not have moved, so under their spell was I, and as 'ridiculous' seemed to be the order of the day, thus far, I found myself murmuring in awe, "How beautiful you are!" So help me I did. It's God's honest truth!

Then he was on me in a single bound, roaring fit to burst my eardrums…which, admittedly, was the least of my worries. One mighty paw smashed into my chest, driving out the rest of what little air still lingered in my lungs, and then those great eyes disappeared, and all I could see was that horrible, gaping mouth, absolutely overflowing with dagger-like teeth, descending to my face…

…and then, at the very moment I expected to feel those frightful carnivores crunch into my skull, the ponderous weight was lifted from my chest, to the accompaniment of an infuriated scream. In its place, I saw the elephant towering over me. Even from such a distance I could tell that the gleam in her eye was quite as angry as the tiger's but, thank the Lord, not directed at my person, but to where that great cat was scrambling to it's feet where she'd sent it sprawling. Just for a moment, the two monsters squared off at one another – the cat screaming his hatred and the elephant (one Radha Piyari) angrily trumpeting

17

her defiance. A moment later, and she was stepping delicately past my prone carcass toward the great cat. Then giving one final bellow, she charged, with my lord rattling around in the *howdah*, working feverishly to reload, and the *mahout* hanging on for dear life.

To his credit, the cat had the good sense not to challenge her, but left off all his caterwauling and slipped to the side. After which, presumably seeking a quieter haven, he bounded off…unfortunately straight at me. I had just enough time for a vision of that deadly nemesis growing impossibly huge, and then, with a leap, he was over me, just as there came the bark of a rifle, and a cloud of earth fountained an inch from my face. "Damn! Missed again!" Lord Brampton bellowed, and the tiger was gone through a bolthole the beaters had thought to make in the interest of survival; and just like that the episode was over, in less time than it took to relate it to you.

I lay there, blinking at the sun, scarcely able to convince myself that I'd survived. Then Ram Singh was on a knee by my side, thrusting the neck of his flask between my lips.

"Charlie, are you hurt?"

I tried to answer, but could only gargle brandy instead.

"God be praised you are alive!" cried the old duffer, wheezing fumes all over me. "It is a miracle, by Jove! Yes, most certainly, a miracle beyond a doubt!"

Then the village headman was there, too, fairly leaping about in his agitation, gabbling away like Billy-bedamned, and then finally there was my master, calling down from above:

"Smithers!" he snapped, gripping the sides of the *howdah* with whitened knuckles, "What the devil do you mean by it!"

"Sir?"

"Confound it, man! Falling over the side like that. Most ridiculous thing I've ever seen!"

"But My lord…"

"Clumsy, that's what it was! Clumsy and stupid!"

"Milord, if you would only let me…"

"What do you think this is, a walk in the park? Tiger hunting's a damned dangerous business!"

"But sir…!"

"Yes, damned dangerous enough without you playing about like a bloody fool!"

I was about to protest further, but realized that it was no use. My lord was not in the mood to listen. So I lapsed into silence, telling myself that I wasn't really as sullen as I felt.

It would seem, however, that his earlier, deafening release had eased the pressure, for when Lord Brampton eventually finished venting his spleen, he was so kind as to notice my distress. "What's that? Hurt are you? God's teeth, man, you'll have to be more careful! Scratched your head in the fall, too, I see."

Dazed, I put a hand to my forehead. When I brought it away my fingertips were smeared with blood, and I suddenly began to feel decidedly light-headed. I'd come that close to having my brains blown out in another one of my lord's chronic accidents. What, with having come face to face with the tiger and all, I'd quite forgotten about that part.

"Damn!" quoth Lord Brampton. "Day's hunting ruined!" Then relenting somewhat, he snapped at Ram, "Well don't just stand there, bandage him up, and don't be all day about it!"

So, with Ram Singh swathing my poor head in bandages (so many that I began to wonder if he was administering medical attention so much as trying to manufacture a turban to rival his own), and a sufficiency of time at hand, perhaps this is a good opportunity to introduce myself – or to some of you, introduce myself again.

Charlie Smithers is the name and personal attendant to my Lord Brampton (of the Yorkshire Bramptons, of course – with five lines in 'Debrett') is my occupation, and has been for as long as I can remember. Those of you who have read the previous volume of my memoirs will have already learned about my childhood, and how I was destined to become milord's man from the first day I drew breath.

It's a good life on the whole, I don't mind saying, although it has its moments, like the one I just described to you; I could do with fewer of those and no error! But being of service to my gentleman is a sacred duty, like my dear old dad used to say (a great one for duty was my dad) and there's no getting around it, neither. Gentlemen need looking after because, what with all their strange foibles and all, they're altogether unable to look after themselves. I know that might sound a bit barmy, but it's God's truth. Whatever goes on in my gentleman's mind, self-preservation ain't part or parcel, and you can take my word for it, too. Helpless as a babe in the woods, he is. Why, I should just shudder to think what would happen if I weren't around. 'Course some of you might recall we *were* separated for a while a few years back, while on safari in Africa, it was, and no harm done, but that was more good luck than good management, if you ask me.

Still, it has its ups and downs. It's not an easy life, as you may have gathered. You're bound to have your bad days along with the good, this being one of them. The thing is to put those days aside and just get on with it, 'cause if you don't Lord only knows what he'll get himself into next.

Knowing your duty can be a hard road, oftentimes – something my guv'nor warned me about, and never let me steer away from it neither. To him, duty was duty, and that was all there was to it. It can be a harsh taskmaster – perhaps the harshest there is – knowing what's expected of you, and even more, what you expect of yourself. Living up to that standard means that failure comes hard: like when I failed my master at Balaclava – that round of canister taking away most of his innards, and leaving me unscathed, but for a ball or two in my shoulder, and perhaps a few more in my leg.

The thing was that I *saw* that Russian gun being trained, and I *saw* where the round was bound to strike, too. I keep telling myself that I tried to come between my lord and the impending danger, and I did – but alas, not in time. What has tormented me ever since is *why*– why hadn't I been in time? Was it because it had all happened too fast, or had I been afraid, and hesitated? I know that you might think that placing myself in line with a round of canister may actually *require* some hesitation, but it was my duty to do so, don't you see? I knew what had to be done, but I failed. Out of that entire debacle – that gloriously stupid charge – was I the only one to hesitate? If there were others, I didn't see them. If they were afraid they never showed it, but died by the score facing their enemy. I had failed in my duty, and am alive to tell the tale. A prickly moral question you'll agree.

But all that's in the past, thank God. No use dwelling.

I believe I've been of good service since then. As I alluded to earlier there was that time in Africa: it was no fault of mine that we had become separated, but the fact that my master considers himself to be a deadeye marksman, contrary to the fact that, time after time, he has proven otherwise. That he sought to end that deplorable record by drawing a typically inaccurate bead on an ill-tempered rhinoceros is the real reason we became separated. It's all there in my earlier volume, about whispers of a curse with regard to the Brampton's unfortunate affiliation with musketry, and the unadorned walls of the gunroom at Brampton Manor to back it up. Take that into account with my lord's grim (and misguided) determination that his abilities were otherwise, and you find us here in India today, on the fifteenth day of July, in the Year of Our Lord, 1863.

For once I had made my way back to England from the bowels of Africa, returning to my master's side (and having discovered the source of the Nile in the process), it was inevitable that Lord Brampton's restless spirit assert itself once more, and it was only a matter of time before we were off again to seek adventure. To be clear, though, adventure was of my lord's seeking, not my own. Given a choice, I was all for the quiet life at home, having learned the hard way that bold undertakings did not guarantee a happy ending, and that went double for whenever my master was in the vicinity.

Not that I had any say in the matter, of course. The next thing you know we were on the train to Newcastle, from whence we boarded a P&O steamer, *Carnatic*, bound for Alexandria, a place I had left in somewhat less style only a few years earlier.

Memories of my many adventures in Africa were strong in my mind even before setting out, and they stayed with me during the entire voyage. They grew stronger as we passed through the Strait of Gibraltar, with the Dark Continent so tantalizingly close, and docking in Alexandria, with its familiar sights, sounds and smells, only served to heighten them further. Here I had laboured at the very dock we were now berthing, shivering with malaria, and a good two stone lighter than what was good for me, sick at heart for those doe-like eyes and that exquisite, laughing face. Her memory never left, but stayed with me over the monotonous clacking of the railcar wheels, as we journeyed to Cairo, and then on to the Red Sea Port of Suez. No camel train for us this time, you'll note, but the real thing.

The great canal, begun the year of my return to England, was by now nearly half complete. Although all we saw of it was at Suez, there were still labourers in their untold thousands, poor devils, toiling away while we looked on, sweltering in our solar toppers. There was only a moment for me to wish them all a silent good fortune before it was time to take our leave.

The second leg of the journey, from Suez to Calcutta, was taken in the comfort of an Indiaman. My memories of Africa were palpable when we rounded the Horn, and I could lean on the rail in the evening, staring out at the shore, and far, far beyond – to where only my imagination could see – to *Ukerewe*, the Great Water, to the burned-out ashes of a hut, mingled with those of the woman I had loved, and those of the little one – our little one – beside her. Memories so strong that they vied with the present as to which were real. Had I once been that person? Had those idyllic moments ever existed? They existed in me now, and so, too, did that old familiar ache that, in my naivety, I had heretofore thought healed.

At last we debouched onto the Gulf of Aden and the Arabian Sea, and as I said my farewells, amidst the imagined laughter of a thousand tiny little bells, we left Africa in our wake.

The sights and sounds of India are like no other place in the world, but it was the smell that I noticed first, still two days out from port – every spice on earth mingled with something that I knew all too well: the rot of jungle. This from the great Sundarbans Forest, situated on the vast river delta, formed where the Ganges flows into the Bay of Bengal, over ten thousand square miles of it, in fact. For, upon being told our destination, I lost no time in looking up Bengal in my lord's Encyclopaedia Britannica, on the concept that being forewarned is forearmed, and gleaned as much of the place as I could beforehand.

22

As my master had telegraphed Lord Elgin while we were still in Suez, informing him of our impending arrival, the Viceroy's personal barge was alongside as soon as our ship had dropped anchor in Calcutta's harbour, and that famous old reprobate, that I would come to know as Ram Singh, was bellowing up at us through his superb whiskers, welcoming us to India in the name of the Raj, and lost no time in setting us up at the Auckland hotel.

The Auckland, I must say, was absolutely first class, complete with electric lighting no less, and a kitchen that was second to none. As much as I would have been inclined to stay longer, however, alas, it was not to be. For less than a week later, accompanied by a suitable entourage, we were ushered out of the city to bag milord's tiger, with what I thought was unseemly haste, and the rest, as they say, is history.

Now, with my ministering angel tucking the end of the bandage into a fold, the *mahout* was examining Radah's flank where the tiger's claws had struck, gently murmuring, "*Shabash*, Radha Piyari!*" praising her courage ('*Piyari*' meaning 'love' or 'darling' in the local lingo, and no creature ever deserved it more). Radha, herself, grumbled irritably (making a sound quite similar to my lord's bowels) while slightly favouring her hind leg. Ram spoke to the fellow, and was answered in some length.

Eventually he was able to turn to me and say, "Rest easy, Charlie Smithers, her wounds will heal in due course."

"What's that?" I felt my face redden guiltily, "I don't know who you're referring to."

If Ram Singh was smiling I was unable to see it through his whiskers, but his eyes were twinkling when he said, "Why your elephant, of course!"

Although relieved to hear the news, I was unwilling to show it, as it seemed unmanly. I replied, "The elephant? And why should I care one way or another?" I was reluctant to concede that I had any affection for the beast, even if she had saved my life, as I felt that it wasn't the English thing to do.

However if Ram Singh doubted my lack of concern, he did not show it, but spoke a few words to our *mahout* and received another rather lengthy reply.

"He says that you saved the elephant from grave injury, perhaps even saved her life, when you dove off the *howdah* to do battle with the tiger, with nothing but your bare hands."

The *mahout* let out another stream, but before Ram could interpret for him, he turned to me and grinned, "*Shabash bahadur, sahib!*" '*Shabash*' being roughly equivalent to the English '*bravo*', and '*bahadur*' to '*hero*' or '*champion*'.

The claim was so preposterous that I was at a loss for words. Surely the man didn't think that I had leapt to the ground with any such purpose in mind, and said as much to Ram. The old duffer smiled, not without kindness. "It is what he thinks, and that is what is important. He may be a simple fellow, but the elephant is not. She will bring you much good fortune." There was just the barest hesitation, "Especially as she fancies you."

Well, he had me there, for even I could see that the old girl had taken a shine to me for whatever reason. Why, back at the camp, prior to riding out, I had been studying her (well, she was an elephant, after all, and you don't see many of those in Yorkshire) and wandered in too close. Perhaps it was the way she was looking back at me with eyes that did not so much as glitter, but laugh outright, or the way she seemed to be playfully swaying from side to side with suggested merriment. Whatever the reason, before I knew what was happening, she'd reached out with her trunk and wrapped me up so tight I couldn't move a muscle! Curious, it had never occurred to me to cry out in alarm; there was just something in me that recognized it as an embrace, she was just that gentle. But that didn't mean that I was going to succumb to Ram's ludicrous suggestion so easily.

"Rubbish!" I told him. "She's an animal!"

"Incapable of such high emotions?" Ram Singh finished for me before gently chiding, "Come, Charlie, can you think of no other creature that has shown you affection – a dog, or a horse, perhaps?"

That put it in a different light, all right. It was only a second and I was remembering my mare, Pet. She and I had been quite close, practically inseparable, we were, and it hadn't all been one-sided, neither. A right game one, she was. Lovely disposition, and could carry me all day, if need be. Ridden her at The Charge, in fact, and hadn't seen her since, but then we all lost friends that day.

Still unwilling to concede, I said, "It's just that, she's so…so…"

"Different?"

"Well she is, isn't she?"

"To you, perhaps," Ram's eyes twinkled some more, "but to those of us who are familiar with these creatures, we learn to respect their judgment, and Radha Piyari's more than most. I have known her for several years, ever since she was just a calf, and never witnessed such an embrace as she gave you this morning."

"Saw that, did you?"

"Of course, Charlie, how could I not? The *mahout* told me that it is a sign of good fortune, superstitious devil that he is."

I ventured a derisive snort, not entirely devoid of a certain amount of bitterness. Myself and good fortune have forever been strangers. "I suppose that you think so, as well?"

Ram laughed and took a guzzle from his flask. "It is true that these Hindu rascals think that all the world is a dream, so if they can believe such a thing, how difficult can it be to believe that an elephant can bring good fortune? But I am a Sikh," he said, "and not subject to such superstitious nonsense." He laughed harder, "So therefore I must seek it out on my own!" and continued laughing until tears began to mingle in his beard. Presently he subsided, wiped his eyes, and said, "All that I can tell you, Charlie, is that, in India, there is much that cannot be explained away with what you in the west would call a rational mind. So if the *mahout* says that good fortune will attend you, who am I to gainsay him?"

"You should get into politics," I advised. "You talk a good deal, but say very little." At which he erupted into another gale of laughter, and was still chuckling to himself five minutes later when we heard the scream.

25

Chapter Two

In a trice I swept up my rifle, and set off at a sprint toward the sound. Quick as I was, however, Radha Piyari and my lord were quicker, and I was the recipient of an excellent view of her exorbitant backside as she crashed into the jungle without bothering to pick her way through the underbrush, with myself bringing up the rear, as it were. However, on foot, it was impossible to keep up with an elephant in a hurry, and they were soon gone from sight, surging ahead, leaving a trail of trampled vines and broken tree limbs, with flocks of brightly-coloured, but highly excited, birds taking wing in her wake. All the while the screams continued.

I was still picking my way through an endless stream of ruined flora when I heard my master's rifle discharge, whereupon the screaming abruptly rose a pitch higher. Thoroughly alarmed now, I renewed my effort, and soon broke into a clearing, taking everything in at a glance.

In the centre stood a temple in sad repair, covered in creeping vines. It appeared to have been long abandoned, except that on the grounds close by there was a rickety-looking structure, crammed with enough wood to make a bonfire large enough to do Guy Fawkes proud. On the structure lay the body of a man composed in death – if you would consider bulging eyes and a protruding tongue composed. In the midst of it all, bound to a stake, was a woman in the highest state of alarm. At the base stood perhaps half a dozen other men with flaming torches in hand, looking for all the world like cats who had just eaten a canary. I immediately understood what was taking place and felt a surge of revulsion. Evidently my lord had been just in time to interrupt these villains from subjecting the lady to the odious custom of *suttee*: the burning of a widow on her husband's funeral pyre. What great luck that he had!

Even as I broke into the clearing, one of the fellows suddenly made to thrust his torch into the pyre. Without thinking, I leveled my rifle anf felt the butt kick into my shoulder. The rascal gave a scream and pitched forward onto the ground.

His cronies, sensing that the game was up, took to their heels, and sped off into the jungle.

The *mahout* had coaxed Radha to kneel and my lord sprang to the ground, dashing toward the woman with all the signs that he was in as high a state of anxiety as she, something I had not ever witnessed on any occasion prior.

"I say! I'm most dreadfully sorry!" he exclaimed, whipping out his handkerchief: "Had the rotter dead in my sights, too! Can't imagine how this happened! Never forgive myself!"

It was then that I noticed a thin stream of blood flowing down the woman's arm, and knew in a flash that this was my master's handiwork. In less than five minutes he had come close to doing the both of us in (myself twice!) which was something of a record, even for him.

"Allow me, my dear," Lord Brampton told her, reaching out to put his handkerchief to her wound, which must have been quite tender, for no sooner had contact been made than the lady's eyes flew open wide, and she screamed one last time before slumping against her bonds in a faint.

Clearly distressed, my master fumbled out his clasp knife and began slicing at the rope just as Ram Singh burst onto the scene with the other elephant, and a small army of beaters bringing up the rear.

"After them!" I told him, pointing in the direction the survivors had fled, "They can't have gone far!"

It was not necessary to repeat myself, for the burly old Sikh had taken everything in as had I only a moment before. Gone was the jovial visage. In its place was a look of grim determination, the whiskers fair bristling from his beard. He gave a single nod and spoke to the mahout, and they went crashing off into the jungle in the direction I had indicated, with the beaters fanning out behind him.

With the pursuit taken care of, I hurried forward to check on the man that I had shot. A cursory examination satisfied me that he was dead. Then, ever mindful of my duty, I hurried to the aid of my master, arriving just as he severed the rope binding the woman to the stake, and was in time to catch her before she fell to the ground. I would have swept her up in my arms, but was thrust aside as Lord Brampton did that in my stead, carrying her inert form away from what was to have been the scene of her death – a scene that I found too hideous to imagine. Eager to be of service, I quickly procured the linen I used for when my lord dined in rough country. Spreading it on the ground, Lord Brampton lay the girl upon it, as tender as I'd ever seen.

"Water, Smithers," he said in a tone quite as gentle, without taking his eyes from her.

I took out my own handkerchief and, soaking it with water from my canteen, handed it to him. He accepted it without a word and began to sponge her face. "Poor child," he murmured.

It was only then that I noticed how handsome her features were. No woman looks her best when in a state of panic, but composed in sleep as she was now, I could appreciate the round face and pouting ruby lips, as well as the caste mark on the prettily troubled brow. So, too, could I now appreciate the rich embroidery of her tightly-fitting sari that did little to conceal the firm mounds of her breasts, or the tantalizing roundness of her hips. Judging by the silken material, and the golden bangles on her wrists, or the many-jewelled rings on her fingers, whosoever had been her erstwhile husband, he had apparently been a man of some means.

I daresay both my lord and I would have continued to admire her further if her eyes hadn't fluttered open at that very moment, reminding me that I still had my duty to attend. I took up my canteen once again, and guessing correctly that my master would like to do the honours, handed it across to him. He accepted it as he had the handkerchief, and held it to her lips. After only a moment's hesitation, she took the prettiest little sip you ever saw, all the while regarding my master with wonder, using her eyes to full effect. The effort wasn't wasted, for milord spoke in such a gentle tone, that I had to do a quick take to reassure myself that it was, in fact, really he.

"There child, are you much hurt?"

In lieu of an answer, she huskily whispered, "You have saved my life, sir!" with a lovely accent, as if she scarcely dared to believe the recent events (which, in fact, had happened so fast that I could scarcely believe them myself). Then, over my master's protests, she struggled up and embraced him, clinging him with a ferocity that would have been quite improper had it not been for the circumstances. "Oh, you are real!" she cried, with her face huddled to his chest. "This is not a dream!"

Taken completely by surprise, Lord Brampton was at a loss, and quite right, too, if you ask me. But as I said, the situation being what it was, and as the lady showed no sign of relinquishing her hold from around his neck, and burst into tears in the bargain, he relented so far as to put a hesitant arm around her shoulder in a feather-light caress.

"There, there, my dear," he told her, and Galahad couldn't have said it better, "it's over. No one will harm you now."

Snuffling prettily she managed to say, "Those wicked men...! My husband...! They were going to...! Oh! It is too horrible for words!" before the sobs carried her off again. Meanwhile my master continued to offer her comfort, and murmur soothing nonsense. The scene could have played out indefinitely had it not been interrupted by the return of Ram Singh and company. My lord gently extricated himself from the lady's embrace, and stood to face them.

"Well?" he demanded, more his old self. I could tell he was livid on the lady's behalf, over the outrage that had very nearly been committed on her person.

Ram spread his hands, palms up, in the universal gesture of helplessness. "I am sorry, sahib, but I am afraid that we had no luck. The lady's assailants have vanished, most regrettable to say."

"But who were those scoundrels?" cried my master, "And what was the meaning of such a...a...*barbaric* act? Why, if I hadn't shown up in the nick of time..." He broke off when this produced more wailing from the lady. "Oh look! Now I've upset you, my dear, frightfully clumsy of me!" Then willing himself to a second attempt, "Here, allow me to see to your wound. Can't imagine what I was thinking!"

Ram Singh and I exchanged knowing glances. I'll ask you to note that my lord did not say, "Smithers! See to her wound!" or "Smithers! Attend the lady!" but had insisted upon seeing to it himself, as he had in every other respect previously. He

29

remoistened my handkerchief from the canteen and addressed the affected area – by the look of it little more than a scratch, thank heaven.

The lady accepted his ministrations with surprising equanimity, requiring mere moments to regain her composure.

"You have gentle hands," she told him, in a voice that might have been velvet– I found myself thinking *speculative* velvet, if ever there was such a thing.

I saw my master's ears turn pink. "What? D'you really think so?" I could tell that he was pleased.

"Mmmm," she sighed deliciously, jarring the monocle loose from my lord's eye, "I do."

Meanwhile Ram Singh and the village headman had dismounted from their elephant, and gone over to study the corpse laid out on the platform. For reasons I could not fathom I felt grateful for the excuse to extricate myself from the vicinity of Lord Brampton and his patient.

"With your permission, sir," I said, drawing his attention.

"What's that, Smithers?" It seemed to take a great deal of effort for my master to break his concentration, but when he looked up at me I gave my head an interrogative tilt in the direction of the pyre, unwilling to speak of it in front of the lady for reasons I thought obvious. To my relief he understood my meaning, bless him, and even seemed eager that I should take myself away. "Quite right," he said, "off you go, then. I'll call if I need you." And then, having dismissed me, he returned his attention to the lady. "Now then, my dear, how does that feel?"

"Lord Brampton sahib, seems to be quite taken with the lady," Ram Singh observed, when I had made my way over to where he was closely examining her husband's remains.

I murmured something noncommittal. I believe that Ram sensed my reticence, for he did not press the issue further. Instead he gestured at the corpse. "What do you make of it, Charlie?"

The man had been an old greybeard, somewhere in his sixties (a difference in years which is not uncommon in this part of the world) was even more richly attired than his widow, and as I had said earlier, had undoubtedly been someone of means. He

30

had been dead for several hours by the look of him, but I doubt that it was any longer, as the body had not yet begun to decompose – something that I imagined would happen quite quickly in this climate. His facial contortions I've already described.

"How do you think he died?" I asked.

Ram replied in all sobriety, without any trace of his earlier tippling, "A very good question, my friend."

"Would you say it was a violent death?"

Ram looked at the bulging eyes and the grotesque protruding tongue, and said without humorous intent, "Whatever it was, by his expression, I would venture that it took him by surprise." He reached out under the man's grey whiskers, and turned back the collar of the richly brocaded coat, and said, "Does this answer your question?"

I leaned forward in order to observe where Ram was indicating. The skin around the man's neck was bruised a ghastly black, and swollen on either side of a deep indentation no wider than the span of a finger, although quite deep enough to be lethal.

"Strangled!"

"So it would seem, Charlie." Ram replied, very grim. "I think that there has been a very bad business here."

"Blow me!" I whistled through my teeth. "As if this *suttee* business wasn't bad enough!"

"Indeed," Ram replied, glancing over to where my master was taking the greatest of care with his patient's arm – managing to look contrite, and blushing at the same time. "Perhaps the lady might enlighten us further."

"Hold on," I said, "that's hardly decent, isn't it? I should think she's been through enough for one day. Upsetting her further is pretty rum, ain't it? Why not wait 'til she's more herself?"

"Aye, it is rum," Ram agreed, although there was no compromise in his tone, "but this is a rum business, Charlie, as we have both agreed. The risk of upsetting her is most regrettable, but so too is it unavoidable, I'm afraid. It is best to question her while the events are still fresh in her mind."

31

In the end, I had to concede to his reasoning, but I didn't have to like it, and said so. He agreed.

"I do not like it either, Charlie," he confessed, "but we have a duty to discover the truth of this matter."

Well, when he put it like that – pointing out that it was our duty and all – it was an entirely different story. Consideration for the sensibilities of a lady of quality was one thing, but duty was a horse of an entirely different colour, and could not be gainsaid. With that lodged in my mind, it took a great deal of weight from my shoulders, however I did have reservations on another score.

My lord, as Ram Singh had himself pointed out, did appear to be quite taken with the lady, for whatever reason. Whether it was because he felt it was a means to make amends for having shot her, or if it was for her physical charms, I couldn't say. It might be the former, although I had my doubts. After all, I'd had my own close calls, more times than I can remember, and precious little he'd ever done to make amends with *me* (like just a few minutes ago, for instance). Still, quality will out, native quality notwithstanding, so there was a chance that he'd see this episode in a different light. In fact, as an example, I recall that he had been most distressed when his horse trod on Lady Wingate's foot, so many years ago (just prior to the hunt, it was), so there was definitely a case to be made there. Although, contrition or not, it had not been enough to save his suit for her hand.

Not that this girl's physical charms could be taken lightly, you understand. A rare beauty she was, coffee-coloured skin and all, and she didn't seem to mind milord's attention one little bit, in spite of having just lost her husband. Still, like I said, the old duffer appeared to be well into his sixties when he copped his lot, and if I'm any judge, the lady had yet to see her twentieth year, so that might account for it. Then, too, regardless that my master had winged her with an errant shot, there was no denying that he'd also saved her life in the very nick of time, and she'd made no secret of her gratitude. But whatever the reason, the fact remained that milord had placed her under his protection, and while Ram Singh had convinced *me* of where duty lay, I had my doubts that he would meet with any such success in that regard with my master. I was to find, however, that it was unwise to underestimate that doughty old Sikh's ability.

Indeed, my lord's face had clouded over the instant Ram Singh made his intentions known to him.

"You what?" Lord Brampton looked him up and down, through his monocle, his face clouding with rage.

Ram Singh bowed, unperturbed. "It gives me no joy to upset the lady, sahib, but nevertheless I must ask her some questions, and as speedily as may be, while the memory is still fresh in her mind."

"Why, you insolent fellow," Lord Brampton was holding himself in with difficulty, "you'll do no such thing!" He gestured to where the subject of the conversation was sitting sedately on the linen a short distance away. "Have you no consideration of what this delicate creature has been through?"

"Most assuredly, sahib, but the fact remains that we must get to the bottom of the matter, and as quickly as may be." There was just the briefest pause before, "Lord Elgin will be most eager to know what happened, down to the very last detail."

It was all I could do to keep the shock off my face, and I found myself regarding the old boozer with new respect. The implication was obvious: my master might be a lord, but Lord Elgin was also the Viceroy, representing The Raj and the Queen, with vast, sweeping powers, whom even my master must consider before offending. If Ram Singh – who had his master's ear (as who should know better than I?) – considered it his duty to question the lady, he would be doing so in the name of the Viceroy, indeed, in the name of the Raj, and heaven help anyone who stood in his way.

However, if he had expected my master to back down, he was very much mistaken. To a man the Bramptons were nothing if not bull-headed, and I've often thought that my lord had a greater share of this than most. His face clouded dark thunder, then grew purple with the greatest rage I'd ever seen in him (and you may take my word for it that I'd seen my share), but before he could even begin to start bellowing, the lady in question calmly rose and came forward, placing a hand upon my master's arm.

33

"Please, my lord," she said, placating him in an instant, something I never thought to see. When a Brampton was angry, he usually *stayed* angry until he was damned good and ready *not* to be. "I thank you for your noble concern, but I will answer this man's questions."

With the dissipation of the thunder on his brow, my master absolutely preened under her praise, and drawing himself up to his full height, managed to look very noble, I must say. Clicking his heels together, he offered her a bow. "Ma'am," he said, and that was all.

Then, somehow managing to look regal as all get out, in spite of the fact that her sari revealed more than it covered, the lady now turned to Ram Singh, with an air of expectant resignation mingled with disdain.

With the deepest, most respectful, bow in his own turn, Ram Singh began:

"With your permission, lady," he asked, "may we know you're name?"

There was a pause, almost as if she was considering how to answer, then with grave dignity she replied, "My am Amrita Pirāli."

"Pirāli," Ram repeated, ever more respectful. "That is Brahmin name, is it not? The highest of your Hindu castes?"

"It is," she replied.

"And Amrita," he continued with a kind of paternal benevolence, "a beautiful name, but also very noble, for I believe it means 'immortal'?"

"Indeed it does," she conceded, then with a glance at my master, and a secret half-smile she said, "but it can also mean 'ambrosia'."

My master could not help himself. "I say!" Then his face grew pinker than ever.

However Ram was unmoved. "And the deceased?"

Amrita did not hesitate, nor did she appear overly forlorn. "My husband, Gopal."

"A holy man?"

"If you wish." She said it with the merest shrug.

Ram's brows knit, as I'm sure did my own, but if her offhand reply had suggested further questions along that line, for the moment he chose to proceed on a different tack.

"If you would be so kind, my lady, could you recount what has taken place here?"

"Surely it is clear," she said, her disdain rising. "My husband died, and those wicked men – his disciples – sought to make a sacrifice of me!" Then as suddenly as it had arisen, her scorn subsided, and there was a softening of her voice when she turned to my master and continued, "And they would have done, if it were not for you, my lord."

Lord Brampton, even more erect than ever, flushed with pride at her attention and said, "That's the truth, by god! Had one of the beggars in my sights just as he was about to set fire to the whole blasted lot!" Here he turned away, and finished on a note of embarrassed confusion, "Only I...I missed, confound it!" Then turning back to the widow Pirāli, he resumed his earlier contrition, "I say, my dear! I'm most frightfully sorry! How can you ever forgive me?"

She waved his remorse away as if it were no concern. "In exchange for this scratch upon my arm, I have gained my life. I consider the trade to be most advantageous."

My master gulped and shuffled about like a schoolboy on his first visit to the headmaster's office, but he was eventually able to regain his noble composure, just as Ram Singh continued, gesturing at the ruined remains of the temple.

"It would appear that this place of worship is no longer inhabited, and most likely has not been for the course of my lifetime, and certainly not in yours," he allowed the slightest smile to accompany his acknowledgement of her youth, managing to convey that complimenting her beauty had been his real intention, the effect of which, I thought, was not ungallant. "Perhaps you would be so kind as to explain your presence here?"

"Certainly," she replied. "We were travelling to Calcutta from our village some distance to the north." As an aside, she added, "I am sure that you are aware that the Pirāli name is well known in those regions along the Ganges?" When Ram Singh inclined his head, acknowledging that this was so, she continued, "My husband wished to meet the holy Ramakrishna and perhaps even his teacher, the celebrated Bhairavi Brahmani, the ascetic. We camped out in the ruins of the temple only the night before." The memory of the previous evening's consequences caused a shiver of dismay, or possibly something else – a gesture that was not lost on the Viceroy's man.

Without any further preamble, Ram came directly to the point, "Forgive me, lady, but I must ask: how did your husband die?" Continuing without pause he added, "Unfortunately, the evidence appears to suggest a possibility of foul play."

"What's that?" my lord interjected, incredulous. "Foul play? What the devil do you mean?" When Ram supplied my master with the details of our examination, he breathed, "Good God!" and for the first time regarded Madam Pirāli with some uncertainty. "Is this true?" If uncertain prior to her response, however, I can't ascertain with any exactitude what his emotions were toward the lady following it.

In a calm, matter-of-fact tone Amrita replied, "There was no foul play, only a most unfortunate accident." Here she paused for the merest of instances, the calm seeming to slip briefly, and with good reason, as I was to discover. "You see my husband was a*bibrānta*." When she saw that this brought no enlightenment to any one of us, she explained further, "I believe that the English word is an asphyxiate." As we continued to exhibit every sign of thickheaded ignorance, she appended, "Of an erotic nature."

Here she paused to allow the meaning of her words to sink in. Well, there was fat chance of that. Ram Singh glanced at me, and presently I shifted my own gaze to my master, and he from Amrita back to Ram, all three of us perplexed – all three also blushing slightly at the word 'erotic.'

When she saw that her explanation had been wasted on us, Amrita explained further, with just a touch of exasperation, using words that were impossible to misconceive. When she had finished, our silence had progressed from perplexed to stunned. Ram Singh, at least, had gone as pale as a ghost.

Then, "D'you mean to tell me," milord began, scandalized (reflecting all of our sentiments, I'm sure), "that when he...that is to say...when he approaches his...what I mean is when he's about to...to..."

"Achieve orgasm?" she supplied helpfully.

Now even milord fell silent. Instead he ended lamely with a half-hearted interrogative tug at an imaginary cord around his throat.

"Quite so," madam confirmed, with what I thought was a note of relief. A relief, I might add, that was not shared by any of us, and even less so with my master. After a great deal of effort, he managed to stammer, "But...but..." before finally coming out with it, "but what the deuce for?"

To which the widow replied, "I am told that it greatly enhances the experience during the act of..."

"Yes...quite," my lord managed to interrupt her just in time, and attempted to cover his embarrassment by clearing his throat, over and over again, quite volubly, I thought.

It was Ram who was the first to recover. "You said that your husband was a holy man." His tone suggested that such behaviour was unlikely in a man of the cloth, so to speak, even for a Hindu. Little did he know.

"Did I?" she asked. "I thought it was you." Now the disdain seemed mingle with amusement. "But rather than quibble over such a minor detail, I will concede that Gopal Pirāli fancied himself as a holy mystic and a Tantrist. I believe that is why he wanted to meet with Bhairavi Brahmani all along." For our benefit she added, "The lady teaches it, you see?"

Ram's brows knit again. "Teaches what, lady?"

Madam's own brows were knit when she replied, "Why, *Tantra*, of course!"

Here Ram Singh sighed. "If you would be good enough to explain."

Madam parroted the sigh, and replied with some irritation. "*Tantra* must be experienced to be explained, and that would take a lifetime." From her tone, and haughty expression, the implication was obvious – in her opinion, a lifetime of study for one such as Ram Singh would scarcely be enough.

37

But the Viceroy's man was not to be put off.

"I would be obliged if you would try, madam."

Amrita Pirāli regarded him for a moment, one corner of her mouth curling into a sardonic smile. Then the moment passed, and she reached a decision.

"Very well," she said, "Tantra seeks to achieve godliness by accessing *prana*," for our benefit she explained, "the energy that flows in the universe, in and around us," and I daresay she couldn't resist when she added, "even in you."

Uncowed, Ram persisted, "And what has this belief to do with your late husband's…ah…*proclivity?*"

"Well, obviously achieving such a state requires a purity of spirit, which in turn requires a shedding of all that is not pure: *kāmêcchā* – what you would call 'lust' – being foremost amongst them."

Well if lust was a sin there wasn't an innocent man amongst us, and no lie! Why just the sight of that brazen beauty, with all that delectable stuff fair quivering under her sari was enough to set my master wrenching at his collar. Even Ram Singh, who you might have reckoned as too old for such earthly matters, appeared to be in a fine stew. But if that wasn't enough, here she was prosing on, about what I daresay we were all thinking, just as cool as you please. Dear God, you would have thought that she was *French!*

Meanwhile Ram Singh had gathered his wits about him to make another stab at getting to the heart of the matter, and kept doggedly on.

"But if lust is the chief…*distraction* to achieving this holy state…"

For once, Amrita took pity and finished for him, with that same sardonic curl on her lip. "Why was he a practitioner of *bibrānta?*"

Ram's relief was plain to all. "Precisely, madam."

"A fair question," she conceded with another one of her regal nods. "Most sects believe that such a distraction must be suppressed. My husband taught that it be embraced, and by embracing, be released from its power."

38

"Your husband embraced...*lust?*" It crossed my mind that Ram was thinking of doing the very same thing, indeed, if he hadn't done already. My lord, I should note, by the way his eyes kept dancing from madam's excellent bosom to her rump, and back again, seemed capable of very little else.

"He did," Amrita affirmed, although she didn't strike me as being all that cheerful about it.

How Ram managed to keep his facial expression impassive is beyond me (no doubt all those whiskers helped) but his voice was quite sober when he said, "Your pardon, lady, but if what you say is true, he appears to have embraced it with uncommon zeal."

It was here that my lord managed to interject, albeit in a hoarse whistle that was not quite his own.

"There can be no question that what Madam Pirāli has spoken is the truth. She is a lady of quality, after all." Then he blushed furiously, leaving little doubt as to his opinion of just what those qualities were – not that I blamed him. "She has been so...um...*kind* as to give witness under the most trying of circumstances, to which I find the...the...*necessity* most regrettable," he lied. "So there, Ram Singh; your questions have subjected the...ah...lady to enough humiliation, I think. I will not have you questioning her veracity on top of it all, d'you hear!"

Ram Singh was wise enough not to press the point, but managed a bow that somehow included both my master and madam.

"I beg your pardon. I meant no inference or disrespect." (Didn't he though, by gad!) But before either could comment further, he continued on as smoothly as you please. "Lady, were you present when this...accident occurred?"

"I was."

"Yet you did not come to his aid?"

"I would have done," she replied just as coolly, "but you see, it was quite impossible."

"And why is that, may I ask?"

To her credit, she looked him full in the eye. "My hands were bound at the time."

At last Ram was left floundering, and he wasn't the only one, I can tell you. Out of the corner of my eye, I saw Lord Brampton stoop to retrieve his monocle from where it had fallen again. He did not bother to reinsert it, I would assume on the grounds that he felt it likely that it would only pop out again upon the lady's next utterance. But the question remained, and at length Ram Singh managed to ask it...or tried to, at least.

"Who was it that...that..."

"Placed the cord around his neck?" Madam interjected not unkindly. When Ram managed a nod she replied, "My husband, of course."

"But who...?"

"Applied the pressure? It was also he."

In spite of his earlier assurance to the contrary, it was beyond Ram's ability to keep the disbelief out of his voice. To his credit, I thought, my master offered no objection, but awaited her answer with bated breath.

"You mean to tell me that your husband throttled himself...to *death*?"

Madam calmly replied, "I mean exactly that." Then she elucidated further,"Gopal Pirāli was no longer a man in his prime, and the act of *surata* had become less and less within his capabilities, so he took recourse to other means. Eventually the time had to come when even these *other means* no longer sufficed." Contrary to what we were going through, she continued without any evident emotion whatsoever, "I have already told you that my husband fancied himself as a seeker of ultimate truth, but he refused to accept a much plainer truth when it was staring him in the face. He had lost the ability to become aroused, and his desire to continue to be blind to that fact drove him to his death." She shrugged as she had done earlier, "As I said, it was an accident. Most regrettable, but there it is."

"My word!" Lord Brampton was positively agog. "Well I never!"

I believe that all three of us took a moment to reflect on the possibility of ever finding ourselves in a similar position:

being faced with doing ourselves in, in an attempt to get on with it, and were much sobered by the thought, to say the least.

Ram Singh made an attempt to put the best possible face on the matter. "He must have been a driven man."

But madam didn't care for the illusion. "Gopal Pirāli was a selfish and stupid man," she said with that same curl on her lip, "who could not see the truth when it was right before his eyes. He cared for his own pleasure more than he cared what happened to me."

Although surprised by her answer, Ram recovered quickly, "Ah yes," he said, "this brings us around to where Lord Brampton, sahib, saved you from a horrible death."

"Yes," she replied, and assuming correctly that she was given leave to continue, so she did. "The only ones more stupid and selfish than my husband were those fools – those wicked *beasts*," she angrily spat the words, "who called themselves his disciples. Last night, when they came running in answer to my scream for aid, what did they do? Did they see to my husband's welfare? Did they return to the last village we had passed in order to find some sad excuse for a doctor? Did they, at the very least, untie my bonds? The answer to all three questions, gentlemen, is an emphatic 'no'!" Here the curl on her lip grew even more pronounced, and her words ever more bitter, until she was positively shaking with rage. "Instead, they did what so many men would do upon finding a helpless, and I may say *not unplain*, woman at their mercy, claiming afterward that they were merely seeking their master's *truth*, as he had taught them to do! The truth!" and this time she did spit, literally. "Their sad excuse for *that* was to arrive at the conclusion that, in order that I forever be a fitting consort to their master, I must undergo purification as a *suttee*, and incidentally erase the only witness to their crime!"

At this Lord Brampton had reached the end of his own tether, so to speak. With cries of, "Oh my dear!" and, "The bounders!" he absolutely launched himself at the girl, sweeping her into a protective embrace. "You must never fear that we will not find these…these…*scoundrels*, and bring them to justice, what? Isn't that right, Ram Singh?"

41

Ram inclined his head. "Most assuredly, Lord Brampton, sahib, the guilty will be punished," but his face was a closed book.

Much of the rest of that afternoon was spent paying our respects to the departed, while we cremated the remains of the late Gopal Pirāli, each, I think, for their own different reason. For the villagers it was enough to know that the dead man had been born a Brahmin for them to pay all due respect. At the forefront Amrita stood in silence while the flames took hold of the heavier timbers, fanned into life by a freshening breeze, until the clothing on the corpse began to darken and curl. When the stake we had cut her from started to go, I could only guess what thoughts were in her mind, but I could see the hem of her sari shiver as though she were trembling.

Standing attendance beside her, solar topper respectfully in hand, Lord Brampton tried his best to look solemn, and keep his hands off what was supposed to be the grief-stricken widow, for the benefit of all onlookers.

Ram Singh stood at attention, his face still unreadable. I rather think that his own motives were more political, being the Viceroy's representative, so to speak, and it wouldn't do not to put on a show for the locals, who were also Hindu, as was the dearly departed.

And me? As the flames grew and grew, until they vied with one another for the sky, and the body itself became as one with the inferno, I reflected that I'd learned the hard way what was proper. It was always wise to honour the local gods whenever finding yourself within easy reach of their grasp.

Hours later, when the flames had died, and the earthly remains of Gopal Pirāli had been reduced to smouldering ash, no one was surprised when my lord announced that the lovely widow would be accompanying us back to Calcutta. What did surprise me (and greatly, I must admit) was that after handing madam up into Radha Piyari's *howdah*, my master turned to me, with a poor attempt to hide his eagerness.

"See here, Smithers," his voice a hoarse conspiratorial whisper, with eyebrows arching like church steeples, "just as a

42

point of interest, you understand, but d'you *really* think that there's anything to this choking business?"

Chapter Three

Owing to this new state of affairs, milord graciously cut short our expedition, declaring that, in the interest of attaining surroundings more suitable to a lady, we should return to Calcutta forthwith. Consequently we camped out on the plain one final night, arriving back at the Auckland the following afternoon.

In that short time, when not preoccupied with my duties, I was able to observe our guest. I could not, in all honesty, claim that Madam Pirāli behaved without decorum, because she did, as one used to her station, but perhaps more gaily than what one might expect, having so recently been exposed to such brutal misuse. Indeed, she was quite merry when in the company of my lord, laughing enchantingly at his attempts to be jovial, or listening with disarming attentiveness whenever he spoke of more somber things. Neither was my lord blind to this attention, and revelled in it as only one can who has found the experience to be novel. Indeed, he succumbed to her flattery (if flattery it was) with an ease that I might have found disturbing in one to the manor born, if I could sense any danger attenuating, but I could not. In the end I arrived at the conclusion that hers was merely a reaction to my master having saved her from a horrible death at the eleventh hour, and though seemingly odd, was entirely natural, given that I had survived the jaws of death on more than one occasion myself, and knew what to expect.

The only other curiosity of madam's behaviour was her attitude toward myself. Again, not that she behaved improperly – she maintained a cool distance that gentle persons will with a servant, but perhaps cool might not be the correct word when cold would have served better. Then, too, the very set of her shoulders whenever I was in close attendance suggested a reserve that, if not actually hostile, was decidedly unfriendly. Why this should be I couldn't say, nor could I say with all certainty that it, in fact, was. All that I could acknowledge was the unease that I felt, and how in the past that had often been the companion of what my Hebridean mother had called 'the sight': a dubious gift that I had inherited from her. Such could not be trusted in its

44

entirety; however, as I had occasion to realize that it was far from infallible. Ultimately I decided that my only recourse was to maintain myself with all due propriety, and perform my duties with the utmost attention...and continue to observe her as closely as possible, for as long as she was a companion to my lord.

For that was the greatest curiosity, and perhaps why I viewed the lady with such suspicion. Although in hindsight it seems only natural. My lord was smitten by her, that was as plain as the nose on his face, and I had to admit that it had an improving influence upon him in many ways, not least of which was his disposition. Why, he had not raised his voice above a jovial guffaw since the previous afternoon, which wasn't like him at all. In fact, his ebullience in general was so alien to his nature that I found myself wondering if I were not now serving an entirely different gentleman. His smiles and grins, in particular when he was conversing with Madam Pirāli, I could vaguely relate to when we were lads together, and might appear as something ridiculous in a grown gentleman; but apart from it not being my place to question such behaviour, neither could I begrudge it in him. Up to this point life had been a hard go for my master, with precious little to smile about. Let him smile now; who was I to wish it were otherwise?

As to the lady, what can I say? I was a stranger in a strange land – a benighted land in more ways than I can tell you, parts of which I've already described. After witnessing what had apparently been about to take place the previous day, it was no great hardship to come to grips with the notion that a widowed woman might lead a precarious existence, if she was fortunate enough to have any existence at all. So if she voiced no great yearning to return to this village of hers, it could well be because there was now nothing for her to return to. Gopal's disciples might be asses to a man, but who was to say that they weren't the common fare? A culture that was capable of tossing a widow onto a raging inferno, in order to protect her good reputation, was capable of anything in my view. I was given to understand, too, upon inadvertently overhearing madam in conversation with my master, that Gopal had died leaving no offspring, so there was no question of returning for the sake of her children. Indeed, from my own conversations with Ram, I discovered that, even had they existed, it was by no means a foregone conclusion that they would have offered her succour, let alone an inheritance. Aye, it was a strange land, and no error. So if my lord offered his protection, there was no earthly reason that I could see that she should not be happy and grateful to accept it. Small wonder, too, given the circumstances, that Gopal's passing should go unlamented by her, but that she should feel a deep gratitude to my master for offering to raise her from a life that must have been little better than slavery, high caste though she was. How long that protection would last remained to be seen, but who could blame her if she were to do her utmost to render it into an indefinite period of time? Perhaps I was getting ahead of myself with such musings, but England had changed over the years, and there was now a growing sentiment that was not so averse to foreigners of colour as it once was, especially if she was an Indian (who were coming to be regarded less and less as foreign), with a claim to some sort of nobility, and a stunner to boot. Yes, without a doubt my musings had taken the bit in their teeth, and roiling in turmoil as they were, I could only hope that events transpired for the best for all parties involved.

In the meantime there were other events afoot.

Once the lady in question had been settled with her own suite of rooms adjoining our own, with a maid hired temporarily from the hotel to see to her needs, and my master made comfortable with his brandy and cigar, I was about to retire to my own little room when there came a knock on the door. Upon answering it, I found Ram Singh in the company of another man with a trim little moustache, and a black leather case, such as doctors might use to carry their instruments.

"Official business, Charlie," Ram told me, eyeing the brandy decanter still resting on the tray, "but I thought to summon the services of my good friend, Doctor Simpson, to see to your and the lady's wounds." His eyes twinkled, "I have discovered that an outing with his lordship may be hazardous to one's health!"

Ignoring the last bit, I said, "I'll summon my master."

But he replied, "All in good time, Charlie."

The doctor interjected, "Quite right, Ram Singh," and to me he said, "Sit down," in a practiced tone that would brook no argument. I found myself obeying before I knew what was what.

As the doctor began unwinding Ram Singh's handiwork from around my head, tutting at the slovenly dressing all the while, the gregarious Sikh took a chair opposite, and when I saw that he still hadn't taken his eyes off the decanter, I relented. "Oh go ahead."

"Very kind of you, Charlie!" he beamed, helping himself to a snifter. He poured a finger from the decanter, and raised his eyebrows at the doctor.

"Yes, all right," I said. It was too much to hope that once having given an inch, the wily old duffer wouldn't go for the mile.

"Much obliged, I'm sure," the doctor murmured, without looking up from his task, only pausing when Ram handed him the glass. When my good health had been drunk to, he returned his attention to my wound without another word, while Ram got down to business.

"So tell me, Charlie," he said, leaning comfortably into the chair, "what do you know about Bhutan?"

"Never heard of him," I replied, wondering what this was leading to.

Ram threw back his head and laughed, his great belly quivering. "It is not a person," he informed me, "it is a place."

"Same answer, I'm afraid."

"It is a country on our northeastern frontier," he said, unwilling to maintain the suspense any longer, "filled with *badmashes* and thieves!"

"Sounds charming," I replied, "but what has it got to do with me?"

He eyed me speculatively for a moment. "The reason why I have come today is because my master has sent me to invite your lord to Government House for a discussion. He will be asked if he would be willing to accompany a mission there." He explained, "It was thought that his illustrious title would add weight to our cause."

I didn't care for the sound of that, and said so, but he continued as if I hadn't spoken.

"It is to be a mission of peace," he announced, slowly roiling the brandy. "It will fail, as have all the others, but the attempt must be made."

I liked the sound of that even less. "But why a peace mission? And why should it fail?"

"Because as well as being *badmashes* and thieves, the Bhuteau are an ignorant people, who know little of the world beyond their mountains, and what they do know they hold in contempt." He paused to consider: "Oh they know our frontier country well enough, in Bengal and Assam, and our protectorate in Sikkim," he looked at me, for once his face impassive, "and that is where they have formed such an opinion."

Just then he was interrupted when the good doctor applied a cotton swab laced with alcohol to my forehead.

"Oh don't be such a baby!" the doctor admonished, shocked at my outcry, "I've known children hurt far worse. Never heard a peep out of *them!*" and expertly began to wrap his own bandage around my poor head. He finished by the time I had subsided to the odd whimper, and after pronouncing that I would be good as new in a day or two, announced that he was off to attend to the native lady, whom I took to mean Madam Pirāli.

Ram rose and saw him to the door in my stead. I was placing a ginger finger to my newly dressed wound when he returned.

"Now where was I?" he asked, resuming his chair, and another finger of Lord Brampton's brandy...both with equal pleasure I might add.

"These Bhuteau people holding the world in contempt," I prompted before adding, "You seem to know a great deal about them."

I thought that that might make him smile, but I was wrong. "Not so," he told me, swirling the brandy again, it struck me as an aid to assist his thinking. "Not many do. In fact, we know as much about them as they know about us, possibly even less."

My head was beginning to hurt, and I believe it wasn't solely from the doctor's attention. "Look here, you said that they're a country of villains, but now you say that you don't know much about them at all. Which is it? You can't have it both ways, you know."

The brandy continued to swirl. "Sadly I can," he said, without looking up. "I know that they descend from their mountains and prey upon our people. They rape, murder, and pillage, stealing anything that they can – livestock, goods, even the people themselves. Then, before the authorities can respond, they are gone again, up into the passes with their booty, where it will be sold to the highest bidder."

"What," I asked, "even the prisoners?"

"Most assuredly," he replied, before giving me further food for thought: "British subjects though they are."

I felt myself growing pale, and it was a struggle to keep my hands from shaking. What he described was nothing short of slavery. I was familiar with slavers; in fact few knew better. Memories of my time in Africa sprang, unbidden, to the forefront of my mind – of that terrible night when Omar Digna and his murderous Baggara had swept down on a peaceful village, leaving fire and destruction in their wake…and death, yes, they had left plenty of that, too…

I could see the bodies, lifeless bundles huddled and misshapen, littered haphazardly in the flickering firelight. Aboyo seeking comfort, and I with none to give, because deeper in the shadows…

"Why hasn't something been done about it?" I demanded, more harshly than had been my intention.

Visions of laughing eyes mingled with those that had grown cold and lifeless; the soft, willing mouth now a feral snarl frozen in rigor.

I could sit no longer, but thrust myself to my feet, and began pacing back and forth.

"Oh, they do from time to time," Ram said, now watching me more closely than I liked. "Sometimes the army makes a foray; sometimes with success. Sometimes the government sends a mission, as they are about to do now, but that has never led to lasting peace."

Hands hooked like claws; shreds of skin under the nails.

49

I hooked a finger in my collar. The room had suddenly grown quite hot. "What about the mountain passes, then?"

"The *duars*?" Ram asked, and then explained, without taking his blasted eyes of me, "For that is how the Bhuteau refer to the passes, you know. Yes, the army has taken possession of them every so often, but never for long."

The tiny still form beside her; with the umbilicus winding aimlessly back to her grotesquely slashed womb...

"In God's name, why not!"

My hands felt the urge for occupation, so I grabbed a gew-gaw from a side table, and watched, in shock, as it slipped through fingers that had suddenly become nerveless, smashing to pieces on the floor.

"In its wisdom," Ram began (aye, he was a diplomat's man, and no error), "the government has always sought a peaceful resolution, but it always falls into the same old pattern: the Bhuteau strike, in retaliation the army occupies the passes to keep them out, and the government sends a mission to their capital city of Poonakha. A fine is levied, the prisoners returned (if possible – regrettably that is not always the case) and an agreement of non-aggression is signed on a piece of worthless paper." Ram Singh's voice had grown less than neutral, and became even less so when he continued, "Then everyone returns to Calcutta, firm in their belief that they have done all that can be done."

"And the passes – these *duars*, I mean?"

"They are returned to their owners," Ram's hands spread, palms facing up, his sarcasm obvious. "How can it be otherwise between *peaceful* nations?"

"And then?"

"Before the year is out the cycle begins anew."

I exclaimed, "But that's bloody ludicrous!" in a voice not quite loud enough to disturb my lord. "The border should be sealed. Those *duars*, or whatever you call them, should be held and never relinquished!"

"As they are on our Assam frontier," he said, "but should our forces occupy the duars on the Bengal side, it would mean war."

50

"Then so be it! Those blasted rascals should get what's coming to them!"

"I happen to agree with you, Charlie," Ram informed me, "and fortunately so does Sir James."

I felt my anger suddenly begin to ebb.

"He does?"

"Yes, he does. Oh, he will try the diplomatic measures first, because he must, but in the end he will get his war."

"Well good!"

Ram regarded me soberly over his pince-nez. "You have been to war, I think, Charlie?"

I told him that I had.

"As have I," he said. "It is a terrible business."

As it so often did, my mind returned to the north valley at Balaclava – to the drumming of the horses' hooves mixed indecipherably with the roar of the guns, and over it all a furious droning in our ears. Fountains of earth springing up all around us, while everywhere man and beast were being torn asunder in ways you could never imagine.

"Yes it is," I agreed. "It's bloody and it's awful, and it's heartless and cruel besides. But this ain't the Crimea, and we won't be fighting for anything as stupid as glory, or for the bloody Turks, neither!" I felt downright noble when I told him, "This is British soil, and these are British subjects. That's what makes it different, don't you see?"

Ram continued to regard me. I thought he seemed slightly amused. "Oh dear me! It is as simple as all that, is it?"

"Of course! Why shouldn't it be?"

Musing, he said, "Only a few, very short years ago I fought in the Great Mutiny." He allowed himself a dry chuckle, "And before you ask which side I was on, I will tell you that I am no mutinous dog, but was faithful to my salt, as I am to this day. The point I am trying to make is that many, many – far too many – were not so faithful as I, and others like me. Those men were British subjects, too, just as I was, but they did everything in their power to erase us from the face of the earth. Had you been here, given half a chance any one of them would have slit your throat, or plunged a bayonet in your stomach, or worse." He placed his

51

empty glass on the table, and stood with an aged sigh. "The mutiny may be over," he told me, "but many, many" and again he said, "far too many of these *British* subjects would do the same to you today, given half a chance. Would you be willing to go to war for them?"

"Well," I said, more thoughtful, "it ain't quite Mayfair here, now is it? Nor even Ireland neither, and there's lots about this country that makes my innards quail, and I don't mind saying it. But we're all under one Queen – one rule of law that pertains to me as much as it does to you. Oh, I know that it's not perfect, and there's some as hate me for the colour of my skin, just as some of my folk don't care for your lot for the colour of *yours*, but that don't matter. What *does* matter is doing what's right." I matched him look for look. "So yes, I'd go to war for those poor fellows, even if they hated the ground I walked on. They have that right, just as I have the right to despise their wicked customs. Because, even though what we have today ain't perfect, it's a damn sight better than what's out there," I encompassed the rest of the world with a wave of my hand. "Just ask any of the poor sods that those Bhuteau buggers hauled away. If they're not yearning for the comforts of their hearths and – yes, British – homes this very instant I'll eat my hat! What's more, they need our protection – 'cause that's also their right, d'ye see? – and it's high time that they got it!" I ended with, what to me was the trump: "It's our *duty*, dash it all!"

Oh, I was in a fine taking, let me tell you. Inadvertently or otherwise (I was beginning to see that I could never be sure with him) Ram had touched a nerve, unearthing a past that would have done best to stay buried. My memories were always too real, and (just as she had been) always *there*, just below the surface, and it could never be otherwise. In a twinkling I had been turned from reluctant journeyer into some bloody ass of a Galahad, straining at the bit, absolutely *demanding* to be given the chance to go a-questing! A radical turn, you'll agree, and it didn't endear the old bugger to me at all, either.

He was looking at me now with something that I thought might have been compassion, and it filled me with loathing; but whether it was for him or myself, I wasn't entirely sure.

I was afraid that he might press the issue, but after a time he merely shrugged and said, "I see that you are that very rare commodity, Charlie: a man of principle." Then he reached into his sash, pulling out a pasteboard card, elegantly engraved. Handing it to me he said, "Lord Brampton's invitation. Perhaps you would be good enough to see that he gets it?"

I accepted it without a word. My thoughts were so much in turmoil, I could think of nothing to say.

He inclined his head and I followed him to the door. At the threshold he hesitated, half-turning. "I think that my words have offended you, Charlie. I am very sorry for that. It was never my intention."

A part of me wanted to hit him, but I found myself saying instead, "I believe you." There didn't seem to be any point in denying it at any rate.

Turning further, he offered me his hand. "You are an interesting man, one whom I would gladly have as a friend."

Now it was my turn to hesitate, but then I decided to take it after all. When I did I found that it was warm and firm.

"Perhaps one day we will sit together over another bottle of that excellent hock, and share our war stories."

I fancy my grip was as firm as his, but I told him, "I don't often talk about those days anymore."

Undaunted, he gave another laugh. "Then we will tell each other lies, like old soldiers do! That will be even better!"

When he was gone, I closed the door quietly behind him, then took a moment to rest my back against the wall. Moments later (a minute or ten, I had no way of knowing) I was able to deliver the Viceroy's message to my lord with, I think, a degree of composure that was acceptable to my station.

***

I accompanied Lord Brampton to Government House later the next morning. I can't imagine why, as it was no great distance, and a household run under the stern eye of Ram Singh put my own poor service to shame. But at the appointed hour my master emerged from his rooms with his walking stick in one hand and his hat in the other saying, "Come along, Smithers, don't dawdle!" and sailed out the door, with myself, caught unaware, racing far behind. He was already out on the street when I reached him, gazing at massive thunderclouds gathering directly overhead.

"Damn fine weather," he declared, "Shan't need a cab!" and then we were off. Minutes later we were caught in a monsoon.

My lord gave no indication that he was aware. Indeed, he had this strange cherubic smile upon his face when he turned to me and asked, "See here, Smithers, what do you make of this Pirāli woman?"

The downpour was drumming on my bowler, and I was cursing silently that I had not thought to bring an umbrella, but Lord Brampton's departure had been so sudden that there hadn't been time to consider. I ventured a sidelong glance, and fancied that the whites of my eyes must be showing. Very correctly, I said that she seemed rather nice, if he didn't mind my saying so.

"Don't mind a bit!" he exclaimed, suddenly stopping with his arms outstretched, inhaling – roughly speaking – about a pint of water. "What a lovely day!" he declared in a voice that was positively happy, and squelched on, seemingly unaware of the deluge running from the brim of his topper.

Left with no other recourse, I had one hand on my hat and the other clasping the lapels of my coat to my chin, blinking at the rain, and doing my utmost not to lose my way as it cascaded down, obliterating everything from sight.

"Fetching gel!" he said, flicking his stick with a fair bit of swagger. "Fine figure of a woman, what?"

With a care (and with water runnelling down my spine), I allowed that la Pirāli did strike me as rather handsome, now that he'd mentioned it.

"Oh posh!" he exclaimed, "She's a stunner, ain't she?"

Completely sodden, I admitted that she was above average, appearance-wise, in a manner of speaking.

"Did you know that she thinks my monocle makes me look distinguished?"

54

I would not have been human if I had not been curious about my master's complete disregard for our situation, but for the moment, managed to keep such curiosity to myself, as it was not my place to enquire. Instead, I splashed unhappily along, dutifully claimed ignorance of the regard that madam had for milord's eyepiece.

He replied, "Well she did," then with pride, " she said '*quite* distinguished', actually. What d'you think of that, hey?"

I said that the lady had a very discerning eye.

"Yes," he agreed, well pleased, "yes she does, by Jove!"

We continued on, with the rain coming down in sheets, and my lord steeped in his own private thoughts, for which I was grateful, hoping that privacy might be maintained. What my own thoughts were you might well imagine. Why, just forget about being soaked to the skin. In all my days I could never remember my master speaking to me with such familiarity. What's more, I wasn't at all sure that it was proper. Well you see what I mean, don't you? A master speaking to a servant like they were the best of chums was quite bad enough, but to be speaking about a lady, and with such intimacy, too…well it beggared belief, that's all. It really did.

Then…

"Popped around to call on her this morning," he said, which explained his absence when I had returned from tidying up his room. "Quite a proper thing to do, of course. She *is* under my care, after all." He explained in such a manner that, had it been a commoner, I would have harboured doubt as to whether observing the proprieties had ever been his intention.

"Late riser," he said.

"My lord?" I enquired.

"Amrit – that is to say, Madam Pirāli. Damn late it was, almost nine."

"Nine, sir?"

"Nine o'clock, man!"

"Oh, I see, sir."

"Or perhaps it was eight-thirty…or after eight…hard to say, really."

While I was absorbing this information (and doing my utmost not to), as well as generous amounts of rainwater, he continued:

"I say, fetching attire!" He said it with such relish that it quite alarmed me.

"Your Grace?"

"For the boudoir!" he explained, which, of course, did little to quiet my unease. "Damn fetching togs some of these Indian ladies wear!" and his face grew more trance-like than ever. "Can't see how it would be comfortable to sleep in, though..." – pause – "must keep crawling up the..." he gestured anatomically, and I quickly looked away.

"She invited me in. Quite gracious of her, I must say!"

By now even my thoughts had become drenched, so I continued on at his side, voicing my disapproval in silence, as it were. Fat lot of good it did me, too.

"For tea," he said, his face crinkling in a most unsettling fashion. "Dear little thing, I hadn't the heart to tell her that I'd already dined, and that Elevenses wouldn't be for hours. Small oversight, really. How was she to know?"

"Indeed, sir."

By now we were both thoroughly soaked, through-and-through, or *I* was at least. My lord, on the other hand...

"Charming conversation. Most charming. Beyond doubt a lady of quality. Good tea, as well!"

I replied, "I'm sure, sir," no longer able to keep the misery from every facet of my bearing. But as bad as things were, they suddenly got worse.

Out of nowhere Lord Brampton's character suddenly changed, in a way that quite drove the notion that we were standing, virtually naked, in the middle of a monsoon, clear from my mind. It was decidedly more – for lack of a better word, I shall say *lascivious*.

In a low, husky voice he said, "Lovely perfume, too!" Then, "I say Smithers," and he actually leered, "there's precious little that the Frogs could teach this bunch about scent, what?" Bless me! He even went so far as to dig a conspiratorial elbow into my ribs! "It got me going, if you know what I mean, hey!"

56

Astonished, I could only gasp, "Really, sir, I don't think..."
But my lord was on a tangent and would not be denied.

"All that flesh just oozing out of her bodice!" he shuddered dreadfully. "And those pouting lips of hers!" in a tone that left me dumbfounded. "And that fine, fat rump too, by Jove!" Then, as God's my witness, he followed this shocking statement with a sound so lecherous that is impossible to record on paper.

"My lord!" This had to be the bloody limit!

"And all the while her looking at me with those come-hither eyes!" he swore savagely. "Wicked, that's what they were, quite delightfully wicked, I must say!"

I could take it no longer. With a great effort, I pulled myself together, and finally had the wit to ask, "Sir, are you well?"

"Never better, Smithers! Never better!" he laughed something shocking, "Delightful gel! Gad! Can't remember ever feeling in such trim!"

If the truth be told, neither could I. I wondered if it might be the sun.

In some desperation, I pressed on. "Milord, you are not yourself."

"Ain't I though?" he bellowed laughter, a sound that can only be described as amazing. "I should like to know who is then!" and he evidently considered this so humorous that he had to stop for air, drinking in huge gasps with various scandalous expostulations regarding madam's charms in between.

I was completely at a loss. Here we were on our way to meet the most important man in India (to discuss an affair of state, no less), only to find that my master had suddenly gone barking mad. Why, it wouldn't do at all! I glanced around for aid, but the street was empty in the pouring rain. Sensible of the city's inhabitants though that might be, I was left with no recourse.

Gently as humanly possible, I said, "Come along, sir," and taking him firmly by the arm, guided him to a nearby bench. To my relief he did not remonstrate, nor deride me for laying my hand upon his person, but allowed himself to be led as meekly as a child, with only the occasional titter to show for his previous

57

behaviour. Reaching the bench, I sat him down as gentle as could be. And there we were: him sitting and me standing, in a torrential downpour.

I had to shout over the rain to be heard, "Sir, have you taken spirits?" I knew this to be unlikely as the sun (wherever it was) had yet to cross over the yardarm, an observance that my master seldom failed to follow. Indeed, this was confirmed only a moment later.

I bent over, putting my ear to his mouth.

"No spirits," he sighed, still not himself, but at least several decibels further down the scale. "Just tea. Wonderful, wonderful *tea!*" His tone continued to subside, "Marvelous concoction, quite different from anything at home."

The tea.

I asked, "Was there anything in the tea, sir?"

He regarded me, all bleary-eyed. "You should know, Smithers. Milk and a squeeze of lemon, as always." He thought that this was funny, too, but instead of laughter all that emerged from him was a rugged squeak.

"No sir! I meant was there anything else?"

"Anything else?" Peering carefully through the rain, I noticed that his pupils had become quite enlarged.

"Yes, sir! Did madam put anything else in your tea?"

"Madam?" His mouth had sagged open, a string of drool mingled with the rain.

"Yes sir! Madam Pirãli!"

"Madam Pirãli?"

"Yes sir!"

"D'you mean Amrita?" he asked, as if at a name half-remembered, "Amrita Pirãli?"

"Indeed I do sir!"

As if by magic, the question disappeared from his face to be replaced by a smile that was almost gentle.

"Amrita," he sighed, "Such a lovely child!" Then he looked at me, and the smile became complete blissful innocence.

"Did I mention that I popped by for tea?"

Chapter Four

"Bloody hell! You're scalding the skin off my feet!"

"'Pon my soul," Dr. Simpson replied with the same clipped tones he'd used the day before, "I've never had to deal with such a baby in all my life! Be quiet and drink your toddie, sir! There's a good lad!" and continued to pour boiling water into the basin with what I thought was a rather heartless vigour.

"I beg the both of you be silent!" Ram Singh warned, as stern as I'd ever heard him. "They are about to begin!"

Bundled up in a blanket as I was, I could only offer him a jaundiced eye. Otherwise there was nothing I could do but grind my teeth, endure the scalding pain lapping around my ankles, and hold my peace. Oh yes, and ignore the good doctor's superior smirk.

We had arrived at Government House, late for my lord's appointment. Indeed, if I'd had my way, we would not have arrived at all, but returned to the hotel at once, to see what could be done for my master's malaise. But my lord's mood had taken yet another turn, and he latched onto it with vigour, I must say.

Still at the bench, the both of us soaked to the skin in the pouring rain, Lord Brampton had finally taken note of his surroundings. His head had come up with a start, and he looked around with every sign that all that he saw was registering in his mind. I thought that this was all to the good, but was wrong again.

"Here," he asked, in a voice fraught with suspicion, "just where the devil am I?"

Relieved (prematurely, as it turned out), I told him. But at the first sound of my voice, his head had swiveled 'round to me, and angrily demanded, "And just who the deuce are *you*?"

Nonplussed, I replied, "My lord! 'Tis I, Smithers!"

At this he leapt to his feet with a vigour I could have sworn had not existed in him only a moment before. Regarding me with that same dark suspicion, he began to back away.

"Smithers?" he asked.

"Why, yes, sir!" I told him, too amazed to say anything else.

Squinting at me through his monocle (now hopelessly smeared by the rain) he said, "You don't look at all like him."

Well out of my depth, I took a step closer to be more easily recognized, and said with some desperation, "I can assure you, sir, I *am* he...that is to say *me*, and none other!"

He studied me for a full chary second, still steeped in uncertainty; before finally delivering his verdict: "No you ain't neither! You can't fool me, blast it all!" Then, as God's my witness, he declared, "You're Varney the Vampyre!" and with that he was off at a run, bawling for the constabulary to come to his aid, no less!

Well, I'd never seen the like, and that's no lie. A Brampton with his wind up, who would have ever thought to see the day? Well, there was no catching him, that was flat. My lord had a head start, and judging by the way he was eating up the ground – legs churning like bedamned, still bellowing at the top of his lungs – he wasn't going to give it up any time soon. All I could do was trot along after, silently willing him to keep his voice down, and do my level best not to look like a cutpurse from the docks.

All was saved by one fact, and one fact only, near as I could tell: whether by instinct or happenstance, the route my lord had taken led directly to the arched North Gate preceding onto the grounds of Government House itself. Perhaps something about the sight of it tripped a link in his fevered mind, or perhaps his exertions had finally got the better of him, or perhaps it was a mixture of the two, but when that neoclassical monstrosity hove into view, milord's headlong flight gradually began to lose momentum, until he finally clattered to a halt a few yards from the gate, both the sentries and myself eyeing him with stark apprehension.

He stood there for a long moment, studying the place as though it was a distant memory, his expression still vacant, but (praise be!) gradually less and less so. Just as the rain stopped, he turned and saw me. This time, I'm happy to say, with recognition.

In a voice half his old quarrelsome self, the other still half in a dream, he said, "Come along, my boy! Mustn't keep the

60

Viceroy waiting!" and ignoring the startled looks of the sentries, squelched inside, with me pelting after, taking the time to give them a flash of the Governor General's invitation along the way.

Ram Singh met us at the entrance, and, to give the man his due, didn't bat an eye at our bedraggled appearance, but bowed my lord inside, where he was taken in tow by servants, and swept away.

"His lordship would be no worse for a hot bath and a change of clothes," he observed, handing me a towel, "and neither would you, my friend." With those damned whiskers of his it was impossible to see if he was grinning or not.

"Awfully decent of you," I told him. Then, "Look, I can explain…"

Whereupon he held up a hand for me to stop. "There is no need whatsoever, Charlie, I assure you most definitely."

"But it must look odd," I ventured.

To which he replied, "Odd?" He gave me a look. "Clearly, Charlie, you have not mingled overmuch in Calcutta society. That," he said with an air of finality, "*is* odd. Now come!"

It turned out that I never did get that bath, nor the change of clothes, neither. Instead, ushering me into an anteroom, Ram insisted that I strip off my togs, whereupon a servant took them to dry by the fire. To me he gave a blanket and a stern frown when he saw that I was shivering, as if the malaria had taken hold again.

"How fortunate that Doctor Simpson is still in attendance," he said, explaining, "Sir James' son has a slight fever. I will send for him at once." When I told him that I would rather have the hot bath he'd spoke of, he replied, "Dearie me, there is no time!" and whisked me out of the anteroom, and through a maze of back corridors, down to another room, all the while offering a deaf ear to my demands for an explanation. What, with having been soaked to the skin until I was gripped with ague, and my master apparently having taken complete leave of his senses as well, I thought I'd already been through enough. How was I to know that it was only beginning?

Shivering more than ever (for those corridors were damned drafty!) I took the chair that he offered, but before I

61

could remonstrate further, Doctor Simpson swept into the room, and without so much as a by-your-leave, jammed a thermometer under my tongue. Then bullying me into silence, he took up my wrist in one hand and his Hunter in the other, all done under a dark cloud of a disapproving frown. Seconds later– grudgingly, I thought – he announced that my pulse would do, but then whipped the thermometer from my mouth to study it more hopefully. After which the basin, hot water and toddy all arrived in double-quick order. Seconds later brings us to the present: with the good doctor plying his trade with sadistic glee, Ram cautioning us to silence, and me feeling hard done by in every conceivable way.

"*Who* are about to begin, dammit all! Who are *they*?" I demanded in a series of whispered squeaks. But before I could say anything further, Ram held a cautionary finger to his lips that promptly disappeared into the depths of his whiskers. At the same instant I distinctly heard the sound of a door opening and closing, right beside me.

Impossible as it might seem, it was coming from the wall, mere inches from where I sat…where I swear there wasn't a door at all!

It took a few moments for it to all become clear: what I had previously dismissed as a candle sconce, was actually a listening device with a tiny horn-shaped object protruding from the wall, wrought of intricately worked brass. I must say that the workmanship was splendid, as it was cleverly disguised to resemble the fixture aforementioned. If it weren't for the sound emanating, I wouldn't have given it a second glance.

My brow clenched as I regarded the old Sikh with an inquiring look, I daresay mingled with a generous amount of guarded respect – for no mere menial would be aware of such a device. In lieu of a reply, he arched his brows at me a time or two, smiled, and inclined his head to the speaker, indicating that I should be still and listen.

I must say that the quality of the sound was quite exceptional, for after hearing the voice of a man, whom I knew immediately to be Lord Elgin, say, "Gentlemen, shall we begin?" I could hear the muffled sound of chairs scraping back on carpeted floors as those in the adjoining room took their seats, and even their papers being placed upon the table.

When all were settled, Lord Elgin continued.

"As you are all aware, the topic of this meeting is to be the country of Bhutan, and a study of actions to be taken in a response to their recent incursions along our north-eastern frontier. Colonel Durand, as Foreign Secretary, perhaps you would be so kind as to begin."

There came the sound of papers being shuffled, followed by a crisp clearing of a throat, but before the colonel could start, I heard someone say, "A moment, if you please. Are we all here? I thought Lord Brampton was to attend."

I spared a guilty glance in Ram's direction, but he had the good grace not to return it, but stared thoughtfully at the wall, immersed in concentration. Meanwhile, Dr. Simpson, presumably having grown tired of tormenting me, had taken a chair and was listening as well.

I thought Lord Elgin sounded weary when he replied, "Lord Brampton has been," there was a slight hesitation, "unavoidably detained."

At which someone else said, with affronted indignation, "Detained? The governing board of all British India invites him to attend a council, and you say he's *detained!* What the devil do you make of it, sir!"

Lord Elgin replied evenly, "Lord Brampton occasioned to be in India on a tour of leisure, and not being *of* the governing board is under no obligation to attend. It was thought that, as the part we are considering him to play is purely of a functionary nature, we might discuss the matter at a later date. In the meantime, we shall proceed without him."

Not to be put off the other voice said, "Still sounds deuced odd!"

But was silenced when Lord Elgin replied heavily, "Nevertheless, Sir Robert, we shall proceed."

At the mention of the name, the doctor whispered in my ear. "Napier."

Well, that impressed me, I can tell you. So this was old 'Fighting Bob' – a hero of both wars in the Punjab, not to

63

mention the recent happenings during the Great Mutiny. The man had been wounded so many times that he carried more hardware in his carcass than any other man in the Empire.

Meanwhile Colonel Durand had at last succeeded in gaining the floor. There was a repeat of that crisp throat-clearing, and he finally began:

"Due to the recent raids by Bhuteau forces along our Bengal frontier, the question has been raised as to whether a diplomatic mission should be sent to Poonakha. The more salient reasons would be..."

The colonel was interrupted when Napier asked, "*Where* did he say?"

"Poonakha, Sir Robert," Durand replied with diffidence. "Capital city of the Bhuteau." Returning to his papers, he resumed with, "The more salient reasons would be to recover the captives from the Bhuteauh..." or I should say, attempted to.

"And what's a Bhuteau, hey?" Napier demanded.

To which another voice replied with some impatience, "They are the people of Bhutan, Sir Robert."

Clearly skeptical, Sir Robert inquired, "The *people?*"

Exasperated now, the other voice snapped, "Yes!"

At which point Lord Elgin intervened. "May I remind everyone that the subject of this meeting is most serious, and must be considered with all due gravity. Sir Cecil, I'll caution you to show a proper respect. I will not allow petty quibbling to distract us from our goal."

That gave a clue as to the ownership of this third voice. It must be Beadon, the Lieutenant Governor of Bengal.

"Quite, Milord," he replied tersely, "my apologies, sir."

"But why not Bhutians?" Napier continued as if no one else had spoken, "or Bhutaneze? Seems more logical to me!"

Continuing to sound tired Lord Elgin replied, "I'm quite sure that it does, Sir Robert, but it's hardly to the point. I must ask you to be silent while the colonel continues." There followed a muttered something I couldn't make out, and Durand had the floor again.

"Thank you, Milord. As I was saying, the most salient reasons for sending a mission to Bhutan are to recover the captives and stolen property. In order to accomplish this the government is prepared to pay one third of the revenues of the territory of Ambaree Fallacotah." Anticipating further interruption, he hurriedly explained, "A Bhuteau territory we annexed back in Lord Canning's time, for a similar reason, I believe."

"Fat lot of good it did us, if it was!" someone said.

"On the condition," Durand bore on patiently, "that the Bhuteau cease and desist their aggressive behaviour."

"Can't see the good in that, either," Napier again. "Why offer 'em money at all? Why not just march in and have done with it, hey? They've given us enough reason!"

"Perhaps our esteemed colleague is unaware of the geographic nature of Bhutan." This was Beadon again, who was now veiling his irritation with condescension. "Mountainous border country, accessible only through the passes, followed by malarial lowlands thick with swamps and jungle, and that," he said, like a man who has proven his point, "is even before you reach the Himalayas." There followed an impressive pause. "A tough nut to crack, sir!"

Tactfully, Napier replied, "And just who the hell are you to tell me what is or is not a 'tough nut', hey?" Apparently Beadon's condescension had not been lost on him, and he liked it about as much as the next man, "Why, I've bin fightin' nigger armies ever since you were sucking on your wet-nurse's tit, you mealy little pimp!"

At which point the entire room erupted into bedlam. By now I thought it was safe to gather that Napier and Beadon had no use for one another, which said something about the latter, if you like, and not much of it good. For my money, if old Bob said that Bhutan could be taken, I believed him. What's more he would go on to prove it, too, with an even more hazardous undertaking, five years later in Abyssinia, and become known to the world as Sir Robert of Magdala.

Which was neither here nor there at the moment, for the meeting was in danger of getting out of hand. At all points voices were raised in anger while a gavel sounded repeatedly, with Lord Elgin roaring for order. Being an old hand in the diplomatic, he eventually got it, too, and the hubbub died to a whisper. Pressed beyond his patience, the Viceroy was just beginning to tie into the room at large when I heard the door unlatch, and much to my astonishment, I heard Lord Brampton's voice say, "Your pardon, gentlemen."

It would seem that my master's appearance was far more effective at reducing the room to silence than anything Lord Elgin had up his sleeve, for I believe I could have heard a pin drop at that moment.

Then I heard Beadon gasp, "Good God, is that a dressing gown he's wearing?"

I felt myself flush with shame. It was clear that milord required my service, but I was helpless to provide it, even though he was only a room away. What effect the Lieutenant Governor's rudeness had on my master I couldn't say, but I found myself disliking him even more.

Lord Elgin was the first to recover: "So it is. One of mine, I believe." Kindly, he added, "It does you justice, Milord."

"Thank you, Jimmie." Lord Brampton acknowledged the compliment before explaining, "I was caught out in the rain." Perhaps to those who did not know him well, he sounded quite normal; but I, who had known him all my life, could still hear a distance in his voice, as though he were still in a dream.

"To be sure," Elgin replied politely. "Would you care to join us? We were just getting under way."

"I believe that I will," he replied, and presently I heard the scrape of a chair as he took his seat.

When all was ready, Napier was the first to speak. "With your permission, milord."

To which Elgin replied, "You have the floor, Sir Robert."

"Look here," he began, "tough nut or *not*," he emphasized the last word, obviously for Beadon's benefit, "is really not the issue. Conquest need not be our goal when a limited action would serve just as well. We could take the passes just as Lord Auckland did on the Assam frontier back in '43. If we plug the holes our problem's solved."

"As you know, milord, I concur with Sir Robert," this was Colonel Durant. "Sending a mission is a complete waste of time."

"Thank you, Colonel," Elgin replied. "Your opinion has already been noted, as has Sir Robert's."

Well, I couldn't deny that this was all quite edifying, but it did occur to me to wonder why I was here, listening in on a government council, that by its very nature must be held in utmost secrecy. I couldn't credit that Ram Singh or the doctor (who by all accounts gave every indication that this was no novel experience for them) would take such lengthy measures purely in the spirit of mischief...no, not even they. However, any attempt I made to ask immediately resulted in the both of them strictly admonishing me to be quiet. So I sat where I was, without speaking a word, with distinct feelings of discomfort about the propriety of it all, while fretting for my master at the same time.

Hard on that thought, the skin of my scalp shrank with horror when I heard him say, "I was delayed by a woman, you know."

There followed a silence so absolute that I could actually *feel* the astonishment coming through the wall. Even Lord Elgin appeared to be at a loss. My master, however, having explained his tardiness, apparently felt that nothing further was required; so he offered them, "A delightful gel," before lapsing into a silence of his own.

But before anyone could offer a remark, one way or the other, I was almost grateful when I heard Beadon say, "If I may, milord?"

I could hear Elgin's relief quite clearly when he replied, "Please do, Sir Cecil!"

"With all due respect to our military representatives," he made it sound as though very little respect was due at all, "not only must a mission be sent so as not to endanger the lives of the captives, but because seeking diplomatic relations with Poonakha is the correct thing to do."

"And who do you send it to?" Durand demanded. "By all accounts the country's in the middle of a civil war! Which government do we recognize, confound it? The entire situation's preposterous!"

I heard Beadon reply, "I'll grant you that it is unusual..."

And someone else interjected, "Bloody fools are always at each other's throats!"

"...But I have every confidence that it will resolve itself in short order." He pressed on, "My sources tell me that the existing Deb Rajah's position is untenable."

"Very well," this was Napier, proving that he knew more about Bhutan than he'd let on. "But even if they did have a central government for us to speak with, it wouldn't do a damn bit of good. It's the barons who hold the real power!"

"Gentlemen! Gentlemen!" Elgin gave his gavel a tired rap or two.

"We had tea, you see," said my master, with a happy sigh.

Better prepared this time around, Elgin ignored him. Instead he asked, "Mr. Eden, I believe that you would like to say a few words?"

I heard a young voice, not much older than myself, absolutely dripping with self-confidence, "Indeed I would, Your Excellency," hard on the heels of which came a discontented rumble from Napier.

"Gentlemen, as the state secretary for the region in question, I feel that I may be – ah – more *informed* on the subject at hand than some." I'd seldom heard anyone more self-assured, if not out-and-out patronizing. "And I say that it is *vital* that a mission be sent! We dare not risk injury to the captives by precipitate military action...."

Napier rumbled, "Nonsense! Put the word out that we're coming, by Jove, and that they'll have to answer for it if one single hair on any of those poor devils' heads is missing, they'll be safe as houses!"

"...And their property as well. Surely gentlemen, you can see that only misunderstandings can prevail if we do not sit down and speak with the Bhuteau face to face."

"Aye," said Durand archly, "and you're just the laddie to see to it, I suppose?"

Mr. Eden was all cool reproach. "If the Board so decides, then I stand ready, yes, Colonel!"

"You're inordinately eager to pad your portfolio," Durand replied. "I daresay if Lord Auckland was my sire I'd be mighty eager, too! But assuming that we do send a mission, what experience do you have, hey?"

I know when a man was standing on his dignity, and I was listening to it now: "Have you forgotten Sikkim, Colonel? I believe those negotiations were finalized quite satisfactorily!"

"Pshaw!" Durand scoffed, "A politico on *one* mission, *and* you had an army behind you, don't forget!" and then Elgin was rapping his gavel again, calling for order.

Lord Brampton sighed again, "Devlish good looking she was, too. Fine figure of a woman!"

Lord Elgin also sighed, although decidedly not in the same manner.

"Milord," he said, acknowledging my master's presence, before hurrying on. "Gentlemen, it is clear from these arguments, and many others in the past, that we have two differing points of view. I must ask you to listen while I present a third." There was a brief pause, and then he began, "In the past I was opposed to sending a party to deal with these people, firstly on the grounds that their government claimed that *they* would be sending one to visit *us* in Darjeeling…"

Durand scoffed, "And quite a party it would be, too, I'm sure! If I remember correctly from dispatches, Milord, the word that was used was '*zinkaffs*'. It means a common messenger, Excellency!" His incredulity was plain. "Why, the mere proposal of sending such persons to treat with us would be as if Lord Palmerston were to promise to send up a groom or two from Broadlands to talk over the Schleswig-Holstein affair with the Austrian Ambassador!"

"Nevertheless, I chose to wait," Elgin continued ponderously, "because there was still room to hope that it might be otherwise, and I still hold onto some of that hope, slender though it may be, for unfortunately no such messengers ever arrived…"

"Can't say I'm surprised," said Napier. "They don't respect us, the bounders! Been too bloody soft with 'em all along!"

"Therefore I have decided that, barring the offchance that they do arrive, a mission, with Mr. Eden as our envoy, will proceed with the cessation of the rains, and as soon as the political climate in Bhutan deems it appropriate.

"I will remind you," he continued, "that Britain has just fought a long and bloody civil war of our own, here in India. Atrocities have been committed on both sides, for whatever reasons, if reasons they be. The time for vengeance is past, and the time to review the causes of the insurrection must begin. Make no mistake, gentlemen…and Lord…that the British Raj is under a microscope; not only from the world, or princeling protectorates, or neighbouring states, but from the meanest sweeper on the street. I can tell you that his suspicion of us is still very strong. Winning his trust will not be easy, but," he emphasized, "it must begin by showing him that we will act correctly and with forbearance, and *in his interest*." He emphasized even more heavily, "And above all, we must begin *now!*"

I'm not much of one for politics, but it was the finest thing I'd ever heard, and quite took my breath away, let me tell you. It was all I could do to keep myself from applauding.

"Amazing creature," quoth my master, his mind, or what was left of it, still on *la Pirãli's* not inconsiderable charms.

And so the moment passed, and the urge to huzzah for old England passed along with it.

***

Soon after, the meeting wound to adjournment. I rose to attend my master, but Ram Singh assured me that he would be seen to by his own people, and bid me to remain seated. I was halfway through demanding an explanation for this, and for what I could only think of as our dishonourable role of having listened through the entire proceedings, acting no better than common spies, when the door opened, and Lord Elgin himself stepped into the room. While we hastened to our feet (with me at the height of embarrassment to be caught wrapped in nothing more

70

than a blanket, and said feet still in a basin of hot water), he regarded Ram Singh and inquired, "Well, did he hear it all?"

Ram inclined his head, "Oh yes, Excellency!"

I must confess that I was so astonished that I blurted out, "You *knew?*" before I was aware of what I was saying. In an attempt to cover my embarrassment, I thought to attempt to cover my breach of etiquette as well with a much belated "My lord?"

James Bruce was not a tall man, but he had broad shoulders and a barrel chest, and it was said just about the finest mind in the Empire. So it seemed doubly inconceivable to me that he had actually *wanted* me to spy on what was perhaps the most important assembly in all of Southern Asia. He turned to me, his eyes constantly calculating. Instead of an immediate reply, he courteously invited, "Do have a seat, Smithers."

It was as well he offered because I wasn't sure that my knees wouldn't have given out at any rate. But instead of offering me a moment to collect my wits, he began as soon as my backside hit the cushion.

"Capital!" he declared. "So now you see what we're up against, do you?"

One thing that was certain was that I didn't see any such thing.

"My lord?"

"Factions," cries he, "blasted factions pulling every which way but together! Let me tell you, it's enough to drive a man to drink! Thank you, Ram Singh." This last was said as the burly old duffer moved a chair for him to sit. He sank into it with a sigh, and for the first time I noticed that Lord Elgin did not look well. His complexion was grey and the top of his bald pate bore a sheen of perspiration, while those calculating eyes were rimmed in shadow. He had not been so when my lord and I had arrived less than a month earlier. I had always known His Excellency as a man of action, and now wondered what had become of him. "But ne'er mind about that," he continued. "It's my concern, not yours." At which I could only agree, and was on the point of asking him what this was all about, when he enquired, "So tell me, what did you learn?"

71

Where to begin! I stammered some foolishness about it being wonderful to be able to listen in on the halls of power, as it were.

His expression never changed. "What else?"

Of course I realized even before I had finished speaking that this was not the answer that he sought. This man, who for decades had controlled the destinies of nations all across the globe, had not asked his question hoping to be flattered by the likes of me. But what he *was* looking for, I had no idea. I'm a simple fellow at heart, and I'm not ashamed to say it but, when all's said and done, woefully unsuited to the machinations of those in a position of authority. Therefore, as was my custom when occasion found me completely out of my depth, I reverted to the trooper I'd been back in the '50's. Rising to attention, fixing my eyes on the grey wisps fringing the dome of his head, I spoke the truth as I saw it.

"I must say that I did not care for Sir Cecil Beadon's temperament one little bit, sir. In my opinion, his attitude toward my lord Brampton was really quite unsuitable – unsuitable and...and...yes, *churlish* besides!"

I thought that he might laugh in my face, or at the very least damn my eyes, and who was to blame him if he did? It must be admitted that my poor master, with his addled brain, had not exactly deported himself with aplomb either. The difference, as I saw it, was that Lord Brampton had obviously not been in full possession of his faculties, and Sir Cecil had, such as they were, and had lacked the grace I would hope to hear pursuant to a conversation between gentlemen. Why it was shocking, that's what it was! What's more, he wasn't the only one neither. So before Lord Elgin could bring the full weight of his wrath down upon my head, I finished with an indignant, "And if you don't mind my saying so, milord, Mr. Eden is not one jot better!"

There, it was out. Whatever became of me for speaking so about my betters, a blow, however feeble, had been struck in defense of Lord Brampton's honour. Call it foolhardy, call it madness, or whatever you like, but as I saw it, that was the path where my duty lay, and that was the long and the short of it.

But instead of upbraiding me, or consigning me to the nearest dungeon (and I'll ask you to remember that Calcutta had perhaps the most notorious one on earth), Lord Elgin stood and, reaching up, grasped my shoulder in a grip surprisingly strong.

"Good lad!" he cried, before turning to his man. "You were right, Ram Singh: he is a sharp one."

The strain of the day was starting to tell. "My lord," I asked, close to despair, "perhaps you would be so good as to tell me what this is all about!"

"Quite right!" he said. "Mustn't keep you in suspense any longer, hey? Most inconsiderate of me." He insisted that I return to my seat, while he did likewise. Whereupon he continued to grill me with those calculating eyes of his. "My boy," says he, "when Eden sets out to Poonakha, I want you and Lord Brampton to accompany him."

Well, Ram Singh had said as much the previous day, but it still came as a surprise, considering everything that had transpired since that time. With that in mind, I thought it wise to bring up this most pressing issue.

"My lord," I told him, "I'm afraid that it's out of the question." I felt myself flush with embarrassment, but looked him in the eye. "My master is not well, as you yourself must have plainly seen." I then went on to tell him all about the events that had taken place on our way to Government House.

Well, it was my day to be astonished, and no error, for instead of becoming angry or concerned, or even surprised, Lord Elgin merely laughed, and said to the doctor, "What would you say, Simpson, must've been dashed good *bhang*, what?"

With an evil grin the doctor replied that, judging from what he had heard, it must have been superior quality indeed, and what was more, Lord Brampton must have taken an inordinate measure of it on board, whereupon all three of them had a goodish chortle at my master's expense. I could only remain perplexed, and await an explanation.

Finally taking pity, the doctor informed me, "*Bhang*, is the local term for cannabis." When he saw that I remained unenlightened, he added, "A concoction derived from the hemp plant. Quite common up in the north country, where I believe his lady friend claims to be from. The effects can be quite similar to what you've just described."

Well, this was all news to me…but stay! No it wasn't neither! I remembered now: lying on a pallet in that Massai hut, with both ankles broken, and only a pot of honey-beer to ease the pain. Then there was that wonderful creature, with those lovely eyes, patiently miming how I should inhale the pungent smoke from a bowl of burning hemp. Aye, I remembered, and felt that old familiar pang, whenever I was caught unaware.

"He was drugged," I said. It was not a question. I remembered my lord referring to the tea.

"Can't be sure, of course," Lord Elgin allowed, "but that would be my guess, wouldn't you say, Ben?"

The doctor went one further. "As sure as God made little green apples," says he. "The man was tight as a hat band!"

I didn't care for my lord being referred to with such familiarity, and offered him a cold stare and a sniff, but the effort was wasted. The doctor's evil grin did not relent. "His lordship will be himself, by and by, and no harm done, you'll see."

I can't say that I was entirely mollified, nor would I be until I saw for myself that Lord Brampton had recovered, but I was able to set the matter aside in order that we might continue. I had thought that there could be no astounding me further, after all that had transpired, but of course I was wrong again. Still there was one question weighing on my mind.

"Sir, if you wish to have Lord Brampton accompany Mister Eden, why don't you simply ask him? I still don't understand why you should be saying any of this to me!"

Elgin nodded soberly. "To be sure, Smithers. Lord Brampton's presence would be quite beneficial to the cause. A peer could only add prestige to the occasion, and show the Bhuteau how serious the Raj is for an agreement to be reached. In addition, by all accounts that I've heard, he would be able to put up a bold front as well."

I replied that my master's courage was beyond dispute, and it was too…when he wasn't drugged up to his ears.

He nodded and said, "I'm quite sure that he takes after his father, brave as the very devil. Given the right circumstances, he was quite capable, as I recall."

I didn't require any further explanation as to what Lord Elgin meant by 'the right circumstances'. Given occasion where bravery was called for and very little else, my lord's father was in his element, and so it was with my lord as well, I had to admit. But if that occasion demanded speculation or planning, both suffered under a distinct disadvantage. But even if such were nothing more than the truth, no matter how plainly evident, I could never allow myself to say so. Consequently I said nothing at all.

Elgin continued. "Yes, he would be beneficial as a figurehead, but Eden will do the negotiating. He has the experience, after all, or that is to say," he amended, "more than Lord Brampton, at any rate." The way he said it made me wonder if he had much faith in Mr. Eden, either. As I'd overheard, he wasn't exactly awash with experience.

"But that's all fish for the stew," Elgin continued, closing to the point, "The real reason that I want our Lord Brampton to go is so that he will take you with him."

I could actually feel my eyes pop out of my head.

"*Me*, sir?"

"Yes, Smithers," he told me, ever so grim, "you."

There was only one question to ask that I could think of, and so I did.

"But why?"

At which Lord Elgin grew even grimmer, and so too did Ram Singh and Doctor Simpson, now that it occurred to me to notice. Both of them standing on either side of the Viceroy as they were, I must say that they didn't make a very pretty picture.

"Now see here, Charlie," Elgin began, then thought to ask, "May I call you Charlie?" Of course I was dumbfounded. It never occurred to me to think that the Governor General of all of India would ever bother with the given name of a mere manservant, but here he was, asking just that, and as polite as you could ever ask for, too. When I gave him a dumb nod of assent, he continued. "See here, Charlie, what I am about to tell you is not to go beyond these walls, do you understand?"

"Why yes, sir!" I told him, 'dumbfounded' having given away, once more, to my old acquaintance, 'perplexed'.

He studied me closely. In fact I could feel everyone's eyes upon me. So heavy it was, too, that it made my flesh crawl.

"Very well," he said, "I gather that what Ram Singh has told you, and what you heard in there," he tilted his head to the room on the other side of the wall, "that you must know something about the political hierarchy in Bhutan?"

I admitted, "Only a little, sir. I gather that this Deb Rajah is their ruler?"

"Nominally, yes, in all things secular," he told me, "although their spiritual ruler, The Dhurm Rajah, supersedes him." He explained further, "Sort of like the Queen and Lord Palmerston."

"Oh, I see, sir!" then for no reason I could think of added, "Thank you, sir!"

"But the real power," he said, "lies with the barons – their *penlos* – and the greatest of these are the two that govern the passes. The Paro Penlo, whose territory borders with Bengal in the west, and the Tongso Penlo, sharing a border with Assam to the east. Now there's one very important fact that you must understand: Bhutan's economy depends upon those passes – those *duars*, I should say. They charge a levy on all goods entering or leaving the country…"

"That's a polite way of putting it," interjected the doctor sourly. "Their system's rotten to the core! The beggars would rob you blind if you let them!"

"Quite," Elgin agreed, "but that is neither here nor there for the moment. What is to the point is what Sir Robert alluded to earlier. In Auckland's time, the Raj did annex the Assam *duars*, and in order that they not bankrupt the entire country, granted the government in Poonakha a stipend in compensation under the caveat of their continued good behaviour."

"Fat lot of good that did, too!" the doctor snorted his derision, echoing what had been said earlier in the chamber.

76

By way of acknowledging, Elgin said, "Yes, well, their central government is exceedingly weak, with no army or police to speak of, or laws either, for that matter. The Deb Rajah accepts our money readily enough, but claims that he's powerless to stop the intrusions through the Bengal *duars*, and I daresay there's some truth to that. The penlos are a law unto themselves. With the annexation of the Assam *duars*, and – in an effort to break the Tongso Penlo's power – paying the revenue directly to the Deb Rajah , we have only succeeded in making an enemy of him." Elgin shrugged, "He's been deprived of his main source of income, so he stands in defiance of the government, and plots his revenge by way of further incursions along the Bengal frontier.

"Now Charlie," he leaned forward, clasping his hands together, "I am under no illusion that Mr. Eden's mission will succeed. It will fail; the Tongso Penlo will make sure of it, and sooner or later there will be war. But it does have its uses," he allowed. "It will give me eyes on the Bhuteau who matter." His stare was unwavering, and as God's my witness, could mean only one thing!"

"Me?" I gasped.

"You," he replied evenly.

"But...but...that makes no sense, sir, if you don't mind my saying so! Surely there are others..."

"Indeed there are," he agreed. "Some with more experience at collecting intelligence, too, but there is one thing that I have yet to point out." After a brief pause he said, "The mission may not be without its perils." The way he said it did nothing to alleviate my anxiety. "If anything should happen, it might be necessary to cut and run." His eyes remained fixed when he said, "In such a situation a man of proven worth over rough country would become invaluable."

I sat huddled in my blanket, with my feet – still soaking – forgotten in the pan, staring wide-eyed with disbelief, while doing my best to ignore the chill rising along my spine.

"But, My lord," I reasoned, "I am nothing more than a gentleman's gentleman. What do I know about rough living?"

Without batting an eye, he replied, "A good deal more than you're letting on," and then he absolutely floored me with, "as your experience in Africa seems to suggest."

Chapter Five

I was a very thoughtful menial on my solitary walk back to the Auckland, I can promise you that. Ram Singh had assured me that my lord had left Government House some time earlier, by way of the Viceroy's personal carriage, and had been accompanied by a man hand-picked by Ram himself. So there was no need to worry on that score, but there seemed to be plenty of need to worry on others, and this I proceeded to do, with all due abandon.

At the top of the list was Lord Elgin's declaration that this harebrained dream child of his (this bloody mission to the back-of-beyond, smack dab in the middle of territory that, by all reports, might well be described as hostile) was about as madcap as any I'd ever heard. Why, the very notion of Lord Brampton being placed, purposefully, in a position of danger was enough to make me feel quite indignant, I don't mind telling you. By God, what did Elgin think he was about, involving my master in his beastly machinations? Why, it was downright unsporting, that's what it was! Unsporting, and…and even *devious*, so there!

And speaking of devious, that brought me to the next item on the list: Madam Pirãli. Just what had *she* been up to, plying my lord with some beastly oriental concoction? What game was she playing? I should think that Lord Brampton was quite mesmerized enough without doping him up to his ears. Why, all she had to do was coil her little finger and he was at her heel like a puppy, and that was when he was *in* his right mind, too. So what had she to gain by luring him out of it?

"Right, then," I murmured with my firmest British resolve, "I think it's time to visit the lady myself, and squeeze some truth out of her. There's more to that one than meets the eye, or my name's not Charlie Smithers."

Having arrived at that conclusion, which was by no means satisfactory as of yet, I was forced to set it aside for the moment, as there were other items that required my attention with some urgency.

Lord Elgin had the temerity to state that he wished for me to be his eyes and ears on this blasted mission, or to put it another way – to spy for him. 'A sharp one' he had called me. Well, I daresay you could dig into the annals of the Smithers family history as deep as you like, and never find what you would call a genius, but we weren't exactly drooling imbeciles, neither. Aye, and possibly a lifetime of service had honed my senses, to where I could judge a gentleman's temperament and personality to a nicety. So I did have to admit (grudgingly, you may be sure) that I could be of some use in that regard. But that only brought me to the last item that was troubling me, and quite frankly, I didn't know what to make of it: Elgin's knowledge of my time in Africa.

It was true: I'd made my way across rough country in my time – more than two thousand miles of it by my reckoning, dodging spears and arrows, and belligerent locals, howling for my skin every step of the way, besides. What's more I'd done it on my own, not like some I could mention: not like John Speke, for instance. Why, compared to what I'd been through, he'd made the same journey in the bloody lap of luxury, he did – servants and bearers to beat the band – and even then it had come to within a hair of doing him in. So I was aware of what my accomplishment had been, and was duly proud of the fact, but what I didn't understand was how Lord Elgin could know of it, for I hadn't told a blessed soul.

Oh I may have tried to, once or twice – to Lord Brampton, for instance, but he hadn't much interest, and I must admit that the same could be said for my own parents. Couldn't I just remember how my guv'nor's eyes had glazed over while he listened politely, and then congratulating me for my imagination afterward? Then there was my Presbyterian mother, whose eyes hadn't glazed, but narrowed with suspicion. For hers was the same opinion as my father, but instead of congratulating me, she had toddled off to the kitchen and, returning with the iron soup ladle, had cranged it off the back of my head. It was the same as she'd always done when I was a lad, when she guessed that I was telling a stretcher.

There were other reasons too, of course. I think that, upon returning to his homeland, every traveler can identify with the frustration of trying to describe distant lands and wondrous

80

creatures and sites. No matter how hard you wrestle with the words, it just isn't possible to make those moments come alive for others the way it was for you, and after a while you just stop trying. So there was that, but I think most of all, my memories of Loiyan were too intermingled with everything else, to want to take that chance.

You see, no one back home would ever have been capable of understanding. Perhaps I'm doing them an injustice, but I believe I am not. If I had attempted to describe her, they wouldn't have imagined her as she was (a beautiful creature who loved me) but as a blackamoor and little else. Their eyes would have judged me, which was neither here nor there, but they would also have judged *her*, and that was altogether different. So I kept my silence, protecting her memory as best I could. Until Lord Elgin had otherwise informed me, I had thought myself successful, and was duly disconcerted to find that I was not. Coming under the notice of the mighty can be a double-edged sword: recognition from the Royal Geographic was one thing, but put in the hands of the most powerful man in India, who must be ruthless enough to use every means at his disposal in order to maintain the machinery of government, there was every chance that it could be rather more perilous.

Not that I've ever shied away from peril, you understand, but like any man with a grain of sense, I don't go looking for it, neither. Live and let live is my motto, and a long life for all, but I'm here to tell you that don't count for much in the heart of hostile territory.

With the weight of these subjects on my mind, I was very deep in thought, and only succeeded in returning to the present when I arrived at the Auckland, and was standing outside my master's bedroom door. My respectful scratch upon its panels went unanswered but for the deep glottal rumble of his snoring. I opened the door a crack to peep in, and sure enough, my lord lay in bed, with the covers tucked under his chin, in deep repose from the day's ordeal. With nothing further to see to his immediate welfare, I decided that the time was ripe to look to his future. Therefore, exiting the suite on tiptoe, I took the few steps required down the corridor, and knocked upon her door.

81

It was answered in due course by a handsome girl dressed in the Auckland's livery, but before she could inquire as to my purpose, a voice came from within the room that I recognized as Madam Pirāli's.

"Who is it, Sarala?"

Answering in the maidservant's stead, I replied, "'Tis Smithers, ma'am." And presently she appeared, dressed in cloth of gold pantaloons that Indian ladies sometimes favour (although few as tight-fitting as this) along with a light muslin bodice and nothing more.

"What do you want?" she asked, and the Queen could not have sounded more imperious.

"A word," I told her, "in private, if you please."

She studied me for a moment, her eyes narrow with suspicion. I returned her gaze evenly, doing my utmost to ignore the chasm of her cleavage. Finally, to Sarala, she said, "Leave us."

When the girl was gone, she did not ask me to sit. Instead she took a chair for herself, regarded me with her expression unchanged, and said, "Well?"

I said, "It is in regard to my Lord Brampton, ma'am, and his condition this morning."

"His condition?"

"Yes, ma'am."

"What of it?"

"Ma'am," I replied, "milord was not himself, as I'm sure you're aware."

Ignoring my implication, she said, "Not himself? Whatever do you mean?"

"I have reason to believe that he was drugged," I told her, and her eyes looked askance.

Still clinging to her role as the innocent, with her nose in the air she replied, "Drugged? What sort of drug?"

When I told her, she said, "And you think it was me that gave it to him." Indeed, it was useless for her to pretend otherwise.

"Yes, ma'am, I do. It could have been no other."

The air between us grew even more tense, but only for a moment, then suddenly she laughed. "Very well, it was I!" Her eyes flashed with anger, and her tone filled with scorn, "What of it?"

I said, "I would know your intentions, ma'am."

"My *intentions?*" She regarded me as if I were a simpleton. "How dare you!" and looked down her nose at me. "You have no right! Furthermore, I'll remind you that I am under your master's protection!"

Uncompromising, I told her, "He may be your protector, ma'am, but he is also my gentleman, and his welfare is not only my concern, but my duty. If you are his enemy, I must warn you that you are also mine. Now, I will ask you again, what were your intentions?"

Her mouth dropped open, and her eyes bulged from her head. In fact her expression was so completely that of stark disbelief that I began to feel disconcerted in spite of myself.

Finally she found her voice. "I find your…*request* to be very ungallant!"

I sighed, "Ma'am, it is not a request, and I would have an answer directly, for it has already been a most trying day."

She looked askance again, and began to fidget in her chair, her skin flushing darker than it already was. Then she turned to me, glaring her defiance, but hard on that, her haughtiness suddenly crumbled, leaving in its place a little girl.

Now subdued, she said, "You cannot know what it is like to be a woman in India." Her voice was scarcely more than a whisper. "Everything that we have, everything that we are, depends upon a man." I might have pointed out that it wasn't so different in England, but held my tongue. "You saw how it was." Now she did look at me; her eyes were pleading. "You saw what those…those, *animals* were about to do to me! I would have died most painfully, had it not been for your master coming to my rescue! Oh, I don't expect you to believe me, but I meant him no harm, in fact quite the opposite," she shrugged and simply said, "He saved my life."

Everything about her was sincerity in itself, but I remained obdurate. "Then what of this morning, ma'am?"

She blushed so furiously that the kohl around her eyes faded into nothing. She looked once more to the floor, and confessed, "I wished to show him my gratitude," and even managed a half smile. "Surely you would not begrudge me that?"

"Gratitude!" I believe that the word fairly exploded from my mouth. "What on earth…" and then I blinked, astonished, feeling my own face beginning to flush, and said, "Oh!"

She said, "A woman who has nothing to give, gives herself," and although she was still blushing, the smile remained. "I am well versed in the ways of pleasing a man. The *bhang*," she explained, "was to be part of that."

"Look here," I stammered, "do you mean to tell me that you drugged Lord Brampton and…and…"

Sensing correctly that I was now the more uncomfortable of the two of us, she gained confidence, and admitted, "It was my intention to have congress with him, yes."

"But surely," I said, "a woman of your…that is to say of your…"

Her smile deepened. "Appeal?"

I nodded, "Yes!"

Her eyes were twinkling now. "So you do not think that I require such a subterfuge to lure a man into my bed?"

"Good God, no!"

Wickedly, she traced the outline of her generous figure with languid fingernails. "You believe that this should be sufficient?"

I confess that I was unable to keep myself from gasping, "Rather!" and give in to the urge to take a moment to ogle the rest of her from the neck down. Well, it had been at the lady's invitation, after all.

Finally she took pity and laughed. "I thank you for the compliment, Charlie," and don't you know, I didn't mind a jot that she'd used my given name. "Perhaps you are right, but I did not drug our lord in order to lure him, but rather to heighten his pleasure."

She didn't seem to mind when I stumbled my way to a chair. Sinking gratefully onto the cushion, I said, "I see." Then, in an attempt to be clear, I asked, "So you put the *bhang* in his tea?"

She shook her head. "The *bhang was* the tea, and of a variety that I knew to be especially potent." She gave a little amused shrug, "John...that is to say, Lord Brampton, took an immediate liking to it...with a pinch of lemon, and drank a great deal – more than I should have allowed, I confess, but he was so ardent, and I was foolish enough to enjoy his flattery." She absolutely fluttered her lashes at me. "Such moments are very rare for an old woman of thirty years."

Well, if she was fishing for compliments from me, she could have them, and the town clock, too. What her attire managed to cover was scarcely worth mentioning, and what it revealed was all present and accounted for in the most pleasing way imaginable. Just knowing that she was so close, squirming in that chair of hers, with her bodice fit to burst, was enough to make a fellow break out in a hellish sweat, I can tell you. But there were other things to consider, of course; there always were.

It took an effort, but in due course I was able to regain my feet, as well as my composure. I turned to her and bowed. "I assure you, ma'am, that your beauty is beyond question, if I may be so bold as to say so. I congratulate my lord upon having such a discerning eye."

She accepted the compliment with a grateful smile, but then followed it immediately with a little frown, and asked, "Does he?"

Puzzled, I could only reply, "Ma'am?"

"Have a discerning eye?" she said, "I mean we were chatting quite comfortably, and I was just waiting for the tea to take effect, when the next thing I know he announced that he had just remembered something rather important. In a trice he had his watch out, claimed that he must be away, and was gone. It was all very astonishing, I must say, and not at all flattering, either."

Realizing how little time had elapsed from my lord's partaking to when I met him scurrying from his rooms made her story all the more plausible. Why, the effects must have hit him between then and by the time that he had reached the street.

When I told her what the occasion had been, when my master had taken his leave so abruptly, she gasped and said, "Oh my goodness! Do you mean to tell me that he was..." her hand swam before her face, searching for a word. Failing in that, she continued, "…in the presence of the Viceroy?"

"Quite," I told her.

Whereupon she seemed to crumple in on herself. "I have been so foolish!" she wailed. "How could I have put dear Lord Brampton in such a frightful situation?" She turned to me, her face imploring, and I could do nothing less than take note of the transformation in her from when I first entered the room. "Oh Charlie, how you must despise me! You must think that I am a very wicked woman! Oh to be sure, I am not what you Christians would call a saint: I am only a Tantrist following her creed, but you must believe me when I tell you that I never intended any harm, you simply must!" Suddenly she reached out with both her hands and grasped my sleeve, every delectable fiber of her was beseeching me. "I will make amends," she declared. "Just tell me what I must do, and I shall do it gladly! I swear by all that is holy!"

Gently, I extricated my arm, and looked away, closing my eyes so that I might think. As the moments passed, it became clear to me what should have been clear all along: whatever, or whoever, else was at stake, my foremost duty lay in watching over my master's wellbeing. Finally, with a silent prayer for forgiveness on my lips, I made a decision and turned to her. She remained seated, although her hands were now clasped together in her lap. She was wringing them repeatedly while anxiously studying my face for any sign of what my judgement might be.

"Ma'am," I told her, "the first thing that you must do, is indicate to me where we might find more of this marvelous hemp."

***

"Not *going?*" Lord Elgin's brows knit so sharply that the grey fringe around his skull seemed to close in on the domed pinnacle. "Do you mean to tell me that Lord Brampton *refuses* to go – nay – refuses *me?*"

Very evenly I replied, "He does, milord," all the while doing my best not to look too pleased.

86

Elgin gnashed his teeth and swore. "Well, that's the very devil of a thing, wouldn't you say, Ram Singh? The very devil, confound it!"

I looked at Ram, and then quickly away again when I saw that he was watching me in turn, with eyes too shrewd for comfort.

"Indeed it is, sahib," quoth he, in a voice without inflection.

"I don't know what to make of it!" Elgin began to pace back and forth, thrusting his hands beneath his tails. "Highly irregular," he growled, flashing me an angry look over his shoulder. "Don't know what to make of it at all!"

Well there was nothing to say in reply to that, so I thought it prudent to maintain a respectful silence, and wait for reason to will out. Personally, though, I couldn't see what all the fuss was about: Elgin had already admitted that my lord's presence on the mission was not really required. It seemed to me that his pique was, in the main, due to being refused what even he must admit was a request, and not a command. In a way I could see his point, though – a man who had made his mark by shaping the policies of Her Majesty's Government all over the globe, and who now sat in control of an entire subcontinent (which was, in fact, an empire in its own right) a request declined must come as something of a shock.

Not that I cared much about that, you understand. Time heals all wounds, including a blueblood's ruffled dignity. It was Lord Brampton's safety that most concerned me…and my own, too, of course. If the time ever came to cut and run, I know for a fact tha it would never occur to him to do so. It was by no means an idle boast when it was said that a Brampton never ran. They did not. They didn't know *how*. For them there was only glorious victory, or glorious death. Inglorious retreat was not in their vocabulary, which is why the remains of that noble family have littered battlefields from the time of Bannockburn to Waterloo. No, when all was said and done, as much as it was, perhaps, a dishonourable path to take, on my part, to deny my master the chance to do what some might see as his duty, there was no question in my mind that he was better off in the arms of Madam

Pirāli, doped up to the ears with bhang, if need be, rather than finding a hero's death in the back of beyond. Let Elgin think as he liked; this was one occasion were my honour and my duty did not walk hand in hand.

Still it must have been hard for the old fellow, so to soften the blow, I said, "On the other hand, Your Excellency, Lord Brampton did not forbid my participation."

At which Elgin stopped short and swung around. "D'you mean to say he would give you leave?" His astonishment was plain; by the quizzical set of his brows I could see that even Ram had been caught off guard.

I assured him, "Indeed, he already has, sir."

What my master had actually said on the subject had been so intermingled with a dream-like prosing on Madam Pirāli's virtues (coupled with much that was, at best, incomprehensible) that I wasn't at all certain that he was aware whether he was giving me leave to accompany Mr. Eden to Bhutan, or to America, but his exact words in response to my query were a bemused, "Hmm? Yes, all right."

Elgin swung around to his man. "Well that's something at least, hey, Ram Singh?"

Although he never took his eyes off me, Ram inclined his head gravely, and allowed that it was.

So, on the surface of things, with Lord Elgin greatly mollified, that seemed to be that, but as I suspected, I would not get off so easily. When I bowed and took my leave from His Excellency's presence, Ram Singh insisted upon escorting me off the premises.

We had no sooner left the room than I murmured to him from the corner of my mouth, "Ask me no questions and I'll tell you no lies."

As it turned out I needn't have worried, for he merely chuckled softly, and reached inside his tunic for his flask. Helping himself to a generous mouthful, he then offered it to me. I thought, "By gad, why not?" as the meeting with Lord Elgin had been more trying than I had predicted. After all, regardless of the right or the wrong of the matter, one does not beard the Viceroy in his own lair every day, does one?

When I had shuddered away the effects of the brandy, Ram said, "Be at peace, Charlie. What is it to me if your Lord Brampton spends his time befuddled in the amorous embrace of the Pirāli woman?"

Something on my face must have registered my shock, for he smiled and said, "Did I not tell you? My wife's third cousin's number two son is employed as a page at the Auckland." He took another healthy sip, and continued happily, "He is, as you English say, 'learning the ropes', but we have high hopes for him one day."

I should have known better, of course. The wily old duffer would have an eye to every portal in town, if not the entire state, or indeed all of India. I may not be the brightest spark, but that didn't prevent me from seeing that Ram Singh was more than your average gentleman's gentleman. What he said next confirmed that, and unsettled me to no end.

"What do you know about her, this Pirāli woman?" he asked. He'd spoken casually, but it didn't prevent an uneasy stir in my stomach.

"Why, as much as you do," I replied. "We were both there when she told her story."

"Just so," he agreed, then asked lightly, "Do you trust her?"

I could feel those uneasy fingers begin to twine into my vitals, but then I remembered how she looked stripped of her haughty veneer: so vulnerable and like a child. I was convinced that she meant my master no harm. "Yes," I told him. "Yes I do. Why do you ask?"

"Oh, it is probably nothing," he grinned self-deprecatingly. "Doubtless there is a flaw in my character that has made me a suspicious old fool."

"What do you mean?" I asked, feeling less and less at ease, in spite of myself. If Ram Singh smelled a rat it behooved me to find out what it was.

He offered me another sip from his flask, but I waved it away. So he shrugged and tucked it back into his tunic. Then, with a thoughtful half-smile, he said, "She told us that she was from the north, did she not?"

When I agreed that she had, he continued, "There have been reports of *thug* activity from those parts." He regarded me with a significant look on his face. "I am sure that you recall the manner of Gopal Pirāli's death?"

Well that brought me up short, to be sure, for there could not be more than a handful of people in the entire empire who weren't aware of the term and its meaning. *Thuggee* had been the practice of ritual murder by a sect devoted to the goddess, Kali, and had been responsible for tens of thousands of deaths all across India back in the earlies. For sheer barbarity it had known no equal, but the very notion seemed preposterous in this day and age.

Yet preposterous or not, I couldn't keep the desperation from my voice when I said, "*Thugs?* But they were stamped out back in the '30's, surely!"

"That is largely true," he agreed, "but every now and then there will be occurrences, here and there." And again he regarded me over his spectacles, "You are new to India, Charlie, but I think even you have some knowledge of their *modus operandi.*"

Gad, and so I did, as did everyone! *Thuggee* would join up with innocent bands of unwary travelers, in small numbers to avoid suspicion, but gradually, unbeknownst to the innocent, increasing along the way, until eventually they would fall upon their victims at a preconceived signal; but that wasn't the half of it, by god! The cause of death had always been their calling card, and the deep welt around Gopal Pirāli's neck leapt, unbidden, to the forefront of my mind: strangulation!

"But hold on," I said, attempting to ward away the notion. "Surely women don't signify."

"It is rare," he conceded, "but not unheard of, Charlie. Back in my fathers time a sect of women *Thuggee* swept through the Punjab, accounting for many lives before they were brought to justice." What he said next sent chills racing up and down my spine: "It is important to take note that they were Tantrists, too, just as your Madam Pirāli."

Astounded, I could only say, "D'you mean...?"

"Precisely, Charlie," he replied, "for when else is a man more vulnerable than during the act of *surata?*"

90

When indeed? "But surely you're not suggesting that Madam Pirāli is some sort of sex-crazed murderous!" The very idea was too far-fetched to believe, and yet, those icy fingers continued to mangle my bowels.

Ram replied, "I am not suggesting anything, Charlie. I am merely pointing out some facts that, if you add them together, you may find the sum disquieting. But it may turn out to have no meaning at all."

In order to press the latter option, I seized on what should have been obvious. "But you saw for yourself what Gopal's beastly disciples were about to do to her! Why, they were about to burn her at the stake, man! In fact, one of them was on the point of setting a torch to the whole business when we burst on the scene!"

"We saw what we saw," he allowed, "but I did not see a man with a torch, did you?"

"You know I did! I shot the bounder myself!"

"Even the best laid plan lacks perfection," he replied. "Perhaps it was reckoned that the distance between you was too great for any sort of accuracy. Perhaps they were planning on allowing us to think that they had been frightened off." He looked at me, "Almost certainly they hadn't expected such a keen shot as yours."

"But...but..."

"Yes," Ram agreed, "Lord Brampton was a witness," but before I could feel any relief, he posed the question, "However, is what you saw actually what was about to take place, or what you were intended to see, and so come to an erroneous conclusion?" And then he pressed the point, "How can we know with absolute certainty what their intentions were? We have only the lady's word to go by, after all."

In my mind I saw her leaning forward, every ounce of her naked emotion as she begged me to believe her. No, it couldn't be. My servant's instinct knew that she was telling the truth.

"Perhaps you're forgetting something," and I found myself gaining confidence, as I knew that I had found the truth of the matter. "There's one glaring hole in your hypothesis. *Thugs* go in for murdering strangers, and Gopal Pirāli was madam's husband, remember? That's a stretch even for them!"

"Ah yes, the *alleged* husband," Ram replied, and I didn't like the way he said it – no, not at all. "I took the liberty of having my people make some inquiries to the north. Being a Brahmin of some station, it was not too difficult to ascertain where Gopal Pirāli's village lay – if you'll recall, madam neglected to volunteer that information; an oversight, no doubt, but what my agent discovered upon speaking to the household is irrefutable."

"*Irrefutable?*" My voice seemed to be coming from some distance away, while my mind scrambled to brace itself for a shock.

"Yes, Charlie, I am afraid so."

It were as though someone else was speaking, when I heard myself ask, "And what might that be?"

There was compassion in Ram Singh's voice; I could hear it clearly when he replied, "Gopal Pirāli was a widower, Charlie." And then to make it perfectly clear, he added, "He left behind no living wife."

Chapter Six

I was in a rare taking, indeed. As my lord's manservant, I'd learned to take a lot over the years, but there was nothing more certain to raise my hackles than being lied to. In fact, so vexed was I that upon arriving at the Auckland, I strode angrily down the corridor, bypassing my master's apartments altogether, and banged loudly on her door. When it was opened, I brushed past her maid and into the room, without so much as a by-your-leave.

She was standing at a birdcage, attempting to coax a luxuriously plumed parrot to accept a bit of fruit from her fingers. She was dressed differently from before, but the effect was exactly the same.

She turned when I came in. "Charlie!" she cried gaily, gesturing toward the bird, "This is Sanji, a present from…" and stopped short when she noticed my mien.

"Madam," I told her, through jaws tightly clenched, "whatever your name is, I will have the truth!"

I expected her to deny it, to continue to play the innocent. I expected an ordeal, but I intended to get to the bottom of this for my master's sake, whatever the cost.

What I did not expect was for her to show her concern – not for herself but for me – and say, "So you know."

"That I do!" I replied, "Come, madam, did you not think that I would discover your secret eventually?"

Her face was a mixture of sorrow, and something that I couldn't understand, for I thought that it might be relief.

She said, "I am sorry that I lied. I wanted to tell you when we spoke the other day," she made a futile gesture with her hand, "but I lacked the courage."

A likely story, thinks I, and put it to her plain. "Madam, are you a *thug*?"

At which her jaw abruptly became unhinged, and she stared at me with such unfettered astonishment that it was hard not to believe that I'd caught her unaware.

She mouthed for some moments without making a sound. Eventually she was able to say, "What?" It was necessary for me to repeat the question twice more before she registered the least comprehension.

"You believe that I am a *thug?*" she asked, and I must admit that her astonishment was almost convincing.

"Speak truly!" I snapped, "Do you deny it?"

She replied with vehemence, "I do!" with tears beginning to well in her eyes.

Striving not to be disconcerted by them, I said, "You cannot deny that the manner of Gopal Pirāli's death was suspicious, and is in accordance with *Thuggee* custom!"

"Suspicious it may be," she flared, "but it happened exactly as I told you!" She turned away, dashing her knuckles to her mouth. "Oh Charlie you are cruel to believe this…this *lie!*"

I brushed this aside. Still quite cool, I asked, "Perhaps you'd be so good as to tell me who you really are."

Her hand came away from her mouth to clasp with the other at her waist. Taking a moment to square her shoulders, she turned to me. "I am called Amrita Joshi, servant girl to Gopal Pirāli."

"A servant? Why didn't you tell me this before?"

She shrugged and looked away. "Because I saw a chance to become someone other than who I was."

"Speak plainly, can't you?"

"Oh, Charlie!" she gestured helplessly, "I am *Dalit*, the lowest of the low, an untouchable!" She murmured more to herself than to me, "Although that did not prevent Gopal Pirāli, a high caste Brahmin, from touching me every chance that he could!"

"I don't understand," I told her, and then ventured, "You were his consort?"

"I was his *bed woman!*" She spat the words with such distaste that her lip curled into a sneer. "My parents sold me to him when I was thirteen."

"Hold on, do you mean to tell me that your parents *sold* you?" I was so shocked that the only utterance I was capable of was, "Good God!"

"I mean exactly that, Charlie."

"And you were only a child at the time?"

94

She might have agreed, if for no better reason than to press her argument. Instead she merely shrugged, "Perhaps by your English standard, I was."

I had to ask, "Were they aware that..." but lost my nerve, "that is to say..."

"Were my parents aware that they were selling me into a life of bondage with a beast?" she asked bitterly. "Of course they knew. The entire village knew, but our family was poor, and Gopal Pirāli was depraved enough to ignore our customs, and was willing to pay besides. They reasoned that there was no other choice."

It was all a bit much for me to absorb, so I mused in silence, while willing the shock to dissipate. Perhaps I waited too long, or the silence was not to her liking, for after a moment she continued, "Perhaps they were thinking: where else would an untouchable have such an opportunity?"

Well, that beat all, and I couldn't make head or tails out of it. So naturally I asked, "What do you mean *opportunity*?"

"To live in the house of a Brahmin," she said, "to become educated, and to better myself. These are not small things, Charlie." She looked away again, "and what it cost was just a little thing – so little as to be almost inconsequential. In exchange for hope, they allowed him to deflower me, and practice his depravity upon my person. All those years I tried to tell myself that the exchange was a fair one," she continued to look away, "sometimes I almost succeed."

Well, it was shocking enough, I daresay, but at least I was beginning to understand. "So when Gopal's followers came upon you and found him dead..."

"After they had their way with me – again, it was such a small thing," but her voice was as stone, "it was decided that I should atone for their sins, and become purified in the bargain."

"In the flames."

"Yes," she whispered. "In the flames." Then, she roused herself with very little pause, "But when Lord Brampton rescued me, and I saw his face, I felt... oh I felt *everything* that I told you! He was so tender! So brave! So *noble*! I wanted to belong to him as I have never wanted anything before!" Her eyes slid

95

downward, "And yet how could a lowly *Dalit* ever hope for something so grand? I knew that first I must become worthy!"

"So you decided to become a Brahmin, to become Madam Pirāli?"

Her gaze remained fixed on the floor, and in a small voice she whispered, "Yes."

I chided, "You could have told me."

She raised her eyes; they were pleading again. "I wanted to tell you, Charlie. Oh, you must believe me! But by then I already had much to atone for, and you and I..." she gestured with her hand, searching for a way to proceed, "...I felt that we had become friends, and I did not wish to place that in peril!" she sighed, impatient with herself, "The lie had gone too far, and I could not think of a way to take it back."

Well, there was no two ways about it, this was as wild and wooly a tale as I was ever likely to hear, but was it the truth? I wanted to believe her, just as I had wanted to believe another story at a different time and place: in Africa, when Omar had convinced me that his Baggara meant a peaceful village no harm. I had believed him then, much to my cost. I couldn't allow myself to make the same mistake again.

However, as unlikely as her story was, this Amrita Joshi, I couldn't say with any conviction that there wasn't any logic to it, because there was. I couldn't condone her lie, but I could at least understand it. In a moment of the utmost trauma, she had seen what she had thought was an opportunity and had seized upon it, and who could fault her for that? Well, all right, plenty could fault her; it was deceitful after all, but who among us, finding ourselves in the same situation, could say with any degree of conviction that they would not have done the same? Would I? Well, no, I wouldn't – I'm a Smithers – but that didn't mean that I couldn't understand the motives of those who would, and while I say that I couldn't condone them, that didn't mean that I condemned them, neither. It was all a mystifying quandary, one that I would need time to resolve.

I took my leave of her, after obtaining a promise that she would reveal the truth to my lord forthwith, which I must say, she eagerly agreed to do. Still, as unsure as I was, I thought it not inappropriate to allow her the chance to redeem herself to whatever degree was possible.

However, as much as I was undecided, I was to find that I might have saved myself all the trouble and worry. For some few hours later, upon answering the bell to the study, I found that the decision had been taken out of my hands.

I entered the room and bowed. "You rang, sir?"

"Ah Smithers," said Lord Brampton, "come in."

He was sitting at his desk, pen in hand, writing upon a sheet of stationary, stamped with the family crest. He appeared to me to be neither garrulous nor stupefied, but in complete control of his senses...as much as that could be said for any man so smitten. For smitten he was, that was certain, although what depth that affection would be for a lowborn creature such as Amrita Joshi, remained to be seen.

When I came before the desk he gestured to a chair and said, "Pray be seated."

That was my first intimation that this was no ordinary summons; for I could not recall ever having been seated in my master's presence. I complied with his wish, but I do confess that I would have been more at my ease on my feet. Feeling desperately out of place, I sat on the edge of the chair, back ramrod straight, wondering where to place my hands. In the end I decided that they should rest on my thighs, which was the closest I could come to sitting at attention.

Lord Brampton set down his pen, and sat back in his chair. Taking his handkerchief from his breast pocket, he removed his monocle, and began to polish it. The Queen Anne clock on the mantelpiece marked the time, while he regarded me with more thought than I could ever remember, rendering me more uncomfortable by the minute. Finally, in a voice not unkind, he said, "I've given some thought to your request to accompany Auckie's boy to..." he stopped and pinched his eyes until they were very nearly shut, "Confound it, where was it again?"

I replied, "To Bhutan, milord."

"Quite so," he said. "Quite so."

He held the monocle to the light, and gave a squint into the lens. The Queen Anne continued to make the only sound while he considered. A decision was eventually achieved, and the eyepiece was returned to the handkerchief for further burnishing. I, on the other hand, remained rigidly seated, while doing my best to mask my surprise. This was not the subject that I felt required immediate attention.

Speaking with care to his handkerchief, he said, "Like to go myself, of course. Should be damned interesting, what? Quite out of the question, though, what with…" he waved his hand vaguely, managing to encompass a tremendous workload, whose weight and importance were in a direct relationship to the mystery of what it consisted. "No," he said, and I could almost see the weight of his responsibilities pressing down on his shoulders, "completely out of the question, I'm afraid."

Finally, I could not maintain my silence any longer. "My lord, if I may?"

He looked up…but not quite at me, if you follow.

"Yes?" he asked, "What is it?" For the first time there was just a hint of his old brusqueness returning. It was almost as though he knew what I was going to say, and accordingly disapproved.

Speaking carefully in my own right, I told him, "Sir, certain information has come to my attention regarding the lady"

The skin on his forehead pinched abruptly, his bushy brows meeting in the middle.

"Lady?" he demanded, and yet, I thought, managed to sound evasive, "What lady?"

"Why, Madam Pirāli, My lord…or rather, Miss Joshi." Desperately, I added, "Sir, she was to have spoken of this to you personally."

The master that I well knew was rising closer to the surface. "Well, if it's any concern of yours," he said, replacing the monocle in his eye, and glaring down his nose at me through it, "it just so happens that earlier I did have a conversation with," and he emphasized heavily, "*Madam Pirāli*. What of it?"

At a loss, I said, "My lord, she is not who she would have you believe." For now, in spite of her promise to do so, I was certain that Amrita had not revealed the truth to him, after all, and was daring me to do my worst. Well, we'd just see about

98

that. It was never wise to put a Smithers to a dare, especially when his master's well-being was at stake.

Which only goes to show you how wrong a man could be.

Her voice came from behind me, "I did tell him, Charlie, I swear it!"

I twisted in my chair, and saw Amrita standing at the doorway, devilishly handsome as always, with the saddest look you ever saw.

"My dear Madam Pirāli!" Lord Brampton was all gallant solicitation, as both he and I rose to our feet. "What a pleasant surprise! Come in! Come in! We were just talking about you!"

She regarded him in a state of vexation, with her arms folded across her breasts, and a little slippered toe tapping impatiently upon the parquet. "My lord..." she began but my master interrupted her with a mock frown.

"Now, now," he said, "let's have none of that 'milord' business from you, hey!"

"Very well," she sighed before adding with some emphasis, "*Johnny*. How many times must I tell you that it is not '*Madam*', but '*Miss*', and it is not '*Pirāli*', but '*Joshi*'!"?

"Fiddlesticks!" says he, eyes all atwinkle. "You're nothing of the sort!"

Whereupon she wheeled around to me, arms shooting out in the utmost aggravation. "Do you see what I mean? He does not *believe* me!"

Well, I hadn't seen this coming, and that's no lie. In the past, left to his own devices, my master has proven himself to be capable of reaching some rather remarkable conclusions, but this one beat all. When faced with the truth – no, forget that – when faced with an out and out *confession* that was contrary to his desires, it would appear that his answer was simply to refuse to believe it. Here, and I thought that I knew my gentleman, too! A word to the wise: never say that you've seen everything, because I'm here to tell you that you bloody well haven't.

"I see your game," he chuckled his indulgence at her. "You're trying to trick me, but I'm too clever, what!"

In reply, Amrita's arms slammed down to her sides, with her hands clenched into tiny little fists. Then, with a stamp of her foot, and one of those curious sounds of exasperation that are unique only to women, she abruptly turned and stomped out of the room, muttering a long stream of something in Urdu as she went. I don't know what she said, but I daresay it wasn't pleasant.

I stared from her retreating back to my master, to all intents and purposes shocked out of my wits. I'm sure he would have seen it in an instant, had he looked, but he did not. Instead, still standing, he reached down and began to fiddle with the bottle of ink upon his desk, with a sort of absent fondness lingering on his face. He seemed to have forgotten that I was in attendance, for when I ventured a hesitant, "My lord?" he returned to the present with a bit of a start.

And that's when it struck me.

As I've said before, a Smithers may not be the brightest spark, but we'll get there, given time, and in one of those flashes you read about in penny novels, I suddenly understood. My master was aware of the truth, all right. It wasn't a question of his not believing it, but rather his not *acknowledging* it, which is something subtly different. His reasons, too, had become clear: it wasn't for his own sake that he maintained the pretense, but for Amrita herself. The fact that it dovetailed rather conveniently to his own ends was neither here nor there, and it made me regard him in an entirely different light.

Amrita Joshi had told me that the reason she had decided to play the imposter was because of her desire to better herself. If it became known that she was a lowly *Dalit*, all the doors that Amrita Pirāli had opened for her would be slammed shut in her face, not to mention that any legal proceedings that might be brought against her for impersonation would undoubtedly be quite severe in this caste-ridden land. My master had realized as much, and as he had declared himself her protector, had denied the truth when it was staring him in the face. Aye, there was that, but it was also his intention that, once opened, those doors to a higher station should never be closed to her. Now here was something, and no two ways about it. In the first place, Miss Joshi was no *thug*, that was as clear as day to me now. She had been telling me the truth, even though the truth might well have placed her in perilous danger. That was proof of her regard for my master, and his for her was to behave more nobly than any man I've ever known.

As I said, all this occurred to me in a flash. In the few seconds that had passed, from the time that I had taken him from his reverie, my mind had switched one hundred and eighty degrees.

Before my master could reply, I held myself as erect as I knew how, and said with grave diffidence, "If that is all, My lord, the hour is late, and I thought that I might look in on *Madam Pirāli* before I retire." I emphasized her name ever so slightly, but knew that he would catch on.

His face was a curious mask as he regarded me. I swear that his eyes flickered with surprise, and his mouth twitched beneath his moustache, but then all was carefully concealed again when he said, "Very good, Smithers. Good evening."

I bowed, "Good evening, milord," then turned to leave, but he called me back.

"Sir?" I asked.

His expression was...*warm*, for lack of a better word, making me wonder, for the hundredth time, if I were not in the presence of a completely different man than the one whom I had always known.

"About this Bhutan business."

"Yes, milord?" In the conversation that had ensued I had completely forgotten the reason he had summoned me in the first place.

"I think I can do without your services for a time."

"Very good, sir." Well, that much was settled, once and for all.

"Oh, and Smithers."

"Sir?"

I have said elsewhere that a Brampton's pride is immense. Therefore I think that it spoke volumes when I say that he condescended so much as to smile.

"Thank you." He didn't say what for, but then he didn't need to.

I inclined my head and left the room, without saying anything in reply.

***

Darjeeling was the capital city of the province most closely affected by the Bhuteau incursions, and would be the forward base of operations for Ashley Eden's mission to Poonakha. It lay three hundred miles to the north, and would have been an arduous journey, had not the railroad stretched two thirds of the way. I had taken leave of my master on a morning at the beginning of October, after he had presented me with a muslin-wrapped bundle as a gift. About three feet long, and a third as wide, it reminded me of a box of long-stemmed flowers, only considerably more heavy. I could not restrain my surprise, for never could I recall such a gesture previously. I had tried to express my gratitude, but just for the moment my gruff old master returned and dismissed me from his sight before I could make a sound, wishing me a curt, "Pleasant journey," as I was walking out the door, wondering when I would ever see him, or Madam Pirāli again.

I must say that it was with mixed emotions that I climbed aboard a rickshaw, with my travel bag between my knees, and my lord's gift clasped close to my chest. I directed the coolie to the railroad station, where I was to catch the ten o'clock to Sahibganj. I found Ram Singh waiting there when I pulled up.

I said, "I didn't know that you were coming, too."

"Nor am I!" he chortled. The dew was not yet dry, and he already had his flask in hand, and was putting it to hard service in the bargain. "A man of my years is content to let you younger bucks perform the more arduous tasks, while I linger with my comforts!" I daresay he thought that this was very funny, for he was wiping tears from his eyes by the time his laughter subsided. After bracing himself with another refreshing sip, he said, "No, Charlie, my only purpose here is to see you off."

Warily I replied, "That's quite kind of you, I'm sure," and instinctively placed a hand to my breast pocket, to reassure myself that my wallet was still there.

Ram's shrewd old eyes did not miss the gesture, and he laughed appreciatively, as if I had just given him the greatest compliment, which, knowing him, I suppose I had.

"Very well," he confessed genially, "I thought that we might have a talk."

"What about?"

"Oh, you know, this and that."

Well, that was so much gammon. I doubt if the old rascal had talked about 'this and that' since he had learned how to speak. It wouldn't serve any purpose in pressing him further, however. He'd come to the point in his own good time.

So we took a seat on some rattan chairs, and spoke about such edifying things as the weather, and the passing of the monsoon season. I listened politely while he gassed on about Company shares, and about the yield of rice in the lowlands, of all things. He was halfway through a lecture on shipping tariffs when, suddenly, he interrupted himself and said, "You will be relieved to hear that my suspicions of Amrita Joshi were unfounded."

Carefully I told him, "I have not entertained any suspicions of Madam *Pirãli*," emphasizing the last name, "for quite some time."

He chuckled. "Joshi or Pirãli, what difference is it to me? What do I care about Hindus and their castes?"

In spite of myself, I could feel myself beginning to relax. "I'm glad to hear you say so."

He gave me an amused look over his spectacles. "Come, Charlie, did you really think I would care? If she is a threat to no one, let us leave the lady to enjoy the company of your Lord Brampton for as long as either wishes it. Nary a cheep will you hear from me, unless..."

"Unless what?"

I couldn't read his expression when he said, "Let us just say that it might be prudent to have my wife's third cousin's number two son keep a discrete eye upon the happy couple in your absence."

Outside, the usual maze of people were carrying on with their lives – everything from *dhotied bhistis* with their *chaggles* of water (one each for Muslim, and Hindu), to the brightly-coloured saris of the women, to the occasional *nabob* resplendent in his finery, to the matted locks and scraggly beards of the all but naked holy men, to a skeletal cow with golden nobs and garlands of flowers adorning her horns, and finally to the marine band, looking smart in their red coats bedecked with white braid, and spiked helmets, assembling to greet Mr. Eden's arrival at the station, and to see him off with all due fanfare. It would seem that the Raj did not believe in doing things by half measures.

As the time of departure was drawing near, we got up and made our way to the ticket agent – a thin little bespectacled Eurasian with a harried look and a mole on his cheek – I showed him my government pass, and he waved us over to the waiting area before returning to the task of trying to bring order to the chaos among the throngs of would-be travelers surrounding the wicket, all demanding his attention at the same time.

We sat at a table, each taking a chair. I set my bag on the floor beside me, and Lord Brampton's gift between us. A waiter arrived to ask if we would like any refreshment. Ram ordered *chota-pegs* for us both, before I had a chance to voice an opinion on the matter. Moments later, with my companion happily guzzling, and myself trying not to appear to be sipping too primly, the conversation continued.

"I appreciate your concern," I told him, "but I promise you, there's no need to worry on my lord's behalf."

Ram set his empty glass on the table. Catching the waiter's attention, he ordered another. Then sitting back contentedly, wiping his moustaches with the back of his hand, he said, "No need to worry on the one score, perhaps, but there's always a chance that someone who has nothing might find the temptation to acquaint herself with means too great to resist. If that should happen," he continued, "what lengths would she be prepared to go to acquire it?"

I stared at him. "Surely you're not suggesting that she might go so far as to steal?"

"I am suggesting the *possibility*, Charlie, but that is all," then he added ominously, "and the possibility of even more besides."

I couldn't stop myself from gaping. "You mean you still think she might try to do him in? Why that's preposterous!"

He shrugged, at the same time accepting his second glass from the waiter. "It is unlikely, I will admit, but poverty can breed desperation, and your Amrita Pirāli, in spite of being well kept in the bosom of wealth, in fact owns very little. I wonder what sort of desperation would she be capable of, if those trappings were to be taken away?"

"Balderdash!" I cried, and then told him how much she had been willing to risk to make amends to my master, who had only treated her with kindness. Losing the trappings of wealth would have been only a part of her downfall. Losing her freedom, or worse, would have been the likely result, if my master had not acted other than he had.

"Ah well," he said with a trace of humour, "it was only a suspicion, and I am a suspicious old goat, especially when it comes to women. Not often do I hear of occasions where a human will act contrary to their humanity. I am happy to say, for your lord's sake, that this may be one of them."

Something about his tone made me feel that he remained unconvinced. I was prepared to push the subject further, but just then, with a thunderous roll of the drums and crash of cymbals, the marine band struck up "Rule Britannia". I twisted in my chair to see a landau pulling up to the station, debouching a soft-looking, brown haired gentleman not much older than myself. He was wearing a black frock coat with a black silk topper, and had a neatly trimmed moustache and sideburns down to his jaw line.

Of course I recognized the landau as being that of the Governor-General, and so reasoned that this must be Mr. Eden. The way that he passed through the double file of marines, with his head up, looking neither to left nor right, as if no one else could possibly matter, confirmed it. Seldom had I seen such arrogance of bearing, and you can be sure that I've seen more than my share.

He was travelling with an entourage of perhaps four, trailing respectfully behind him: flunkies by the look of them, except for one, who I recognized as Doctor Simpson. I rose to

105

meet Mr. Eden as he entered the station. I bowed, and he paused, regarding me with icy disdain. Of course his minions followed his cue, with the single exception of the doctor, who smiled at me and winked.

"Sir," I began, offering him the letter that Lord Elgin had written as recognition of my being an official member of the expedition. "Allow me to introduce my…"

He interrupted me with a voice as cold as his stare. "Power!"

One of his followers, a thin, nasty-eyed, balding chap, with a pinched mouth and no lips, obediently scurried forward.

"Yes, Mr. Eden, sir?"

"You will inform this fellow that I've already been apprised as to who he is, and why he is here."

The little man turned to me without batting an eye at the unusual request, and minced, "Mr. Eden already knows who you are, and why you are here." He spoke with a relish, and it seemed to me that he was enjoying the attention he was getting as his master's go-between, and was making the most of it.

Still looking down his nose, Eden continued, "You may also tell him that I do not approve of him, and that he is not to address me unless he is first spoken to, is that clear?"

I could feel my face redden while Power repeated his master, word for word, in a tone that was altogether louder than what was necessary. The station had grown silent, jam-packed with interested onlookers. It didn't matter a jot that most of them couldn't understand a word that was being spoken, the situation was clear enough, heaven knows – Smithers was catching it with a vengeance.

Of course this would never do at all.

"Right, then," I said, addressing Power, while tucking Elgin's letter back into my pocket, "you're a right piece of work, aren't you? And you can tell your master for me…"

"How dare you!" Eden thundered, or tried to, I'll give him that. His face was working something furious, right enough, but he couldn't hold a candle to my lord when it came to thunder, not on one of his more liverish days at any rate.

106

"Oh, we're speaking to me now are we, sir? How very kind." I looked him up and down, cool as you please, as if he was something that had just crawled up from the gutter. Meanwhile, someone in the crowd gave a little snigger, and Power grew decidedly pale. "In that case, seeing as how we're clearing the air and all, sir, I should mention that whoever gave you your information about me should have told you that it's not wise to take on airs with a Smithers: it ain't polite, and we don't like it one little bit!"

"Take on airs? Why you...!"

"And if you're not prepared to be polite," I said, gathering up my packages, "I'll take my leave of you, if you don't mind, and go someplace else, where the air is somewhat more to my liking. Good day to you, sir."

Well, you could've heard a pin drop just then. Ram and Eden were both gaping at me as if they couldn't believe their ears. Doctor Simpson was looking elsewhere, with one hand covering his mouth, and Power appeared to be trying to work up a bit of temper. However, he seemed to change his mind when I riveted him with a look prior to walking away.

I had gone less than a dozen steps when Eden shrilled, "How dare you turn your back on me, you...you *miscreant*! Come here at once!"

I stopped and turned. "I don't believe that I will, sir, if it's all the same to you. I'm angry, you see, and I'm very poor company when I'm angry. Why, I might even say something that I would regret."

At which it was Ram's turn to clamp a hand to his mouth. Meanwhile the good doctor spasmed so suddenly that it left him doubled over at the waist.

"Why you impudent dog!" quoth Eden. "I shall report your insolence to Lord Brampton immediately!"

Level as I was able, I said, "As you wish, Mr. Eden, but it's no odds to me if you do or if you don't. Lord Brampton is my gentleman, you see."

Eden's voice rose another octave, and his face was turning such a lovely shade of pink I thought he might want to loosen his collar. "I'm well aware that he's your master!" says he. "I'm sure he'll be quite interested to hear of your attitude toward your betters!"

Well that did it, you may be sure. I walked up to him 'til I was quite close. His eyes started to shift nervously as I tilted my tile to the back of my head with my thumb, and stuck out my jaw.

"And what '*betters*' might you be referring to, *Mr.* Eden?" It was foolish of me, I daresay, but I couldn't help putting a subtle emphasis on his title, or rather his lack thereof. In an evil hour the almighty Lord Auckland may have spawned the bastard, but, by heaven, for all that he was still just a mister, same as me, and if I was any judge, it rankled him to no end.

"You scoundrel!" He was absolutely seething, "Is that any way to behave towards a gentleman?"

To which I replied, "No, sir, it is not, and if I were speaking to a gentleman, I would deport myself with all due propriety, I assure you."

I thought that he might take his cane to me, or try to at least, or even set his flunkies on me, but such a pack of spineless creatures you never saw, and were no match for a Smithers when his dander was up. So he just stood there regarding me with poisonous hatred, his mouth working like bedamned. Finally, just when I thought he would explode, he opened his mouth to speak…or I rather think it was to shout something at me. However, what that something was would remain a mystery, for at that very moment there came a piercing whistle from the locomotive, drowning him out completely. Then the conductor was announcing to all and sundry that it was time to board.

Thankful for the intrusion, I made good my escape, nodding a hasty farewell to Ram Singh along the way, and scurried off to find my berth in one of the second-class cars. Finally settled in on a bench seat with my luggage stowed away, I was able to take stock of how this new adventure had started off with such an inauspicious beginning.

There was a lurch and the train started to roll, but I scarcely noticed, so deep was I in contemplation. Perhaps an hour later we reached the outskirts of the capital and began to accelerate. Only then could I find the words.

Sadly I muttered, "Charlie, old son, you've done it again."

Chapter Seven

Darjeeling is a pretty little town nestled beneath Observatory Hill in the Mahubharat Range, or what is also known as the Lesser Himalayas. We reached it on the first day of November, 1863, after travelling on horseback from Sahibganj, across a hundred miles of the Great Gangetic Plain. The road was in decent repair, so we were able to make good time along the way.

The Darjeeling Hills look impressive enough from a distance. Having travelled across the often treeless steppe with little more to see than the occasional village and gangs of labourers in countless fields of rice, wheat, cotton, or maize, they could easily be mistaken for mountains, but were in fact foothills to the even more majestic range that lay beyond. As we drew nearer, and the ground began to rise, the heat of the plain gradually gave way to a climate that was altogether more temperate, which was a relief to all concerned, I can tell you. It also allowed that of which every true Englishman holds dear, and has made it famous throughout the world: the growing of tea.

There were vast plantations of it everywhere, interspersed here and there with orchards of every fruit imaginable, or the odd field of coffee; but in Darjeeling country, beyond a doubt, tea was the thing.

The town itself was like no other I had ever seen in India. In a sense it was as though we had never left England. Much of the architecture was decidedly European, with Gothic churches and public schools, to Tudor houses nestled among the evergreens (yes, *evergreens*). Much of the population was European as well, for the primary reason for the town's existence was as a refuge from the heat that blanketed the rest of the subcontinent for much of the year. In fact, as I learned later, one of the first public buildings to be erected was a sanatorium, and by the number of white faces you could see everywhere, it appeared to be doing a thriving business. Even passing the army encampment I saw a company of the 38th, with their red coats and white cross belts, being put through their drill out on the *maidan*; it felt so thoroughly British, and seemed every bit like coming home.

However, it was not long before that impression was disabused, for although it was by no means extraordinary to see white families taking the air, there was also a goodly representation of every race under the Raj's domain: Hindus, Muslims, and Sikhs to be sure, but there was also a sufficient number with features that were decidedly oriental, who, for the most part, hailed from lands beyond our borders. People from Tibet, Nepal, Sikkim, and even a few tall, fine looking specimens, who I was told were Bhuteau. They and the pagoda style of their Buddhist temples were a constant reminder that this was the frontier, and that Brampton Manor was a world away.

I examined all these sights from well in the rear of our little caravan, consigned there by Mr. Eden, and thankful I was to be so. After our set-to at Calcutta, I had no wish for such a scene to be repeated, so I would have taken pains to steer well clear of his path at any rate.

Not that I had the opportunity to say so, mind. Power, that unctuous little pimp, had delivered the pronouncement of my semi-banishment the minute we got off of the train at Sahibganj, and said it with such a smug little sneer that it was necessary for me to put all of my concentration into not placing my fist into it, for all that I had chastised myself quite severely already. It would make a poor showing of my remorse if, at the first opportunity, I broke the insufferable twerp's nose for him. So I maintained my silence, and kept my thoughts to myself, enduring the ordeal until he left me alone with a final disdain-filled sniff, and ponced off like the Queen in high dudgeon.

Like I said, though, it was all for the best. As my orders had come from Elgin, Mr. Eden might lack the authority to forbid my presence, but he had not left any room for doubt about whether or not I was welcome, either. So it would seem that I would have been put under a cloud regardless of whether the altercation had taken place or not. In the end I accepted the situation as best I could, and determined to use my enforced solitude to putting my thoughts in order.

This was no small task, either; for it seemed that my mind had been in a state of shock, of one description or other, from the moment that I had disembarked from the Indiaman back in

July. What, with being shot, attacked by tigers and involved in government intrigue, not to mention trying to look out for Lord Brampton's well-being on top of everything, it was all that my poor unimaginative mind was capable of just to react to the situations as they arose. There was never any question of my being capable of anything else until now.

The first question that I needed to answer was perhaps the one that was the most obvious: why was I here at all?

By now it must be abundantly clear to you that a Smithers is driven by a strong sense of duty, and that to his master above all other considerations. If it had not been for that conversation with Ram Singh, the evening that he apprised me of the affairs along the border country with Bhutan, I would have supposed that conviction (which I had held to all my life) would have continued unchanged. After all, something that's been literally hammered into you when you're a lad doesn't let go that easily, so why was I here in Darjeeling, leaving my master unattended, with a lady who might well have no cause for suspicion, but if Ram were to be believed, wouldn't be any the worse for having a cautious eye on her all the same? Lord Brampton's approval for me being here notwithstanding, it was the closest thing to gross dereliction to duty I'd come to ever since Balaclava. And speaking of Balaclava, there arose another question, one that had dogged me ever since I had buckled them to my hips before mounting my Pegu pony at Sahibganj: what of my lord's gift?

So distraught was I over having had words with Mr. Eden that it had lain, forgotten, on the bench beside me on the train, only to be rediscovered on that leg of the journey's end. Surprised, and not a little relieved to have something to take my mind off of my troubles, I had undone the wrapping to find, still in their wooden packing cases, a light cavalry sabre, and the latest model of the Tranter revolving pistol, complete with a generous supply of .44 caliber rim-firing cartridges – oh, and yes, scabbard and holster included.

Also included was a generous purse filled with rupees, and a note from my lord, informing me that the bulk of the money was to be used to purchase a horse and saddlery at my earliest convenience (which to be sure I had, directly after my upbraiding from Power), and the hope that I would not require the other items at all, but best to be safe, what? He had signed it with his usual stylized 'B', and added a 'Godspeed' as a postscript. This, of course, brought me around to yet a different question – that of my lord's recent behaviour.

There was no denying that he was a changed man ever since laying eyes on the dusky Amrita. In fact, I had never witnessed a change so complete in anyone in all my life; and the cause wasn't that he was constantly topped up with *bhang*, neither, 'cause he wasn't, not above half. No, it was something, or someone else, and logic pointed squarely at the lady as the culprit.

If you knew Lord Brampton as well as I, you would have understood just how remarkable that change really was. Ever since recovering from his wounds at Balaclava, he'd been at odds with the world as a whole, and never been the kind to suffer in silence, but shared his most liverish moments with others, particularly myself, in ways that tried one's patience. I don't know, perhaps it was more than a sense of duty that got me through those ensuing years. Perhaps there was also a sense of responsibility to go with it. After all, I had failed to prevent his wounds, whether through my own personal cowardice, or from the physical impossibility of the occasion, I thought it probable that I would never know, but if that was his legacy from the war, the constant reminder of what he had become was my own. Therefore I bore it as something that was no less than what I deserved…until now.

Was the power of a woman's regard enough to change a man's outlook on life, even one whose outlook had become so entrenched as my master's? If the woman was remarkable, few knew better than myself that the answer to that question was an emphatic yes, but was Amrita remarkable in a way that was beneficial to my lord's welfare, or solely for her own? On the face of it, she appeared to be devoted to him, and I happened to believe that this was the case. Still, Ram Singh's misgivings that she might be an opportunist were unsettling, all the more so because, being three hundred miles away, I could be of little assistance if he happened to be proven correct. That being said, there was all the more reason to rely on the good offices of Mrs. Singh's third cousin's number two son, whom the family held in such high regard. If worse came to worst, those good qualities would be sorely needed. All I could do was try not to fret, and pray that the lady was being misjudged. In the best of all possible worlds, she would have my gratitude for the change she had wrought, and suspicion could go hang.

These and other questions roiled through my mind, over and over again without end, until we were well on the final leg of our journey, and the hills of Darjeeling came into view.

It can often hit you like that: when you're so consumed by imponderables that you can't see that the answer is right in front of your eyes, until your mind becomes distracted by something altogether different. Sometimes it takes but an instant.

When I looked upon those towering hills, so green with forest and field, it was as though a shutter had been lifted from my mind's eye, revealing a scene much in the same way the shutter of one of those new-fangled photography machines that Doctor Simpson was always raving about, and had indeed brought along with him on this journey.

I had become rooted in my past, as who has not at some point in his life? But whether it was conscious or otherwise, I had chosen the lesson of caution it had taught me, of the dire consequences that could result from believing too much what I had wanted to be true, and I was pierced again by that old familiar pang.

Did I want to believe that Amrita was my lord's salvation? Of course I did. How could I not? Lord Brampton's happiness was very important to me, and not only for completely personal reasons, neither. Did I wish it too strongly? Possibly, perhaps even probably, but the difference was that Amrita Joshi was no Omar the Baggara, with a tribe of murdering cutthroats at her behest. What was more, Lord Brampton was not a helpless woman, heavy with child. If it all fell out ill, whatever transpired would not see the death of him, and in that moment I saw that he understood that as well. He had chosen the path toward the *possibility* of happiness, and with a conscious choice, had left caution in his wake.

Once, in an ill-starred moment, I had trusted a man, and as a result had lost everything. Was it wrong ever to trust again, or should I cling to the safety of caution so much that I would sacrifice happiness to maintain it? With the question placed thus, there could only be one answer, and I saw that a part of me had known this all along.

In spite of having once foresworn both, I was here with a sabre on one hip and a pistol on the other, as ready for desperate service as ever there was – all for many reasons: duty, honour, and a sense of what was right, yes, there were those things, but above all, I was here because of my memories of her. It was what she would have wanted me to do; I knew that for a certainty.

She, who had seen the better person in me, still maintained that power to make me want to become that person, and so here I was. It was all quite simple.

Then of course there was that crafty old devil, Elgin. This was his doing, and no error. '*A handy man who knew his way across rough country*', that's what he'd said, and even alluded to my time in Africa. He knew a damn sight too much for my liking, but *how* had he known? Africa was my memory – my *secret*, if you like – it was *mine*, and I had no wish to share it. To have it resurface out of the blue the way that it had was an invasion of my most private thoughts, and quite disconcerting besides. A man may not own much, but his memories are his, and his alone, to choose whether or not to make public domain. At the time I had been too taken aback to comment on the subject, but the more I thought about it, the more I realized that I would have to settle the question, once and for all: how had he known?

My conviction to have the truth revealed took a serious blow just a few weeks after we had arrived, when word came that Elgin was dead.

I knew that he had not been well, but still, it hardly seemed real. Elgin may have been a scheming old codger, as I suspect most great men must be, and I can't say that it had been a pleasure to have come too close to his shadow (graveyards were filled with others who had suffered fates that were similar) but he had moved mountains in his time, and was one of the shining stars of the Empire, who had seemed greater than life to many.

115

To discover that he was not was more difficult to accept than I ever would have thought possible, perhaps, in part, because the answer to my question may have gone to the grave with him.

As a footnote, we were told that Sir William Denison, governor of Madras, was given an interim appointment as Governor General, pending the arrival of Sir John Lawrence, one of the famous Lawrence brothers, who had been recalled from England. I received the news without any qualms. Both were thought to be capable, and no man living knew India better than Sir John.

So that summed up the political situation on our side, which brings us to the reason why we were here in the first place: Bhutan.

Apparently it was in a shambles.

As I came to know more about this strange Himalayan country, I was to discover that this was not an extraordinary state of affairs, although it *was* inconvenient. You see, no sooner had the decision to send a peace mission to Poonakha been made, than it was discovered that it was no longer possible to go. All this was explained to me by Doctor Simpson, through the good offices of the Cheeboo Lama, who was the Daiwan in Sikkim, but was otherwise enlisted by us to act as interpreter to the Bhuteau (both Sikkim and Bhutan speaking dialects of Tibetan). I was to find that he was a cheerful old sort, with a cherubic face and a wispy Chinese beard, the very picture of a rather moth-eaten mandarin in his blousy kimono (the dress of choice in these parts), complete with pillbox hat and button. Although he was a great man in his own country, I soon found out that he carried no side, preferring the company of lesser men to our chief (and that should tell you all you need to know about him). Both the Cheeboo and the doctor had stopped by my rooms one evening, shortly after his having returned from talks with one of the minor governors, or *Jungpens*, on the Bhuteau side of the border.

The doctor and I had maintained relations after my having made a spectacle of myself in Calcutta. Although I was grateful for his friendship (the sole exception to my ostracism), I also thought that he was mad to offer it. Being seen conversing with the pariah of the lot could not do his standing with Mr. Eden any good.

"To hell with him!" he'd barked and shrugged. "Eden's a fool. What's worse, he's an ambitious fool. You did well to stand up to him in Calcutta!" Then he'd tempered his praise with, "'Course you know that he's bound to make your life a living hell?"

That charming conversation occurred in transit. Since then our friendship had blossomed, mainly, I suspect, because he was partial to port, and had found out early on that I usually had a drop or two to spare.

I answered the knock on the door, and he brushed past me without waiting for an invitation to enter.

"Capital!" he exclaimed, which was nothing extraordinary, in and of itself: he was always exclaiming, or barking, or shouting as the case may be. "Absolutely capital!" He stood rubbing his hands together in front of the small fire I had burning on the grate, possibly to rub out the cold (there was often a chill in the air in the evening at these heights), but I thought it more likely that it was in anticipation.

It was when he turned and barked, "Well, don't just stand there, come in, man!" that I realized that he had not come alone. I looked over toward the door and saw the Cheeboo Lama standing at the threshold, just as I have described, grinning self-consciously.

He bobbed his head. "Pardon the intrusion," he murmured, in quite good English. "My very rude friend, Doctor Simpson, told me that you would not mind."

"Nor does he!" his very rude friend declared, helping himself to one of the room's two chairs, and further aiding the cause by unerringly opening the cabinet where I kept a bottle and glasses. Taking out three, he unstopped the cork, and with a cry of "Shall I be auntie?" began to pour for us all.

Recovering from my surprise, I said, "He's right, of course. Yes, do come in, please," and motioned him to the remaining chair. Courteously, I waited for him to be seated before taking my place on the only other item of furniture, which was my cot.

With the doctor busily engaged, the Cheeboo and I were left to our own devices for some moments. Any hopes that he was an accomplished conversationalist were soon dashed, as he sat there like a contented Buddha, smiling at me through his shop-soiled whiskers. So as a preliminary, I told him that I had occupied myself throughout the day by preparing for the expedition, and I believe that I may have made some remark about the inflated prices in Darjeeling.

"Well, that's what you get in a resort," the doctor finished pouring, and passed the glasses 'round. "You should've thought of that in Calcutta, laddie!" Then, before I could retort that I hadn't had the opportunity, he said, "Anyway, there's no rush. We're not going anywhere soon." In answer to my look of inquiry, he cocked an eye and said, "Tell 'im, Chee!"

The old gent's smile somehow grew warmer. "You see, Mr. Smithers? Doctor Simpson's rudeness knows no bounds. Not only has he failed to make any introductions, he insists upon addressing me with an abbreviated version of my title."

"Absolutely true!" the doctor scoffed into his glass, "Can't pronounce your blasted name!"

The Cheeboo sighed, and managed to sound serene at the same time. "I see then that we are left to introduce ourselves. The good doctor's quite right: you English have never been able to pronounce my name satisfactorily, so rather than insult me with your clumsy attempts, you may call me Cheeboo."

"Charlie Smithers," I told him, wondering if I ought to offer him my hand, but he merely inclined his head.

"An honour," says he. Then, with the niceties seen to, he took a healthy draught of port, and continued, "I am afraid that it is also quite true what Doctor Simpson told you: the mission has been delayed."

"Delayed?" I asked, "For what reason?"

"Because we don't bloody know who's in charge over yonder!" quoth Simpson.

"But how can that be?" I wondered. " It's that Deb Rajah fellow, isn't it?"

"Yes, but which one?" And again, "Tell'im, Chee!"

118

So, with infinite patience, the Cheeboo made a second attempt and, interlaced here and there with further interjections by the doctor, managed to tell the story, and quite a tale it was, too, and might give you some insight into the general state of affairs for that country.

It would seem that, shortly after it was considered desirable to send the mission, Bhutan was approaching some sort of crisis, which apparently was more common than not. In order to avert it, the Deb Rajah had enlisted the aid of the governor, or Jungpen, of the capital city of Poonakha, while the court was still seated in the summer capital of Tassishujung, promising in return a much superior position if he complied. Such compliance was offered, but when the alleged crisis failed to happen, the Deb Rajah failed to keep his word, offering the promotion to another, instead.

So far it was politics as normal, in my opinion, although what came after was a bit extreme.

The Jungpen of Poonakha felt himself aggrieved, and I daresay for good reason, but instead of intriguing behind his leader's back, as any politician worth his salt would do in Whitehall, this fellow waited for the court to return to the capital. He allowed the retinue into the palace (which also doubled as a fortress), but closed the gates on the Deb Rajah himself, and immediately announced his own nomination for the Deb Rajah's office. The supreme leader, suddenly finding himself out in the cold, as it were, fled back to Tassishujung, and barricaded himself in that city's palace, and promptly invoked – and received – the support of the powerful Paro *Penlo* (or Baron) among whose responsibility were all the duars in the western regions of the country. Unfortunately, in response, this forced the Jungpen of Poonakha to seek the aid of another baron – the Tongso Penlo – commander of the eastern duars, who, along with the remainder of the ministerial council (or Lenchen) eagerly complied, and promptly invaded Tassishujung, laying siege to the Deb Rajah's palace.

"That is the situation as it stands," the Cheeboo said. "The government is in chaos, with warring factions surging to and fro across the country. So you see, it would be pointless to send any

119

official mission into Bhutan at present. For all intents and purposes, the government simply does not exist."

"Not that it was ever effective when it did exist," says the doctor, taking a cheroot from inside his tunic. "Their central government's not fit to laugh at...even less so than our own; it's the Penlos that have the real power." He bit off the end and spat it on the floor; then ignoring my exasperated glare, struck a Lucifer on the sole of his boot and lighting it, proceeded to puff contentedly.

"But this is ridiculous!" I cried, for I was eager to get on with it. "I mean it's right out of the Dark Ages, isn't it? All this over a broken promise? Why, if that were the case in England, we'd be awash in blood year round!"

"We've had our share of blood and broken promises," the doctor happily reminded me.

This I well knew, of course, but I didn't care to be reminded of it just then. Reconciling with the notion that I should come here was one thing, but that notion didn't include delays.

More out of desperation than anything, I turned to the Cheeboo. "How reliable is this information? Who was your source?"

He told me, "I spoke with the Jungpen of Dhalimkote myself."

"Dhalimkote?" barked the doctor. "Wasn't he the same rascal that caused all the trouble a few years back?"

"You are correct, Doctor Simpson," the Cheeboo replied, and then for my benefit, "The Jungpen of Dhalimcote invaded my country two years ago, abducting some cattle, and many captives besides."

"And that ain't all," cried the doctor. "The beggar tried to do the same thing here, just a few months later!"

I said, "There, you see? Surely you don't trust the man?"

Quietly, the Cheeboo replied, "The Jungpen of Dhalimcote? No, I would not say that I believe everything that he tells me," he continued before I could reply, "but the people thereabouts tell me the same thing." He explained, "They have no love for the Bhuteau, Mr. Smithers; they are Mechis, an

120

Indian tribe that the Bhuteau treat as slaves. They are well disposed to your countrymen, and would have little inclination to supply me with false information, in order to further their masters' interests."

"So that's that, then," said the doctor, leaning back in the chair and, stretching out his legs, placed his feet upon my bed. I noticed that his boots were covered in a generous coating of mud. "We'll just have to wait it out!"

The Cheeboo stood, tucking his hands into his sleeves, and gave one of his little, head-nodding bows. "Gentlemen, as the bearer of such melancholy news, I cannot help feeling a certain responsibility, and wish to make amends." The doctor (not looking the least melancholy, I might add), arched an inquisitive eyebrow at him. "Darjeeling has a beautiful countryside that few people from the west have ever seen. While we wait for the unfortunate situation in Bhutan to clarify itself, I would be honoured if you would allow me to show it to you."

***

The Cheeboo hadn't been lying, neither. If anything, he'd been grossly understating his case; but then, it was hard not to. I doubt if there are adequate words to do the place justice.

In those days the town didn't rival what it was to become in later years, but it was still quite charming, and had been used as a resort by local royalty years before the Company ever got wind of it, the Maharaja of Cooch Behar even building his own palace there. I understand that the British Raj purchased it from him later on, and use it for much the same purpose, which is sensible of them.

Although the Botanical Gardens, St. Joseph's and the Planter's Club were still some years in the future, there was the imposing structure of St. Andrew's, as well as pretty little Loreto Convent, and another school, Saint Paul's, was nearing the end of construction. It was, as I said, all very nice, and you would have thought it a proper British town if it wasn't for the brown faces on the street, and the low, wooden Buddhist temple, surrounded in gaily coloured prayer flags. Yes, it was all very charming, but it was what lay beyond the town that really caught the eye: the Himalayas.

I had heard of them, of course, and imagined that they must be quite grand, but I really had no idea. You could see them quite easily from the town: majestic snow-capped edifices, the highest, Kanchenjunga, said to be the third highest mountain in the world. Well, you could have told me that it was the highest, and I would have believed you. Compared to that monster, it seemed laughable to think of our Yorkshire fells as mountains; I'm here to tell you that they aren't even in the same running.

We climbed Observatory Hill and it felt as if we were standing on the roof of the world. You could see forever, or as close to forever as made no difference. Why, just by standing, and rotating a mere one hundred and eighty degrees, *four countries* came into view. To the west was Nepal, to the north, Sikkim and British Sikkim sat side by side, while over to the east, across wide stretches of low country, looking as cold and ominous as anything you've ever seen, crouched the brooding foothills of our ultimate destination, Bhutan.

I must have been loud in my amazement, for I could tell that the Cheeboo was pleased. Even the doctor was too awestruck to do more than gasp every now and then.

"Tomorrow I will take you to Tiger Hill," the Cheeboo told us. "On a clear day you will be able to see the greatest mountain of them all."

Reverently, I heard the doctor whisper, "Everest!" and could scarcely contain my own excitement.

***

We started out early the next morning. On an impulse, we had invited a friend we had made among the garrison's officers, Captain Austen: a bright young blueblood with a likeable nature, who we found was to be included in our mission. He showed up bright and early with six Pathan lancers in tow, claiming that we could never be too careful in these parts. Consequently, it was on his advice that we also went armed. Although the country was pacific for the most part, it was said that brigands were known to

122

inhabit these hills from time to time, so it was best to bring along some insurance.

We'd packed provisions for an overnight stay. The distance to Tiger Hill was short (only eight or ten miles as the crow flies) but our hearts were set on exploring, and we didn't want to be caught unprepared if nightfall found us away from shelter.

Outside of town, the scenery was much the same as when we'd arrived: field after field of tea, looking as if it had been there ever since the beginning of time. I think that I said as much aloud, for in that gentle voice, that was so much in contrast with Doctor Simpson's, the Cheeboo smiled and said, "Alas, no, Mr. Smithers. Tea is relatively new in this area."

I asked him how he knew so much about it, and Simpson interjected, "Didn't you know, Charlie? These hills used to belong to Sikkim until the Nepalese took it from 'em, an' then we took it from *them*, back in '16!"

"Which you most graciously returned to my country," said the Cheeboo.

Simpson barked a laugh. "Well, we couldn't have your sort going around with such long faces *all* the time, now could we?"

Smiling, the Cheeboo turned to me, "The British Raj purchased these hills from us thirty years ago, when I was a boy. They encouraged settlement, and the planting of tea..."

Simpson guffawed, "To break the Chinese monopoly, don't ye know!"

Ignoring him, the Cheeboo said, "So you see, Mr. Smithers, Darjeeling has been growing tea for a comparatively short period of time."

It was all news to me; mostly, I suppose, because I'd never given it much thought. Well you don't, not when you consider that tea comes from a grocer's shelf. How it got there had never concerned me, really. But when I looked out on all those rolling fields of green, stretching every which way for as far as I could see, I thought of all those grocers' shelves back home, and every sitting room, or kitchen, or dining hall throughout the land, with auntie pouring amidst the cream, scones and jam. I thought to myself, '*This is where it all comes from. It all starts here, at this very place,* and promised myself that I would never look upon it the same way again.

As the miles stretched on, the plantations gradually gave way to semi-evergreen forests of oak and *sal.* Wildlife was abundant: we saw elephants grazing in a clearing, with some rhinoceros close by. I kept a wary distance from *those,* I can tell you! They looked placid enough, but the last time I'd seen one of those blighters he'd chased me clean off a cliff, and glared at me all the way down! Later on, I saw a curious, long-tailed creature about the size of a dog, with a dark brown coat, and a strange, elongated trunk, and a head too small by half. The Cheeboo was informing me that it was known as a civet, when the calm was suddenly interrupted by shouts, and the clash of steel.

Once you've been in the ranks, it's something that you never quite get out of your system. One moment all is quiet, and then comes the cry of combat, and the unmistakable sound of blades against blades, and then everything is a world of reaction.

I looked at the Cheeboo, and he at me. Whatever registered on my face I couldn't say, but his was complete consternation. Then I was touching spurs to my pony, and drawing the Tranter at the same time. She broke into a gallop, hooves drumming a rapid tattoo on the packed surface of the road, with Austen and his lancers hard on my heels, and the Cheeboo and Simpson coming up behind. Rounding a bend, the melee soon came into view, a hundred yards off: perhaps a dozen pressing against half their number. The former were mounted, wearing mail coats and steel casques, armed with swords, bearing down on the latter, who were unarmoured and afoot, some with blades, some only with staves. Even as I squeezed my knees into the game little mare, desperate to come to grips, I saw one of the attackers rise in his stirrups, sword raised high, and bring it down on the head of one of the assailed with tremendous force. I could hear the sound of steel biting into bone even over the shouting and drumming of hooves. It's not a sound that one soon forgets.

I had about halved the distance when I noticed, from the corner of my eye, that one of the attackers – a rider richly caparisoned, cap-à-pie in armour, with a silk scarlet robe fastened over his shoulders – had remained aloof from the fighting, seeming content to wait in the wings. I took him to be the leader of the attackers, but then instantly dismissed him from my mind as the immediate peril demanded my full attention.

I let fly with the Tranter at the gallop, while still some distance off. The heavy pistol bucked in my hand, the recoil jarring my arm up to the shoulder. Where the round went to God only knows, but it bought us some time. As it turned out, it was enough.

The sound of the report brought everyone up short, particularly those who were pressing their attack. The big fellow, who had just cut down that unfortunate, granted himself a moment of shock: staring at me with his eyes owling out of his head, and sized up the situation in an instant. The next moment he was clapping in his own spurs, and coming at me full bore, sword leveled straight at my heart, and screaming bloody murder.

I had to time it to a nicety. The urge to blaze away at him was almost more than I could bear, but with both of us closing at the gallop, there was only enough time for a single shot, so I had to be sure. If that didn't stop him, I knew that I was a goner.

We were closing at an amazing speed, rendering the distance between us to almost nil, in less time than it takes to say it. Taking a breath, I held the pistol over the pony's right ear with my arm straight as a lance. Then I was sighting down the barrel, and saw his raging face just beyond the foresight. I lowered it a fraction, and squeezed the trigger.

It's all too easy to miss with a pistol, and doubly so when you're perched on a horse, going hell-for-leather; but I had waited until the last possible instant, when the tip of his sword was not more than six feet away, and saw the round catch him squarely in the chest, lifting him out of the saddle. Then he was flying backwards, arms and legs almost comically extended, until he hit the ground with a crash.

The ferocity of our charge had shocked the remainder of the attackers into a temporary immobility; then, even though they outnumbered us two to one,the sight of their comrade's sudden demise startled them into flight. We were after them without breaking stride, and I was blazing away for all I was worth. Momentum was on our side, so we were among them in seconds,

125

the Tranter accounting for two more, and one of the lancers a third. Then it was out with the sabre and I was hacking away at anything within reach.

Although still heavily outnumbered, the impetus of our charge gave us the advantage, and in truth, once our foe discovered that we were not helpless, they seemed disinclined to fight, but instead preferred to flee – all except for the man in the scarlet cloak.

While his fellows made good their escape, he turned at bay, his horse rearing back on its haunches; I had just a glimpse of dark, merciless eyes flash beneath his helm, and then our swords were crossing, striking sparks up and down the blades, and we were past, wheeling around for a second charge. He was a well-built specimen; as big as the man I had shot, in fact, nearly as big as myself. When we closed, his arm darted out, intending to grab hold and wrestle me to the ground, but I swung my sabre, and more by good luck than skill, felt it strike home. I heard him cry out, then he was racing away, reeling in the saddle, nursing his arm, with his blood soaking the flank of his horse.

The altercation had taken less than a minute, but his companions had made the most of the opportunity he had bought them, and were well away by the time I could take stock. Austen rode up with blood on his own sabre; we paused just long enough to make sure that the rascals weren't going to return before walking our horses back to our friends, and the people we had rescued.

The doctor had dismounted, and was checking the still figures lying prone on the ground. In addition to the one I had seen cut down, there were two others that I hadn't noticed, and another writhing in agony from a cut to his neck, blood pouring in gouts from the wound. Suddenly he stiffened, and flopped back in the dust, as still as his companions. I swung down from the saddle with the intention of offering my assistance, but the doctor only shook his head.

"Poor souls," he said, "nothing can be done for them now."

Well, that was rum to be sure. In fact, it was a rum business all around, as it was only by the grace of God that we had managed to save any at all. With this in mind I turned to the surviving members of the party, presently being seen to by the Cheeboo.

The first was a youth still well in his teens, pale and shivering with shock, speaking to no one. He had the look that I well recognized: staring, unblinking, off into the horizon, but what he saw God only knows. To my surprise, the second was a girl, standing with her back to me, speaking rapidly to the Cheeboo. Being otherwise engaged, I hadn't noticed her earlier.

I inquired, "Is anyone else hurt?" and she turned at the sound of my voice.

I stopped in my tracks, dimly aware as my sabre slipped through nerveless fingers to the ground.

That face! I stared at it as I have stared at no other. For there was no way on earth that it was possible, but here she was all the same:

Loiyan.

Chapter Eight

Unthinking, I cried out her name and staggered forward, only to stop short when she hastily drew away, her eyes (those beautiful eyes) wide with alarm.

What was this? Puzzled, I spoke her name once more, but this time as a question, "Loiyan?"

With one hand clasping her shawl protectively against her throat, she spoke in credible English, "Forgive me, sir, are we acquainted?"

Frowning, I studied her carefully, completely at a loss. The world whirling around my head went unnoticed as I pered ever so close. The eyes, the high forehead, the fine-boned cheeks, the prettily dimpled chin, the finely crafted nose, the wide and generous mouth...and those full, beautiful lips. Everything was *her*: her height, the slender body beneath her sari, even the graceful motions of her hands – everything, and yet...

I studied her even more closely, only afterward aware of how foolish I must have looked. Beneath her shawl, her luxurious hair was so black that it appeared blue to my eye, descending over her shoulders in long straight tresses to the contours of her waist. Her skin was the same colour as the local natives. How could I not have noticed what must surely have been so obvious?

My voice was not steady when I told her, "My apologies, I...I thought you were someone I once knew."

She studied me in turn. After a moment a gentle understanding appeared in her eyes, and softly she replied, "Ah, I see." She stepped away from the Cheeboo, and approached nearer (as I, myself, had done only a moment earlier) studying me even more. Then in a voice barely above a whisper, she said something that unsettled me even more. "I owe you my life, *sahib*. From this moment on you are my champion, my *bahadur!*"

Flustered and embarrassed (and, yes, overwhelmed) I fear that my attempt at reassuring her was a feeble thing. Having stared at her to the point of rudeness, I could not look at her now, but instead directed my clumsy words to the ground, muttering some excuse about helping Simpson with the dead, before abruptly turning away.

The bodies of the survivors' companions were placed on the backs of our horses. Those of their erstwhile oppressors were dragged to the side of the road, and left in the hope that the authorities might recover them before they were discovered by predators. Thus encumbered, we were forced to make our way back to Darjeeling on foot, our adventurous journey to Tiger Hill now forgotten. I never did set eyes on Everest.

Having witnessed my distress (regardless of my feeble attempt to mask it) both of my companions maintained their distance, as I'm sure was wise. Little good could come from any effort to console the inconsolable, although any curiosity they had upon the matter they kept to themselves.

The lady (she who so closely resembled the woman I had loved) was not so reticent.

Lost in thought as I was, struggling with old memories, I didn't notice her until she spoke at my side.

"Pardon my intrusion," she said, "but I would know the name of my saviour."

My God! Her voice! Even her *voice*...!

I told her with my eyes scanning the trees in the opposite direction. Branches shivered as a troop of monkeys scrambled past, one stopping to stare with naked curiosity before leaping onward to rejoin his fellows.

She volunteered her own name, Charula Khaur, even though I hadn't asked, and the boy as Mir Singh.

I regarded the lad, still pale and trembling from the ordeal, walking like one in a trance. More harshly than was my intention, I suggested that he required her presence.

My words stung her, I'm sure, and I was torn between remorse and something that approached savage elation. She dropped back without another word, allowing me to continue on my own.

And yet I felt her eyes on me all the rest of the journey.

***

Once returned, we made our report to the adjutant at the military base, a harassed looking man, I thought, with a clipped moustache, and a face bronzed by the sun. After seeing to the bodies, I left Simpson and the Cheeboo to see to the welfare of the living. I exchanged no further words with any of the survivors, including Charula Khaur, telling myself that she was no longer my concern.

Later that evening, I was in my room cleaning my weapons when there came a knock on the door. Upon answering, I found it to be the Cheeboo; he had come alone. I must confess that, at first, I was wary, lest he ask me questions that I would never have the capacity to answer. My fears were groundless, however. Instead of prying into my private life, he told me that the war in Bhutan had been resolved, with the rebels the victors; thus removing the last obstacle to our mission.

I thanked him and saw him out. If he was surprised by my brusque behaviour, he didn't show it, but bade me a good evening before disappearing into the night.

I shut the door behind him, and resumed my seat at the small wooden table. Picking up the stone and sabre, I applied the former to the blade in long smooth strokes, while absorbing the Cheeboo's news.

I was relieved, certainly, for any further idleness was most unwelcome, leaving me prey to what might occupy my mind. Sleep might be difficult tonight, but tomorrow would bring a myriad of details to see to, and I felt certain that this brief and painful chapter had come to a close.

***

As it turned out, I was right to anticipate difficulties, for now that the go-ahead had come at last, Mr. Eden was in a great taking to be off. Consequently, everything that had to be done had to be done at double-speed.

Provisions had to be procured, an escort to be requested, transport arranged and a host of other details that I won't bore you with, but every last one of them had to be considered and seen to, as soon as humanly possible. If I do say so myself, as an old campaigner, and also as a gentleman's gentleman, who was used to anticipating my lord's needs on any number of his excursions: everything from attire, to delicacies from Fortnum and Mason, my help was invaluable. Not that it was ever asked for, you understand: Mr. Eden was too high and mighty to ever condescend to that, but he didn't object when I dove in anyway, giving assistance to the army quartermaster, procuring enough tents from stores, going out in wagons to purchase rice from the locals, and making sure that there were enough boots to go around for the escort, which, after much deliberation, had finally been decided on: fifty Sikhs, and fifty sappers from the local Sebundy Corps.

I did not limit my assistance to the lower orders neither, but more than once was taken quietly aside by Power, asking my advice on everything from headwear to hardtack, it only then occurring to me that the man had never set foot in country any wilder than Devonshire in his life. I did what I could, and I believe that he was duly grateful, for his attitude toward me began to grow less frigid. The same could not be said for his master, however, for Eden continued to offer me his back, if he offered me anything at all, a circumstance which I did not regret, as I was content to remain ignored.

Meanwhile, the greatest difficulty lay in determining how all of this mountain of supplies and provisions should be got from here to Poonakha, the country in-between being deemed too rugged for beasts of burden. Consequently the call went out for a small army of bearers. Initially, they arrived in droves, eager for the Viceroy's coin; however, upon being told their ultimate destination, few were found who were willing, so fearful were they of the Bhuteau. It was only through the Cheeboo's influence, and the greatest of efforts, that a sufficiency were enlisted, and you never saw such a varied assembly in all your life. Some, of course, were locals, while others were recruited from Sikkim, and still others were Tibetan Lepchas, short, stocky people bearing the narrow eyes and broad, bland faces of the Mongol, virtually indiscernible between man and woman unless stripped down to the skin. It must be noted that a good many of these sturdy peasants were indeed women, who were capable of carrying as much as their menfolk, over great distances of the roughest ground in the world. These would prove to be the most dependable of the lot, but their numbers were comparatively few, and we could only hope for the best. As it turned out, it was a hope so forlorn, I can't think why we ever left at all.

Bereft of hindsight, however, and equally ignorant of the future, on the first day of the new year everything was finally deemed ready, the provisions loaded, and the baggage train sent off to the frontier, twenty-two miles away. The main party followed three days later, overtaking them at the River Teesta as planned.

It would be the last element of our journey that would proceed according to plan for quite some time.

Whether through misunderstanding, or sober second thought, once having transported the supplies to the Teesta, many of the coolies either considered that they had fulfilled their contract and returned to their homes, or decided that this was as close to Bhutan as any sane person would want to go. Whatever the case, the result was the same. When we arrived at the camp the place was a shambles.

Everywhere you looked bundles had been deposited in the most haphazard fashion imaginable, and left unattended, while those responsible could be seen huddled in groups, large and small, arguing with a red-faced member of the quartermaster staff, shaking their heads, or gesticulating wildly with their hands. Others simply turned and walked away, streaming past us in their hundreds.

Eden was in a rare taking, as you can imagine: absolutely bouncing in the saddle, twitching left and right, shouting at all and sundry until he was quite beside himself, all to no effect whatever; he was simply ignored as the desertions continued. It was only through the good offices of the Cheeboo that order was eventually restored, but three days were lost while an urgent summons was sent to his own estates for labourers to replace those already decamped.

This was just the first instance of this particular problem. There were to be others. Indeed, we would find that it never really stopped. Whether it was their fear of the Bhuteau, or the nature of the terrain we were headed into, many of the coolies found the prospect so unappealing as to reject it altogether. We were to discover that they were not fools.

Given the trouble we had in procuring a labour force in the first instance, and the fact that it was necessary for it to be augmented within the week, before anyone had even set foot on Bhuteau soil, you might think, 'Hold on! This has a bad flavour! What do those coolies know that you don't?' and I would agree with you; in fact I'd go one step further, and call the whole thing off. After all, if this was the sort of trouble we were getting from our own folk, what could we expect from those living on the other side of the river? After all, we hadn't been invited. From what I gathered from the Cheeboo's talks with the Jungpen of Dhalimkote, the Deb Rajah was neither expecting nor even *wanting* us to come. So the question arises: why were we going? To be sure, it seemed a fool's errand, but unfortunately we had the perfect fool in charge, and I'm not saying that out of hindsight or personal animosity, neither. The man was as pompous a dunce as ever signed on with the diplomatic corps, and you may believe they've had more than their share. You might think that I'm misjudging him, and with good reason. In answer, all I can do is relate events as they unfolded, and allow you to judge for yourself.

The sappers had not been idle while we were awaiting the Cheeboo's return. The escort commander, Captain Lance, set them to work constructing rafts from stalks of bamboo, which, fortuitously, grew in abundance in the area. Therefore, when the new force of coolies arrived, and Eden turned a blind eye to what was becoming more and more obvious, insisting that we press on, the means of ferrying our people and supplies across the Teesta was already in place. So by nightfall of the next day we had established camp on the Bhutan side of the river, in what was known as the Athara *Duar*: a strip of lowland, ranging from ten to twenty miles in width, running along the base of the Bhutan mountains, from Darjeeling to Assam, said to be quite pestilential during the rainy season.

I had heard from Captain Austen (who had been billeted as Eden's aide) that the Jungpen of Dhalimcote had been asked to

133

send people to meet us at the river. Of course no one ever showed, which was another ominous sign, if you like. In fact, we didn't meet any Bhuteau at all until the next day, after we'd crossed the Athara *Duar*, and ascended into the hills, to a place called Kalimpoong. They certainly seemed friendly enough, gifting us with produce and the like, which was fortunate, as our supply train had broken down again, with even more desertions. So nothing could be done but have Captain Lance send some of the Sikhs to round them up again, and bring up the bundles from where they'd been so unceremoniously dropped. In the meantime, we waited.

I can't say that it was unpleasant, however. The people were really quite charming, and made much of our presence. Using the Cheeboo as translator, we were told of their admiration of the British, and their disgust with their own government. Not so rare, perhaps; show me a politician and I'll show you someone who had better have a bloody thick skin; but these people were heaping their abuse with a will, some even going so far as to suggest that we should take the place over (take note of that, all you denouncers of the wicked Empire), and I would soon see that they had good reason.

Other than that, our stay was uneventful. The Kalimpoong Welcoming Society continued to be friendly, and even took us to other villages, I suspect so that they could show us off to their neighbours.

It was while we were visiting the first of many monasteries we would see on our journey (I remember this one employed a fingerbowl to contain holy water – made in England it was, too) that I mentioned to the Cheeboo how curious it was that these people were so eager to please, and yet the Bhuteau had such a fearsome reputation.

"But of course, Mr. Smithers," he told me. "As I mentioned earlier, these people are *Mechis*, a race that is similar to those in Bengal, except for their very curious resilience to malaria. Did you know that they are the only people capable of inhabiting the Athara *Duar*? The Bhuteau – the *real* Bhuteau – take advantage of this by enslaving them to tend their fields."

134

Well, that put it in a different light, of course, and I can't say that I blame them for their scowls, and the abuse that was showered every time Poonakha was mentioned.

The next day we met the genuine article in the surly old form of the ex-Nieboo of a place called Dhumsong, a fort that was on the way to our destination. To be fair, however, he might have been surly because he was the *ex*-Nieboo, and not the current one, a situation I was to find that was not all that uncommon, as officials were constantly being deposed to make way for a favourite at court. The incumbent, having nowhere else to go, would often settle nearby, and bide his time, waiting for the cycle to continue.

Proof of the old codger's surliness came with the first words out of his mouth: "I forbid you to go to Poonakha!" This to Eden, after the Cheeboo told him of our intention. When informed that we were going anyway, and that he hadn't the authority to forbid anything of the kind, he sighed in a philosophical way, and agreed. Then he went even further and said that, if we were determined to go, he might as well supply us with guides to make sure that we at least reached Dhalimcote without any hindrance.

I mention this strange but minor episode to give you an idea of the workings of the Bhuteau mind, for we were to discover that this fellow was in no way untypical. They could be (and often were) pugnacious as all get out, until faced with any sort of resolve. Then they crumbled faster than you could say Jack Robinson. Quarrelsome, deceitful and rude, it was little wonder that Bhutan (*nominally* a vassal state of Tibet) should have been abandoned to their own devices, as the Tibetans (sensible lads) no longer wanted anything to do with them.

On the ninth day into the new year, we recommenced our journey, and almost immediately all the coolies that the Sikhs had rounded up in the days before, promptly abandoned their bundles and deserted again. As a consequence, we were forced to leave much of the baggage behind at the first village we came to.

The next day we journeyed for only a few miles, for Eden, the ass, had decided that nothing would do but that he should detour off the road and allow his countenance to shine on the

135

fort at Dhumsong, which turned out to be little more than a small rectangle, built of stone and mud, perched on a hill that was said to be five thousand feet high.

What he hoped to accomplish was beyond me, and he never did say. I suppose, in all fairness, he may have been attempting to see to the safety of the stores we'd left behind, but I rather doubt it. I daresay I wasn't too far wrong with my first assessment: having been touted and feted by the friendly people of Kalimpoong, I think he expected to be treated the same everywhere he went. If so, he was soon disabused: our surly old friend's replacement, the current Nieboo, was not only surly and old as well, he was also so covered with ground-in dirt that he could have passed for a chimneysweep, and perhaps was, for all we knew. Anyway, he slammed the door on Eden's face, without any ceremony whatsoever. Lovely view from there, though, as I recall.

With no other choice but to swallow our pride, we moved on, and made some progress the next day, scrambling to the top of Labah Mountain, which my encyclopaedia tells me is six thousand, six hundred and twenty feet high. I mention this to give you an idea that, although our path was constantly undulating, we were traversing territory that was gradually taking us higher and higher into the mountains. As an example, after having camped out that night, the next day we descended the other side, by a very steep and difficult path down to the Durlah River, and were still three thousand feet higher than we had been two days previously.

We were a footsore bunch in those early days, no two ways about that. Muscles were aching that I wasn't aware that I had. What you didn't use going up a slope, you used coming down. Every muscle in my legs: thighs, calves, shins, all seemed about to burst at any given moment, and that's without mentioning anything about my back, or the largest muscles of all, so that even sitting my pony became a chore. Mornings would find me so stiff that it was necessary for me to bend over (with every tendon in my body creaking fit to raise the dead) and touch my toes before I was able to climb into the saddle. Not that I was ever in it for very long – as sure-footed as my pony was, in many

136

places the trail would have been too steep for her to manage my weight. So I would dismount and lead her, grateful that she did not add to my burden but stepped along as briskly as she could, which was far brisker than I. Even my long trek across Africa paled in comparison to what we were crossing now, and I was even further removed from those days when I had been on campaign.

Knowing that I was not suffering alone was a faint comfort. Eden looked like death warmed over, in spite of his best efforts to hide it, while Power would stagger ahead like a man in a daze. In fact, it was only our escort that showed no sign of bother. Sturdy Sikhs and wiry sappers, they trudged along, day after day, until I was certain that they could continue so to the ends of the earth...which, judging by the look of our wild surroundings, couldn't be that far off. Their example inspired me to keep pace, and grateful I was that they were too polite to allow any sign of their disdain for all of our years of soft living to show upon their faces. Gradually, however, as the days passed, and mile after mile was left behind, I could feel my body harden until, in time, I was able to carry myself along almost as well as they.

Upon reaching the Durlah River, we were met by the strangest sight you ever saw, coming through the woods on the other side. There were perhaps a dozen men dressed in the native garb, which was similar to that of the Cheeboo – a sort of tartan kimono with a baggy pouch in the front, which was used as a pocket; but as outlandish as this was, I soon found that it was only the beginning,

In the hands of each of these charmers were musical instruments – cymbals, drums, flutes, what have you – and at sight of us they broke into what, for lack of a better word, I shall call 'music', with more pomp than you'd ever find at Horse Guards, too.

I'm no expert, of course, but in my time I've heard fiddles and the odd banjo played in various pubs, as well as drums in Africa on a few memorable occasions, and I know what can get my toe to tapping as well as the next man.

This did not.

Such a caterwaul you never heard in your life! Far worse than even the Scots with their infernal pipes. Stupefied by the sound, I could only watch them as they came on, with just enough presence of mind not to clamp my hands over my ears. Presently they arrived at the water's edge, and ground (or fizzled) to a halt, whereupon we were addressed by their leader: a pompous old codger who could have taught my master a thing or two about putting on airs.

By overhearing the Cheeboo translating to Eden, I learned that they had been sent to greet us by the Jungpen of Dhalimcote, and were to provide an escort of honour. So without further ado we were given the signal to move forward – for although rapid, at this point the Durlah was little more than a stream, and could be easily waded. After we had crossed, this gang of fellows struck up what I can only assume was a march, and led the way, leaving me to hope that the remainder of our journey would be a short one, and that their martial airs would not frighten the horses any more than they already had.

Mercifully, both prayers were answered, for we soon reached a valley, with the fortress towering high on the cliffs. Here, apparently deeming that their duty had been fulfilled, the musicians discontinued their efforts; but before I could register any gratitude, the silence was filled with the rattle of musketry from the fortress, apparently also in our honour, and it continued unceasing for the remainder of the day. Amidst this din, we dismounted and began to make camp, while Eden, accompanied by the Cheeboo, ascended to the fort.

The evening fires were just being set when they returned. Eden's face was a mask, let me tell you, and it wasn't a very nice one, neither. He was railing away at the Cheeboo as they descended, obviously in a rare taking. So it wasn't difficult to overhear.

"Can't think what to make of the man!" he cried. "He must have been drunk!" Then rounding on the Cheeboo, he demanded, "I say, in your talks with him before, are you quite certain that he offered to provide us with supplies?"

The Cheeboo murmured something, and Eden snapped, "I'm perfectly aware that he was willing to supply us...if paid in advance...at a monumentally inflated rate of exchange! He actually expects us to pay him seven rupees for every bag of rice! That's fourteen *shillings*, man! I'll be bound that he got it from Jolpigorie, for there's nowhere else within a hundred miles, and I happen to know that they are selling the same bag for a mere fifteen pence! Why, it's a blasted outrage! I'll see him damned first!"

Eden continued on in this vein, with the Cheeboo trailing patiently behind, until they were at last out of hearing. It boded well, I'm sure you'll agree.

The next day was no better. In fact, it was much worse.

Problems with the coolies had not waned since leaving Paigong, but had remained a constant drain on our limited resources, with them leaving the train by the dozen every day. I can't say that I blamed them, exactly, for theirs was no easy task, hauling backbreaking loads over the roughest country you could imagine, with no end in sight, neither; but they had signed on for the duration, and been paid in advance besides, so there was that to consider, as well. Although *why* Eden agreed to pay them in advance is beyond me. People from the hills consider a swindle nothing less than their god-given right, and good fun besides. From their viewpoint, I can imagine that it seemed to them that Eden was begging to be taken, and they were only doing their best to oblige him, but I suppose that I could be mistaken.

I know that it vexed Eden terribly. Not only for the delays that it caused, which were quite bad enough, heaven knows, but also I think that each was beyond the understanding of the other. More and more, I began to suspect that he simply couldn't comprehend their unwillingness to see our mission through. After all, with a cessation of Bhuteau raids on the frontier, theirs would be the most immediate, and visible gains. For the coolies' part, though, I don't think that they believed in it from the beginning, but that they were being asked to break their collective backs to further this arrogant *feringhee's* career, and I wonder if they were too far wrong?

I already knew what Elgin had thought of our chances – God rest that wily old bastard – and all the others besides. Beadon had pushed for it, and got his way, but in my opinion,

Eden was the only one to think that he could actually pull it off; more fool he. The man was so blinded by what he supposed were his own abilities that he could never entertain any idea that he might not be right. In this case he couldn't be more wrong, and what's more the coolies knew it.

Be that as it may, day after day it became routine to send out a patrol at first light to round up the runaways, and bring them back in an effort to force them to fulfill their contracts. It was an uphill battle, that's certain, but it wasn't my *indaba*. All I'm trying to tell you is that you might as well attempt to get blood from a stone as to try to force willingness into a hill man if he's reluctant to give it. That notion was reinforced by what happened next.

This particular morning the Sikhs had enjoyed good hunting, and returned to camp before luncheon, herding a dozen of the surly brutes before them. As it turned out, those poor sods couldn't have picked a worse morning to get caught.

As usual, I had pitched my tent on the outer fringe of the camp, like every good pariah should. The doctor had strolled over for a congenial chinwag, so we both noticed when the Sikhs brought them in, sitting them down under guard, while the *havildar* went to report. There they stayed, glaring sullenly, to await Mr. Eden's pleasure.

Never the most agreeable man to start with, Eden's mood had soured even further when confronted with the Jungpen's duplicity of the previous day, and it soon became apparent that an evening's sleep had done nothing to sweeten it, neither. He came storming from his tent like a thing possessed, with Power and the *havildar* hard on his heels.

Under his breath the doctor warned, "Have a care, Charlie, this could be trouble."

He might have saved his breath, for it was all too plain to see, even for a Smithers on a bad day.

Eden glared at the malefactors and demanded, "Are these the fellows?" When the *havildar* assured him that they were, he glowered even further. "So you seek to try me, do you?" he addressed them with a menacing growl. "You think that my patience knows no end, is that it?"

140

No one replied. In fact, it was plain as a pikestaff that not one of those unfortunates spoke a word of English, but even if they did, they must have realized that it wouldn't have been wise to speak up just then. Instead they just sat where they were, staring at the ground in sullen defiance, and as it turned out, that was quite enough.

"Well, I won't have it, do you hear!" Eden roared, all in a passion. "I'll tame your blasted insolence, and you will like it!" With that he rounded on the *havildar*, his eyes blazing with fury. "A dozen lashes for every one of them! See to it at once!"

The *havildar's* eyes widened with a momentary astonishment, but then he stiffened to attention and snapped a command, launching his men into action. The prisoners were seized, 'cats' were produced, my Tranter was out, and the doctor was wrestling me to the ground.

"I thought you might try something daft!" he hissed into my ear, but I was struggling for all I was worth, and wasn't in the mood to listen.

Exasperated, he continued. "God's blood, man! Will you not have a care for your own worthless hide! There's nothing you can do!"

Then I heard the Cheeboo, who had arrived out of nowhere, "Doctor Simpson is correct, Mr. Smithers! You will only make matters worse!"

"There, you damn fool, do you see?" Simpson growled, "Listen to him, if you won't listen to me!"

But I wasn't having it. The moment I heard the first lash fall, I lost all sense of reason, save one – to put a stop to it. The last time I had witnessed a flogging had been in Africa on an ill-fated day. It was that unspeakable memory that now rendered me into a man possessed.

A Smithers is usually the most easy going of fellows, but you wouldn't want to be near one when he's got blood in his eye. With one mighty heave I broke free of the doctor's grasp, and was struggling to my knees, scooping the Tranter from where it lay on the ground. Then, just as I was about to shout for Eden to stop, a blinding pain exploded in the back of my head, and for a moment I saw the most amazing fireworks.

Then the world fizzled to nothing before my very eyes.

Chapter Nine

I slowly came to with a throbbing head, and the irritating sounds of two people in the midst of an argument. Wafting toward consciousness, I was gradually able to recognize who the voices belonged to: Doctor Simpson and the Cheeboo, no less. Simpson was shouting in a most annoying fashion, although, to my ear, he didn't actually seem annoyed himself, but closer to what passed for his own particular version of amused. The Cheeboo, on the other hand, was speaking in a more considerate tone, but was clearly distraught.

Through the pain in my head, I heard the doctor say, "Good God, man, did you have to hit him so hard!"

"Forgive me, Doctor, but I knew not what else to do," quoth the Cheeboo. "Is Mr. Smithers much hurt? Oh, this is most unfortunate!"

"I reckon he'll live," the doctor allowed, "no thanks to you!"

"I cannot think what came over me!"

"If it were my guess, you were only trying to beat some sense into that thick skull of his, but, my stars, Chee, you needn't have taken it quite so literally!" Simpson, ever the card, granted his own wit an appreciative bark of laughter.

I could sense the Cheeboo wringing his hands. "If I had allowed him to proceed any further, there might have been serious trouble."

"If by 'might'," Simpson replied, "you mean there would have been 'an absolute certainty' of trouble, you'll get no argument from me!" Bark! Bark! Oh, he was well pleased with himself, right enough.

"I acted without thinking," said the Cheeboo mournfully. "When I saw him draw that great pistol, I knew that I must stop him, but the only means at my disposal was this faggot of wood."

"Which I see is now splintered into pieces!" barked the doctor. "Ne'er mind, Chee, we can still use it for kindling!"

"I can't help but sympathize with him, however. He was merely attempting to lend aid to those poor unfortunates."

"Those '*poor unfortunates*' could teach a gypsy a thing or two about double-dealing," said the doctor heartily, "and I'll be bound that they've received worse than what they got today." But then he relented somewhat. "It was a bad business, though, by heaven. Hold on, he's coming to!" This last was in response to my groan, induced by my poor throbbing head.

"Welcome back to the world of the living, laddie!" cried the doctor with a nasty grin. He assisted me to a sitting position more vigorously than what I would have wished for, causing me to hope that my head would simply explode and have done.

Foolishly, I thought, the Cheeboo asked anxiously, "Did I hurt you, Mr. Smithers?" So I took a moment to glare at him.

"Here," asked the doctor, "how many fingers am I holding up in front of your face?"

"You're not holding up any," I replied with some irritation, at the same time gingerly exploring the giant goose egg on the back of my head.

Bark! "See, Chee? What did I tell you? He's fit as a fiddle!"

Feeling decidedly to the contrary, I gazed over to where the coolies' punishment had been executed. They were still there, still under guard, some administering salve to the long vivid welts on the backs of their fellows. Some were moaning in agony, some were sobbing from the pain, while others stared angrily at the ground in front of them, brooding in silence. Of Eden there was no sign.

The doctor sighed and rose to his feet, dusting the dirt from his knees. "Well, I'd best be off to see if any of those chaps require my assistance." Nodding in my general direction, he added, "Chee, you'd better stay and keep an eye on our idiot friend here. Make sure that he doesn't nod off again, or, worse, start a mutiny!" Then he strode off with his medical bag grasped in one hand, apparently in order to inflict his own particular brand of kindness upon the natives, who I would have thought had suffered enough already.

Watching him go, I asked, "He saved me from disgracing myself, didn't he? You both did."

"Forgive me, Mr. Smithers, but you would only have succeeded in making a bad situation much worse. I'm afraid that disgrace would have been the least of your worries. It is most fortunate that Mr. Eden was too preoccupied with seeing that the punishment was carried out to notice our little struggle.

"Eden's a swine!"

Philosophically, the Cheeboo replied, "Mr. Eden is the second son of Lord Auckland. Sons that do not inherit must make their own name in the world and, accordingly, he possesses the ambition that such circumstances engender." Then, not unkindly, he chided, "If he so chooses, he is also the man who has the power to put you in chains. Doctor Simpson has told me about your unfortunate acquaintance with him in Calcutta. It would be ill-advised to try his patience further."

When I remained silent, he continued, but on another tack entirely, or so it seemed. "My friend, when I came upon you struggling with Doctor Simpson, I thought that you had been possessed by a demon. When I saw the look on your face I was sure of it."

"Don't be ridiculous!" But, unbidden, my thoughts turned to soft doe-like eyes, and a beautiful laughing face, and I could not, in all honesty, deny it.

Then came the gentle touch of his hand on my shoulder.

"Forgive my impertinence, Mr. Smithers, for intruding upon what you hold most dear, and no doubt wish to keep only for yourself. It is not my intention to pry. I would leave you in peace if I thought that peace would find you."

A retort was forming on my lips, but by great good fortune I was saved from acting even more the fool by a shout from somewhere close by, drawing our attention to the fortress, high upon the cliffs.

We looked up to see that the gates had swung open, from which presently came a sizable procession in no apparent order. Equally without any discernable order, the squawks and tweets and thumps of their instruments, descending to us on the still mountain air, proclaimed that at least some of them were musicians, apparently returning for an encore.

"It would seem that we are to be the beneficiaries of an official visit," the Cheeboo mused. "The Jungpen cometh. I had best be away to lend whatever poor assistance I am able to our worthy leader."

Grateful for the interruption, and perhaps curious besides, I rose and accompanied him, still nursing the lump on my head. He made no objection as we made our way toward where Eden could be seen emerging from his tent, dressed in his best frock coat, top hat in hand. It was no great distance, and we soon arrived. The Cheeboo took his place at Eden's side, while I, with no official capacity, and wishing to remain out of view, retired a pace or two behind them, nursing my wounds at Captain Austen's side, with Power goggling on his other.

By now the Bhuteau were close enough that individuals could be made out without very much trouble. Apart from the musicians, there were men-at-arms, clad in helms and mail, armed with an assortment of weapons (anything from matchlocks to bows and arrows) all uniformly antiquated. In addition, several others were carrying standards, which were nothing more than boards fastened to staves, bearing the inscriptions of their delegate's badge of office, in a manner similar to the Chinese. All of this being led by a single man on a horse, whom I assumed was the Jungpen himself.

In the process of wending their way down the slope, every so often the entire procession would stop and vie with the orchestra over who could make the most noise, shouting at the top of their lungs; but whether their purpose was to ward away evil spirits, or invite us up to tea, it was difficult to say. Equally curious, I thought, was that every time this happened, the figure on the horse would put down his head and shake himself in the saddle, much like a dog. The entire effect was so utterly astonishing that there could be little doubt that this was to be a meeting of two vastly different cultures.

At length, with a final cacophony of shouting, and a last honk and squeal from the band, the assemblage arrived, and ground to a halt. The distance between our two parties was sufficiently near that I could clearly make out their features, and realized that these were people from Bhutan-proper, and fine looking specimens they were, too. Taller and better formed than your average Bengali, their round faces and almond eyes bore the stamp of the orient. I decided that they bore a certain amount of intelligence, too…with the unfortunate exception of their leader.

To my eyes, the Jungpen of Dhalimcote appeared to be neither intelligent, or of note in any particular way that might commend him. Considerably wider in girth than his companions, he slumped in the saddle in a manner that would have had our old riding master, back in the 17th, burst into tears. Regarding us through the slits of his eyes, he held his too-large head in an affectation of what he apparently imagined was regal, but merely succeeded in appearing ridiculously pompous instead.

As if that weren't enough, the ridiculous achieved the sublime when a party of his followers swarmed to the Jungpen. Lifting him bodily from the saddle, they spun him around twice, and carried him the remainder of the distance to where we stood waiting, stunned into silence. It immediately got worse: for instead of setting him down, they continued to dandle him on high, rather like a trophy. Clearly this was an attempt to display their conviction that this fat, dirty man with the low, sloping forehead and greasy moustache was too dignified to walk, and indeed, too exalted to stand on the same ground as Eden, who must be regarded as a supplicant.

There was some eloquence to the gesture, I will admit. As I said, the meaning was clear, requiring no translation whatsoever. The effect, however, was quite contrary to what the Jungpen must have hoped for. I could not see Eden's expression, nor the Cheeboo's neither, nor even my own, when you come right down to it, but Austen looked like he was ready to burst, although he was making a heroic effort to hide the fact. You might agree that it was not an easy thing to do, and our success must have been rather less than total, for after a while, when our complete awe failed to materialize, the Jungpen had the decency to look embarrassed, and began beating the heads about him, berating his bearers to set him down.

Finally he stood, face to face with Eden, and it wasn't very difficult to read his thoughts: "*Well, that didn't work, worst luck! Oh well, ne'er mind, on to Plan B: I'll impress him with the power of my personality!*" And this he proceeded to do, although I daresay not as he had planned.

147

It started well enough: the Cheeboo remade the introductions, and bows were stiffly exchanged, before the principals sat down on hastily provided chairs. After that, I'm sorry to say, events soon began to go awry.

Still smarting from the previous day's encounter, it was easy to see by his bearing that Eden held no high opinion of the Jungpen, not that I blamed him you understand, and you'll note that I was no great admirer of Eden, either. On the one hand you had that product of the British upper class, supremely confident in his abilities and the rightness of his thinking; on the other you had someone who was little more than a warlord at best, or a robber captain at worst – brooding alone in his mountain fastness, estranged from the niceties of court (*estranged*, in this case, meaning 'utterly ignorant of'), and was none too subtle about it neither. So in that light, the meeting was probably doomed from the start. With Eden being a square peg as ever there was, I couldn't say that the Jungpen was the round hole, exactly, for the man lacked symmetry in every sense of the word, but if a great deal of allowance was made, you could just settle for 'oblate'. In any case, the two would never get on.

After a few false pleasantries had been exchanged, accompanied by a frosty smile or two, Eden planted his fist on his thigh, leaned forward, and said to the Cheeboo, "Now then, let's get down to business, shall we? You may tell my esteemed," pause, "*friend*, that with regard to the shipments of rice…" and that was as far as he got, for the Jungpen interrupted in his own jibber-jabber, looking affronted as the dickens.

Suddenly frowning, Eden snapped, "What's that? What did he say?"

The Cheeboo looked embarrassed when he replied, "The Jungpen has asked for brandy."

Eden's brow creased even further, as if he couldn't believe what he'd just heard. "Asked for *brandy*?"

The Cheeboo hesitated, "Demanded it, actually, Mr. Eden."

"Well, I never!" Eden exclaimed, fidgeting back and forth. His fist was still jammed into his thigh, lending a slightly ridiculous appearance, I thought, but then I always had. He was no longer leaning forward, however, being quite taken aback, you see. He continued thus for a moment longer before suddenly snapping over his shoulder, "Damn it all, Austen, what do you think?"

Beside me, Captain Austen had been making heroic efforts to regain his composure, but the Jungpen's demand had caught him off guard, so he was unable to keep the mirth from his reply.

"A bit early in the day, sir, to be sure." At which someone had the temerity to snigger, and wouldn't you know it, from the corner of my eye I noticed that Doctor Simpson had rejoined our party.

Eden twisted his head around to see who had caused the offensive sound, and in the process his eyes fell upon myself, and turned instantly into little shards of ice. He seemed about to say something, but I had yet to shake the darkness from my mood, and in that brief second, whatever he saw in my own eyes caused him to change his mind. Instead, he said to the gathering as a whole, "Must I remind you all that these are official talks between the British Raj, and the government of Bhutan!" which was stretching it a bit, I thought. The Jungpen was no great odds, but of course Eden knew best. "I must insist that you observe the proceedings with all due solemnity!"

He had a point, I daresay. For, having sensed our mood, the Jungpen's face began to darken with something that was other than dirt, which was beginning to be mirrored by his fellows behind him, some even going so far as to finger the hilts of their swords. Taking note, Eden, in his infinite wisdom, decided to give in.

"Oh very well!" he sighed, "See to it, Power."

Agog, Power couldn't keep from blurting, "But Your Honour, not the Napoleon, surely!"

Perhaps to make amends, or more likely, in my view, to assure that there was the least interruption in this divine comedy, Simpson intervened: "Allow me, Mr. Eden." And reaching into his bag, he retrieved a bottle clearly marked 'Medicinal Brandy'. Somewhat relieved, Eden accepted the bottle while Power went to find cups. Presently he returned with two tin mugs and, once having poured a measure into each, the proceedings were ready to commence.

Eden raised his in a toast, "Your good health, sir." and taking the merest of sips, pointedly set the cup aside. Meanwhile, the Jungpen had thrown his back in a single swallow, and was holding out his cup, clearly expecting it to be replenished.

Caught off guard yet again, Power hesitated, and looked to his master, his face registering all sorts of uncertainty. Eden smiled the thinnest smile ever, and after the slightest hesitation, inclined his head, indicating that Power should proceed, which he did, albeit with every sign of reluctance.

However, no sooner was this measure poured than the procedure was repeated: the Jungpen downing the contents in a gulp, and holding his cup to be re-filled, and a distinct look of 'and-don't-be-so-stingy-this-time-dammit' registering on his fiz.

Eden's hesitation was longer this time, and I can't say that I blame him. But, observing his reluctance, the Jungpen waved his hand dismissively, and said something to the Cheeboo with his chest out, and his head tilted back, and his mouth twisted into a contemptuous sneer.

We were informed, "He says that you are not to concern yourself, Mr. Eden. He is capable of drinking vast quantities of spirits to no ill effect," and I noticed that this sentiment was echoed by the Jungpen's entourage, who were smiling and nodding proudly amongst themselves, their confidence in their leader's capacity to imbibe clearly knowing no bounds. Further, they had that settled look of anticipation about them, as if they were expecting to be awed even further.

In the end Eden complied, although I can't think why. Certainly he would want to appear civil to his host, but there were serious issues that needed to be addressed, if we were to push on without delay. But it takes two to have a discussion, and notwithstanding Eden's efforts to do so, with his own cup remaining firmly ignored at his elbow, it was a farce from the beginning, for of course the result was that the Jungpen got beastly drunk.

If there's one thing I've learned over the years, it's that when a chap boasts of an immense capacity for alcohol, it's a

150

sure bet that he hasn't, and the Jungpen of Dhalimcote was no exception. In no time at all he was as pickled as Davy's sow, in spite of his increasingly slurred assurances that he wasn't (which was the bulk of the conversation throughout the afternoon) and all the while Eden's smile became thinner and thinner, with the palaver going precisely nowhere.

He had to shoulder his share of the blame, of course, and he knew it, which did nothing to sooth his temper. For of course, by the time he realized his mistake, it was too late. By then the Jungpen was reeling about, occasionally bursting into what must have been song, and inviting everyone else to join in (I hardly need mention that no one did), while his own company of Merry Men began to shuffle about with increasing embarrassment. Finally, when any suggestion of Eden's smile had disappeared altogether, the brighter sparks amongst them took the cue and, with shame stamped firmly on their collective faces, gathered him up, intending, I am sure, to return with him to the fortress.

However, if such *was* their intention, they obviously didn't know their man, for the Jungpen would have none of it.

Angrily shaking off those who were attempting to guide him back into the saddle, he suddenly rounded on us, filled with drunken dignity (which was a paradox if ever there was) and slurred something to the Cheeboo.

Eden sighed, "Well, what is it this time?" plainly not expecting anything uplifting. Nor was he to be disappointed.

The Cheeboo hesitated even longer than before, until suddenly Eden, having reached the end of his patience, snapped, "Out with it man! What did he say?" as if the Cheeboo were a mere menial, such as myself, and not the Dewan of a nation in his own right.

Ever patient, however, the Cheeboo showed no offence. Instead, in as level a voice as he could manage, he said, "Mr. Eden, the Jungpen wishes to visit ..." there was, again, the briefest hesitation, "with me..." followed by a slight emphasis on, "*alone.*"

Eden remained perfectly still, but the blood was draining from his face, leaving him pale as a ghost. The inference was all too clear —he had been snubbed, but not only he, but the entire

British Raj (which he happened to represent) for the sake of someone whom he undoubtedly considered no more than a petty official. It was a prickly diplomatic conundrum, you'll agree.

If he acceded to the Jungpen's request, his loss of face would be obvious, not just to the Bhuteau, but to his own entourage as well. For a man, whose vanity was only matched by his ambition, it must have been a painful notion for him to contemplate, and yet he did contemplate it, and agreed, although, I must say, not with the best of grace.

Finally he said, "Oh very well!" but would look at no one. "Perhaps *you* can talk some sense into the man!"

Unwilling to tarry any longer than what was necessary, the Cheeboo took the Jungpen by the elbow, and with the aid of a few stalwart Bhuteau to keep him from toppling over, guided him off to his tent. Perhaps Eden was still hoping that something positive might arise from the day, but for myself, I believe that he was afraid of what the Jungpen's reaction would have been had he denied the request. The man was an eccentric when he was sober, heaven knows; there was simply no way of telling how he would answer in his present state; he might declare war, or curl up and go to sleep, or anything at all. In the end, I believe that Eden had just wanted the man out of his sight, and took the path of least resistance to achieve that. Had he but known what was to happen later, he might very well have taken his chances ushering the Jungpen out of our camp altogether, and be damned to the consequences. But, of course, he didn't.

As for the rest of us, that seemed to be an end to the day's proceedings. So we all quietly shuffled off to be about our business, while Eden returned to his tent in high dudgeon, no doubt, to brood and scheme so that his ambition should not be thwarted. Meanwhile the Bhuteau from the Jungpen's party hung around in the wings, huddled in various groups, looking as though they wished they were invisible.

Much had happened in a day that had seen so little result, and I do confess that my mind felt greatly encumbered by it. Old memories had been stirred, and once stirred, were not prone to going away. Wishing to avoid the unavoidable, I endeavoured to stay occupied, so found myself at the horse lines, giving my pony a good curry. I'd taken to calling her Maggie, after the chambermaid back at Brampton Manor, because of her cheerful exuberance in all things, as well as her eagerness to please. She'd given her usual friendly nicker when she saw me walking over, and daintily nibbled some mealies from the palm of my hand. Several minutes later, her coat was just beginning to shine when I heard Simpson behind me.

"Quite the auspicious beginning, wouldn't you say?"

"I don't think Eden knows what he's got himself into," I replied, for I was eager to mend any fences that might have become damaged between us, as well as to discuss anything else other than what lay so heavily upon my mind. "See here, Doctor, about this morning..."

Simpson interrupted me with his familiar bark, and I felt Maggie suddenly stiffen, ready to shy. This, you'll note, from a mare who could take the sound of a pistol shot, mere inches from her ears, without flinching.

"I daresay you're right," he chortled, apparently finding something about Eden's discomfort amusing, 'but he'll never admit it, not even to himself!"

I, on the other hand, was not quite so sanguine at the thought of going into territory that might well turn out to be hostile, with so little faith in our commander. But of course the doctor was barking mad.

Taking his interruption as a sign that he didn't wish to discuss it any further, I allowed the subject of this morning's misadventure to languish. It turned out that I was wrong. It was merely a case of the doctor wanting to broach the matter from the direction of his choosing. When he did, predictably, it was with his usual tact.

Without asking permission, he picked a spare curry brush from my saddlebag, and began to apply a half-hearted effort to his gelding, next in the line to Maggie. It was just as well that he could afford a *syce* who was ten times more capable than he, for there was a quality he brought to the task that suggested that he was not altogether comfortable with it. The gelding, however, was a placid creature who bore his master's ham-fisted attention

153

with an equanimity that would have done credit to Francis of Assissi on one of his more serene days.

"You're a strange one, Smithers," says he, brushing away like he was beating a carpet. "I've been hearing talk."

Well, it was a bit like the pot calling the kettle black, if you ask me, but when faced with the comment I was instantly on my guard.

"Oh? About what?"

"Chee tells me that you have a past."

"What man doesn't?" I replied carefully, although I endeavoured to make light of it.

Bark! "True enough! And we've learned not to ask too many questions in the army, hey?"

Still proceeding with caution, I said, "Well I've answered to 'Boots and Saddles' in my time, if that's what you want to know."

"In the cavalry, were you?"

"The 17th," I allowed, wondering where he was taking this.

"Lancers!" he exclaimed, well satisfied. "I thought you were handy with weapons! Seen any action?"

"In the Crimea," I replied softly, willing him not to ask what so many others had before him – 'what was it like?'

But whatever the doctor wished to hear, my reliving those memories wasn't one of them.

"Yes, bad business, that," Simpson shook his head sadly. "I was over there myself."

"Oh?"

"With the infantry, though; nothing as glorious as the cavalry. With one of the rifle battalions."

Relieved, I said, "So you know what it was like."

"Mmm?" he asked, then, "Oh yes, I know all right. No need to go into all that, though, is there?"

I hastened to reassure him, "No, certainly not."

"Something like that can alter a man for life."

I agreed. "Yes it can."

"Change his outlook on things – even the way he behaves."

"Most assuredly."

He continued to bounce the currycomb, hither and thither, off of the gelding's already shining pelt. "I said the same thing to Chee just the other day. Know what he replied?"

"No, I don't."

The doctor left off trying the patience of his mount for the moment, as he looked skyward in aid of his memory.

"'The darkness in Mr. Smithers' soul runs deeper than that.'" He whacked the gelding's shoulder, apparently to be interpreted as a gesture of affection. The placid creature swung his head around, blowing gently from his nostrils, and nudged his hand. "Can't imagine what he meant by it though," and with just the slightest pause he asked, "Can you?"

I might have been taken aback, I suppose, but I wasn't, not entirely, anyway. I was well aware that my earlier behaviour regarding the porters must have elicited some curious speculation. So I looked at him as levelly as I was able and, not unkindly, said, "You needn't worry about me, Simpson. Should the time come when I'm needed, you'll find me ready."

It was a simple enough act of reassurance, but in making it I think that it was for my own good as much as his. We were about to venture into the unknown. A Smithers fighting his own private battles along the way was the last thing that was needed. If, as I said, the time ever came when the talking stopped, our little mission would urgently require every man to stand firm. If today's extraordinary meeting with the Jungpen of Dhalimcote was any indication, simply starting talks with the Bhuteau might well be a task beyond any man's capabilities.

Then, wouldn't you know it, speak of the devil, there came to our ears inebriated shouts in a foreign tongue, but clearly those of indignation. Our present tasks and conversation were immediately forgotten as we looked across the way to the main camp and saw the Jungpen weaving mightily were he stood, gesticulating with angry gestures at the huddled group of coolies that Eden had placed under close guard, with the Cheeboo hovering anxiously at his elbow.

"Hullo!" the doctor cried with some degree of anticipation. "This could be fun!" And with that both of us dropped our currycombs, and without another word, made haste to intervene.

155

When we reached hailing distance, the doctor cried out with rather more cheer than I thought the situation called for, "What's this, Chee? What's our dirty friend got himself into this time?"

The Cheeboo looked up, his expression a mixture of dire concern and relief at our presence. I noticed that some of the Sikhs guarding the prisoners were already beginning to fidget nervously with their rifles. However, their *havildar*, obviously an old hand, barked an order, and they snapped to attention, their weapon safely grounded before any harm was done.

"Oh, Doctor Simpson!" cried the Cheeboo. "Mr. Smithers! Thank goodness the both of you are here!" He gestured toward the fat little man. "The Jungpen demands that the prisoners be set free!"

Bark! "Well I'll be bound; that's the first sensible thing he's said all day!" cried the doctor. "But we can't do anything without the man of the hour's say-so, now can we?"

Out of the corner of my eye, I saw Mr. Eden rapidly approaching, red-faced with fury. "What the devil is it this time?" he snapped, too enraged to offer even a pretense of diplomacy.

Not to be outdone, the Jungpen also continued to rage, which was drawing the attention of his followers, who also began to approach rapidly, with their hands on their hilts, and dark scowls on their faces.

Everyone could see that the situation might get ugly, and indeed it did without warning. For, with his angry screeching having reached a crescendo, the Jungpen suddenly drew his knife and charged, with his followers hard on his heels...not at any of the Sikhs guarding the recalcitrant porters, you understand, but at an inoffensive commissariat sergeant who was standing close by, looking on with as much interest as the rest of us...and who was also unarmed.

There was no time to think. Lunging forward, quick as a wink, I punched the knife out of the Jungpen's hand. When he pulled up short, bubbling over with astonishment, I placed myself foursquare in front of him, smiling and nodding with every sort of reassurance I could muster...with my right hand lightly resting on the Tranter. Meanwhile his fellows hovered around uncertainly, waiting for their master to make the next move.

Now the *havildar* barked another command, and there came the ominous ratcheting sounds of dozens of hammers being brought to full-cock. The Bhuteau glanced around to see the surrounding Sikhs with their Enfields leveled at the pack of them, also waiting with some interest for the Jungpen to make the next move.

That unfortunate, upon finding himself at the centre of attention, now looked very much like he wished that he wasn't, and I could tell without any difficulty whatsoever, that he suddenly very much regretted his rash behaviour. In a twinkling, rage changed to abject fear, and he turned and rushed out of the circle, to all but throw himself on his knees before Eden, babbling nine to the dozen.

Without being asked, the Cheeboo translated. "He says that he is sorry, Mr. Eden, and begs your forgiveness." The translation, however, was hardly necessary as the Jungpen's rather eloquent gestures were making his meaning abundantly clear.

However, Eden remained unmollified. Tried beyond all patience he rasped, "Tell him to leave, and to take his pack of jackal's with him!" He paused briefly to consider, "And one more thing: tell him that he may not return until he has submitted his apology to me in writing!"

When this was done, the Bhuteau took heed with all due alacrity, and scuttled off back to Dhalimcote with rather less ceremony than when they had arrived; and that seemed to be the end of it.

It was a curious and rather telling episode. Eden spun on his heel and stalked off without another word, leaving the rest of us (even the chastised bearers) to exchange glances amidst much rolling of eyes and relief over the close call.

Simpson jutted his chin at Eden's receding back. "The least he could have done was to thank you for preventing any blood being spilled."

157

"Yes, Mr. Smithers," the Cheeboo agreed, eagerly bobbing of his head, "I concur with the good doctor: your actions were truly heroic!"

Even the commissariat sergeant (I never did learn his name) insisted on shaking my hand. "'Pon my soul, sir, you saved my life!" and it seemed to mean a good deal to him, for he said it twice more within the minute before it occurred to him to add, "How can I ever repay you?"

I tried to shrug it off as I was embarrassed by the praise, but he would not be dissuaded. "It may not mean much in the great scheme of things, sir," he said, "but I have a certain affection for my hide, and I daresay my missus would agree. It was the finest thing, you staring him down like that, sir, the finest thing I ever saw!"

It was too much, and I suddenly found it difficult to breathe, what with everyone crowding around me so. Before I knew what I was doing, I pushed past the man, and mumbling something about attending to my duty, made my way back to the horse lines, desperate to find solitude.

In truth my mind was a mass of confusion, for so much had happened in so little time that I was caught struggling to come to terms with one thing before the next caught me, as always, unprepared. I had not intended to intervene with the Jungpen, indeed was scarcely aware that I had until I was standing before him, coming very close to drawing the Tranter for the second time that day, and what the repercussions would have been if I had I could scarcely consider. But that may well have been because I was still struggling with what Simpson had spoken of earlier: about the darkness in my soul.

What of it, I wondered? What was so unique about my suffering that made my life such an ordeal? The answer, of course, should have been 'nothing'...but was it? I had always assumed that misfortune was to be experienced and then the thing to do was to get on with it – one does. I also assumed that a pure man's soul was a great rarity, and that the everyday people around me carried on with their lives without any visible signs of being in torment; but not me – not Charlie Smithers.

I was still tormented by doubts about a possible lapse of courage all those years ago, while riding into the guns at Balaclava. Lord Brampton had never fully recovered from his wounds, and the discomfort often rendered him irascible. I, being the one closest to him, bore the brunt of his ill temper, but I bore it gladly, with the suspicion that I may have been responsible never far from the forefront of my thoughts.

Still, it must be admitted that the introduction of the beautiful Amrita Pirāli (nee Joshi) into his lordship's life brought a welcome change in him, and I can't say that I was happy solely for his benefit alone. In this case what was good for my master was also a relief for me, but I continued to be nagged by my doubts about my own motives for believing her to be everything that she claimed that she was. Was my trust tempered by the fact that I *wanted* to believe her? I could not, in all conscience, say that it wasn't. I had believed what I had wanted to believe previously in my life, and it had cost so many innocents their lives, including my Loiyan. The weight of that knowledge was heavy, but I bore it the same as I bore Lord Brampton's wrath, because I suspected that it was no less than what I deserved; and yet my trust had succumbed so easily, in spite of knowing full well what the outcome might be should that trust be misplaced.

However, if I was so shallow as to relinquish my caution, the same could not be said for other scars on my conscience. The punishment delivered to the porters this morning, deserved or not, had stirred a reaction in me that I had not expected (and yet the Cheeboo and Simpson had) and had so nearly been the cause of my disgrace, without achieving anything in the least useful. A Smithers is seldom in the habit of backing away from a situation, so if a weapon is drawn it must be acknowledged that it is with the intention of using it. The only question that remained was, in my mind, who would I have been putting a bullet into: Mr. God-almighty Eden, or a Baggara with a hennaed beard, who could never die enough for my liking? Whatever the answer, the outcome would have been the same: I would have been fortunate not to be escorted back to Darjeeling in chains, and the porters would have been flogged regardless.

All this, you may gather, was scarcely heartening for me, with regard to my state of mind, and it was little wonder that I considered that I might be losing it. I was forced to acknowledge that I was possessed by a rage that would surface at a time and place of its own choosing, leaving me helpless to resist. What was more, it was not necessary to look far afield to find the reason, for it had been growing in me ever since leaving England's shores. Once containable, the constant assault of the sights, sounds and smells of a savage land upon my senses had torn them free, and once free, threatened to gain mastery over me. I would need to guard myself very closely to make certain that never occurred.

Hard on that thought, unbidden, the image of my beloved swam into my mind, like a face swimming to the surface of deep waters: laughing, full of life…and love. Something clenched in my chest, and I was driven to my knees, the hot salt of tears burning in my tightly clenched eyes. Loiyan! The image was so real that I found myself reaching out for her, but even as I did so, her features transformed to the coffee-coloured face of the girl I had saved from those Bhuteau brigands, she who so closely resembled my long-dead wife.

I recoiled, hearing a voice, much like my own, cry out in anguish, "Go away! Why do you torment me so?"…and to my further astonishment, even though her face was in my mind, I felt her touch on my shoulder, and her voice whisper in my ear, "Be at peace, *Bahadur*. It is not my intention to cause you pain."

My eyes flew open with a start, and there she was, the very girl, looking down at me with a face so hauntingly familiar, filled with a terrible compassion:

Charula Khaur.

Chapter Ten

She was dressed in the garb of a coolie, with her long black hair caught up in a turban, but it was her, right enough; I would have known that face anywhere, having seen it countless nights in my dreams.

I was vaguely aware of having flung myself backwards to the ground. I'm afraid that my wits were not about me for, after staring speechless for what must have been an eternity, when I finally found my voice, it was only to stammer, "You! But...! But...how! Why!" and other such pearls of wisdom. It was to the girl's credit more than my own that she seemed to comprehend.

I daresay I continued to goggle, for the last time I saw her had been when I had left her with the authorities in Darjeeling, refusing to look back as I struggled with the doors she'd opened from my past, doors that I was desperate to close again. Her face, her voice, even the lines of her body were Loiyan in every respect. Save only her hair and the colour of her skin, I would have been convinced that my wife had returned to me from the grave. Now here she was, out of nowhere, standing above me with those same striking features that I had tried so mightily to erase from my mind, patiently waiting for me to stop acting like the village idiot.

At last, when I did manage anything even remotely coherent, it was immediately clear that wisdom was still some distance away.

"I hardly expected to see you here," I told her.

"Evidently not," she agreed, still looking concerned.

I was finally aware of how foolish I must appear to her: lying on my back, gaping like a floundering cod. So I gathered myself up, and dusted off my shirt with brisk, angry strokes of my hands. I didn't like that she had caused such a reaction in me.

There was a chill in my voice when I asked, "Perhaps you would care to explain yourself?"

The girl simply shrugged and said, "I wanted to be near you, so we disguised ourselves and came."

"We?"

161

"My friend, Mir Singh, and I," she replied, and I had a brief memory of her companion, not much more than a boy, who had also been rescued that fateful day.

I felt my brows knit, and heard myself sharply demand, "You want to be *near* me? Why?"

Her eyes were without guile when she explained, "*Bahadur*, you saved my life!"

"But…but that's ridiculous!"

"Nonetheless it is true."

The simplicity of her answer did nothing to mollify my temper. "Do you mean to tell me," I began quite slowly, for I was now aware of the necessity of keeping my fouler moods under some restraint, "that you and your friend willingly assumed the guise of common labourers, joined up for this mission, and have come all the way from Darjeeling, across some of the worst country that God put on this earth, all for the sake of being *near* me? Are you aware of how preposterous that sounds?"

Another shrug, and this time with the ghost of a smile she repeated, "You saved my life."

"Confound it, woman!" I struggled mightily, and managed to lower my voice before proceeding, "That's the most insane thing I've ever heard!"

The corner of that pretty little mouth twisted upwards into a sardonic grin. "Is my life of so little worth to you, sahib?"

And there I was, stammering and gobbling again.

Sensing correctly that nothing coherent would emerge, she interrupted, "It is no matter, for my life means a great deal to *me*. True," she continued, "I am not without means, and I could have turned my back on you, as you have done to me." Here she paused, looking me full in the face, and I felt my blood rise as I looked away. "I could have continued on with this life that you have saved, and never set eyes on you again, sparing only a thought, every now and then, for this strange *feringhee* with the sad eyes who once gave me everything, and allowed me to give back nothing in return."

It was useless to attempt to respond. I contained my reaction to staring at the toes of my boots, and surrendered the floor.

"But I am not such a person," she said. "I owe you a debt of gratitude…"

Eagerly, I seized upon the opportunity to interrupt. "You owe me nothing!"

But she continued as if I hadn't spoken,"…And I must confess that I have been filled with a great curiosity."

I stared at her, blinking foolishly, then ventured, "About *me?*"

"About you," she confirmed. "About one who has the heart of a tiger, even though it is a heart that bears much sadness." Again the simple shrug, that made her appear so small and helpless. "I would know more about him. When you stood up to that Bhuteau beast today I saw one man. When I came upon you now, I saw another."

We stood as we were, regarding one another – she with her curiosity and compassion, and I with my confusion. I felt helpless under such scrutiny: her eyes were penetrating, stripping away my defenses. Soon she must know all…

"I am no one!" I cried harshly, and snapped, "Damn your impertinence! Leave me alone!"

Instead, undeterred, she took a step forward, studying me closely, her eyes darting back and forth, now tinged with concern.

Finally she said, "She meant a great deal to you, did she not – this girl I so closely resemble?" As God's my witness, I thought that I might strike her, but she forestalled me with, "Forgive me for the intrusion, Mr. Smithers *bahadur*, I will leave you to your thoughts." Then she hesitated before saying, "God grant you peace," and turned to leave, but stopped after only a few paces, with the air of someone who has had a momentary recollection. Without turning back, she spoke to the night air before her, "You might mention to Mr. Eden, sahib, that there is trouble brewing among the porters." There was that slight shrug again, as if it mattered little to her whether I did or I didn't. Then she was gone, draining me of all feeling before she was out of sight.

***

163

The next morning arrived with it's own problems.

"I knew that it was stupid to flog those porters," Simpson said, for some reason looking smug and pleased with himself.

"Why? What happened?" I asked, tucking my shirt into my trousers. I had just arisen, having emerged from my tent after a restless sleep, and had not yet made the connection.

The doctor fixed me with a look, and demanded, "Where on earth have *you* been?" But before I could answer, he barked his laugh and said, "They've all scuttled to the hills, or at least enough of them so that Eden will have to change his plans!"

My wits were slow, and I continued to stare, so he said, "The coolies, man! Eden thought that he could whip some discipline into 'em, but instead they said 'snooks to you, guv!' and scurried off!" He stopped to consider, "Leastwise they're not here!" and thought that was very funny indeed.

That was when I recalled Charula Khaur's warning from the previous evening. The memory was accompanied by a brief surge of guilt, for I had not acted upon it, but any such emotion dissipated quickly when I realized that, ultimately, I wasn't entirely sure where my sympathies lay.

Before I could contemplate further, I saw Captain Austen emerging from Eden's tent, sporting a look of disgust as ever there was. Simpson waved him over and demanded, "What news?"

The young captain gave me a nod, and said, "Situations normal, Doctor, everything's topsy-turvy as can be." Pressed to explain he said, "A letter came from the Deb Rajah via our friend the Jungpen. He claims that he doesn't know why we are coming, and, without saying so, managed to convey that he didn't want us to. But he suggests that if we have an issue with the Jungpen, then let the Jungpen deal with it, or words to that effect."

The doctor scoffed, "But surely this was all discussed ages ago?"

"That was the former Deb Rajah," the captain explained, "There's been a civil war since then, remember? Anyway, that's not the half of it."

The doctor barked and, with a trace of facetiousness, demanded, "Oh explain, do!"

"It seems that I'm to take the lion's share of the bearers and go down the road to Jolpigorie, a few days journey south of here."

"Whatever for?" asked Simpson. It was difficult to ascertain whether his expression of astonishment was real or in mockery.

"Why, to purchase some supplies of course." It was plain from his expression that Austen wasn't sure whether the doctor was speaking seriously or in jest, either.

"Do you mean to tell me that after yesterday's memorable occurrence, the Jungpen still remains obdurate?"

"If that means will he sell us any rice at a decent price, then the answer is no." The captain appended, "He did offer his apology in writing, though, just as he promised."

"Well that's a relief, I'm sure!" cried the doctor. "We'll make quite a meal out of that, won't we? Should go nice with a bit of sage!"

"Clever man!" said the captain sourly, pulling on his gauntlets. "Let's see how much you laugh when we continue with only half an escort!"

"What's this?" I demanded sharply.

Austen paused to give the doctor an evil grin before turning to me to explain. "There's not enough food to go around, is there? So someone's got to be left behind. Can't be the coolies: they're needed to carry what there isn't enough of in the first place, therefore it falls on the military, as usual. So it's a grand total of the Sikhs and ten sappers to escort us on our merry way to the back of beyond, while the rest remain here to guard the baggage."

I heard myself blurt, "What do you mean, 'guard the baggage'?"

Still uncowed, the doctor burbled, "Oh, this is getting rich!"

The captain sighed, "You poor benighted souls. Haven't you been listening? There were scarcely enough porters to begin with, and without any promise of provisions along the way, we'll be forced to provide our own. That means that the bulk of them will be carrying food. Couple that with their deserting in droves

165

means there won't be enough left to carry everything else, will there? So the baggage has to remain here, don't it?"

"It's as bad as all that?" I asked, while the doctor absolutely slapped his thighs with glee.

"It's not good, Charlie," said the captain, at the same time offering Simpson a glance bereft of levity. "So we'd best keep a sharp lookout out for trouble."

Scratching the whiskers under his chin, the doctor mused aloud, "And what's the chance of that, I wonder?"

"Oh I don't know," came Austen's cool reply. "You've got your choice of hill country or jungle, filled to bursting with all sorts of interesting fellows, whose only idea of commerce is nothing short of piracy, and excellent opportunities for ambush virtually every step of the way, so you tell me; but I'm keeping my weapons close by all the same." Then, finished with his gauntlets, he clapped them briskly together. "Right, well I'm off. Wish me a pleasant journey!" and strode away without another word.

***

The 'few days' to Jolpigorie and back, took Captain Austen more than two weeks, which was fair travelling, all things considered, over broken roads with a baggage train laden with eighty pounds of rice per man.

I had hoped that Charula Khaur had been amongst those porters chosen for the expedition, so as to rid myself of her presence for even that brief interim, but alas, such was not the case. I noticed her around the camp shortly after Austen departed.

Insofar as she had made every precaution to appear as a man (a task not so difficult as it might seem: your average Bengali being prettily handsome, in the oriental fashion), now that I was aware of her presence, it was impossible for my eye not to rove over the remaining porters, in spite of myself, seeking a form that was both slight and subtly lissome, with the hips filling out the baggy pyjama trousers somewhat more than was the norm. Once knowing what to look for, she was all that much easier to find.

166

Once found, I would experience that familiar sinking sensation, coupled by a curious...*longing*, I suppose, and an unreasoning anger that she was not Loiyan, and therefore an abomination to my eyes...eyes that could not help seeking her out nonetheless, mindlessly hoping, and invariably disappointed.

I felt woefully pathetic, and this humiliation was not lessened one jot by the suspicion that I was becoming perhaps too familiar with the sight of many of our bearers' backsides.

Throughout this time, and for sometime after, both Simpson and the Cheeboo left me to myself, as if they somehow knew of my torment, and of the necessity that I must come to terms with it on my own. For my part, we could not resume our journey soon enough.

This we did on the twenty-ninth of January, 1864, the day after Austen's return. True to his word, all but ten of our twenty-five sappers were left behind to guard the mountain of excess baggage deemed unessential, due to our lack of transport.

Austen set off before us, with the Sappers and guides that the Jungpen had agreed to provide, while the rest of us in the main party followed some three hours later. Upon our departure, I can't say that we made a grand sight beneath Dhalimcote's massive walls. What that worthy, standing at the battlements of that high brooding fortress, made of our small procession I could only guess. Eden leading the main party with Power at his elbow was not a sight to induce confidence, nor was the long train of bearers, struggling under backbreaking loads, with the Sikhs on either side, acting equally the part of jailors as much as protectors.

I did my utmost not to think of Charula Khaur in their midst, but as the train crept past, found myself searching for her yet again; and there she was, with a bundle strapped to her back that must have been half her own size, striding along gamely. Angry, I turned Maggie's head toward the vanguard, and wondered at her reason for being here, and could not countenance that it was myself.

Oh, we were a happy little mission, and no mistake. Simpson in a slouch hat, with his patient gelding encumbered with his medicine bag (as well as a small mountain of

167

photographic equipment) provided one meager ray of sunshine; the Cheeboo, looking like a deflated balloon in his silks, was perhaps another; but in my present mood, I did not seek out their company, and not wishing to taint them with my malaise, prayed that they would not seek out mine.

That day we descended some fifteen hundred feet (as I discovered later from Austen, who was a keen cartographer), crossing the Sukyamchoo River before making camp near a swamp. Auspicious you'll agree.

The next day was somewhat better, the ground being more or less even, we were able to travel some eleven miles, crossing the Nurchoo River around noon, and made camp by the Mochoo at day's end. Here the waters teemed with fish, and the shores with game, thus allowing us a rare opportunity to augment our meager diet for a brief but welcome interval.

It was on the third day that events returned to the farcical. Once having crossed the Mochoo, we proceeded for ten miles through well-forested country, where we arrived at the deep flowing waters of the Dechu River. Here some few hours were lost while the sappers prepared a bridge for us to cross, and it was getting on to late afternoon, when, after having scaled a steep wooded cliff, we were met by a party of Bhuteau, claiming to be officials of some stature. But then I don't suppose that we could hardly expect them to describe themselves as petty – what official would?

I had just made my way to the front of the train, Maggie's reins in hand, no one objecting when I joined the party. There were Bhuteau present, with their modest retinue waiting in the wings. Attending the officials were Eden and the Cheeboo, and I remember Simpson and Austen being there as well. Eden was being his usual sweet-tempered self when I hove to within hearing.

"What's he saying?" he demanded of the Cheeboo, barely disguising his annoyance. The gentleman he was referring to was a rather moth-eaten specimen with unfocused eyes and a lopsided grin, attempting (unsuccessfully) to hide the fact that he was three sheets to the wind. He was nodding along eagerly to every word of the Cheeboo's translation, although it was plain as day that he couldn't understand a blessed syllable.

"He says that they have come to warn you of great danger," said the Cheeboo.

"And what danger might that be?" Eden demanded.

The Cheeboo patiently asked the question, and the Bhuteau responded at some length with great animation. "He says that he has come to warn us away from Sipchoo. The commander of the fort there is concerned that his men will become inebriated and venture forth to cause mischief amongst us."

This gave Eden pause; he turned to Austen and snapped: "What do you make of it?"

"Well it doesn't say much for the man's abilities as an officer," the Captain scoffed. "If he can't keep his men in check that's his affair. But if they're from the same mould as the brutes we saw at Dhalimcote, I say let them do their worst – they'll get more than they bargained for."

Eden equivocated for a minute or two further, clearly not wanting to provoke an incident, but as Sipchoo had been our goal for that leg of our journey most of us were for pushing on. Finally he told the Cheeboo, "You may thank him for his concern, but we shall proceed as planned."

We set off without further delay, with Captain Lance posting outriders on the wings, and a section of Sikhs to reinforce Austen in the van, only to find upon our arrival that the fort at Sipchoo, as well as the soldiers, were both entire works of fiction.

When Eden confronted the officials they showed not the least bit of remorse for their attempted subterfuge, but fell amongst themselves laughing, much like school boys caught doing the dirty, claiming that it had been their aim to cause us to choose a more desirable camping ground than the one we had. Eden's reply was to turn a deep shade of crimson and have them banished from the site.

What did I tell you? Farcical as all get out. I only mention the episode in an attempt to give you an idea of what we were getting ourselves into. I was quickly learning that Bhutan was a

169

nation that marched very much to its own drummer. You could put it down to the seclusion of the territory, I suppose, but even that don't tell the whole story. I've since spoken to Tibetans, who were credited with having settled the territory in the first place (much to their annoyance – they'd rather *that* was kept under the rose). The reason that Bhutan is an independent state today isn't because the Bhuteau thirsted for freedom, or any other purpose so noble, but because they were so contrary that the government in Lhasa washed their hands of them out of frustration. I dare you to name one other nation on the face of the planet with a similar pedigree.

In case you're wondering, it's not my intention to paint everyone with the same brush: the Bhuteau peasantry were as stalwart and handsome a folk as you could ask for: friendly, hard-working, and generous to a fault, they bore the weight of a rapacious feudal system with long-suffering patience...that evaporated into mist everywhere we went, whenever out of hearing of an official. Then few of them seldom refrained from giving voice to their opinion that they should come under the flag of the British Raj.

No, it wasn't the working class; it was their rulers who fit the bill of absurdity that I'm attempting to describe. Few were little more than warlords, uneducated strongmen brooding up in their mountain lairs, preying on any and all passersby, with no sense of loyalty to a central government that was consequently largely stripped of its power – much like England during the Middle Ages, when the barons held sway, and the king ruled in name only. That's what we were getting ourselves into, and Heaven help us, too.

Our arrival at Sipchoo came with it's own problems, and might give you an idea of how woefully unprepared Eden was before ever departing Darjeeling. For it was here that the majority of the bearers' contracts expired. Eden's plan to hire new ones here came to nothing, as he was unaware that Sipchoo was only a hamlet consisting of five houses.

To be fair (if one must) the blame could not be laid *entirely* at Eden's feet, for it also showed how woefully ignorant our own government was of Bhutan, not more than half a dozen

170

Europeans having visited the place since the Battle of Plassey, well over a hundred years earlier. Anyway, the doctor thought it was worth a laugh.

The next day, the first of February, we were visited by the local Nieboo, who blandly told us what was to become a familiar refrain throughout the journey: he had not received word of our coming, nor, consequently, instructions about what to do with us when we arrived. No, he was very sorry (although he didn't look it) but he was unable to supply us with porters (here he paused to gesture at the barren countryside, I suppose to emphasize the obvious), and advised us to proceed no further until instructions arrived from Poonakha.

Eden's response was also becoming predictable. Rather than face any delay, and risk any further duplicity, our numbers were again stripped to the bare minimum, while any bearers who were willing were enticed to carry on. Not many were, for when we set out the next day, a mountain of baggage was left behind for lack of transport, with all but fifteen of the Sikhs to guard it. My sergeant friend from the commissariat was also left behind, along with the native doctor. Further, and perhaps most telling, Eden was forced to pare away his own personal retinue, leaving the *moonshee* (or literary assistant) behind as well, but the most telling of all was that his ever-loyal assistant, Mr. Power, was included in their number.

What wrenching of the spirit was caused by this separation from his master, I could only guess. Power and I had not started out well together, and I still couldn't claim that there was much love lost between us, but for one not bred to hardship I have to admit that he had carried himself well, and from all subsequent reports, also continued to do his duty in this new role on Mr. Eden's behalf.

It's not for me to say whether Eden's decision to push on was the correct one. Certainly there were valid reasons to avoid delay, as previously described, but the porters were all in when we arrived, and faced with the disappointment of being asked to extend their contract (and I use the word 'asked' loosely here – when faced with the daunting presence of a burly *subadar*, '*asking*' them to continue on, I can well imagine that it took a certain

171

amount of courage to decline). Morale was low, and they might have been all the better for some rest. Although it can equally be said that they might have used the time to decamp. As it turned out, many did anyway, and I can't say that I blamed them. If we thought that the going had been rough so far in our journey, we really hadn't any notion at all.

So we were a pretty lean crew when we ascended a mountain spur to the plain of Tsigong (elevation over fifty-seven hundred feet) a fine open plain just below the Tulélah Pass. By the time we had arrived, however, we were to discover that our numbers had grown leaner still, as the coolies had deserted in large numbers amidst alarming accounts from the locals of the depth of the snow in the mountains, and for once the reports had been accurate.

We entered the pass early the next day, soon, for the first time on our journey, encountering snow as deep as two feet. That would make the going rough on even country, but here it rendered our ascent tortuously slow.

Not all of our party were immediately dismayed, however. I recall that Maggie had stopped still at the first sight of the stuff, and with inquisitive ears forward, had reached down and touched it with her nose, jerking back with surprise at the coldness, I suppose, for I doubt that she had ever seen it before in her life. Thereafter she gave a little prance before I could compel her to proceed, for I believe that it filled her with wonder, even more so when she found that her hooves sank through its surface to the more estimable support of the earth. An amusing first reaction, perhaps even charming, but within the hour, after wading through drifts that rose past her hocks, making every step a laborious process, I could tell that she loathed it as heartily as I did myself.

At the forefront, Austen and his party had the worst of it, breaking the trail for the rest of us, but churned snow is not packed snow, and can be every bit as arduous as a virgin drift. Predictably, soon packs could be seen, here and there, scattered along the way, evidence that more and more of the coolies had had enough and decided to call it quits. There was never any question of pursuing them, even had I been so inclined. There was only the planting of one foot in front of the other, occasionally urging Maggie to follow whenever the reins tugged in my hand, and I found her lagging with an untypical reluctance.

All the rest of that long afternoon was so employed, ascending the trail one step at a time, hour after interminable hour, until at long last we'd reached the small plateau of Thlungchoo, three thousand feet higher than from where we had started that morning. Fortunately the place was well forested, and soon the smell of wood smoke filled the air as fires were lit to keep out the cold. Although no lives were lost on that inhospitable night, sleep was had by few as we huddled around the flames, and in spite of our exhaustion, eager to start out again on the morrow.

We began at light's first break, ascending to the pass at ten thousand feet, and then down twenty-five hundred in a steep descent on the other side to the plain of Dongachuchoo, hampered every step of the way by the deep drifts. It was a tired and miserable company that made camp that night, and I believe that it was only due to the difficulties behind us that kept the remainder of our bearers from melting away.

We were finally able to leave the snow the next day, with a short journey of a few miles to the Am Mochoo River where we set up camp. Here the sun was hot, and our spirits improved as if by a miracle.

The next day we proceeded in a leisurely fashion to a pretty little hamlet called Tsangbe. Here we were greeted by the peasantry, the same as had been the case in many other places: supplying us with gifts of eggs and milk, and all the while voicing their wish to come under the realm of British India. All these occasions made me realize that, as well as being sound, there was something to be said for a governing body that was also predictable, which, by all accounts, is something that these poor blighters had never known.

But proceeding onward.

Just two days down from the Tulélah, the contrast was remarkable. The air was warm and the soil rich, with neat fields of barley, buckwheat, millet and turnips to be found everywhere along the way.

The only other episode of note on that leg of our journey occurred while passing a flour mill. The miller was a venerable ancient who had come out to greet us, and we were shocked to see that he was hideously disfigured by a large tumour on his lip, concealing his mouth and a large portion of his face. How he managed to eat with it I couldn't imagine. It was here that I was given a new insight into our fabled man of medicine.

"Poor benighted souls!" the doctor tutted with a concern that I had hitherto not seen. "I say, Chee, tell the old gent to stop by after we've made camp and I'll remove the bloody thing for him."

The Cheeboo did as he was bidden, and, filled with surprise and hope, the miller agreed with an alacrity that belied his years. Later that evening he arrived with a large number of relatives (or simply inquisitives) in tow. With the aid of chloroform, with infinite tenderness the doctor removed the offending tumour as promised, amidst the great astonishment of all assembled. Thereafter, whenever we arrived at a village, and even at Poonakha itself, we were always greeted with the question, "Which among you are the doctor who removed the tumour?" Which was good for Simpson's stock, obviously; what Eden's thoughts were upon being so summarily upstaged was anyone's guess.

Another, lesser occurrence happened soon after we had cleared the snow line. The ground had evened out and I was able to take to the saddle again if I held Maggie to a walk, although such was not as effortless as it might sound. Having been introduced to snow, the little mare was equally as exuberant to be rid of it, and I could sense her longing to kick up her heels with every step. Consequently a great deal of effort had to be expended reining her in.

Shortly thereafter, I came upon something that was altogether more serious.

We hadn't gone very far when I began to hear the sounds of wailing, and soon came across coolies sitting by the side of the road; soon there were dozens, sitting with their packs beside them examining their feet, all in a great deal of discomfort.

Dismounting, I went to investigate, one after the other, and found several cases of frostbitten toes. Anywhere on the subcontinent you will find that your average bearer has feet as tough as shoe leather, impervious to heat and cold alike, but they do have their limits. Seething with anger that no one had thought to address this issue (and perhaps mingled with guilt that I had not thought to address it myself). I went up and down that line of those poor stricken wretches, cursing foully with every fresh case that I found. Among the last was a young lad who, even in my agitation, was oddly familiar, being treated by one of his fellows, no doubt as ineffectually as all the others. Rudely, I shoved this one aside so as to take a closer look. Both large toes were inflamed and swollen, and must hurt like the bloody blue blazes. That's when I looked into his face and saw that it was Mir Singh, Charula Khaur's companion, grimacing back at me. That's when the penny dropped, and I turned to the one who had been attempting to offer assistance...and found myself face to face with *her* again.

I felt my blood run cold, unsure of which was the distraction – the plight of the afflicted bearers, or the sight of that beautiful face staring back at me, her eyes rimmed with tears. Not a word was spoken, and the spell only broken when the lad groaned aloud. My thoughts returned to the present with something of a start and, scooping him up, swung him into the saddle. Mounting after him, I paused only long enough to...what? I didn't know then, and I'm not sure now. I looked at her, and she at me, and then I was urging Maggie onward to the front of the line.

Eden was just dismounting when I arrived. All around there was the hustle and bustle of making camp. Simpson was close by and was the first to notice me, and then the boy, one eyebrow arching interrogatively.

I told him, "Your services are required," handing the lad down as gently as I could.

The doctor received him with equal care, and saw immediately where the problem lay. "Good God!" he said, reaching for his bag.

175

By now Eden was aware of my presence as well. He eyed me with the purest dislike and demanded, "What's the meaning of this?"

This was the closest that I had been to the man since setting off from Darjeeling a month previously. The best that could be said since is that we had tolerated one another, and for my part at least, only barely.

My words were at first respectful, but my tone was quivering with anger when I said, "Sir, this is just one case out of many," and then even my words reflected my true feelings. "For the love of God, man, have you no decency?"

Eden's eyes bulged with astonished outrage, his mouth working furiously, I suppose over the pure effrontery of what I had said; but I took little satisfaction from the sight. It might have ended badly, right then and there, but for the doctor rummaging around in his bag, and producing a bottle of laudanum. "The boy has frostbitten feet," he told Eden, his tone reflecting something remarkably like contempt. "Knowing where our destination lies, and what it will take to get there, could the Raj be so mean-spirited as to fail to take the most meager means to supply something so simple as shoes for these poor fellows?"

That caught Eden up short, you may be sure. While I may have been a despised pariah, the doctor was held in high esteem, and commanded respect; his opinion could not be so easily dismissed. That being said, however, you could see the man's pride working on him like a dog worrying a bone. Accepting fault was a concept that was foreign to him. In his mind he was the exalted Ashley Eden, the Lord's very own anointed, and the rest of us were not. Therefore it was preordained that he could do no wrong. Now, faced with damning evidence to the contrary, he continued to mouth furiously, but no words would issue for the simple reason that there was nothing he could say. Instead, with what must have seemed to him the most logical response, he spun on his heel and stomped away without another word, no doubt furious with the bearers for having the effrontery to have contracted frostbite in the first place.

The laudanum was quick to take effect on young Mir Singh, so the doctor felt it safe to leave him in the care of an attendant. Rising to his feet with his bag in hand, he wasted no time on Eden's receding back, but looked to me. "You said there were more."

We rode back together down the length of the baggage train at a gallop, with more of his attendants bringing up the rear, and soon came upon the afflicted bearers in varying states of agony. The doctor's boots were on the ground before his horse had come to a full stop, with myself only slightly behind him. In no time at all he was examining his patients, snapping orders left and right to his harried aids as they arrived, all out of breath.

Taking stock that all was now in order, I retrieved some rags from my saddlebag. and proceeded to where I had last seen Charula Khaur. She was still there, sitting alongside the others, examining her own feet, with her sandals in the grass close by.

She looked up as I approached, and stared, no doubt wondering why I had come. I stopped just short, without deigning to look at her face. Yet I could feel her stare when I held out the rags, willing my hand not to shake. But it soon became too much for me when she failed to reach out to take them. She continued to stare as if for all the world I were something other than a man.

So I dropped them on the ground in front of her, and walked away.

Chapter Eleven

We spent two days in the village, giving the porters as much time to recuperate as possible. Of course no word of explanation was forthcoming from Eden, nor was there any elucidation as to why they were soon issued with scraps of rawhide and cloth, but of course none was necessary. These were the same materials from which the locals manufactured their own footwear, and our people were invited to follow suit. Better late than never, as the saying goes, and if the former were to Eden's shame, the latter, to some small degree, was to his credit, for the gesture was not at all an empty one, as you shall soon see.

The next day, as at other villages where we had made camp, we were visited by the local Jungpen, a portly fellow of ill humour who had no idea what to make of us. No, there had been no word from Poonakha, and no, he had not the facilities to aid us in any way. What was more, he said that we were forbidden to advance any further, but then with a typical Bhuteau resignation, allowed that he hadn't sufficient means to prevent us if we were determined to do so.

It was the typical farce that we were becoming well accustomed to, except for one of our party, which was Eden himself. With every such setback he took it as a personal insult, and an obstruction on the road to realizing his political ambitions. So when this latest version of the same old story issued from this robber baron's mouth, Eden's frustration became evident.

His tone was quarrelsome when he demanded of the Cheeboo: "Ask him if this means that Poonakha is officially ordering us to turn back."

It was a simple enough question, but only to one who is entirely ignorant of diplomacy, and the Jungpen, for all that he looked fit to play the part of a Calcutta street sweeper, was not a fool.

"Well," Eden snapped after the Jungpen had replied, "what did he say?"

Without the least inflection of any kind, the Cheeboo replied, "Mr. Eden, the honourable Jungpen says that this means

178

nothing of the sort. He says that it means precisely what he said it means: you are to stay in Tsangbe to await word from Poonakha."

Eden positively gnashed his teeth. "I'll be damned if I will!"

Aside from his bearing and tone of voice, Eden's frustration was most evident in that he had asked the question at all. Given the unsettled situation along the border, he knew perfectly well that, should the mission be turned back prior to reaching Poonakha, Calcutta would have little option but to regard this as a political snub, and nothing short of a declaration of war. If the Jungpen had been favoured with the same acumen as he looked to possess, he may well have seized upon this as a chance to rid the land of the hated foreigners, once and for all, without realizing the consequences. Fortunately he was not such a fool, and had turned his back on the delicious carrot that Eden had dangled before his eyes.

Our exhaulted leader slapped his thigh, and rising to his feet, began to pace back and forth.

"Well that tears it!" he said. "Captain Austen."

"Sir!"

"I would be obliged to you if you would see to it that we are prepared to move out at first light."

"Very good, Mr. Eden."

When Austen was gone, Eden continued to pace for another minute, visibly annoyed. Finally he sighed, his shoulders slumping into a measure of acceptance. Then he regained his campstool across from the Jungpen.

"Very well," he said to no one in particular, before continuing to the Cheeboo. "Ask him if he would be agreeable to provide postal runners between here and Sipchoo, and to provide for their protection as well."

To this the Jungpen was agreeable…provided that he be given a present from the start, and another upon the completion of our mission. I thought that our fellows back home at the Foreign Office could learn a thing or two about negotiating from this one.

With a few minutes further haggling, the business was completed, and Eden was able to draft his first letter to Power...telling him that he might as well pack up and go home, taking all of the unemployed *sepoys* with him.

In fact, the only good thing I can say from our brief rest period was that I was spared the haunting presence of Charula Khaur, for she remained invisible amidst the ranks of the porters. I prayed that she would remain so, but I confess, without much optimism in that regard. I could feel it in the air, feel it with my mother's gift of the 'sight', with a growing sense of despair: my past was coming back to claim me.

We left at first light, an even smaller procession than ever, for many of the frost-bitten porters had to be left behind. On our way out of the valley, our column trudged past Tsangbe's fort, set high upon a hill – a small enough building made of rubble stone, remarkable only for the beauty of its situation.

On the downward slope, we were subjected to a typically steep descent, to the Sukchoo River, where a good wooden bridge provided a safe crossing. Here the surrounding country was quite agreeable, with the air crystal clear, and the mountains in the background looking majestic as all get out. Perhaps it was inevitable that our spirits should respond.

Once past the Sukchoo, the other side of the valley ended in a steep rise, but the path was greatly ameliorated by a zigzag system of ramps cut into the rock itself, all the way up the face of the cliff. What this impressive feat of engineering had cost in terms of labour and coin of the realm I would hesitate to wager, but it must have been an immense undertaking.

The ease of our ascent did nothing to dampen the spirits of my fellow travellers, for we had long since learned to appreciate any leg in our journey that did not test our fortitude to the utmost. I confess that even my own spirits lifted somewhat when I saw that this stage of our trek was within sight of a waterfall cascading down from the heights above us, dissipating into mist before ever reaching the ground. Caught in the sunlight, we were privy to every colour of the rainbow several times over. I daresay that even the most unimaginative amongst us waxed poetic at its beauty.

The same magic must have been working its wiles on another, for when I paused from my position in the rear of the column to take in the sight, I heard Charula Khaur's voice speaking softly at my stirrup, "Oh *Bahadur*! It is beautiful!"

I stiffened in the saddle, unwilling to look at her, afraid that the spell had been broken, but instead I found myself saying, "Yes, it is."

We stared in silence for some moments longer, content to let the vision play on our minds. Eventually it was time to move on, so I turned Maggie's head away. She obeyed, but I thought with regret, and it wasn't in me to blame her. Meanwhile the girl seemed content to traipse along at my side, shouldering her enormous burden without a word of complaint.

I did my best to ignore her, and when a Smithers sets his mind to a task, he can be a formidable adversary. The beauty of our surroundings would seem to have served as an ally as well, for as we travelled higher, the entire world opened up before us, and there was much to capture my attention; but it also lulled me into a state of contentment that I do not believe I would otherwise have been vulnerable to. In truth, 'contentment' is not an accurate word, for I was far from content, and had long since forgotten what it was to feel so. This was more like a soothing balm smoothed over the bruise of my soul. The pain still lurked beneath, but the numbing on the surface could almost be translated as pleasure. Thus it was that I happened to glance down at her, took note of her load, and against my better judgment, found myself saying, "How on earth have you managed to cope?"

She regarded me quizzically, but when I indicated her haversack, she smiled, and swinging it from her shoulders, tossed it up to me.

On reflex, I reached out and caught it one-handed, and found to my surprise that it hardly weighed anything at all.

By way of explanation she said, "Our *subadar* is a kindly old fellow."

I handed it back to her, and before I knew what I was saying, demanded, "Who *are* you?"

At this she burst into laughter. It was a sound that even I could not find disagreeable.

"I have already told you, *Bahadur.* I am simply a girl, nothing more."

"I doubt that," I told her, but she looked at me so guilelessly that I had to smile, albeit ever so little. "Most women would not trek so willingly to the back-of-beyond."

She looked at me askance, and when she spoke, there was a hardness to her voice that I had not heard before. "In case you have not already noticed, *Bahadur,* I am not *most women!*" Then a corner of her mouth twisted into a grin, "As for this trek, in my years I have journeyed long and far. I was on the road when first we met, do you not remember? Why should it not be likewise now?"

No, she was not like most women, but she was so like another that her invitation to compare cast a shadow. Perhaps she sensed as much, for she was quick to change the subject.

"I wanted to thank you," she said.

"For what?"

"For the cloth to bind my feet." I glanced down and noticed that she was wearing boots, made from the material that Eden had supplied. "It is the thought that counts," she said, still smiling.

"A gift of a few rags is of little consequence," I told her, hearing the chill creep back into my voice.

"Yet it *is* a gift," she said, very bold. "One that you chose to bring to me." With that the conversation ended as she abruptly hastened her stride in order to catch up to her companions. And was it my imagination, or did she accent the sway of her hips as she went, knowing that I would be watching?

Meanwhile, our journey continued.

Shortly thereafter we ascended to a plateau, and almost immediately came upon the local peasantry lining either side of the road. Here each villager stood beside a smouldering pile of wormwood, which, I was told, was a traditional greeting in these parts. If so, it was a tradition that carried no great distance, for we never encountered such a welcome again in our travels.

The village of Saybee was very fine, with neat little cottages lined either side of the single street. Here, as in all other places we stopped, bereft of any of the authorities from Poonakha, the locals wasted no time in letting us know of the low opinion in which they were held, and, by way of contrast, their admiration for the British. Reinforcing my conviction that, by and large, people were the same the world over.

Then suddenly the assembly parted like the Red Sea as the villagers fell into murmuring amongst themselves. Soon we saw an entourage dressed in the garb of *Zinkaffs* fill the void, approaching the inner circle, shoving aside those who were too slow to make way of their own free will.

They were the usual puffed-up nonentities that we had become accustomed to, only this time they arrived with a very definite message.

After some initial jabbering back and forth with the Cheeboo, Eden, with his usual impatience, snapped, "Well, what is it this time?"

After a few more words were exchanged, the Cheeboo turned to him, "Mr. Eden," there was a slight tremor in his voice, which would have been the rough equivalent of you or I issuing a blood-curdling scream, "he says that we are to turn back."

Eden's brows knit together so quickly that I could have sworn that I heard his forehead go 'crack'. "Turn back? What on earth does he mean?"

"He says that it is official, Mr. Eden, from the Deb Rajah."

We all stared at the man, looking supercilious and self-important, fit to beat the band. There could be no questioning the veracity of the Cheeboo's translation. So it was official then, after so much toil the diplomacy was over before it had even begun. We were all going home, leaving the political cards to fall where they may. No one could say that we hadn't tried.

I should have known better – I really should. Eden wasn't about to have his moment of glory slip away so easily.

"Does he have proof?" he snapped.

A few more words were exchanged, and the head *Zinkaff* produced some sheets of parchment from inside his *gho*.

The Cheeboo said, "He has letters."

"Read them."

After a few seconds of the Cheeboo perusing the parchment, Eden sighed, "Out loud, if you please!"

Patiently the Cheeboo replied, "There are two letters, Mr. Eden."

To which Eden snapped, "Then by all means, read them both!"

I can't remember, word for word, but by and large the first was a letter addressed to the Jungpen of Dhalimcote, expressing the utmost in friendship and warm relations to the British Raj.

Eden heard him out in silence, and then pronounced, "Well, that doesn't sound too bad, hey, Austen?"

Austen's tone was reserved when he replied, "Indeed not, sir, but we would do well to hear the other letter before we make any judgement."

So the Cheeboo continued, and we were to find that the tone of the second letter was remarkably different from the first.

Also addressed to the Jungpen of Dhalimcote, it was a merciless upbraiding by the Deb Rajah, threatening his very life for allowing us to have crossed the border in the first place. Further, he was to pay a fine of seventy rupees, and do all that he could to encourage us to turn back. Then, with typical backtracking, he was ordered not to allow us to go away angry, and that if we could not be persuaded to turn back, he was to provide provisions for us along the Sumchee road. A most remarkable document, by all accounts, but we were finding it increasingly commonplace in our dealings with the Bhuteau.

Again Eden heard the Cheeboo out, but this time he remained silent for some time thereafter. For here, at long last, was proof that his presence was not desired at Poonakha, and I could see that the news had hit him square in the stomach. Although he was careful to maintain an unreadable expression, the pallor of his face was quite noticeable.

After a moment Austen ventured, "Sir, it's clear that you were intended to see the first letter," then he looked to where the *Zinkaff* stood waiting, supercilious, superior, and stupid beyond words, "but they can't have intended for you to see the second one. In fact, I have my doubts that this fellow can even read."

Doubts that I happened to share. It was inconceivable that this arrogant little man, with his piggy little eyes, had been given written instructions in that regard, and without anything in writing, was forced to depend on his own dubious memory. If he had not been told of the letters' contents (and there was every reason to believe that he had not) he would have no way of knowing the portent of the message, or even to whom it was addressed. It was clear to see that, having found his plans foiled to hand over the letters to the Jungpen in person, he had opted to hand them over to Eden instead, with only the vaguest idea of their contents.

Eden continued to remain silent, his brow furrowed into a troubled frown. Finally, with his usual peevishness, he snapped, "A moment, gentlemen!" and rising to his feet, strode off down the street, with his hands clasped under the tails of his coat.

I ventured to the doctor, "Well that's that, then. They plainly don't want us."

"Don't you count on it, Charlie," came the reply, preceded by an amused bark. "They may not want us," he gave a nod to Eden's back, "but yon will do everything in his power to see that they get us. He's not about to let something so paltry as written proof stand in his way. It's madness, of course, but in my experience the diplomatic has never been very big on sanity."

Nor was the medical corps, I thought, as I listened to him chortling madly at his little joke.

Presently Eden returned, and by the triumphant look on his face, I didn't need to be told that Simpson's prophecy was about to come true.

"Our course is plain," he announced to the *Zinkaff*, but in all actuality, it was to everyone assembled. "We must press on."

Incredulous, Austen cried, "But sir, the letters…!"

"Were not addressed to me!" Eden replied with a crafty little grin. "Therefore, *officially*, I have not seen them!" He glanced around, I think to invite us all to rejoice in his superior duplicity. What he saw, however, could not have been very encouraging, for he suddenly cleared his throat and, with some irritation, re-addressed the *Zinkaff*: "We will proceed to the *Durbhar*."

185

The *Zinkaff* received this momentous news with typical *sang froid*, as if it was nothing to him, one way or the other, and abruptly turning an about-face, disappeared with his entourage.

We did not stay long in Saybee, leaving the village early the next morning, traversing a slight descent to the Saychoo River, each of us privy to his own thoughts. Once across, we began the ascent of what would become the most imposing episode of our journey: Taigonlah Mountain, and beyond it, the Cheulah Pass.

We reached the first leg by noon, arriving at a grassy plain known by the locals as Bhokur, which we shared with a tremendous herd of yaks, driven down from the heights by the snow. Here we stopped and made camp, not wishing to be caught on the mountain when darkness fell, and it fell early in that wild terrain. For the rest of that day we rested, gathering whatever strength we could while trying our best to ignore Taigonlah looming like a giant over our heads.

Once more we started out well before sunrise. No doubt some of us looking upon that great shadowy mass, that was the herd of yaks, with envy, for though pathetically unfit for this stage of our journey, we were going where they (who were infinitely more suited) had been forced to retreat.

Our progress was slow from the beginning, as we struggled up the heavily snowed trail. Gradually, as the ground rose, the forests of oak switched to pine. Horses were led, as it was impossible to ride such a steep incline. But hard as it was for us, it was infinitely harder for the bearers, struggling through the drifts with seventy-pound loads strapped to their backs. Now and then I saw Charula Khaur, struggling along with the others. I do confess that I felt a surge of pity, but was able to quell it with the coldness in my heart. She was foolish to have come, but now here, must make her way as best as she was able. Whatever her reasons, she was not my responsibility.

Closer to the summit the traveling was easier, as the constant wind swept most of the snow away. Eventually we came to Shafebjhee – a rest home for travellers, clinging to the rock face of the mountain, and there we spent the night, keeping out the chill with fires, fuel being plentiful in the forest.

186

The next morning we awoke to a heavy mist obscuring the ground below, for as far as the eye could see.

I came upon Austen moping about as if someone had just kicked his dog. When I asked him what was wrong, he flung out an irritated arm, encompassing, by the look of it, the entire world.

"Apart from playing chief cook and bottle-washer to our esteemed Mr. Eden, it was my duty to map this area!"

"That's right!" said Simpson, just then walking up to us, tucking in his shirttails. "I remember that you were awfully keen on cartography."

Austen ignored him…which is usually good advice. "From this height I should be able to see all the way back to Sumchee," he spat in disgust, "but this fog is a regular pea-souper if ever there was! I can't see a bloody thing!"

Bark! "Cheer up, youngster!" the doctor cried, clapping an affable hand on his shoulder, at the same time tilting his head sideways, in the direction of Eden's tent. "Thataway lies your salvation!"

Austen blinked his incomprehension…until suddenly Simpson's meaning became clear.

"Why," he said, "that's right! I'll just ask his nibs for permission to stay behind for a few days! After all," he asked, "what could it hurt?"

What indeed? We would find out later, but at the time it all seemed so innocent. Even Eden was readily agreeable, although I was somewhat troubled, for no reason that I could name.

So when we set out within the hour, we were half a dozen fewer than we were the night before. I remember Austen sitting on the ground, frowning happily as he poured over his papers, while one of the handful of bearers left behind with him, was busy fastening a large telescope to the top of a tripod.

All these years later, I think it was the gift of 'the sight,' inherited from my mother, that made me pause to study the man's face: those oriental features beneath his turban, with the wisp of a moustache on his upper lip, and a mole high on his cheek. He seemed content enough in his duties, light as they were, while his fellows were set to toil through yet another backbreaking day. Again, for some indefinable reason, I found myself hoping that he was content, perhaps even happy. Then I shrugged it off as I took up Maggie's reins, and led her away.

That was the last that anyone in our main party ever saw him alive.

***

The descent down the other side of Taigonlah was steep, made all the more difficult by the ever-increasing snow. In places icicles twenty feet high depended from outcrops of rock. Had it not been for our difficulties, I daresay that they would have been quite grand to contemplate.

As always, the snow gradually gave way as we descended, until we came to a very lovely and park-like valley known to locals as the Hah. There we made camp on a pleasant little plain, alongside the Hachoo River.

The next morning, the thirteenth of February, we forded the Hachoo, and crossed the remainder of the Hah Valley, passing through several abandoned villages along the way. I was told by the Cheeboo that these people (much as had the yaks of the Bhokur Plain) descended to the more agreeable climes of Sumchee for the winter, leaving their summer homes a ghost town.

It was still early in the day when we began to come across more and more villages that were still populated. The townspeople, no doubt unused to visitors, turned out in force to bid us welcome. They seemed desolated when we refused to stay, but pushed on. Not to be put off, however, they fell in behind us until we came to our destination for the day – the village of Hah Tampien, at the foot of our greatest obstacle of all, the Cheulah Pass.

The villagers greeted us in the same old way, with the same old complaints, and voicing the same desire to live under our protection. I know, every time that I mention this you must be thinking, 'There goes Charlie, telling a stretcher,' but I'm not, and that's God's honest truth. Perhaps if you had seen how these people were governed (and I use the term loosely) you might

188

more readily understand. While our own government in Calcutta was far from perfect, all things being relative, when compared to that of Bhutan, it would really make you weep. But then these people had never heard of things like the Magna Carta. When they wanted something, and it was within their power, they would simply take it, because they had forgotten how to ask; and if it wasn't within their power, they would grovel and squirm to see if that would do any good...and if it didn't. they would shrug their shoulders, and take themselves off to where the pickings were easier. In a nutshell, that was the governing order of the Bhuteau for you, as fawning a bunch of bullies as you'd ever have the misfortune to meet. It was small wonder that the peasantry longed to be rid of them.

And then, wouldn't you know it, the very next official *wallah* to come along made a liar out of me, after all.

To all intents and purposes, the Jungpen of Hah Tampien was a jolly old cove, with a streak of kindness in him a mile wide and twice as long. He came to greet us on the day after we had arrived, bringing with him some much appreciated supplies of rice, and fodder for our horses.

But food was not all that he brought with him, for he also had his wife and daughter in attendance. Proudly, he proclaimed that his daughter (a pretty young thing, given to blushing, and giggling at us over her fan) was the wife of the Penlo of Paro, the most powerful baron in the western regions of the country. The Penlo, so the Jungpen informed us, wished for us to know that we would be cordially greeted upon our arrival at that city.

Now this was more like it. I could tell that even Eden was pleased, and after filling ourselves to bursting with a hearty repast, we all turned in with high hopes that the worst was behind us...as it turned out, never was a hope more forlorn.

The next morning we found that two feet of snow had fallen during the night, and it continued all that day, clearly making travel impossible. The Jungpen came by for another visit in the morning, bringing with him poles and straw for the *sepoys* to fashion their own shelters, and even arranged for our bearers to be taken into homes in the village. As a gesture of goodwill, I could not imagine its equal, and told myself that it was only humane to find some comfort knowing that, amongst all the others, Charula Khaur would not be suffering from the cold.

The snowfall did not abate that evening, but continued on all through that night, and all the next day. Nor did it subside even then, but persisted for another twenty-four hours, forming a heavy blanket of virgin white for as far as the eye could see, and believe you me, from our vantage point, it seemed as though we could see to the end of infinity.

Although those days must have rested heavy on our minds, I don't remember them very well, perhaps because they were so forgettable. I do remember Simpson grumbling at the delay, non-stop, and the Cheeboo sitting patiently in a corner of the tent, speaking only when spoken to. Occasionally Captain Lance would come for a visit, looking lost without anything to do. Sometimes the conversation would lag, and I would catch him, staring at those canvas walls, as if he could see the mountains beyond, and the passes crammed to bursting with snow. It took no great intellect to see that he was wondering (as were we all) how we were ever going to venture up into such an imposing obstacle. We were to discover the answer all too soon.

It was on the third afternoon that the Jungpen came for another visit. We were notified of the fact by the Cheeboo, who invited us to attend. I remember that we were all pretty cramped in Eden's tent, but by now any news was better than no news, and the Jungpen had clearly not come to pass the time of day.

Although you wouldn't have known it for the first fifteen minutes: the Jungpen seemed content to sit on his campstool, beaming good-naturedly all around, and giving a friendly nod to everyone he chanced to see. On the other hand, Eden was visibly at the end of his tether.

He demanded of the Cheeboo, "Ask him what this is all about."

The Cheeboo did as he was instructed, although one might hope that he chose his words with greater care than had our illustrious leader.

Listening, the Jungpen became quite somber and replied. I could tell by his frown that the news wasn't good.

After hearing him out in silence, the Cheeboo turned to Eden and said, "A *Zinkaff* arrived earlier in the day, close to exhaustion, and half-dead from the cold. When he was revived enough to speak, he was able to notify the Jungpen to expect the imminent arrival of a delegation from Poonakha." He hesitated before continuing, "He says that it is their purpose to turn us back."

The tent became deathly silent. I daresay that most of us were waiting with bated breath, hoping against hope that Eden would finally see reason. The doctor might have been the sole exception; I could tell by the sardonic look on his face that he was daring Eden to be as stupid as he suspected him of being; for it was plain as day to the rest of us that it was useless to proceed. The Deb Rajah, as good as declaring that he didn't wish to meet with us, narrowed our options considerably. But then, he didn't know Eden.

The Great Man seemed in a quandary. Not, you'll note, about the difficulties that lay ahead, but about the one that he'd left behind.

Suddenly he slapped his thigh, sorely vexed. "This news is of the utmost portent," cried he, "and I would act upon it at once if only Austen were here!"

Over the past few days, the absence of his aide had been a point of some anxiety for the camp as a whole. If he and his party had been caught out in the open when the snow had begun, it was even odds for his safety. As much as his vanity wanted to set out immediately and push on (thereby denying Poonakha the advantage of intercepting us while still at a distance from the capital), Eden was too much of a politico not to realize how much face he would lose if it were discovered that he had abandoned Captain Austen to his fate. In the end, after much this-ing and that-ing about, the Jungpen was thanked for his news and sent packing, while the rest of us trickled out, one by one, leaving Eden to pray for a miracle.

Less than two hours later he got it.

Chapter Twelve

We heard the cry just outside our tents, first raised by the *sepoys*, and it was soon pandemonium, drawing nearer by the minute. "Austen sahib! Captain Austen has returned!" I stuck my head out of the flap, and there was the man himself, looking like death warmed over, staggering along with the remnants of his party, amidst much hubbub and rejoicing.

I dashed out, stumbling through the drifts.

"Austen! Thank God you're safe!"

He had that faraway look. It was the strangest thing, freezing the breath in my lungs, for I had seen that expression before – haunted, disbelieving – it had been on all of our faces, coming back up the north valley after the Charge. It's not something you easily forget, no matter how hard you try.

His face was haggard, with patches of frostbite on his cheeks beneath a thick growth of beard. His lips were cracked and bleeding, his hand trembling when he reached out to grasp my sleeve.

"My men are missing," his voice was scarcely above a whisper. "Have they returned?"

I was searching for a reply when the doctor suddenly appeared, shouldering me aside. He sized up the situation at a glance. "You'd best come with me," he told him. Then off they went with Simpson shouting over his shoulder for his aides to see to the others.

He came around to see me that evening, shaking the snow off his shoulders as would a dog, then rubbing his hands over the small oil flame I kept burning in my tent.

"He's resting," he said. "I've seen to his frostbite, and given him a dose of laudanum to help him sleep. He'll be fit as a fiddle in no time at all."

"He mentioned that some of his men were missing," I said.

Simpson's shoulders slumped. He must have known that I would ask, but it wasn't difficult to see that it was a question he would have gladly avoided.

"Four of his bearers are unaccounted for," he said, distractedly studying a corner of the tent. "The storm caught them while they were still on the mountain. Austen thought it best to spend the night in shelter, hoping that it would blow over before dawn."

"But of course it didn't," I said.

"No," he replied, "it didn't."

I tried to imagine what it must have been like for them. Finding their situation untenable, they would have had little choice but to break camp and press on before the snow got any deeper. For two days they had struggled through those drifts. Every step must have been a test to their endurance, lulling the mind into a state of hypnosis. It seemed a miracle that only four men were missing, even though I knew that would be small comfort to Austen. Once having dropped by the wayside, their chances of survival would have been slim to nil.

"You know what this means, don't you?" the doctor asked, but before I could reply he supplied his own answer. "It means that, with Austen and his party…returned," I had thought that he had been about to say 'safe', but had changed his mind at the last moment, "there's nothing in Eden's way to keep us from pressing on."

"Nothing but three days' worth of snow!" I replied, gesturing angrily to where the pass lay waiting. "Good God, man, even Eden couldn't be so foolhardy!" Yet, even as angry as I was, I realized that I spoke without conviction.

For the first time Simpson looked at me; his expression was wry. "Would you care to make a wager on that?"

It just so happened that I didn't care to at all.

***

The storm blew over that night but the wind had descended, bringing with it a freezing cold that threatened to rip the air from our lungs in a matter of seconds, forcing us to stay in our tents yet another day.

However, on the nineteenth of February, five days after having arrived, the wind abated and the temperature rose. The mission packed up its belongings and left Hah Tampien without any fanfare, proof that I was wise not to accept Simpson's wager, after all.

It was madness, of course, but what part of this mission was not? No one save Eden had any hopes of its success – no, not even Elgin, God rest him. It was all being done to save diplomatic face with the rest of the world, the rest of India in particular. 'The Raj plays by the rules', that's what we were saying, but with the Deb Rajah's hostility staring us in the face, it was now possible to say that the rules had been observed and go home. It was Eden, only Eden, that ambitious maniac, who hadn't the least doubt of his own abilities, who would risk all our necks in order that the world might be given a glimpse of his supposed brilliance. He was the sole cause of our venturing into the teeth of the Cheulah Pass when conditions couldn't be worse.

The extra day's rest had done Captain Austen the world of good. As is the way of the young, he rebounded so quickly that I scarcely recognized the hardy adventurer as he took his accustomed station in the van.

There were a few changes in our marching order, however. Eden's sole acknowledgement that the pass might hold some difficulties in store was to have the stronger of our members to the fore, in order that we might break a trail for the others. So it was that, with Maggie in tow, I found myself alongside Doctor Simpson and Austen, as well as twenty strong bearers, newly arrived from the Rajah of Sikkim. With this force we set out, taking turns plowing through snow that came past our knees.

By this stage in our journey I was probably as fit as I've ever been in my life, but a few hundred yards on that grueling road soon put paid to that. I was sweating like a pig within the hour, and gasping for breath soon after; for it is not to be forgotten that whatever little progress we made was all *uphill*, on the road to the pass some thousands of feet above us. Three hours later, when the main force was due to follow, our progress was still pathetically slow, with the snow becoming ever deeper – in places up to our thighs – and still we pushed on, all through that long, punishing morning and into the afternoon.

We were still a half-mile from the summit, close to exhaustion, when there came a hue and a cry from the rear. We all turned to see that the heavily laden main party had already caught up to us. Reaching into his pocket, Simpson drew out his Hunter. His bark of laughter was more like a gasp of dismay when he cried, "Why, it's only three o'clock!" The plan had been for the two parties to arrive together at the end of the day. Clearly the going was more difficult than anyone had allowed for.

Soon Eden was among us, brisk and arrogant as always. Obviously annoyed, to Austen he snapped, "You should have arrived at the summit by now!"

Stung, Austen replied, "Sir, we've been doing our best, but in case you haven't bloody noticed, we've been plowing through bloody drifts three bloody feet deep! It tends to slow one down!"

Eden received this impudence with a glare, but perhaps sensing equal hostility from the rest of us, decided that silence was the best course to follow. Instead, chewing on the ends of his moustache (presumably to assist thought) he stared up at the summit, looming ominously just a few hundred yards away, crammed full of snow, daring us to do our worst.

At last he said, "We must press on," and to my ears, at least, it sounded like a whine from a spoiled child...which I daresay it was.

This was greeted with an amazed silence. Even Simpson's mouth dropped open in disbelief.

"Sir," Austen began, barely controlling himself, "we're all done in." He gestured around at the surrounding trees – trees that could supply a bounty of fuel for fires to warm us, as had been done on previous occasions. "Surely it would be best..."

"I said we must push on!" Eden roared, giving vent to his own spleen before gradually restraining himself, but we could all see that it took some effort. His arm was shaking when he reached out, forefinger extended to the summit. "I have it on good authority that a village lies directly on the other side!"

We all stared at him, wondering if he had gone mad. Then we stared amongst ourselves, and then at the ground.

I was somewhat surprised to hear my own voice inquire, with a feigned politeness, "Directly on the other side, Mr. Eden?" Most heads were hanging loose over slumped shoulders, many being too tired to raise them, but a few swiveled up at that.

195

I hadn't spoken to Eden since confronting him over the cases of frostbite amongst the coolies, and little enough before then, ever since having made a scene at the rail station, a lifetime ago, back in Bengal. You might say that I was trying to lay low to escape notice, and you would be right. The man just wasn't my cup of tea.

Eden swung around, a pained expression forming on his face when he realized that it was I who had spoken. He regarded me with the same keen dislike of old.

In a tone bristling with anger, he said, "You will be quiet!"

Ignoring him, I continued, gesturing up to the summit, towering bleak and inhospitable against the sky, inviting others to do the same. "An odd place for a village, wouldn't you say?"

I could hear a few (a very few) amongst us give a tired little titter, more like a guffaw, but it was enough. Eden's face began to turn red, his eyes attempting to bore holes through me. I thought that he might try to have me arrested (I daresay that the idea had occurred to him), but he had just enough sense to realize that, if he gave the order and no one obeyed it (as seemed likely, given our mood) he would be faced with a situation that was entirely more serious.

Instead he answered in a voice that, I must admit, was dangerously low, "It's there, I tell you, and the snow is bound to be not as deep on the other side, as well! The day still holds enough light for us to make it, and I say we go!"

We stood there glaring at one another, like two desperadoes from the American West, neither of us able, or willing, to back down. The tension was extreme, and we might have been standing there still had the doctor not issued a familiar bark of laughter, and come forward, placing his hand upon my own, where it rested under my coat on the butt of the Tranter.

"Very well," he grimaced sourly, which I assume was intended to be a winning smile, "we've all had our fun, so let's get to it, shall we? The sun isn't getting any higher!"

With that the tension eased, and the moment passed. I thought to give Eden one last defiant glare, but he had already turned away. Incensed, I caught up to the doctor, grasping him by the sleeve. "What was that all about?" I demanded.

He shook his arm free and regarded me with what might have been amused disdain. "You fool!" he sneered. "You still haven't learned a bloody thing, have you?" and left me with that to chew on while he began to wade into the nearest drift.

Fortunately such a procedure makes for a poor exit. Some seconds later he was still only a few feet away, struggling through the snow, so it wasn't necessary to raise my voice, but I did anyway, just for the sheer bloody hell of it. "Oh you think so, do you? Well just you wait and see!"

You don't try to take the mickey out of a Smithers, especially when he's feeling bloody-minded.

To give you an idea, it took us the better part of three hours to cover those last few hundred yards to the summit, and the sun had long since begun to wane. I paused just long enough to look out on the land below, but of course could not see any lights from a village. Unsurprised, I noted that Eden was nowhere within hailing distance, either.

Whereas he had been wrong about the location of the village, Eden was equally wrong about the depth of the snow on the downslope, too; if anything, the going was even slower than had been the ascent. In places the drifts were eight feet deep. More than once Maggie plunged through the crust up to her neck, for once her eyes wide with fright, and soon the panicked neighing of other horses following suit began to echo off the canyon walls. Much hard work was required to extricate her: packing the snow all around where she had broke through, then with constant urging – both with words, and a steady strain on the bridle – compelled her forward until she was free.

The second occasion left me in quite a quandary, for I was still exhausted from the effort required to free her the first time. I was tugging away on the bridle, feeling no end of frustration, with Maggie's shrill neighing ringing in my ears when, for once, Fortune politely intervened in the form of one of the bearers, a Lepcha, who was no stranger to these parts. I couldn't understand a blessed word he was saying, but thank heaven I didn't need to. He was holding out his hand, and by his gestures, asking for the reins. At this point I was more than ready to accept any help that was offered, so it wasn't a hardship to drop them in his hand. He accepted them with a smile, then turning his back on me, approached Maggie, who was terrified, struggling ineffectually in snow up to her ears.

Setting aside his pack, he knelt down on his knees, stroking her forehead, murmuring softly to calm her. I thought it a wasted effort, for the mare was too far gone with fright, as anyone could see. More to the point, I didn't understand for the life of me what earthly good it would do. This time Maggie was truly mired, and her struggles were only making matters worse. She was straining to keep her head above the snow, but it was halfway up her cheeks, and soon it would be higher. I could feel my heart sinking as my hand reached under my coat for the Tranter. At least I could save her from so ghastly an end.

I was on the point of ordering the man to move away from her, when I noticed that, though Maggie's eyes were still wide with fear, her struggles had ceased. I hesitated, feeling the pistol in my hand, though I had yet to raise it – not daring to hope, yet hoping all the same – feeling helpless as the devil as I looked on.

The man leaned forward, speaking softly into Maggie's ear. All the while his arms burrowed beneath the snow until he could reach her flank. Then, with the tone of his voice increasing, he began gently, but insistently, to push.

At first she resisted, and I didn't blame her, for she was being coaxed onto her side, and any fool could see that would be the end of her, but still the man persisted. Slowly, but ever so surely, he got his way.

Now my pistol arm was raised, and this time I don't think I cared if the ugly little brute copped his lot as well. For what he was doing to my horse, it was no less than what he deserved. My finger was actually on the trigger, when Maggie, finally succumbing to the man's wishes, rolled over onto her side. At that point the wizened little fellow was a flurry of activity as he leapt forward, pushing her on her belly, his voice and gestures urging her to continue to roll, again and again. And again and again she obeyed…and with every rotation the snow became packed, as she rose closer and closer to the surface. Within seconds he was urging her to stand, until finally there she was, shaking all over, her head hanging low while she blew loudly through her nostrils, but merely fetlock deep in the snow.

I had just enough time to reholster the Tranter before he turned to me and bowed, beaming from ear to ear.

I accepted the reins from him, and managed to stammer, my thanks, thoroughly ashamed. Still smiling, he gave another little bow and reached for his pack. He would have been on his way without any further ceremony, but I stood in front of him, blocking his passage, offering my hand. He hesitated for a long moment, as if the gesture was foreign to him, but then, slowly, he reached out and grasped it in both of his own, giving it a single, firm, shake. Then, with one last bow, he was gone, soon lost in the train amongst the others.

I can't tell you how many more times Maggie plunged through on that long, arduous day for, exhausted as I was, my state of mind was not at its best, but I can tell you that the second time I was able to coax her on my own, and the third time (or was it the fourth?) she didn't require any coaxing at all, but rolled over with a sense of resignation, and over again, until the footing was firm enough for her to stand.

By then the evening had long since fallen, but fortunately the weather remained calm, and the moonlight magnified by the snow, making visibility rather less of a hardship than one might have thought. Still, if it was a blessing, it was the only one we had. Progress remained excruciatingly slow, to something like a quarter of a mile to the hour, and the cold began to take its toll.

Here and there along the train, I could see dark forms lying in the drifts, huddled by the side of the path. One by one, the bearers, overcome with cold and exhaustion, were lying down to ease their suffering, uncaring if it was their last act in this world. As little energy as I had myself, much of it was expended in rousing them from their torpor, or waylaying others to put their own packs aside to carry them onward.

It was during this time that I came upon Austen with a small party of men, going from one prone figure to the next, scouring the mountain for the exhausted and disabled. After a day spent breaking trail, he was close to exhaustion himself, but I had never seen a man more determined.

199

"I've already lost four men," he told me. "I'll be damned if I lose another."

It was perhaps an hour before midnight when the dark mass of a forest came into view, and we were soon huddled in its shelter; those of us who were still able, set to gathering wood for our fires. I had just returned, encumbered with an armful of deadfall, when I overheard Eden speaking to Austen.

"We'll bivouac here," he said. His voice sounded weary, but there was nothing apologetic in his tone. "Set the bearers a dozen to a fire, and see to it that each has a *subadar* responsible enough to make sure that it doesn't go out during the night."

A tired mind is prone to playing tricks, and for some reason Eden's mention of the porters made me think of Charula Khaur. I thought that was strange because I had been too predisposed to dwell on her at all throughout the ordeals of the day. Now that we had found shelter at last, and a long-needed rest was at hand, my mind refused to be easy, but slowly, like a creeping shadow, gradually began to grow more troubled.

Of course at first I tried to ignore this unsettled feeling, but the image of Charula would not leave, and soon, on the pretense of seeing to their well-being, I was wandering from fire to fire, studying the faces of each of the coolies with care, and failing to find her amongst any of them.

Still, I thought, this proved nothing. She could be anywhere in the encampment; there must be a thousand reasons why she wasn't with the others. There was no cause to fret, she was not my problem, after all, yet I found myself fretting all the same, more and more as she continued to fail to appear.

I chided myself and vowed that I didn't care. The girl could manage on her own, after all, and if she couldn't, well it was no affair of mine, was it? Of course it wasn't; after all, it wasn't my fault that she had been so foolish as to come…and yet…

Gradually I found that my wandering took on intensity as I began floundering about from one fire to the next, peering into every shadow, but not seeing the face that I was searching for.

Eventually I found myself out at the edge of the wood again, staring back up the pass that we had just descended, twelve and a half thousand feet in the sky. It hovered ominously, casting immense shadows in the moonlight, like a colossus seeking vengeance on the insignificant beings who had invaded its domain. Then, whether it was the 'sight,' or whether it was fancy, I heard its voice in my head, plain as day: *"Yes,"* it said, in a cruel, dark whisper, *"I have her, Charlie. Come find her, if you dare!"*

Reluctantly, I was forced to admit that, in spite of Austen's determination, we may have lost another straggler after all. The sensible thing to do would have been to report that she was missing, but 'sensible' was a word that hadn't applied for quite some time.

The next thing I knew I was at the horse lines, untethering Maggie from where she was pawing a lackadaisical hoof through the snow, searching for fodder. If she objected to having her well-deserved rest interrupted she didn't let on, but trailed along at my elbow, apparently content to discover what other adventures I had in store. Willing as she was, however, her day had already been sufficiently long for me to assume the saddle, so I led her along by the reins, instead.

I was fortunate to run into Simpson along the way.

"Whither to, Charlie?" he asked, which I suppose, given his own state of exhaustion, was intended as wit.

When I didn't answer straight away (for in truth I was at a loss how to do so) he looked from myself to Maggie, frowned, noting my direction, and gestured toward the mountain. "You're not going back up there, surely?"

Again I could offer him no reply, for my thoughts were too confused, with the result that the moments stretched without any words exchanged. I had the impression that he would very much like to question me further, but instead, having come to a decision, he reached into his satchel and pulled out a flask of spirits.

"Here," he said, "I've a feeling you're going to need this more than me." And with that he turned away, and was promptly sallowed by the forest.

I hefted the flask in my hand, watching him go. Then I thrust it in my pocket, and continued on.

Had I but noticed, the trail was less arduous going back up as it was coming down. By now the drifts that I had helped break a trail through were flattened and well packed by all those hundreds who had followed after, and due to the cessation of the wind, had not drifted in again. The moon was still bright, so I had little difficulty picking my way along.

The silence was the first thing to assault me. Being in the midst of so many throughout the day, and now finding myself alone in the middle of the night, the contrast might have been unnerving if I'd let it, but there was too little time. I was single-minded of purpose, scrambling up the path, peering into shadows, hoping, and yet afraid of what I might find.

Once or twice I did come across some poor soul struggling down the mountain with their load. I stopped to question them but they could not understand, either not understanding, or being too exhausted to listen as the case may be. So I would direct them toward our fires glimmering amongst the pines before carrying on.

At what point I began to waver I couldn't say, but it gradually began to filter into my psyche how impossible was my mission. When had I last seen her? This morning? The day before? My tired memory couldn't be sure. What if she lay on the other side of the pass, already having succumbed to the elements? What if she had never left Hah Tampien in the first place, but had sensibly chosen to return to Darjeeling instead? What if I had already passed her along the trail? Moonlight or not, it was all too easy to do. Then, just when I had stopped to consider what my next course of action might be, it was Maggie who saved her.

I heard her whicker at my elbow, and turning to look, saw that her ears were pricked toward something unseen. Then, uncaring that I still held the reins, she surged forward, forcing me to keep up with her or to drop them. The former was beyond my stamina, so she forged ahead on her own, disappearing around a small outcropping of rock, with myself following the sound of her hooves crunching in the snow. I caught up with her just as she came to a stop and was stretching out her neck to nuzzle at something on the ground.

I stumbled forward, not daring to hope; the object's dark form mingling into invisibility in the moon shadows of the rock.

It took a moment to see that the form was human. It took another to realize that it was either unconscious or dead, but it took only an instant after I rolled it on its back to recognize Charula Khaur, and notice how shallow her breathing was.

Carefully, I lifted her, propping her back against my knee, and reached for Simpson's brandy with my free hand. I pulled the cork with my teeth, and dribbled a thin stream into her mouth.

At first there was nothing – a terrible instant when I believed her already dead – and then there was a cough, followed by the brandy dribbling down her chin. Hoping against hope, I gave her more, and the cough became more violent, but this time she managed to keep it down. After a third dose she opened her eyes, although showing every reluctance to do so.

I held her close, my breath escaping in a sudden exhalation. "Thank God!" I cried, "I thought that I had lost you again!"

Drowsily disorientated, she murmured, "*Bahadur?*" and the spell was broken.

I tarried a moment until the cold, iron fist grasping my heart relented. At length, with my strength fast dwindling, I picked her up and managed to sling her astride the saddle, placing my overcoat around her shoulders. Then I led Maggie down the mountain, all the while careful not to let Charula tumble by the wayside. My anxiety continued as I braved the cold in nothing but my shirt, unaware of the extent of her injuries, knowing only that Simpson needed to examine at her.

Perhaps it was strange that her secret should hold any meaning for me, but for reasons unknown to myself it did, and it had all along. When I had first discovered her amongst us, it had never occurred to me to reveal her identity to anyone. For one thing, I don't think that I wanted to give Eden the satisfaction of knowing, but of course there was more to it than that. Welcome or not, her secret became my own – something we shared – and the sharing united us in a covenant, accenting our intimacy, as though we were lovers. Thus far I could reason; after that everything became confused.

I needn't have worried about searching for Simpson amongst the campfires, for he was waiting for us just inside the belt of forest. He stepped out of the shadows as we neared.

"So you found who you were looking for," he observed. Although still tired, I could hear the wry amusement in his voice.

I thought it best not to waste any time. "She was unconscious when I found her."

There came a short expletive followed by an explosive, "*She!*" before his training took command. "Bring her deeper into the tree line, out of the wind," he instructed, clearly irritated, "and then build a fire." He led the way in what, apparently, was a thoughtful silence, for after his initial anger had dissipated, he stopped only once to turn and say, "You young juggins! I might have known!" and barked his curious laugh. I, myself, was too exhausted to correct the lascivious conclusion he'd drawn.

We eventually came to a small clearing, far enough away from the other fires, yet deep enough in the woods to provide shelter, where Simpson helped me to ease Charula Khaur from the saddle. I spread my bedroll upon the ground, and the doctor did his best to make her comfortable, as I gathered wood for the fire.

In no time at all cheerful flames were licking around the pine boughs I'd managed to collect, issuing enough light for Simpson to make his examination. Charula Khaur remained semi-conscious, unaware of the proceedings.

There was a quick intake of breath when the doctor unwound her turban and her hair cascaded around her shoulders like waves of darkest shadow. But instead of speaking, he took his stethoscope from his bag, parting the buttons on her shirt before inserting the diaphragm close to her heart.

Frowning, he listened for a moment before demanding, "You gave her some brandy?"

"A little," I told him. "Enough to revive her."

He spat his disgust. "You call this *revived!* Give her some more, man! Get the blood pumping through her veins!"

I hastened to obey while he carried on with the rest of his examination. Charula Khaur was coming fully alert, sputtering brandy in every direction, when he finally delivered his verdict.

"She seems well enough," he decided, folding his stethoscope back into his bag. "Exhaustion, that's all, and small wonder, too. Just a wee chit of a thing." Then it seemed as though he could contain his curiosity no longer, "See here, Smithers, how long has she been…"

"From the very beginning," I told him.

He glared at me as if it was all my doing, and seemed about to say more, but instead spat out with, "Bah! There's no help for it now!" Then diving once more into his bag, he brought out his diminishing bottle of laudanum, and carefully measured out a dosage. "Give her this," he ordered. "It'll help her sleep. With any luck at all she'll be right as rain come morning, but I'll return to have a look." Fastening the clasp on his bag, he regained his feet. "Oh, and one other thing," he said gravely. "Whatever you do, you'd best keep her warm!" and found something particularly humorous in this, for he was chuffing like a steam engine as he disappeared amongst the trees.

Charula accepted the laudanum without complaint, saying very little, but presently the cold grew too much for her, and in a trembling voice she asked for more brandy. I gave it to her, not knowing how it would react with the laudanum. Time revealed that it reacted quite strongly.

I had piled the branches high upon the flames, and soon the fire was roaring away, flinging heat and light in every direction. She nestled under the blankets, her eyes luminous in the firelight as she regarded me for a long time in silence. Then in a tired voice she said, "You have saved my life again."

I did not reply, but instead contented myself by piling more branches upon the flames.

I felt more than saw her eyes on me, for I found that it was difficult to look at her. Moments passed before she observed, "You are cold." This was followed by a rustle of blankets, and she said, "Come, *Bahadur*, bide with me."

It was impossible not to look, and I saw that she had flung a corner of the bedroll aside, with a single lithe, pyjamed leg poking out from under the covers.

"Not a bit of it!" I said, although I daresay that the chatter of my teeth gave me away. For no matter how close I huddled to the fire (in fact, until it threatened to bake the front of me) my back felt as if it were cold enough to grow icicles.

"Poor man," she said, her voice husky with laudanum. "I still have your coat!"

"That's quite all right," I assured her, tucking my hands into the pits of my arms. "I hadn't really noticed."

She continued to regard me, her eyes contemplative, until I felt no end of a fool.

"Very well," she said, "it is *I* who am cold!" She wriggled under the blankets, and gave the prettiest little pout. "I need you to keep me warm."

"Oh crumbs!" I sighed, without realizing that I had spoken aloud, and then seized on my last defence: "Here, I'll get you some more brandy!"

"That would not be wise," she observed, and then clinched it. "I'm sure that your doctor friend would agree."

She was right, God rot her!

Then, with those innocent eyes large as orbs, she said, "And he instructed you to keep me warm, did he not?"

"Well, yes, but..."

She said simply, "Then come."

You wouldn't have credited the fact that I had found her on the mountain just a few hours ago, more dead than alive.

"You're shamming," I accused.

Her arms collapsed onto the blankets, and for the second time she asked me, "Is this life that you have saved so meaningless to you?"

She lay there regarding me, her eyes as soulful as sin, and in spite of myself, I found myself sidling closer.

"That is better," she said, her mouth curling into those dimples that I remembered so well. Once more she tossed the blankets aside and invited, "Come."

This time I obeyed.

It was crowded under the blankets, my bedroll being intended only for one. I turned my back to her, grimly maintaining what little distance between us as possible, grasping the edge of the blanket like grim death.

She said, "You are shivering!"

206

There no longer seemed to be any use in denying it, so I maintained a frosty silence with whatever dignity was left at my disposal. The damnable thing about it was that, even though I was tucked in under the blankets, there was little immediate warmth to be found. For once the cold had penetrated my clothing, it provided an insulated barrier that kept heat *out*. There was nothing that I could do about it, however, except continue to ignore her…and shiver.

Presently she said, "Remove your clothing."

In as scandalized a tone as I could muster, through clattering teeth I cried, "I will do no such thing!"

"But you will be warmer!"

"Not on your nelly!" I huffed. "Why, the very idea!" Then for reasons that weren't immediately clear, I added, "I'll have you know that I'm British!"

Convinced that I had succeeded in putting her, and her foreign notions firmly in place, I forced my jaws to clench shut, and commanded sleep to overtake me on no uncertain terms.

And wouldn't you know, that after all of the trials of that long, evil day, for a while, at least, I succeeded.

***

The fire was burning low when I awoke to what felt like her entire body pressed into my back. It took only an instant to remember where I was, and what, in my folly, had become my situation.

In a trice I was out from under the blankets and standing in the snow in my stocking feet, shivering from the cold…and from something else as well. "How dare you!" I cried, seething at the very thought that she had tried to take advantage.

The moon, as well as the fire, had gone down. Her face was in shadow, but her voice drowsy, when she explained, "You were still shivering. I was trying to warm you."

"What nonsense!" I huffed. "I was sleeping like a baby!"

"Perhaps," she conceded, although the doubt in her voice was strong, "but still shivering." Then, sounding every bit like a

207

wife, she folded back the covers and said, "Come back to bed." I couldn't help but notice that her shoulder was bare.

"I won't!" I vowed, virtue personified, "Why you're...you're..."

"Naked?" Her eyes glowed in the flickering flames much like a cat's. She pulled the covers even lower, exposing a lovely brown breast. "Does that displease you?"

"No! I mean *yes*! Yes it does!"

"You find me plain?" she asked, at the same time stretching luxuriously, also like a cat.

Then it was as if I were overtaken by a great weariness, and I found myself too tired to care.

"You know that I don't," I told her, but looked away, searching instead for something to occupy myself, something other than her. My eye chanced upon the store of wood that I had gathered. Seizing an armful of faggots, I knelt by the fire and fed them, one by one, onto the coals. My mind was confused, but I still would not look at her when I said, "I never have. Not in all these years."

She was silent for a long moment, as she absorbed what I had inadvertently revealed. Then, evidently consigning it to the recess of her mind, she said, "Come back to bed, Bahadur, else you will catch your death of cold."

Perhaps it was her guileless tone, perhaps it was the cold after all, but this time I didn't decline. Instead I threw the rest of the wood on the fire and went over to where she lay, managing to crawl under the blankets without feeling threatened.

Nor did I feel threatened when I felt her strip off my clothing, for I was near frozen, and this time when she pressed her body against me, I was only aware of gratitude for the heat that she shared.

For the second time that night, I was soon overtaken by sleep.

Chapter Thirteen

I awoke much refreshed in the false light of predawn, the fire once more having burned very low. Unmindful of my state of undress I arose and, dancing nimbly through the snow, gathered more wood from the pile, and threw it on the coals. Dashing back to my bedroll, I saw Charula Khaur watching me, just before I dove beneath the blankets.

"*Bahadur* indeed," she murmured approvingly before turning over on her side.

I spooned my body around her with very little hesitation, luxuriating in her warmth, but the more I clung to her the more I found myself groping ever further…and found myself answering a call that I hadn't felt in quite some time.

Uncomplaining, she rolled over onto her back, our faces bare inches apart. There was only a moment to regard one another before I kissed her.

She tasted of honey, and soon I was demanding more. For my answering the call had soon become a yearning, and then a need, primordial in its very nature. It had been far too long.

Pressing her beneath me, impatiently I thrust her legs apart, and pushed forward to claim what she offered – a moan escaping from her lips when I entered her. Soon she was thrusting against me, and everything was a frenzy of animal greed, followed all too soon by the inevitable conclusion, our cries frightening still-slumbering birds from the surrounding boughs.

After, we lay panting breath back into our lungs, staring up at, but not seeing, the sky. Eventually she repeated herself, "*Bahadur* indeed!" and laughed.

This time I didn't press her for an explanation, but was content to put my arm around her shoulder, and let her nestle against my side. Soon after, she was asleep.

Soon after that, so was I.

***

We were awake and dressed, busying ourselves about the fire, when Simpson arrived, bag in hand.

Casting an appreciative eye over Charula, he said, "Well I can see that my medical services aren't required." She offered him a smile, and a mug of tea. He accepted both gratefully.

Warming his hands on the mug, he said, "Ah! That's better! Nothing like a good cup of tea first thing in the morning! My thanks to you, ma'am!" He returned her smile, and for once, it took no great effort on my part to recognize it as such.

We sat around the fire while he caught us up with the news. Although he must have been curious for me to catch him up in turn, Simpson was content to do most of the talking.

"We'll be moving out shortly," he said. "It seems that Eden found his village after all."

I asked, "When did this happen?" for it had been late when we had arrived in the forest, and the day was still early for this to have happened without our knowledge.

"Last night, while you were still gallivanting up on yonder mountain, some of the porters were all for pushing on in search of better shelter, and Eden gave them permission. So they left their packs behind and set out again, finding the place within a few hours."

I said, "Stout fellows, good for them!" It wasn't difficult to recall my own state of exhaustion from the previous evening; the effects were still lingering. Those who had chosen to go forward deserved my admiration.

We would have talked further, but just then our conversation was interrupted by the plaintive notes of our bugler sounding the call for us to form up.

"Aye, well that's that then," the doctor sighed, pouring the dregs of his tea on the fire. Rising to his feet, he offered Charula a nod and graced us with another extraordinary smile, "I'm obliged to you, ma'am." And turning to me he said, "I'll see you shortly, then," and cleared his throat, as if suddenly embarrassed, before stalking off.

I watched him go, Charula approaching in the interim. I thought that her intention was to seek an embrace, but she stopped short of me, and said, "I will be off, as well."

I did my best not to appear too relieved. Obviously much had changed between us, but I wasn't yet ready to explore the extent. Then, to give you an idea of how dis-ordered was my mind, I blurted, "You could stay with me."

But she shook her head and smiled. "It is best that I do not. I think that my presence might be difficult to explain."

Feeling more foolish than ever, I said, "Yes, of course."

We stood thus for some moments longer. I think that she expected me to say something else, but the silence became uncomfortable instead.

Then she smiled again – a curling grimace at the corner of her mouth – and was gone.

I stood alone, feeling no end of an idiot, until I felt Maggie's muzzle nudge my arm – the only living creature who didn't seem to care.

***

I don't recall the name of the village, but I do recall that the deputation that was to have met us at Hah Tampien was there, having arrived in the early afternoon.

The Cheeboo warned us, "Nothing good will come of this," and he was right. Thwarted in their attempt to intercept us at Hah Tampien, the *Zinkaffs* were feeling bloody-minded, unceremoniously turning out many of our porters that were taking shelter in the village, and otherwise just being generally high-handed.

Finally the door burst open on the home where we were gathered, and the Zinkaffs barged in, typical of all the others that we had already met, which is to say that they were as arrogant as Billy-bedamned.

Their leader, a low-browed fellow of middle years, came forward and promptly commenced shouting at the Cheeboo, who heard him out in his usual deferential silence. I tell you, it was all that I could do to prevent myself from intervening between this uncouth lout, and the gentle soul, but of course it just wasn't on.

211

When the *Zinkaff* had finally finished his tirade, and with Eden and the rest of us regarding these ignorant upstarts with cold disdain, the Cheeboo turned and began to translate.

He said, "I am told that we are to return to the frontier. There we are to discuss any boundary issues, which will include turning over the *duars* of Assam," he hesitated briefly, then continued, translating verbatim, "which the Raj confiscated illegally." Ignoring the sharp intake of breath coming from all points in the room, he pressed on. "Then, and only then, will the British be allowed to air their grievances. If after that time we, the *Zinkaffs*, deem it necessary, the mission will be allowed to proceed to the *Durbhar*."

During the silence that followed, I overheard Austen murmuring his outrage to Simpson. "Of all the bloody cheek! *Return* the Assam *Duars*? Bloody fools! Do they think that we'll just hand them over? Why, we only confiscated them to stop what they're doing right now in Bengal! If we leave, what's to stop them from taking that up again, hey? Bloody impertinence!"

Well I had to agree with him there. If it wasn't impertinent to suggest that, after all of the hardships we had endured thus far, we should just meekly turn around and head back to the border, I didn't know what was; and *then*, and only then, were our demands to be heard. Not only that, but if, after hearing our case, these bloody fools considered we had just cause (fat chance of that) we would be allowed to proceed to their capital, *starting from the frontier* again! They must be mad to think that Eden would agree to any such thing.

Very well, I know that I've said that the mission was pointless from the beginning, and it was, any fool could see that, barring Eden, of course, which should give you some idea. Without an invitation from Poonakha, our own claim to having any official standing could be held in doubt. It had been made abundantly clear that our presence was not desired, and God only knows what Eden expected to accomplish in the face of such hostility, except perhaps to make the point that we weren't the sneaking land robbers that so many claimed that we were. But to my mind that point had already been made, time and time again, and we could have turned back at Sumchee, or Hah

212

Tampien, or any number of places without losing face. But this was not Hah Tampien. This was…whatever its bloody name was, on the far side of the Cheulah Pass. I, personally, had endured untold hardships to get this far, and I was only one out of many, so I think that it was safe to guess what our collective opinion was.

Not that I was worried, you understand, because I knew that Eden would nix their plan in the bud, and he didn't disappoint, neither.

In as unperturbed a voice as you could imagine, he said to the Cheeboo, "I would be obliged to you if you would ask these gentlemen for their credentials." 'Credentials', in this case, being a letter of authority.

The Cheeboo asked, and was duly answered.

They didn't have any.

Eden stroked his moustache, concealing his smile. "Then I am sorry, gentlemen, I cannot engage in talks in which you have no authority." This drew a great many angry frowns amongst the *Zinkaffs*, to be sure. If you ask me, I don't think that they had any idea what Eden was referring to. Even if any of them did possess any written authority, it was doubtful that they could actually read it. But all this talk about credentials was so much poppycock; Eden knew it, and so did they. They were the real thing, all right, you only had to look at their rich robes and surly expressions to see that. However, unfortunately for them, they just couldn't prove it.

The murmuring amongst the Bhuteau began to grow louder, to the point where I thought that there might be trouble, but these quickly dissipated when the *Zinkaffs* heard what more Eden had to say:

"Therefore I am determined either to continue on to Poonakha, or to return at once to Darjeeling."

The head *Zinkaff* was quick to answer Eden's threat, for threat was all that it really was; Eden had no intention of turning back now. That much I did know.

Through the offices of the Cheeboo, the *Zinkaff* replied, "You must not think of returning to Darjeeling, Mr. Eden." Which was precisely what the Bhuteau wanted him to do, but not

213

without first reaching some sort of diplomatic solution. If such an agreement was not reached, the severity of the situation could only mean war.

Seizing the upper hand, Eden continued to play the wounded party.

"If the Deb Rajah refuses to see me, I'm afraid that I have no other choice."

Upon being told this, the head *Zinkaff* flew into absolute fits...for form's sake. When he had subsided somewhat, the Cheeboo translated, "Not want to see Your Excellency? But whatever gave you that idea?" Or words to that effect. The *Zinkaff's* face cracked into an ingratiating smile...which rather reminded me of Simpson for some reason. "The Deb Rajah has *never* said such a thing!" Which was cutting it fine, but I suppose that it was accurate enough, seeing as how those exact words had never been spoken in any official capacity. Although it was clear that the Deb Rajah didn't *want* to see Eden, that didn't mean that, if push came to shove, he wouldn't. Eden knew this, and was pushing for all that he was worth: daring the man to what would almost certainly be a declaration of war when he knew that he hadn't the authority to do so, even if he was mad enough to desire such a thing. The only option left open to him was to back down, something that Bhuteau officials were getting good at, without any visible loss of face, either.

"Very well," he said, apparently resigned, "if that is your wish we will return to Poonakha at once to arrange for your reception."

Our party broke up soon after the meeting was over. I was off to the horse lines to see to Maggie's fodder, and happened upon Captain Lance along the way, looking thunderous as all get out.

"What's all this?" I asked. "You look like you've just lost your best friend!" I had hopes that my sally might induce him to smile, but no such luck.

"The bounders!" he grated, "While they were keeping us busy at the conference table, their bloody servants got into our baggage train, and were robbing us blind!"

I commiserated, but wasn't unduly alarmed. "They couldn't have got away with anything more than a few pots and pans, surely?"

I could have swore that I saw smoke curling from Lance's nostrils. "Aye, they took those, too!" he admitted, with his eyes narrowing into dangerous little slits. "But the worst of it is that they took one of my men's rifles as well, damn their hides, and his, too! It's going to come out of his pay, I can promise you, and I'm not finished with him yet!"

So I left him under a storm cloud of ill temper, raging aloud on what tortures he might devise in the form of field punishment for the unfortunate fellow, leaving me feeling relieved that I was no longer in the service.

Maggie seen to, along with the gift of a scrounged carrot, I returned to my tent to begin packing my kit. For now that these latest officials had been disposed of, I assumed that Eden would brook no delay on our road to Poonakha – more fool me.

"Ah wouldn'ae count on it, laddie," was Simpson's verdict when he dropped by for no specific reason other than a chinwag, as far as I could see. He had entered unannounced in his usual fashion, and lolled comfortably in my camp chair, ignoring the fact that I had been about to pack it away. Lately he had been affecting what I can only assume was a Scottish accent, even though I knew that he was no more Scottish than the Queen. I believe that he thought that it made him sound more egalitarian. To me he sounded like a moderately educated man inflicted with a severe head cold. His opinion was expressed in response to my own reply to his inquiry as to what I was "aboot". After which he elaborated.

"Yon *Zinkaff wallah's* no as daft as all that! Poonakha's strategy is to delay, and delay, and delay, 'til they can get all their ducks in a roo."

Cautiously I asked, "'Roo'?"

"Row," he conceded, albeit reluctantly. Then, unabashed, and rolling his 'r's with vigour, he continued. "D'ye no ken whit yon rascally robbers are dain'? They're no but kenchen the whittles all the wee!"

215

Again I inquired, "*Kenchen* the *whittles*?" but this time received nothing more than an indignant glare for my pains. Perhaps he had finally guessed that I was deliberately antagonizing him.

But my good humour was largely feigned as I struggled with this morning's vexation. My dalliance with Charula Khaur had been a mistake…or at least I thought that it might have been. True, I had surrendered to her charms, but only under the most trying conditions. If the girl had the temerity to think that would give her any claim to my affection, she had another think coming.

I noticed that Simpson was regarding me in that quizzical way he had whenever he thought that he had said something especially clever.

"What?" I asked, returning to the present. "Sorry, you caught me woolgathering."

"So I see," says he with a knowing twinkle, damn his impudence! "I was just saying that Johnny Bhuteau isn't finished with us yet. Why it's even odds that we won't be leaving this encampment for a fortnight. They'll dream up some sort of skullduggery to delay us, mark my words."

Only half-listening, I told him, "Eden doesn't intend to lose a minute getting to Poonakha, and he's already demonstrated that he won't be brow-beaten."

"Aye," Simpson agreed, lapsing again into an accent that would have reduced any self-respecting Highlander to a huddle of tear-sodden tartan. "They cannae use force, that they ken, laddie, but there's moore ways than wan to lure a troot frae th'pond!" He stopped to consider, "An' there's moore way's than wan t'keep him innit, too!" Again he stopped, I think to consider whether or not he had stumbled upon something especially profound. Apparently deciding that he hadn't, he shrugged, "But that's by-the-by. If they cannae use force, they might work their wiles on his vanity (he pronounced it 'va-nut-tee') instead!"

Meanwhile my mind had wandered again.

But what *did* I feel toward her? Apparently there was something to have driven me back up that mountain, and I wasn't *completely* forced to have relations with her, so what was it?

What did I feel? This was a question to which I had no easy answers. One of the reasons was that Englishmen seldom admitted to having feelings about anything, not even to themselves, and I hope that I'm as English as they come. True, she closely resembled my dead wife, but wasn't that the reason why I was so repelled by her? Why had I cared enough to save her? Why had I succumbed to her charms? At times the memory of the morning was enough to wrack me with guilt, for I could see it as nothing less than a betrayal to Loiyan. Yet at other times I almost felt elated.

Simpson was looking at me *that way* again.

Finally, dropping the accent, he said, "Charlie, do you have any idea what you're getting yourself into?"

I suppose that I shouldn't have been surprised by the question, but I was. Caught off guard, I did my best to look down my nose at him, and demand as huffily as I was able, "Whatever do you mean?"

It was wasted on him, however, as his expression remained unchanged. Almost paternally, he said, "You're not cut out for this, you know."

"Cut out for what?" I asked, the pure voice of innocence, but he wasn't fooled for an instant, God rot him!

"Come along, Charlie! Let's drop the pretense, shall we?" They were impatient words, but his voice might still have been my guv'nor's. "A casual fling with a native girl is all very well. It's not at all uncommon when on an expedition – camp followers and so forth – but it takes a special breed, don't you see?" Then he fixed me with a stare. "And you're not it."

"Very well," I said stiffly, "I'll drop the pretense." But I was stung by his words, and they put me very much on my dignity. "Would you have had me leave her on the mountain to die?"

His eyes narrowed. "You blithering idiot! You know very well that isn't what I'm referring too!"

"Spell it out for me then!"

His riposte came without pause, and he was fair shouting it, too: "You can't be having it on with her, you bloody fool!"

There, it was out. I glared for all that I was worth, wanting to hate him. He returned it, glare for glare, not giving an inch, and suddenly, just like that, all the fight in me was gone.

I felt my shoulders sag; miserable, I confessed. "I don't know what to do."

I thought that he might exploit my weakness and really give me what for, although I felt that I was beyond caring; but the silence reigned for a good long while, each moment sinking me deeper into despair, until I felt the rough clap of his hand on my shoulder.

"I've known some serious chaps in my time, Charlie," he said, "but you're a horse of a different colour. Why, just look at you, man! Just the thought of what to do with this girl is eating you alive!"

"She…" I began, but the words faded to nothing.

"Yes? She what?" he prompted, and I knew that he would hear me out, whatever I had to say. But it was hard, so hard!

"She reminds me of someone I once knew." The words felt empty. There was so much more left unsaid, but how could I tell him, or make him understand what it meant whenever I looked at her, when I didn't understand it myself? I had kept my memories of Loiyan a secret for so long that it had become a part of who I was. I could no more speak of her to another than I could call fire down from the sky.

Simpson's hand never left my shoulder. He was a strong man; I could feel the grasp of his fingers through the heavy material of my coat. It pained me, yet it was oddly comforting, too.

The silence continued, and when I made no further attempt to fill it, his grip on my shoulder eased.

"Ah well," he cleared his throat, sounding rather like an ill-tempered bear. "Such as that may be, Charlie, I'm not an ignorant man, I hope, and I fancy that I'm a good judge of character. The point I've been trying to make is that you're one of those noble asses who could never do wrong even if you tried…which would be the last thing on earth that would occur to you to do. With men like you it's all 'play up fellows, do!' with fair play and decency fairly oozing out of your pores!"

"You make that sound as if it was a bad thing." I knew that I should have been stung to indignation, but a great weight of hopelessness had descended upon me, and would not allow it.

"Ordinarily I would agree," he replied testily, as if the conversation wasn't to his liking. "It's people like you who have instilled something in the Empire that makes it worthwhile. We're not *completely* about money and power, you know. We try to do what's right, too. We don't always succeed," he allowed, "but we don't always fail, either, because we *try*! And why? Because there's enough of us who are like you! That's the point, Charlie. It just isn't in you to do anything dishonourable; but if this woman isn't to destroy you, sooner or later you will be forced to do exactly that."

I was too despondent to lash out that he was delving into matters which were not of his concern; but I was not too far gone to take him up on this point.

"What do you mean, 'destroy me'?"

He regarded me with pity. "How well do you know this girl, Charlie?" When I failed to answer, he nodded and said, "Just as I thought." And then he said, "In time this mission will come to an end, at which point I assume that you and your master will be returning to England. What then? Are you prepared to leave her here, pining at the dock while your ship sails off into the sunset?"

Something roused me enough to say, "Who said that I would leave her?"

At which Simpson exploded, "Because you would *have* to, you dundering fool! Haven't you been listening to a word I've been saying? You can't take her with you, that's flat!" I was about to protest, but he cut me off. "If that notion crossed your mind you can just bloody well forget it! Oh I know all about your Lord Brampton, and how he's gone all spoon-eyed over that Pirāli woman, but he's a lord, dammit to hell! He can get away with it! Back home, exotic and beautiful women are quite the fashion in Society, or so I've been told, but will you get this through that thick head of yours: *you are not in Society*, and never will be!"

"No, I'm not," I replied, more crestfallen than ever.

219

Simpson paused to collect himself. Finally he said, "You and I must play by different rules than the high and mighty. If you were to take her back with you, people won't see her the way that you will. All they will see is the colour of her skin!"

"What do I care what people will think?"

Simpson didn't bother to reply. He just stared at me as he would a child.

But I had to admit to myself that I was arguing out of pure mule-headedness. For I'd had this same argument with myself years earlier over Loiyan. Simpson's diatribe was nothing that I hadn't examined in the greatest detail already. Of course he was right, but the truth was that I had never thought everything through to that point. He was correct, too, in surmising that I couldn't simply abandon Charula Khaur, and that I was of insufficient means to provide for her even if I could bring myself to do such a despicable thing. The only other option – remaining with her in India – was really not an option at all. My duty was at Lord Brampton's side, and duty trumped all. No (and I realized this with something like relief) my only clear path was to nip this strange infatuation in the bud.

"You're right," I told him at last. "I'll end it."

He gave a terse nod before asking, double-sharp, "When?"

"At once," I replied. "As soon as I see her again."

Having got his way, Simpson's hand resumed its place on my shoulder. "I'm sure that she's a delightful child," he said, prepared to be amenable, "and I'll concede that she's a real stunner besides; but you do see that this is the only way, don't you?"

I told him, "Yes," because it so obviously was.

***

I spent the rest of that afternoon, and well into the evening, searching for her. My mind was all grim determination to see the business through to the end; but although I scarcely was able to admit as much to myself, my heart was growing lighter by the minute, now that I had been shown what I must do.

220

For it was clear to me, now more than ever, that the girl must be told that our future was utterly impossible. Thank heaven that I had such a good friend in Simpson to point that out to me. Far better that she be injured a little now than ten times worse later on.

It was all so ridiculous anyway. Even given the more liberal views that some circles of the Eastern world held towards intimacy, I couldn't countenance the idea that what she might feel toward me was in any way real. I had saved her life, very well, but that didn't require anything more from her than simple gratitude, and not even that, really. Having the silly thing believing that she had fallen head over heels was well out of court altogether.

Thus, girded with this uncontestable logic, I had set out determined to make things right.

Such was my intention, but it went unfulfilled, for I was unable to find her. I checked amongst the porters, but was met with only the blankest stares. Nor could I find her in the rest of the camp either, or even in the village, thinking that she may have been sent there on some errand, but she was nowhere to be found. Finally, several hours later, I conceded defeat, but only for the moment. She was bound to show up sooner or later, and I would have it out with her. Until then I would simply keep my disappointment in check, and bide my time. A Smithers was never more determined than when he was forced to wait.

It was quite dark by the time I finally threaded my way back through the dying embers of our campfires, and the last remaining individuals gathered around them who had yet to seek out their own pallets. Many I knew, and some of them hailed me to come join them, but I begged off, siting our early departure on the morrow. They accepted my excuses and bade me a good evening, as I stumbled through the shadows, seeking out my tent.

I was quite weary when at last I found it. The past few days had been quite trying in both body and soul, and I had much to make up for before the sun next reached the horizon. So with thoughts only for my blankets, I pulled back the tent flap and ducked inside.

221

Until my eyes had a chance to adjust, the darkness was even more absolute than the night itself, yet I still possessed that old soldier's sixth sense, and suddenly knew that I was not alone.

Instantly alert, I stood stock still, tensed like a coiled spring, with my hand trailing to the Tranter, ready for whatever danger might be lurking in there with me. Then from the direction of my pallet, I heard Charula Khaur's sleep-filled voice say, "*Bahadur?*"

I think that I leapt out of my skin, and my reply was slightly more high-pitched than I would have liked. Nor was it terribly intelligent.

"What on earth are you doing here!" I squeaked.

For an answer I heard the blankets fold aside, and in the dying reflection from the fires on the walls of the tent, I could see the outline of what might have been an elegantly shaped thigh.

"Forgive me," she said. "I waited for you, but you did not come. I must have drifted off." Then she chuckled sleepily and stretched, long and languorously. "Where have you been?"

"I…well…I…" I couldn't say at what point my firm resolve had deserted me, but it had, sure as blazes, slinking off into the night like a cur, leaving me to face all that delectable flesh on my own. To my credit, I did manage to say, "This is impossible!"

"Yes," she agreed, "it is." Then in that husky, sleep-filled voice she asked, "Why don't you come to bed?"

And don't you know, even though I wasn't nearly as tired as I had been only a moment earlier, I couldn't think of a single blessed reason why I shouldn't; and as she pulled the blankets even further aside, all sorts of reasons came to mind why I should.

So with only the faintest wail of despair coming from the hidden reaches of my mind, I did.

Chapter Fourteen

As it turned out, Simpson was wrong about being waylaid at the village, but only just. With the city of Paro (the stronghold of the Penlo, the most powerful baron on the country's western reaches) within an easy day's march, and just a hop-skip-and-nibble from Poonakha itself, Eden was impatient to be off. So we broke camp at first light, most of us as eager to be doing so as he.

However, we hadn't much more than started down the road, when we were met by an official party, sent by the Penlo, requesting that we delay our arrival so that he could make arrangements to receive us in style.

The memory of my conversation with the doctor returned: the Bhuteau could not use force to stop Eden, so they did the next best thing: by appealing to the only thing that he valued more than his ambition – his vanity. Mountains could not delay him, nor brigands, nor exhaustion, nor threats of starvation, nor raging rivers, nor frostbite, nor blizzards, he was just that bloody keen…until they dangled the carrot of pomp and ceremony in front of his face, and then suddenly it made perfect sense to hold off for a day or two.

We fell out by the roadside, some few miles from the city, while it was decided where we should make camp, and they were taking a deuce of a time in reaching a decision, too. Over by a stream was obviously unacceptable as we might disturb a demon, or over by a grove equally unacceptable as therein dwelt a wood sprite, and so on. I daresay that, had it not been for the sun baking us to a crisp while we waited, we would have been more sensitive to the local superstitions. After all, I could well imagine what my reaction might be if a party of Bhuteau suddenly descended on London and proceeded to pitch their tents just outside Westminster Abbey, enough said; but it was small consolation when, several hours later, it was finally decided that we could set up camp by the stream after all, and that, presumably, the demon could go whistle.

Charula Khaur had taken her leave of me the hour before dawn. I had risked the small flame of a spirit lamp, and could see

223

the concentration on her face as she finished wrapping her *pugharee* around her head, tucking the loose end into its folds. Once more I took the time to marvel at how much she resembled the one I had loved – her eyes, her mouth…her lips; and then I found myself wondering what other ways she might resemble her even further. Her beauty, her lovemaking, indeed her love, were all so close to my memories as to make very little difference. Simpson had said that this was impossible, and yet was *she* not impossible, her very existence? But there she stood, as real as the racing of my heart, with her brow a pretty wrinkle of concentration, while making certain that her appearance was just so before leaving, unable to know the subtleties of movement and expression that made her so dear to me. How could I ever turn away from that?

Then, stooping low, she had given me a long, lingering kiss, and with the silent swish of the tent flap, and a last brilliant smile, she was gone into the shadows to rejoin her own folk, and to make ready for the day.

I lay back on the pallet with my hands clasped comfortably behind my head, filled with a sense of sated well-being, and the magical wonder of it all.

When reveille sounded I was still awake and already dressed, but upon sticking my head out of the tent flap, I noticed that Simpson had already risen. Whatever he saw on my face (no doubt it was guilt) made him turn away, shaking his head in sad resignation. Then he stopped and turned, much as he had done the other night, staring at me with deep concentration. Suddenly he barked his laugh, and still shaking his head, knelt down by the ashes and began to stoke the fire, occasionally barking and muttering good-naturedly throughout the proceedings.

It was remarkable really, how Simpson's argument, based on sound reason and good judgement, had vanished into thin air at the sight of only one of those lithe, silken thighs, but there it was – that and the other part, too, of course. In the blink of an eye everything had changed, and the prospect of continuing with her made perfect sense.

I crawled out of the tent, and sauntered over to the fledgling fire, scratching my backside, as is my wont upon arising.

I was prepared to have it out with him: to defend her honour, or whatever else he might take exception to, but he didn't even look at me. Instead he continued to fan the flames as the kindling took hold. Only when the fire was burning cheerfully did he sit back on his heels and deign to acknowledge me whilst rubbing his hands together over the coals.

"What did I tell you?" he declared with smug satisfaction. "Johnny Bhuteau ain't half as daft as Eden thinks!"

Well, it had been a long night, and my faculties had no doubt suffered as a result. So I shouldn't have been surprised that my confused mind had some trouble keeping up in the early going. At the moment I had thoughts for Charula Khaur, and very little else. If the conversation wasn't to be about her, in some form or other, I found it a hard go to hold up my end.

Perhaps sensing my confusion, Simpson took pity and explained, "We could be sitting here for days, while our exalted leader waits for his hosts-to-be to tidy up their dusty old palace in honour of our arrival!" He barked again. The very prospect seemed to put him in good cheer, but then, I should have been used to that from him by now.

Rummaging in his gear, he produced an enamel pot, and was about to nestle it in amongst the coals before I was able to rescue it from him. Simpson might be a highly skilled medico, and a dapper hand at photography as well – and even have an eye to the keyhole of the door to the Halls of Power into the bargain, but he was a handless clown when it came to preparing our morning tea. Even sleep deprived as I was, I was more than his equal at such domestic chores. If Simpson had dared to offer a cup of his sorry muck for, say, Lord Brampton to sample…why, I shudder even to think!

The doctor relinquished his hold without protest. Instead, while I filled the pot from my canteen, he fished his pipe from one pocket, and his pouch of tobacco from the other. Soon he was puffing away contentedly while I busied myself around the fire.

I suppose that the good doctor wasn't behaving out of character. He had told me his views and that was that. Upon

225

finding that I had dismissed them, he had contented himself with a laugh and moved on. Not one to hold grudges, you see.

Meanwhile, with his thoughts on one thing, and mine on another, I'm sorry to say that the conversation lagged. Perhaps, given time, that might have become awkward, but fortunately time was never given the chance.

We were interrupted from our own private musings by the drumming beat of approaching horses, followed shortly thereafter by the challenge of our sentry.

"Hello!" cried Simpson. "Something's afoot!"

The doctor's exclamation might have been enough to inspire excitement in others, but apparently not in himself, as he had not bothered to rise. Instead he remained seated, with the stem of his pipe protruding from one corner of his mouth, while the adjacent eyebrow arched inquisitively in the direction from whence came the sound.

It was more *Zinkaffs*, of course – no surprise there. Presently they bustled past, under escort by a squad of Sikhs, looking self-important as all get out (the *Zinkaffs*, not the Sikhs). What did come as a surprise was that they returned in double-quick time, but instead of Eden, I saw the Cheeboo hurrying along with them at a pace that I thought unseemly. Apparently the doctor thought so, too.

"Avast there, Chee!" he bellowed, ignoring the stares this produced from all around. "Where away?"

To his credit, the Cheeboo was able to make the translation without any undue hardship; but then he'd known the doctor longer than I had, so was bound to have become accustomed…if you can imagine such a thing.

He attempted to stop, but he was sandwiched between two of the burlier *Zinkaffs*, and each had a firm grip on his elbow. They never hesitated, but continued to propel him forward without pause.

Denied that simple dignity, the Cheeboo made the best of it.

"Good morning, Dr. Simpson!" he cried over his shoulder. "I have been summoned to the palace of the Penlo! A lovely morning, is it not?"

They would have continued to proceed unmolested, but I was on my feet, and headed them off before they'd gone very much further.

"That will do, corporal," I said to the *naik* commanding. I couldn't be sure that he had the English to understand me, but there might have been something in the tone of my voice to make him hesitate. Probably that was the case, because it worked with the *Zinkaffs*, too. They pulled up short, with their charge still in hand, eyeing me with suspicion.

I had neither pistol nor sabre to hand. In fact, I had nothing but my fists, but it was all too evident that I was prepared to use them.

"Oh no, Mr. Smithers," the Cheeboo murmured softly, so as not to excite his captors. "You must not cause any trouble."

I felt my jaw begin to protrude, the way that it does when I'm feeling especially pugnacious. Unable to think of anything to say in reply, I gave my fists an extra clench, and spat gently from the corner of my mouth. I swear, that if anyone (the doctor for instance) had yelled 'donnybrook!' I would have been amongst them, hip and thigh, and to hell with the consequences, but for a wonder Simpson's sense of mischief seemed to have found its limit.

"Not to worry, Chee," he said affably, clapping my shoulder with a companionable hand (he seemed to be doing that quite a lot lately), "our thick-headed friend's just having a bit of a lark, that's all!" Almost imperceptibly his tone hardened to a cold, warning edge, as his fingers bit like talons into what seemed like every nerve ending at the base of my neck. "Isn't that so, Charlie?"

Well I was damned if it was.

Angrily I demanded, "Are you just going to let these bastards haul him off like he was a mule?"

Softly, with his back to the *Zinkaffs*, the doctor hissed through his teeth, "Easy, you fool! There may well be an international incident before this day is through, but I'll not have it started by the likes of you." Then, turning to the Bhuteau, he was suddenly all smiles, hail and hearty as you could wish for.

"All right, you sods," he beamed, at the same time offering them his hand, "let's get you sorted then, shall we?"

The head *Zinkaff*, a soft, portly, fellow, who looked as if he spent the greater part of his leisure hours sucking on lemons, regarded the doctor's hand as if it had just fallen from the sky.

"Come on, you git!" Simpson murmured encouragingly, "Shakee-shakee, you pig-faced bugger! Can't you see that the good doctor's offering you his hand in eternal friendship?"

The *Zinkaff* continued to regard the proffered extremity with suspicion, but Simpson was so insistent that he was eventually coaxed into offering his own.

Seizing hold before it could shrink away again, Simpson gave it a good hearty pump while grinning from ear to ear, causing the *Zinkaff's* little, close-set eyes to widen considerably with alarm.

"There, that's better!" cried the doctor, nodding as if he and the *Zinkaff* were the very best of mates. "We'll have you strolling through Pall Mall with the best of 'em in no time!" He advanced a step further, flinging his arm around the *Zinkaff's* shoulder, causing quite a bit of murmuring from his fellows, and a squeak of alarm from the man himself.

"There, there, you daft bugger," soothed the doctor, with a companionable squeeze, causing something to pop under the *Zinkaff's* robe, "mustn't get alarmed. It's just that our bone headed friend over there," he nodded vaguely in my direction, "gets upset when he sees his chums mistreated, d'you see?"

It was evident that the *Zinkaff* didn't see at all. He continued to regard Simpson as if he were not altogether of this world, sensible fellow. Undiscouraged, Simpson removed his arm from his shoulder, and with a, "Here, allow me to show you!" seized the astonished Cheeboo from the clutches of his equally astonished minions, inserted his arm through the crook of his own, and, as God is my witness, proceeded to promenade back and forth in front of them!

"There!" he cried gaily, continuing to stomp 'round and 'round in circles, with the Cheeboo hanging on for dear life, "D'you see how easy it is?"

The *Zinkaff* stared from the doctor to myself. Heaven only knows what he saw in my quarter, but he immediately turned to his fellows in some agitation. There ensued much murmuring, and eventually he looked up to beckon the doctor forward. When Simpson (still with our mutual friend in tow) complied, he held out his own hand gesturing to the Cheeboo. Then, locking their arms as the doctor had shown him, he too began to pace around in circles, with an eye on Simpson for approval.

"Now you've got the hang of it!" the doctor cried, as if to a prize pupil. "There's no need to be a sodding bastard, now is there?"

In spite of his dignity, the *Zinkaff* found himself preening under the doctor's praise, and even awarded us with a punctilious little smirk. He then returned our friend to his attendants, presumably with admonishments to escort their charge in the manner in which he had just exhibited. It was all carried out so matter-of-factly that I can't think how we managed to maintain our composure. Certainly more than one of the Sikhs appeared to be on the verge of hysterics.

When all was squared away again, and the assembly ready to proceed, Simpson – to all intents and purposes, seemingly unaware that he was still standing four-square in their way, asked, "So, Chee, perhaps you can tell us what this is all about?"

Still in surprisingly good spirits, the Cheeboo replied, "As I mentioned earlier, Dr. Simpson, I have been summoned to the Penlo's palace where, no doubt, I shall be threatened and treated quite severely."

Still maintaining a pleasant tone, Simpson inquired, "Whatever for?"

To which the Cheeboo cheerfully explained, "Because, as I am the Daiwan of Sikkim, my presence may appear to the Bhuteau, not as a simple interpreter, but as a representative of my country. Therefore they may deduce that we are in league with you British which, of course, is not the case at all. Still," he conceded, "they might well consider this a violation of our treaty, and hold my life forfeit."

"God help them if they do!" I growled. I still maintained my station in their path, and felt no need to stand aside.

229

The Cheeboo offered me his warmest smile. "Your concern is most comforting, Mr. Smithers, but have no fear that it will ever come to that."

"That's exactly what I do fear," I told him, offering the *Zinkaff* a glare, "I don't trust these bastards an inch! How could Eden have allowed this? It surpasses belief!"

"Because he thinks that I have been sent for to discuss the preliminaries of his meeting with the Penlo," he inclined his head slightly, as if considering, "and that is what I shall give him." His smile became almost impish. " I am not the Daiwan for nothing, you know. My few simple skills will suffice, I believe."

Having deemed that he had held his peace long enough, the doctor intervened. "I'm sure you're right, Chee, but just to be safe," he addressed the *naik*, "You and your men will accompany our friend to the palace, do you understand?"

The corporal came to attention and saluted with such precision he might have been with the Guards. "Han, sahib!"

The Cheeboo protested, "I thank you for your concern, but that is not necessary, Dr. Simpson."

"Aye, maybe it is, and maybe it isn't," the doctor inclined his head, "but you'll have them nonetheless," Then he gestured briefly in my direction, and with a hint of humour added, "if for no other reason than to sooth this suspicious fellow's anxiety."

There was nothing that the Cheeboo could say in the face of such logic, so he acknowledged it with good grace. Whereupon the doctor, with one hand on my arm, guiding me aside, bowed and waved the party onward with the other. With dignity restored, the *Zinkaff* proceeded at the head of the procession with his underlings following, rather like gentlemen out for a stroll.

I watched them go, still much concerned, which was not at all alleviated when the doctor, standing at my shoulder, said, "That's all that we can do, Charlie."

I swung on him. "How can you just let him go?"

And was surprised at the good-natured bark I received in reply.

Simpson wagged his great shaggy head, still chuckling to himself. "He's a canny one, our Chee. Save your sympathy for the Penlo, Charlie, I'll warrant he's going to need it!" And with that he sauntered back to our fire, where he began to make a clumsy attempt to fish our now-boiling pot from the ashes.

I allowed myself one last parting glance at the receding procession. Then, with a sigh, I turned and followed the doctor, determined to save at least one of my friends from his own folly.

***

As it turned out, all of my worrying was for nought. The Cheeboo was restored to us unmolested in the early afternoon, and in due course was able to relate how the meeting had transpired: as it turned out, almost exactly as he had anticipated. As well as that, however, he was able to give us an insight into the political arena in Bhutan. By comparison, it was enough to make Westminster seem like a veritable fountain of sound reason and sanity.

"I was received by the Penlo, and his stepfather," the Cheeboo informed us, settling comfortably onto a campstool, "and they immediately set about me as I foretold: shouting, threats, the entire business." He accepted the flask that the doctor offered him and took a refreshing sip. "They are not happy that I have brought you English to Bhutan, you see."

The doctor swore, "Balderdash! We were coming with or without you!"

"Yes, I am aware of that, Doctor Simpson," the Cheeboo gently replied, "but they are not, nor do they care." He shrugged, "It is all one to them: you are here, and I am with you; it is enough."

Grimly I asked, "Were you..."

"Ill-treated?" the Cheeboo smiled. "No, Mr. Smithers, I was not, thanks be to Buddha. There was much shouting and stomping around, but mere voices cannot harm me."

"But still," the doctor prompted, "it must have been an ordeal."

"In the beginning, yes," the Cheeboo allowed, "for I found his ill temper most disagreeable." He picked up a stick and began to prod the logs on the fire, a habit he had whenever he was

231

within reach of anything with a flame. "Before I proceed, there is something you should be aware of. In Paro all is not as it seems. It is the stepfather who holds the reins of power, not the Penlo."

The doctor shot his brows. "What's that? How d'you know? Is this some sort of a plot?"

Smiling, the Cheeboo held up a weary hand to forestall him. "Yes, it is a subterfuge, but it is not one against the Raj, but rather against his real enemy, the Paro of Tongso."

I could feel my own brows knit, but before I could interject, the Cheeboo continued.

"Gentlemen, you must understand the political situation here. The Bhuteau have just fought a civil war."

"Yes," I said, "we know all that."

"Of course, Mr. Smithers, but did you know that the Paro Penlo of the day supported the Deb Rajah who was deposed?"

Simpson barked and demanded, "What of it?"

"It means that he supported the losing side, Doctor."

There was a moment while the Cheeboo studied both of our blank expressions in turn. Then he sighed and continued.

"Knowing that his title and power was almost certainly about to be forfeited to the state, and that he could not retain both, the Penlo chose to abdicate in favour of his stepson."

"Hold on," Simpson interrupted. "How does that help him?"

With infinite patience, the Cheeboo explained, "The birth father of the current Penlo had also held the same office, under which his stepfather, the ex-Penlo, had served as his chief officer."

"So the dead chap's chief functionary married his widow?"

"In a manner of speaking," the Cheeboo admitted, and then enlightened us further: "When the ex-Penlo first assumed his office, part of that succession included the previous Penlo's wife and family – hence his becoming the current Penlo's stepfather."

"Good God!" Simpson cried, looking more interested than ever, "D'you mean to tell me that when the old boy kicked the bucket, his number one inherited his wife…" and as an afterthought, he added, "…and children?"

"Indeed, Dr. Simpson."

"Well I'll be!" cried Simpson, immediately assuming a contemplative look of a speculative nature.

"Exactly so."

"But that still doesn't explain how abdicating in favour of his stepson works in the old boy's favour."

"The deceased Penlo, and therefore the present Penlo as well, was related to the Jungpen of Angdu Forung, who is of a family that is in good standing with the current government in Poonakha."

The doctor mused, "So now the younger Penlo retains all the trappings of office, while the elder retains the power? Deuced odd, wouldn't you say?"

The Cheeboo smiled his tired smile. "You forget, doctor, this is Bhutan."

Chastened, the doctor replied, "Yes, I see."

Which was all one to me. My concern was more for my friend's well-being.

"But you were not ill-used?" It seemed important that I hear his confirmation.

For the second time the Cheeboo assured me, "Oh no, Mr. Smithers! In fact, once the father-in-law arrived, they were both quite courteous, and very willing to listen to my reasoning."

"Which was?"

"That our mission to Bhutan has the potential to be beneficial for all parties concerned, and should be given every chance of success."

I didn't have to ask what he meant, for it was as plain as day. By everything that we'd witnessed so far, Bhutan was a rich country, but by the standards of the Orient, it was not wealthy. Even if we had been the piratical land-grabbers that the rest of the world accused us of being, I should think that we would have deemed the price too high for such a relatively modest prize. No, we would have the *duars* for our own safety, but anything further would be dependent upon what an honest Englishman exceeded at, which was trade. It was the best possible solution that had the potential to benefit both sides. What was required was understanding and trust, and that meant permanent embassies in

233

our capitals. All that stood in the way was the shortsightedness of the xenophobes in power, and that, I thought, was as an immoveable object as ever there was.

I asked him, "Do you really believe that?"

As if reading my thoughts, the Cheeboo sighed – just a little 'puff' that fluffed out his moustache. "Alas, Mr. Smithers, in my heart of hearts, no, I do not. I have had dealings with these people for many years now, and I can tell you without a shadow of a doubt that you will never find anyone so intent on resisting the world outside their borders. They are a primitive people with primitive concepts that have not progressed much beyond your Middle Ages. What they want they take, if they can – whether it be from the lowliest peasant, to ignorant foreigners, like you and myself." He took a breath and continued. "Left to themselves, the people might prosper, but the people that matter do not understand trade and commerce, nor do they wish to. They understand their religion which, although nominally is the same as my own, still believes in demons and wood nymphs. They understand building and architecture, and have managed tolerably well with it. But above all they understand might, and use it everywhere: to govern their people, to levy taxes, to create revenues from the *duars*, and to confiscate everything that they desire, within or without their borders. This they *understand*. This they *know*. To instill in their minds the idea of a modern economy is a task so daunting that it would be foolish not to acknowledge that it might well be out of our reach.

"But in all my years, one thing that I have learned is that there is no such thing as a certainty. If only the *potential* for peace exists, it should be pursued with all of the vigour at our disposal. One day the walls of Bhutan will crumble, as everything must eventually crumble that stands in the path of progress, and with it their archaic thoughts will crumble, also. Who is to say that that day is not before us, and they are finally prepared to listen? Regardless of the outcome, Mr. Smithers, we must at least *try*."

Well, this was a new twist. I had never stopped to consider that the Cheeboo might have his own reasons for coming with us on this madcap adventure. He believed in what we were attempting; but not only that, but this was the closest I'd ever

234

heard him approach a subject with anything even close to resembling passion. One thing this journey had taught me was that when the Cheeboo spoke it was best to listen. Now, listening as he very nearly waxed voluble, I had to admit that, in spite of Eden being little more than a pompous ass, he was right to pursue this conviction. There was more at stake here than the relations between Bhutan and Bengal: other countries stood to profit from our success as well, Sikkim not being the least of them. Less than a year earlier the Jungpen of Dhalimkote had led a raid into the Cheeboo's domain, guided by little more than ignorance and superstition. What better way of dedicating one's life than to strive, not for war, but for mutual understanding? If that gap were ever to be bridged, the benefits would affect millions.

However, be that as it may, when Eden was summoned to the palace later that day, we were soon to discover that such a hope was perilously founded.

As usual the Cheeboo accompanied him in his role as interpreter, and when they returned a few hours later, he stopped by for the second time that day to impart the proceedings.

The long and the short of it was that we were forbidden to proceed to Poonakha, pending an overture from the Deb Rajah, the arrival of which was expected within four days. In the meantime we were to make ourselves at home in Paro.

Simpson barked, "What did I tell you? Four days might turn into four weeks before we leave!"

"What's wrong?" I asked the Cheeboo. For even though it had already been a trying day for him, he was more taciturn than what I would have expected.

The Cheeboo sighed as if he had just buried his mother. "It is nothing, Mr. Smithers." Then he appeared to reconsider, "Only that while in attendance Mr. Eden was also told that nothing of use could be accomplished in Poonakha, but that if we seriously desired to enter into discussions about the Bengal *duars* we should speak with the Penlo, and the Penlo's stepfather. Mr. Eden declined, stating that he must speak to the head of their government, or to no one."

"But that's the normal way to proceed, surely?" I asked.

The Cheeboo regarded me with a pitying expression, much as he had the doctor earlier in the day, and gave the same reply: "This is Bhutan, Mr. Smithers. Here your idea of what is normal does not necessarily apply." He continued, "England has a strong central government; it is now unthinkable that your barons should rise against the Crown, but it was not always so. Here it is now as it was in England during the Middle Ages: the government governs in name only. They may issue decrees, but they are decrees formulated by those behind the throne, and are obeyed, or ignored, at a Penlo's discretion, because the Penlos are the power behind the throne. The Penlo of Paro is in a constant struggle with his arch nemesis, the Tongso Penlo, who, given that he has lost the Assam *Duars*, is no friend of the British. As the saying goes: 'the enemy of my enemy is my friend.' The Paro Penlo – the *real* Paro Penlo – who does not recognize the current Deb Rajah, would make a very useful ally to Calcutta, but I fear that Mr. Eden has lost that opportunity."

"So, what you're saying is, that in order to have discussions with the Deb Rajah – which you say will most likely be pointless – Eden has refused to have talks with the one person who holds sovereignty over the *duars* bordering on Bengal?"

The Cheeboo considered. Then he tilted his head to one side and considered some more. He opened his mouth as if to speak, then closed it again. Finally he spread his hands with both palms facing upward, and said, "Yes."

This was followed by a savage bark from another quarter, and around his pipe stem, Simpson made the caustic observation, "Bloody typical!"

***

Charula Khaur was in my tent again when I entered, reclining upon my pallet, her skin a deep bronze in the low flame of a spirit lamp. How she got there was a mystery, for I had not noticed her approach before retiring, even though our fire was but a few yards away.

"How did you get here?" I asked.

She shrugged her naked shoulders, her long black hair cascading over them, past her breasts, all the way down to the slender bole of her waist. With such a simple gesture, I suddenly realized that I didn't care what the answer was. She was here, that was enough.

In any case she merely dimpled a smile and, gently chiding, said, "It is not right for you to ask, *Bahadur*. A woman must have her secrets." Then she lay a hand, palm down, on the blanket beside her. "Come," she said.

I did as I was bidden, pulling off my shirt along the way. A smile played across my own lips when I said, "I was expecting you." It was the truth. I was.

"Then I am happy that I did not disappoint you. Come lie down. I have prepared a gift."

I lay on my stomach as she directed, and only then noticed a small bowl warming on the brazier. To this she addressed herself, dipping in her hand. It glowed from the oil when she withdrew it. It felt warm on my back, her fingers gently kneading.

I murmured into my shoulder, "You shouldn't have gone to so much trouble."

She simply repeated, "It is a gift." Then coyly she added, "Would you refuse it?"

"God, no!"

It was heaven.

I felt the glow spreading over my skin, penetrating into my body, creating a sensation of peace and well-being. All the while her skillful hands soothed me even more. I couldn't restrain a small gasp of pleasure.

She laughed softly, "You approve?"

"Mmmm," was all that I felt capable of replying.

Time passed without any words. It had been a long while since I had felt so cared for – such a long, long while.

I was closer to sleep than awake when I felt her stop at last, yet all too soon. "That was bloody marvelous," I told her, rolling over on my back, but she was already busily employed with my boots and didn't answer. A gentle tug, and then another, and then those long, skillful fingers were working their way up my legs to my thighs.

I think she was teasing, but I couldn't be sure when she said, "I have been dreaming of this throughout the day."

I thought I was being witty when I replied, "I'll have to have a word with the commissariat sergeant about that. He's obviously not been keeping you busy enough."

She continued to massage my thighs, and laughed, a deep throaty chuckle, "But the commissariat sergeant was left behind in Sipchoo."

"That's right, I'd forgotten." In truth my thoughts were in turmoil. Her ministrations were working, you see.

I felt a tug at my buttons and then my trousers were gone as well. I felt her hand engulf me. It was warm, still lubricated with oil. Then I felt the softer warmth of her mouth, and once more the conversation lagged.

Before very long I was delirious with passion, twining my fist into her hair, dragging her face up to my mouth. Her kiss was as wanton, her tongue cleverly teasing, and I marveled that this was real. Impatient beyond all bearing, I meant to spin her over on her back, but she forestalled me with her palm on my chest, and said, "No."

I daresay I was panting like the town bull, but tried to keep the indignation from my voice when I cried, "For Christ's sake, why not?"

The low chuckle again. "Patience, *Bahadur*! Have I not already mentioned a gift?"

"What's that? D'you mean to tell me there's *more*?"

To which she laughed outright, and said, "I shall let you be the judge."

I closed my eyes, wondering how events would play out. Presently there was the sensation of one silken thigh on either of my hips as she climbed aboard, if you will. I grasped her waist with both hands, but she gently extricated herself, and tucked them behind my head, admonishing me to lie still. I told her that I would, but was by no means certain that it was a promise that I could keep. For a moment I felt her tongue play over the corners of my mouth, and the firmness of her breasts on my chest before she pulled away. My eyes flew open, for I had not wanted the kiss to end so soon, or at all, but forgot about it in the next instant.

She was astride, bolt upright in the saddle, her arms reaching high over her head, with her hands clasped together as if in prayer. She was beautiful! Magnificent! My mouth opened, I believe with the intention of telling her as much, but before the words could form in my mind, she began to dance.

I don't know how else to explain it. There she was, poised like a statue, as if exhibiting herself for my pleasure, and then slowly, almost imperceptibly, her body began to move. Her head and arms remained as they were – so too from her knees on down – but everything else in between began to writhe and gyrate in as lurid an exhibition as I'd ever seen, as if to music that only she could hear, gradually lowering herself, inch by inch, upon my straining self until impaled. At which point the music's tempo slowly began to increase.

I could hear it now, primitive tom-toms playing through my mind while she undulated above me, pulling me in ever deeper. Her belly rippled in and out like a long, continuous wave, grinding her hips around in circles and, being an old cavalry hand, before long I felt the squadron forming into line.

We began slowly, building momentum – Walk! March! Trot! – until finally we broke into the charge, like two thoroughbreds racing madly over the fields. On and on we went, with the thunder of pounding hooves filling our ears, conscious of nothing save our desire to continue ever further. And then, having risen to a delicious state of delirium, we were heading, pell mell, toward a hedge, and it was up and over, without any thought for what lay on the other side. I was dimly aware that someone was babbling aloud: cursing violently, and pleading in soft whimpers, all at the same time. Then we were down on the other side with a jolt so jarring that it brought stars to my eyes, and still we galloped on, and on, and on.

At length, exhausted, we eased to a halt, and she was collapsing upon my chest, gasping for air and murmuring endearments into my ear.

"I had no idea!" she whispered, in a voice that seemed verging on tears. "Truly, I did not! No idea at all!"

Nor did I, but at the moment I was too winded to tell her.

"The other times were for simple pleasure, but this...*this*..." she rolled over to my side, arms still extended, "Ah! Magnificent!"

We lay so for the longest of times, I gratified by her praise but unable to respond. Finally, when I could convince myself that I hadn't been sent for, I thought to say something in kind, but before I could speak she began to laugh.

"What?" I asked.

"Oh *Bahadur*!" she snorted through her nose, making her laugh all the harder, "What does it mean when you English say, 'Yoiks! Tally ho!'"

Chapter Fifteen

It turned out that Simpson's prediction proved correct after all: our stay in Paro lasted nearly a fortnight. I thought that he might crow over his triumph, if 'triumph' be the proper word, but to my surprise, he became as taciturn as everyone else.

It did not begin well, and I must confess that it wasn't *purely* because of the haughtiness of our hosts. The Penlo had told us that we would be treated with every consideration, and then promptly forbade us to move outside our encampment. Eden wouldn't have it. Instead he chose to play the part of the high-handed Englishman, which has done so much damage to our image throughout the world. The Bhuteau were no different, and responded predictably.

The Penlo had ordered a ring of sentries 'round the camp, ostensibly for our own protection, but the façade didn't last for long. When the order from the palace was ignored, and our people began to make excursions to nearby villages in search of provisions, the Bhuteau soldiery retaliated.

They were the most rag tag bunch of ruffians you ever saw: armed any old how, with anything from bows and arrows to *jingals*. Some were accoutred in back and breast plates, others in chain mail, and still others with nothing at all, although most wore a cup-shaped helmet of steel. To a man they were all in fine physique, though: tall, well-built chaps that didn't look like they should be taken lightly, and they weren't slow to prove it, neither.

More than one of our people was accosted outside our encampment, and true to form, instead of being placed under arrest as you might expect in a civilized country, he would find himself threatened, jeered at, or otherwise insulted. If any attempt was made to respond, there would quickly come the rasp of steel, then that unlucky person would find himself looking at the sharp end of a knife; and, of course, to add insult to injury, all the while they would be robbing him blind. That's the way we saw it, at least. To them it was probably all in a day's work. Without benefit of a wage, Bhuteau soldiers seldom hesitated to augment their income by preying on the weak, as per the custom of the land. The harassment was not reserved for just the British subjects, either. Any Bhuteau they caught dealing with us received their fair share as well.

Captain Lance and his Sikhs did their best to maintain order, but their numbers were few, and most were required to guard the baggage. Therefore I had to chip in as much as possible, usually making certain that the villains kept their distance with a scowl or two, and one hand on the Tranter, although that didn't always work.

At one point I found myself racing to the assistance of one of our coolies, in the middle of a jostling circle of a half a dozen Bhuteau guardsmen. I had just succeeded in shoving my way into the centre when there came the sound of rending cloth, and a great cry of surprise, mingled with savage delight. As I elbowed past the last of the rogues, the meaning of the uproar became immediately clear: there, dressed in her coolie garb, was Charula Khaur, pale as a ghost, with her shirt torn open to the waist, and struggling in the grasp of a great ugly brute in a spiked helmet, whose intentions were all too clear. I lost no time in putting my fist in his face, along with one or two others who offered any fight. One attempted to draw his knife, but a boot to his groin soon put paid to that ambition, and the rest backed off, scowling with menace.

I drew the Tranter to even the odds, and at the same time angrily ordered Charula back to camp. Still trembling, she paused only long enough to rearrange her blouse to some form of decency, and obeyed, without either a word or a glance in my direction.

Seeing their sought-after prize take wing, the standing members of the Paro Welcoming Committee decided to call it a day, exiting the scene by a different route, with a rude gesture or two along the way.

I returned to camp at once, feeling nauseous at the thought of how close Charula had come to being assaulted. I found her in my tent, standing rigid in the corner with her back to me, and her arms folded across her breasts.

"What in the blazes do you think you were playing at?" I raged, "Why, you little baggage, you could've been killed! As

God's my witness, I've a good mind to take you over my knee and…!"

There was a '*zeep*' of steel and she spun to face me, her eyes wild with rage. The pale light filtering through the walls of the tent glimmered on the dagger's blade.

"No one shall touch me! No one!"

Well that took me aback, as you might imagine. Her expression was so fierce that I thought that the episode had driven her barmy, and I'm not saying that I was altogether wrong, neither. At that instant, she was more a creature of the wild than the soft pliant woman of the night before, and I swear that in that brief span she no longer recognized me, but saw only a potential threat.

Then the moment passed. The knife wavered, but her expression remained cold and defiant. "Let them try to take what only *I* choose to give!" she spat angrily. "Let them try, and I will feed them their manhood, one morsel at a time!"

A chill ran up my spine. In a flash of memory, I saw not her, but Loiyan kneeling by the remains of a fire, her knife buried in the ashes from where it had fallen from her listless hand. A few yards away, the bodies of Tepilit and Sakuda, the two brothers she had murdered, lay unattended in the morning sun…

Then I was once more back in the present, and it was Charula staring across at me, as if the merest of nudges could send her completely over the edge of sanity. To cover my confusion I cleared my throat and, with a gesture at the tatters of her shirt, quietly suggested, "Perhaps we should mend that."

For a moment her expression didn't change, although her eyes may have flickered with surprise – the only indication that she had heard me. Eventually the corners of her mouth gave a brief upward twitch, engaging the merest of dimples, before, in a tone much more gentle, she agreed, "Yes, perhaps we should."

I retrieved my sewing kit from my pack, held out my hand, and said, "Here, give it to me."

She hesitated. "No, I can do it."

"Perhaps you can," I agreed, "but not as well as I." Still she hesitated, so I reassured her, "I've been stitching up milord's togs ever since I can remember. This will be a piece of cake." Her smile became less tremulous, but the uncertainty remained. Sensing the problem, I took the blanket from my pallet and handed it to her. "In the meantime you can use this to cover yourself."

You might not credit her reticence with the *houri* I'd coupled with the night before, but much had happened in those few hours inbetween. In the fragility of her present state, Charula Khaur was less a woman than she was a child. A lifetime of service had taught me to tell the difference.

A moment passed then, eventually, her hesitation ended. She accepted the blanket, and the return of her reason drew nearer, but not so near that she didn't turn her back to me while removing her shirt, even though while turning, she accompanied the gesture with a shy, apologetic smile. At length she reached behind her, handing me the garment. I gave it a brief study.

"It's not so bad," I told her, "the material's still whole. It's just that the stitching gave way at the seam. We'll have you shipshape in no time at all." And with that, I sat down on the pallet, threaded my needle, and began the business of sewing it back together.

I could sense her unease dissipating, but there was still tension in the air, and I can't say that it was only coming from her. Then Fortune chose to intervene just when the silence threatened to become overwhelming. Without warning, the tent flap suddenly flew back and Fortune, in the guise of Simpson, thrust his grizzled head inside, with all usual disregard for the formalities.

Bark! "Sun's officially over the yardarm, Smithers old bean! Got your port handy, have y...?" He stopped and took the situation in at a belated glance – didn't bat an eye, then ever so brightly said, "Right then, I'll be off!" and disappeared as suddenly as he'd arrived...but for a stifled chortle fading into the general hubub of the camp.

Charula stared at where he had vanished, and then to me, her eyes wide with surprise.

I bent back to my task. "It's all right," I told her, "you never really get used to him."

And just like that the danger was past.

Maybe it was because of the tension suddenly breaking, or maybe it was the domesticity of the scene (something as simple as sewing can do that), I don't know, but Charula burst into laughter.

"You have extraordinary friends, *Bahadur!*"

I looked up for a brief instant, just long enough to give her a meaningful glance. "Yes," I said, "I do," and offered her a wink before concentrating once more on her blouse.

I can tell you that it is possible to hear someone blush. I fancy that it was with pleasure.

The blanket made a swishing sound as she drew near, and took a seat on the camp stool by the pallet.

"A man sewing," she mused, " and for a woman, too."

"What?" I asked. "Find that a bit strange do you?"

"Indeed," she allowed, although it didn't sound as if she found it repulsive.

"Ne'er mind," I said, intending nothing more than a bit of facetious amusement, "there's plenty about me you don't know." but she took it at face value.

"You speak true, *Bahadur.* I only know what I have known since the day you saved me. I would hear you speak of yourself."

And believe it or not, it was only then that it occurred to me that, as little as she knew about me, I knew even less about her.

"Nothing much to tell." I said, "I'm my Lord Brampton's man."

But of course, that only served to egg her on.

"I have heard mention of this Lord Brampton (she pronounced it 'Brumpton':) Let us begin there."

At first I was reluctant, but she was so persistent that soon I was telling her about what it was like during those carefree years, growing up in Yorkshire. I told her about Brampton Manor and its majestic grounds, and about Lady Brampton's prize geraniums that took the brunt of milord's and my own swashbuckling derring-do. I told her about the people there: about Maggie the chambermaid, and Mrs. Kilns, the housekeeper, and toothless old Mrs. Dyck, the cook, and the immaculate figure of Davis, the footman. I told her about all of

245

them: about old Tomkins and how he'd lost an arm at Waterloo, and even about that idiot ostler lad, whose name always seems to escape me. I told her about my guv'nor and my dear old Hebridean mother, from whom I had inherited the nebulous gift of the 'sight' (although I kept that part to myself). Then I switched from the people to the country: the green pastoral fields and gently rolling hills, the majesty of the fells, and how beautiful it all was in the setting sun. It was around here that I began to feel the bittersweet pang for the old place. Out here, in the back-of-beyond, it seemed so improbable that it could exist other than as a figment of my mind. If you've ever travelled to a land that has a completely different culture, you'll know what I mean. Nothing seemed real other than what was before my eyes; home might have been nothing more than a sweet and cherished dream, the kind that caused your heart to ache so with longing in those first moments upon waking.

At length my tale was done, and I was somewhat surprised to note that I had finished mending her shirt at very nearly the same time. I held it out for her to take. She accepted it with a word of thanks, but her eyes were studying me the way all women study men when there's something on their mind.

At length she said, "I am indebted to you for telling me this, *Bahadur*, but there is one thing that you neglected to mention."

I busied myself with stowing away my needle and thread. "Oh? And what might that be?"

"The woman," she said, "the one I remind you of," fortunately, my face was turned away from her, "the one true love of your life."

The silence stretched as I fought to maintain my composure, then, "No," I agreed, closing the lid on my sewing kit, and somehow found the courage to face her, "I didn't."

I couldn't tell you how long we remained that way: standing, facing one another in silence, but it felt like an eternity. All things being equal, it was almost merciful when, finally, she spoke. "It is said that time heals all wounds."

My reply was neutral. "So I've heard."

Her eyes darted back and forth, searching. "Perhaps I can assist time."

Sitting here now, at my writing desk, over thirty years later, I suppose there were a myriad of responses with which I could have replied (denial, anger, and so forth), but by then there were no more words left in me. I won't deny that revealing myself to her had been a pleasure, but it had also carried a generous ration of pain. I couldn't bring myself to risk the consequences of sharing what was buried so deep inside. I had experienced that pain once, and had no wish to do so again. There was a reason why it was buried; let it remain so.

She left shortly thereafter, with that same apologetic smile creasing her lips, and a puzzled frown wrinkling her forehead, but she returned later in the evening, and I must admit that I was happy that she did. Nothing was said about what had transpired earlier. Instead, I was reminded of what I had realized hours before, that I knew next to nothing about her. Therefore later, as we lay on the pallet, letting the cool night air dry the perspiration from our bodies, I took the opportunity to steer the conversation in that direction. She replied without any reticence whatsoever.

"I come from a village on the plains called Nal Hattie, equally distant from Calcutta and where your railroad meets the Gunga Pershad, what you English call the Ganges River."

"At Sahibgange," I said. "Yes, I've been through Nal Hattie."

Her interest was piqued, although guarded for reasons I didn't pursue. "Truly?" she asked. "And how did you find it?"

Although my experience of the place had been restricted to taking breakfast at a small establishment near the rail station, I told her that I thought that it was quite pretty. It seemed the polite thing to say.

She sighed, not exactly sad, but winsome. "I was happy there once."

I can recognize an invitation as well as the next person, so I asked, "What happened?"

She gave a bitter little laugh, "Life, *Bahadur!* Life is what happened!"

247

I waited, knowing that she wasn't finished, but rather pausing to formulate the words.

"By the standards of that village my family was wealthy. My father was a silversmith, as was his father before him. He was a very skilled; rich people came great distances to buy his wares, even from as far away as Calcutta."

I asked, "If he was that good, why didn't he settle there, surrounded by wealth?"

Her tone changed subtly, darker. "Truly, my mother wanted to. She was very ambitious, and often complained that the real wealth would be found in the city, not in 'this stinking village', as she called it." Without looking at me she asked, "Can you imagine, *Bahadur*, your own mother referring to your home in such a way?"

I thought of my wizened old mum, all five God-fearing feet of her, with her thin-lipped mouth pressed primly shut as she poked into the pot of porridge over the fire with a wooden spoon. She often confided that, compared to those northern islands where she had come from, our little cottage close by Brampton Manor was like living in a palace. Although, to be sure, that happiness seldom reflected on her demeanour.

"No," I told her, but she seemed lost in her thoughts.

"My father was a simple man and would not hear of our leaving the village where his family had lived for generations. He could never understand what wealth, *real* wealth, meant to my mother, who was born into a Brahmin family, but which was also destitute." She laughed the same bitter laugh, "My mother and father were complete opposites. My father was a simple and unassuming man, my mother was ambitious and despised my father because he was only a lowly *Vaisya*, and not a Brahmin. She was constantly scheming and plotting to regain the stature she felt she had lost when her parents forced her to marry."

"It must've made life very difficult," I said.

"For me? No," she shook her head, a half-smile forming on her lips. "When my mother tried to make me stay inside and learn the ways a proper Brahmin woman should behave, my father would gainsay her, and allow me to go out and play with my friends." Again she laughed, but this time without bitterness.

248

"He was always thus, telling my mother that I must first taste my life in order to live it."

I could not reply, for the very air had suddenly been stolen from my lungs.

She took no notice of how distracted I'd become, but continued, lost in her story. "He would always say as much to me. He would sit me on his knee and say, 'My child, you were placed on this earth to live. Let none interfere with what God has seen fit to bestow.'"

"And he loved you as you were his only child, and allowed you to choose between becoming the woman of your mother's expectations, or the one of your own making?" But it wasn't a question, not really. The 'sight' came to me so seldom; although I was listening carefully, it was difficult to be sure.

"Pardon?" she asked.

"Nothing," I replied, but my voice sounded distant.

She didn't press me; this was her story, after all. So after pausing to give me a puzzled look, she gave a small, inward shrug, and continued.

"I was happy then. Oh, my mother and my father often argued, sometimes bitterly, but I was always free to escape into the village with my friends, always confident that my father would remain steadfast."

It seemed unnecessary to point it out, but I did anyway, phrasing it as a question, "But he didn't?"

The silence lingered for a very long moment. I thought that she had said all that she was going to tell, but eventually there came a heavy sigh, and quietly she murmured, "No."

"Why not?"

The sigh was repeated, long and unspeakably sad.

"One day, when I was still a child, I was out playing with my friends when I saw a man ride into our village, with a full score of his followers riding behind. From the east he came, clad in mail, with a great war bow slung over one shoulder, and a quiver of fearsome arrows fastened to the saddle at his knee. Beneath his helm I could see a long, forked beard, and eyes....Oh Bahadur, I had never seen such eyes before. They were merciless as stone." Then she looked at me, her own eyes

249

filled with meaning. "Over his armour he wore a crimson robe of silk."

Suddenly I was jolted back to the present. Noting my reaction, she nodded and said, "Yes, *Bahadur*, it was the same man you fought the day you saved my life."

My own voice grew suddenly hard, and not in the least distant. "Who is he?" I demanded. She didn't answer immediately, but carried on.

"We chattered amongst ourselves, my friends and I. We were excited, as you can well imagine. Strangers often came to our village, but not so many with the flat features of the Bhuteau, and none armed so fearfully, or dressed so fine."

I asked a second time in that same hard voice, "Charula, who is he?"

The bitter laugh returned. "We were asking the very same question amongst ourselves, when my *ayah* came rushing out to summon me home. Bewildered, I did as I was bidden.

"I found my mother in the small courtyard in the back of our house. We always used to laugh and say that this was the private domain of Chinchin, our pet peacock. He would often come up to us, hoping for some tasty morsel, or to fan his tail, but that day I noticed that he was careful to keep to the far side of the yard, beneath the banyan tree, and would not come any closer. That was when I walked past the arbour and noticed the stranger sitting on a bench next to my mother.

"She beckoned and said, '*Come here, child.*'

"The stranger turned at her summons, and I saw that he had removed his helmet. His skull was shaven, and I noticed an old scar running down the side of his face. I could *feel* his stare, and realized that his eyes were even colder than I remembered – so much so that I could not move.

"More impatiently this time, my mother commanded me, '*Come, Charula!*'

"I felt my legs move, even though they seemed of wood, and, too, I felt myself appraised. I stood before them, feeling the most awkward I ever had in my young life, and for some reason I could not fathom, ashamed. '*Stand up straight!*' my mother told me, '*You were not raised to slouch like a common sweeper's child! Now*

250

turn!' Mystified, I obeyed. *'Now to the left! Yes, like that! Now turn around completely! Slowly, girl. This is not a race!'* and all the while I felt the cold eyes of the stranger upon me, and I thought that I would die from shame.

"Finally my mother seemed satisfied, and gestured to the stranger with a triumphant gleam in her eye. *'Did I not tell you?'* she asked. *"A rare beauty!'*

"But the stranger merely grunted and beckoned to me. I hesitated, glancing at my mother, but she seemed to be waiting just as expectantly, so I approached until I was only inches away. Brusquely, he reached out and spread my lips with his thumb, peering closely at my teeth. Then he fondled my arms, pinching them – not roughly, no, but neither was he gentle. He studied the tone of my skin, the muscle beneath, and many other things besides. He told me to walk, so I walked. He told me to turn around and return to him. I did that also. He demanded to know my name and I told him, but could not keep the tremor from my voice. He asked me my age, and respectfully I said, *'I have thirteen years, sir.'* He pondered briefly, then shrugged as if it were of little consequence. Finally, without taking his eyes off of me, he said to my mother, *"It is agreed."* His very voice was cold, as if he were bargaining for a horse. So saying, he took a leather purse from his belt and handed it to her, but all the while continuing to look at me.

"I was visibly trembling now, and beseeched her, *'Mother?'* but she was weighing the bag of gold in her hand, and would not look at me. Then, unable to resist the temptation, she emptied its contents into her palm, counting the rupees with avarice-filled eyes. At length, with her own voice trembling, to the stranger she replied, *'It is agreed!'*

"Again I tried, *"Mother?"* She looked at me with an expression I could not read. Then she said, *'This gentleman is called Sangay; he is a lord, the Nieboo of Sipchoo.'* Then with little tenderness she informed me, *'He is to be your husband.'*

"Hold on," I said, "I've seen the Nieboo of Sipchoo. You don't mean that old man, surely?"

"No, *Bahadur*. At the time Lord Sangay was merely a Nieboo," she told me, "but he has risen high since then. Now he is better known as the Jungpen of Poonakha."

I stopped to consider. Ordinarily a jungpen was no great shakes in Bhuteau hierarchy, but from what I could remember from what the Cheeboo had told me, the Jungpen of Poonakha was another kettle of fish altogether. Next to the two Penlos in Paro and Tongso it was the most powerful seat in the country. A sobering piece of information that was. Then having absorbed it, my mind was capable of making the next leap.

"Your *husband?*"

I must admit that I wasn't as shocked as I might have been, however. I wasn't yet an old hand in India, but much of Amrita Pirāli's tale rang true in this case, as well.

"Yes, *Bahadur*," she said, her eyes glistening in the glow of the spirit lamp, "that was their intention."

"But it didn't happen, obviously. How did you…?"

"Please, allow me to finish."

So I held my peace, forcing myself to be patient. Eventually, having composed herself, she continued.

"I remember staring at my mother, unable to comprehend her meaning. Perhaps she mistook my incomprehension for defiance, for she began to grow angry. '*Your father is a fool,*' she said, '*and does not understand the meaning of power! Ungrateful girl! You will be wed to a nobleman, is that not enough?*' She would have said more, but at that instant there came a great commotion from inside the house, and presently my father burst through the door, followed by two of Lord Sangay's men, who had taken station out on the street. One of them said, '*Forgive me, Lord! This man could not be stopped.*' Sangay waved him away with an idle hand, as if it was of no account.

"I had never seen my father so. His turban had come adrift, spilling his hair onto his shoulders, and his eyes were like those of a wild creature. In a voice shaking with passion, he demanded of my mother, '*Woman of shame! Is it true?*' but before she could answer, he remembered himself, and turning to me, said, '*Charula, my daughter, go inside!*' I hurried to obey, but once inside the house, I hastened to the back room nearest to them in

252

a matter of seconds. From there I watched and listened through the window screen.

"My mother and father were glaring at one another in a way I had never seen before. I could sense the energy growing between them as if it were a preamble to a storm. The Nieboo, Sangay, as if regarding my father's presence as insignificant, had not moved. Quietly, he turned to my mother and, indicating my father with a dismissive tilt to his head, asked, '*Who is this?*' To give him his due, my father ignored the Nieboo, and instead asked of my mother, '*Vile creature! How could you? She is our daughter!*'

"But my mother would not be cowed. '*Husband, you have spoiled her, and as usual have left it to me to set things right! How could I do else but what I have done? The Nieboo is a nobleman, and will bring benefit to our family. The match is a good one!*'

"My father spat angrily. '*A good match, you say! Foolish woman! I forbid these proceedings to go any further!*'

"Sangay turned to my father, making no effort to disguise his contempt, and in a quiet voice that resonated of danger, simply said, '*Fellow, the bargain has already been completed.*'

"I could tell that those menacing words had stung my father, but still he insisted upon addressing his wife as if Lord Sangay were not in attendance. '*You cannot want this! He is not even of our faith! There is no possibility of our ever attaining the status that you have so obviously coveted all these years!*' To which my mother sneered, '*No, we will never be Brahmin, you have already seen to that, but at least we will have attained nobility!*' My father staggered back as if he had been struck, holding his hand in front of his face as if warding off a blow. '*Daughter of sin!*' he cried, '*What is so noble about today's deed?*' Then came my mother's angry retort, '*This is what you have driven me to!*' It was at this point that Sangay gave a vexed sigh and rose to his feet, fingering the hilt of his sword. To my father he said, '*I have told you once that the bargain has been sealed. I will not tell you again.*'" Trembling with fury or fear, I know not which, my father replied, '*Vile creature! Be gone from this house!*'"

I saw a single tear meander down Charula's cheek. "It happened so quickly that I can scarcely remember, but there was the flash of sunlight on steel as the Nieboo drew his blade, and then suddenly the point was protruding from my father's back. Horrified, I clapped a hand over my mouth to stifle a scream, for this could not be happening; and yet it was. My father and Sangay stood face to face, my father wide-eyed with surprise, Sangay without any emotion at all. Then my father slowly bowed his head like a token of surrender, and sank soundlessly to the ground."

I lay there, listening to the coldness of her voice. The deeds she spoke of were all in the past, yet I could tell by her expression that she relived them every day. I wondered if they had ever left her in peace.

"I could not speak," she said tonelessly. "In that instant, having just witnessed the murder of my father, all my life had suddenly changed. All the promise, all the security...all the happiness and love was gone in a flash of steel. I realized that my mother had become a stranger to me, a traitor to my life in order that her vile ambition might be fulfilled. Even as I stared I could hear the triumph in her laughter!"

Quietly I asked, "What did you do?"

"I acted without thinking. I stole from the house of my birth and I ran. I have not been back since."

"Where did you go?"

Again the bitter laugh. "How do I know! I ran, *Bahadur*! I ran from the horror of what I had just witnessed, and from the life that awaited me. I ran *away*, without giving any thought of what I was running *to*! I was alone in the world, with no one to befriend me."

I was moved to add, "And a mere child of thirteen, too!"

Child orphans were not uncommon in Britain, nor was it uncommon to see them at large, begging in the streets of our cities, but it was a sight that I could never reconcile with my conscience.

I thought that she acknowledged my comment in a curious way. A bitter half-smile played across her lips, as she gently scoffed, "You English!"

True, my western sensibilities had been stung. I doubted that I could ever remain in the orient long enough to become accustomed to their habits. So as much as a way of avoiding the subject as anything, I asked, "Then what happened?"

"When I had finally begun to tire, I saw that I was standing in front of the house of one of my friends, so I went over to the door, shouting to gain entrance. Kamina's father answered; I told him what had happened, and pleaded to be allowed to stay with them. It was then that I truly understood how alone I was. This man, whom I had ever known for his kindness, looked up and down the street, fear written on every feature, and said that I must leave. '*Child,*' he told me, '*Lord Sangay's name is well known, and a more evil man you will never meet! If he finds that I have been hiding you, he will seek his revenge on me and mine. I dare not risk it!*' Then, after some hesitation, he seemed to reach a decision. Biding me to wait, he left, returning later with a parcel wrapped in muslin. '*It is food,*' he said, '*Now go, and may God be with you!*' and with one final, fear-filled look up and down the street, he slammed the door shut on my face.

"I spent that night huddled in an outbuilding along with some goats to keep me warm. Early the next morning I left an hour before sunrise, taking the road out of Nal Hattie, and I have been on it ever since." Before I could ask her meaning, she explained, "After a day or two, when all my food was gone, I met a travelling troupe of dancers and they took me in." Her smile became less bitter. "At first I worked as a menial, serving food and fetching water, and anything else that I was apable to serve. All the while, when time allowed, I would watch them dance, and practiced on my own.

"One day the lead dancer, Anandi, told me that I showed promise, and took me under her wing. I studied very hard under her tutelage, and improved, until I was accepted as one of them. For the past six years I have been travelling from village to village, dancing for the pleasure of others. In that time I continued to improve until I vied with Anandi herself. That is when I experienced the treachery of someone I loved for the second time in my life."

Charula paused, arranging her thoughts, but the bitterness had returned.

"Anandi was tall and beautiful, with hair down to her waist, and the lithesome form that I soon learned drove men from their sanity, but she was nearing her thirtieth year, and her charms were beginning to fade. Whereas once she saw me as a child, she began to see me as a rival. At first it was little things, a flash of temper, nothing more, but eventually it grew and grew, until the kind lady who had befriended me became as someone possessed.

"One night after a performance, I saw her talking to a man who had the features and garb of the Bhuteau. I remember that he was an evil-looking man with pocked skin and close-set eyes. Anandi noticed me watching and turned aside with him into an alley. I thought nothing of it, and continued on, only to realize much later that this must have been Sangay's man, and now that he had risen high in Poonakha, the new Jungpen still harboured thoughts of revenge on the girl who had run away from him all those years ago."

I asked, "So when I came upon you and your friends under attack by those fellows, it was no ordinary robbery...?"

"No, *Bahadur*," she said, "Lord Sangay's presence there could not have been a coincidence." She regarded me with a look so sober that I could not mistake it for anything other than the truth.

"It was an attempt to abduct me."

Chapter Sixteen

Our stay in Paro became more bearable after Eden complained to the Penlo. His talks were with the *official* Penlo, you understand, but you may be sure that word got out to his stepfather, too, and in double-quick time at that.

It was the usual ploy: stop the harassment, or be prepared to deal with the consequences of either our pushing on to Poonakha, without an official invitation, or our abandoning the mission altogether, and returning to Darjeeling. In the first case they would be risking the wrath of their own government or, more to the point, with their eastern counterpart, the Tongso Penlo, who, after the success of the revolution, was the ultimate power in the land. In the event of the second case, our own government in Calcutta would view the failure with a rather jaundiced eye. All sorts of inconvenient questions would be asked, and all sorts of accusing fingers pointed in their direction. Not an enviable position by any measure.

However, make no mistake, it *was* a ploy; Eden would have crawled to Poonakha on his hands and knees if he had to, just to get the chance to mesmerize the locals with his diplomatic genius, the fool; but the Penlos in Paro didn't know that, thank heaven.

In his role as aide, Austen was included in the party involved with the discussions, and against what he chose to call his 'better judgement', gave in to Simpson's constant pestering, and allowed him to join in, on the caveat that he kept his mouth firmly shut. True to form, the doctor ignored the warning, and immediately pressed his advantage, demanding that he be allowed to bring along his cherished camera as well. The science of photography still being relatively new and exciting, this 'request' was sent up through channels to the Bhuteau and, much to my surprise, was not dismissed out of hand – perhaps as good an indicator as any that at least one of the Paros was possessed of a healthy curiosity for the world outside their borders, and was not completely bound by superstition.

Typical of the man, I suppose, once he had received permission, Simpson lost no time inviting me along, under the guise of being his assistant. As he put it, "Chances are excellent that it will be the greatest bore, Charlie, but you never know. Besides, it'll give you the chance to see a proper Bhuteau city, so why not come along?"

More than anything else, it was the latter part of his reasoning that moved me to accept. Austen shook his head at the folly of it all, but raised no objection, and as I maintained a discrete distance, neither did Eden, being preoccupied, as he undoubtedly was, with matters of state and his own vaunted importance.

So it was that we set out one morning in early March, with Maggie and the doctor's gelding loaded down with camera, tripod, lenses, crates of image plates, flasks of flashpowder, and box after box, each containing bottles of evil-sounding alchemy: things with vile names such as collodian, silver nitrate, cyanide, and whatnot else besides. Undoubtedly it was a grand opportunity, and Simpson was much excited; but I was reclusive and would not respond to his mood, forcing him, after only the slightest of frowns, to take out his exuberance on the poor, suffering Cheeboo instead.

The skies were clear and the sun was warm, so there should have been every reason for me to partake of the holiday atmosphere that the doctor exuded, and I daresay that I would have if it hadn't been for extraneous matters having intervened on my thoughts – said matters, of course, being Charula Khaur.

To be sure, much of it involved the story she had recounted the other evening: of the tragedy of her father's death, and of her being forced to flee her home at such a tender age. I was not so hardened to the cruelties of the world that I could not feel the deepest sympathy for the lass, and I did. The memory of that evening pierced me through and through, and her tone as she had spoken (so distant and cold) left little room to doubt its veracity.

The lawlessness that abounded along the frontier in those days, with just a few companies of *sepoys* and detachments of police to govern the plains along the foothills, was well documented, with grievances going back for as long as Bengal had been a part of British India, and Lord only knows how long

258

before then. Nor were tales of abductions of people and property a secret to anyone. The Bhuteau were a piratical race, preying upon the unfortunates dwelling on the lowlands beneath their mountain strongholds for as long as time itself – that was no secret either. So I believed Charula with very little hesitation. It appeared that the Lord Sangay (the erstwhile Nieboo of Sipchoo, and now the powerful Jungpen of Poonakha) had been more smitten by Charula's beauty than he'd let on, and had neither forgotten, nor forgiven, the insult when she ran away.

If this were all that was going through my mind you might agree that it would be more than enough. By rescuing Charula and her companions that day in the Darjeeling Hills, I had succeeded in making an enemy who, by all accounts, was a power to be reckoned with. What was more, our mission was headed directly into his lair, which was food for thought. But no, I had other things to dwell on besides.

I could not put from my mind the moment when I had spoken, or rather when the 'sight' had spoken in my place, for it had visited me, of that I was certain. So rarely did it come, and with such twisted meaning, that it couldn't help but raise caution, although I never really knew from which direction the danger would come. In this case, however, with Sangay sitting on a rock somewhere in Poonakha, biding his time, honing the edge of his sword, awaiting the day when I saw fit to stick my head in his noose, all seemed evident. Perhaps yes, perhaps no, as I said I could never be absolutely sure; but one thing, and possibly the most profound thing to come from that evening, was the recounting of what I reckoned had triggered the event in the first place: the parallel between Charula and Loiyan.

The 'sight' had spoken only after she recounted how her father had told her that life was to be tasted. Ordinarily, I suppose, it was a rather innocuous phrase, and I scarcely would have noticed, had it not been for the fact that Loiyan's father had told *her* the very same thing, using those *exact same words*! How often had I heard Loiyan speak them herself: that she would 'taste' her life, and live it to the fullest? Hundreds? It had been her mantra, perhaps her only religion, and had lived her life accordingly, every minute of every day, for as long as I had known her.

Once more I experienced the pang that had now become so familiar, ever since sailing from England. It was curious that, ensconced as I was in my duties at Brampton Manor, my memories had begun to dim, until I could almost convince myself that she had been nothing more than figment of my imagination, a beautiful dream, but finding myself once more in the East, the reminders of her were constant, and impossible to avoid, like treading across ground that appeared to be firm, but in reality was riddled with pitfalls.

Charula's remarkable similarity in appearance, now combined with the even more remarkable similarity of her life's story (so much so that it had summoned a visitation) could not be ignored.

For a time I had hated the very sight of her. She had so resembled my beloved, but was not *her.* Now everything had become tangled in my mind, until I couldn't make sense of any of it. *Could* she be the same woman? At some indefinable level, was it possible? Of course it wasn't, the very idea was preposterous, and yet…

I had cremated her body myself, so no, it wasn't possible. But then my head jerked painfully to one side as I remembered how she had come to me after, how she had touched me, and said that I must live, when everything inside felt that I was already dead. She had been real then, too, even after death. Whether it was through the 'sight', or whether it was by some other means altogether, I couldn't say, but she had been just as real then as anything you could set your eyes on, reach out and touch, and say with all certainty, 'this *is.*'

There was more to our existence than met the eye. Whether it was through some sort of deity, or something else, there was a force at work beyond our capabilities of reckoning, and it defied reason. Charula was here, but so too might Loiyan. Rational thought said that they could not be the same person. Almost everything else said that they were.

Almost.

I tried to ward the thoughts away, but they wouldn't be silenced, like knowledge once known, could not be unknown.

Once more I remembered that morning in Africa, along Ukerewe's shore, when I awoke to find that Loiyan had murdered Tepilit and Sakuda while they slept. I recalled her face so easily, as if it had happened only yesterday; there had been no ferocity or hatred, only shock and sorrow. True, she had killed, but only because she had known that, if she didn't kill *them*, given time they would kill *her*. It had been an act of necessity that had come close to destroying everything that she was.

Then I recalled Charula facing me just the other day: knife in hand, and the gleam of blind hatred in her eyes. Had I imagined it, or had it been real? Either way, she could scarcely be faulted; after all that she'd been through, few had more right to hate than she did, and besides, who was I to judge? I had killed in my own time, and hatred born of fear had played its part in that, too. No, I couldn't judge her for that, or for anything, really. It was just that, ordinarily, when I looked at Charula I could see Loiyan, but when I saw her at that moment, it conjured the image of my dead wife on that fateful morning, but not as the same, but rather as two very different people. Try as I might, I could never imagine Charula Khaur showing remorse.

***

Eventually, my thoughts having run around in circles, until I was driven to distraction, I was more than ready to be hospitable when the Cheeboo decided to join me, and point out places of interest along the way.

The city of Paro is situated on a broad level plain surrounded, as are all places in Bhutan, by mountains. It was to these that he indicated with a broad sweep of his hand, and told me that they were liberally dotted with monasteries, each with its own claim to distinction, again something that was not uncommon throughout the land. He pointed to a mountain in the far eastern range, covered in snow, and said that there could be found the celebrated monastery of Dongâlah.

"The frescos covering the walls there are said to have been painted by artists from Tibet."

I could tell that he hoped to impress me, so I endeavored to comply, not knowing whether a Tibetan artist should be celebrated or not. Thus heartened, he pointed to a ridge halfway up a mountain to the west. I could just make out a toy-like structure perched on the lip of a sheer cliff face. "That one is called Gorikha. It is very small, but much venerated." I asked him why that was, and I daresay he told me, but his answer escapes me now.

I do recall that on a later excursion, a group of us climbed that mountain and discovered a large grass plateau at nine thousand feet, by Austen's reckoning. The view surpassed all belief, for we could easily see the magnificent Snowy Range on the Tibet side of the border, fronted by the cone-shaped mountain that the Cheeboo said was called Chumularhi, sacred to the people of that country. Austen and the doctor agreed that by any other standards, the government would situate a summer capital on that plateau, as the air was very clean, and the climate not too warm. But it was all useless conjecture, for the plateau was barren at the time and, as far as I know, still is.

Meanwhile, the Cheeboo continued to point out monastery after monastery. Over on a bleak hill to the northwest, he spoke of a structure built into the rock, overlooking another sheer-faced cliff plunging down the side of the mountain. "That place is known as Tuckshung," he said, "meaning 'the Tiger's Cave'. It is a very holy place, Mr. Smithers, visited every year by many pilgrims." Before I could interject with my monotonous 'why', he told me, "It is said that the most holy Goraknath lived there after he ejected the tigers from the cave." Then he smiled dreamily, "I look forward to the chance of visiting there myself."

I was to find out that he wasn't the only one. Days later he, along with a number of our bearers, made the pilgrimage, some spending what must have amounted to a small fortune, by their standards, on *butter*, no less, to burn in the monastery's ritual lamps, presumably in aid of their prayers for anything from commercial success, to a son and heir. I don't much hold with the rituals of religion, but the Cheeboo was my friend, and besides, as I've said before: I'd learned that it's never wise to show disrespect to the local gods, so I kept my opinions to myself.

The city of Paro lies a quarter of a mile from the citadel, which was our destination. It appeared to be prosperous, for in addition to the standard mud and wattle huts of the commoner, there were also several dozen stout houses built of stone, three stories high, which I took to be the homes of something I had yet to see in this strange, foreign land: a prosperous middle class.

Near the centre of the town along the Paro River, there is a large, stone-paved market place, which the Cheeboo assured me drew many hundreds every evening. We skirted it at a distance, but near the centre I could see a small, rather pretty ornamental building. I asked the Cheeboo what this was for, and was told that it housed a detachment of police to keep order. The Cheeboo's moods were never easy to read, but by now I felt that I was sensitive to his nature by the subtleties of his tone. Sensing that he was not being as forthcoming as he might have been, I pressed him for the reason.

Assuming that I already knew what he was referring to, he shrugged and said, "It is forbidden to enter the square on horseback." After another small shrug, he finished with, "Perhaps Mr. Eden was unaware."

Of course I pressed him further, and was soon able to deduce that there had been trouble here on one of Eden's earlier visits to the palace. Finding himself caught out, the Cheeboo, being the Cheeboo, was eager to make allowances, and swore that Eden had not known of the law, and no doubt about it. I knew this for a falsehood, mainly because the Cheeboo was so terrible at telling them, but also because, it being the Cheeboo's duty to notify Eden of such injunctions, he would certainly have done so. I pressed him even further, telling him of my suspicions, but he only looked away, saying that Eden must not have heard him, at which point I gave up.

The long and the short of it was that, against all advice to the contrary, Eden had insisted upon riding his damned nag through the centre of the market, flouting the local custom with a vengeance. It was the worst sort of arrogance you can imagine, and naturally enough, I thought, the local constable had demanded that he dismount. Eden, being Eden, had declined to do so, and might have come to an injury by the hands of the angry crowd gathering 'round, if it hadn't been for the timely arrival of the Penlo's guard, come to escort him to the castle.

"Hold on," I said, "when was this, exactly?"

The Cheeboo replied, "It was the day after we arrived, Mr. Smithers." Then, obviously hoping that it might ameliorate matters, he added, "It was his first visit to the palace, but why do you ask?"

"No reason," I lied, but in my mind I understood that the Bhuteau may have had greater cause for their hostility towards us than I had first imagined. It would be just like the blundering fool: his blind conceit could have got Charula killed, or at the very least ravished by those ruffians, who had been exhibiting their outrage over the port being passed to the left, so to speak. They were a fairly moth-eaten bunch, and I would have happily thrashed them into next week for what they had intended, but this further intelligence revealed that our side (meaning that stupid bastard) was even less innocent than I originally thought.

But as prosperous as it seemed, it occurred to me that, from where it was situated, Paro *should* have been one of the most thriving cities in the entire orient. Sitting on a vast, easily-cultivated plain, at the crossroads to China, Tibet and British India, with relatively easy access to all, that market place should have been several times larger than it was, with depots for everything from salt to silk, and much else in-between. However, the Cheeboo said that foreigners seldom venture here, mostly because of the general lawlessness of the land, where an enterprising merchant might be picked clean by the warlord Nieboos and Jungpens (either under the guise of taxation, or just out-and-out theft), long before they ever reached the market. Some may have tried; few tried a second time, thus ensuring that the shortsighted xenophobic foreign policy of the present rulers (indeed, if *foreign policy* isn't too grandiose a term for highway robbery) kept their country stagnating in the Dark Ages.

All in all, I found that the scant few miles we rode to the palace that morning to be as educational as all the time I had spent in this strange country thus far, and even more so when we arrived.

The Bhuteau word for palace is '*dzong*', but in fact the word has several different meanings because the structure has several different roles. It can be a palace, as it was in Paro's case, but also a monastery and fortress, as well as the administrative offices of the civil service (such as it was – you would be right in guessing that *they* didn't require much space).

Upon our approach, I was much impressed with the Paro *Dzong*, as it far surpassed any other structure I had seen in Bhutan up to that moment. Although by no means a modern fortress (it was two hundred years old), it was a solid looking five storey, rectangular structure, surrounded by a dry moat, with the typical red band, designating a monastery, painted on the upper works. Inside the square, a seven storey tower, or keep, surrounded by a large copper cupola, was plainly visible as it rose above the outer walls. The entire structure was roofed by what appeared to be clay tiles, but I later learned was split bamboo.

Entrance was gained on the eastern side, via a covered bridge, guarded by a handsome, iron-studded gate, gaudily painted by western standards, with several beautiful inscriptions engraved on stone and iron, some of them in gilt. Just outside the gate were cages containing four huge Tibetan mastiffs, who, thankfully, regarded our procession with very little interest.

Once inside, the first thing to catch the eye was a huge cylinder, about ten feet high, which could be turned by a crank protruding from one end. Although this was much larger than most, by now I knew what a prayer cylinder was (you couldn't travel very far in Bhutan without coming across hundreds of them, and flags as well, which were much the same thing), and what they were for. Roughly speaking, the theory was that the rotation of the cylinder sends the prayers inscribed on it to the Buddhist version of Heaven, while at the same time the rotation rings a bell procuring the attention of the Almighty. Presumably that worthy would then read the notices, and act accordingly. Prayer by machinery, in fact. Anyway, I digress.

Upon entry I immediately realized that we were situated on the third floor. I discovered later that the fort was built on solid rock overlapped by the bottom two stories, made up of granaries and various other storage areas. It only took a moment to realize that, although this was no modern fortress built along the same lines as might gladden Vauban's heart, it was by no means as assailable as what I had first thought. Any besieging artillery attempting a breach would easily pierce the walls of the lower rooms only to have their shot absorbed by the rock on the other side. It would be like trying to tear down a mountain.

Further examination of the walls showed them to be composed of rubble stone and very thick, with a gradual slope inwards from the foundation to the battlements. I noted the soldiers manning the embrasures: tall, splendid fellows, with their chain mail and burnished helms. There were one or two *jingals*, which could shoot further than even our Enfields, but most were armed with the fabled composite bow that Genghis Khan's hordes had made such splendid use of, back when much of Europe had yet to discover the benefits of a decent bath. True, they might be outdated, but they would still be an effective weapon at close quarters, and given the local terrain, that's what a fight was bound to come down to. In addition to that, their rate of fire was far greater than our own muzzle-loaders. Given enough of them, and the will, the Bhuteau might prove to be a tough nut to crack after all.

We were asked to dismount inside the gates, while servants hurried forward to lend assistance with all of Simpson's photographic paraphenalia. When all were decently encumbered we set off down a dark passage, which first turned to the left, then a sharp right, before debouching onto a vast stone-paved courtyard, surrounded by what looked like various living accommodations. Our escort led us past all of these, through another small gate, past a rather steep stairway leading to the upper floors, and into a large, low-ceilinged room, garishly decorated in the Eastern style. The beams were brightly painted in blue, orange, and gold, with Chinese dragons and other creatures vividly depicted. In addition to the beams, the roof was supported by a series of intricately carved arches, and the walls bedecked with all sorts of armour and weaponry, from matchlocks to swords, lending the place a decidedly martial appearance.

At the far end was a dais, with a little wizened old fellow, richly caparisoned in robes of silk, sitting on a splendidly appointed chair, gilded (if I'm not mistaken) with leaf of gold.

The Cheeboo whispered for my benefit, "The Penlo of Paro," which, judging from his advanced years, could only be the *ex*-penlo, the holder of the real power in these parts.

He seemed a decent old stick, beckoning us forward with a smile and a gesture. As with all orientals, it was difficult to tell his age, but I would guess that he had left sixty well behind him.

At length the proceedings were ready to begin, and if any of us assumed that we would be dealing with a doddering old codger, we were soon disabused.

With the Cheeboo acting in his usual role as interpreter, we were told that, as far as he, the Penlo, was concerned, the civil war, which we had thought concluded, was anything but, although hostilities had been suspended for the duration of our visit. Furthermore, he did not recognize the current government in Poonakha, as the former Deb Rajah had been forcibly dethroned, with all authority usurped by his enemy, the Tongso Penlo (damn-his-eyes!) and the current Deb and Dhurm Rajahs were nothing more than bloody puppets, so there! Or words somewhat to that effect.

The Cheeboo continued, "He also says that the closest adviser to the Tongso Penlo is a Hindu, who fled to Bhutan after the Great Mutiny, and is constantly proposing to join in a general insurrection with the British until they are driven out of India."

That should have caused a general hubbub, for this was news to me, but all that Eden did was look composed as all get out.

"Damn all rebels to hell!" shouted the Penlo, exhausting his knowledge of English in one go, but obviously vexed, and perhaps hoping to enlist sympathy for his cause by showing support for ours.

Eden continued to look politely interested, but said nothing.

267

I thought, "You fool! Can't you see that he's willing to *give* you the support of half the country in exchange for aid to put this bloody shambles on its feet again? Are you so blind that you can't see past your own bloody ambition?"

Apparently he was.

The Penlo continued to wait in vain, tapping a jewelled slipper with impatience. I thought that an outburst was imminent, but just then his eye fell upon Simpson's camera, resting on its tripod at a discrete distance from the dais. He was up in a trice, with more agility than I would have given him credit for. He pointed and muttered something, which the Cheeboo translated.

"Is this the device that paints the images?"

Upon being told that it was, the old man left the dais while the rest of us stepped respectfully aside.

Standing proudly beside his prized possession, Simpson received the Penlo with a nervous bow, as out of sorts as ever I'd seen him. But the old fellow scarcely noticed, his attention remaining riveted on the camera. Gradually the doctor overcame his unease enough to detach the lens and offer it to him; then with hand motions, he showed him how to hold it in front of his eye.

The Penlo was enraptured.

Success achieved, Simpson regained enough confidence to show him how the shutter worked. When this was equally well-received, he was soon his old self, holding up a glass, collodian-covered plate for the Penlo's inspection, and as God's my witness, was attempting to explain how it all worked...in English. To his credit, the Penlo ignored him, but turned to the Cheeboo instead.

"This machine will paint my picture?"

"Yes, sir...Your Highness, sir," Simpson beamed proudly. "That it will!"

The Penlo gestured to the room at large. "Can it paint a picture of us all?"

I thought that the doctor was close to tears. "Nothing would give me greater pleasure, sir!"

"Then it must do so at once!" the Penlo cried. "But wait! First I must don my armour, and the...!"

"All in good time, sir," Eden said with a thin smile, the one he used whenever he forgot that he hadn't any lips to speak of. "With Your Excellency's permission, we should continue our talks."

The old man looked crestfallen, which was enough to make me despise Eden even more, but after a shrug, he resumed his seat with polite dignity, although his eyes never strayed far from Simpson, or the camera, for the rest of the proceedings.

Eden, having found that he could be so easily replaced as the centre of attention, was now more forthcoming. He declared that it was unconscionable that our mission had been languishing in Paro for sixteen days waiting for word from Poonakha.

The Penlo agreed: it was a great pity, inexcusable in fact, but what else could you expect from the riff-raff they had making such a mess of things in the *Durbhar* these days?

Eden played his old ploy: in that case, he had no choice but to return to Darjeeling, or press on for Poonakha without any further delay.

However, if he was counting on the same old reaction, of the Paro convulsing in horror at the mere thought of our taking either course of action, he was much mistaken. Without batting an eye, the old fellow told him to press on, by all means. What was more, he was confident that Eden would achieve great things, and with that he rose to his feet.

"Gentlemen," quoth the Cheeboo, as instructed, "the *Durbhar* is at an end!"

The Penlo rattled off something else.

"Now this wonderful machine will paint our pictures!"

***

"Gad! I wish I'd brought along more plates!" the doctor enthused, beaming like he'd just achieved Nirvana, which, in his own little world, I suppose he had. "I say, Smithers! Why didn't you bring more plates?"

"Because that's all you gave me," I told him.

269

Bark!

I couldn't fault Simpson for being so happy. The day had ended with a great success, with the Paro sitting patiently through exposure after exposure, often with Eden sitting beside him, looking like a dyspeptic vulture. There were a few photographs taken with the lot of us. You can see me in the back row, staring like a mesmerized owl; that is to say, in the ones where I managed not to blink.

The old fellow had just called for his armour for the next round when Eden declared that, as much as he'd like to accommodate him, alas, we had to return to camp without delay, in order to make preparations for our imminent departure.

The Penlo was in high good spirits, and wasn't too disappointed. In fact, he did something that I thought was extraordinary. Summoning the Cheeboo, he placed his hand upon Eden's shoulder. "May Buddha go with you, my friend, and may you have success in all your endeavours; but promise me that you will keep a careful watch on the council in Poonakha, for it is composed of treacherous and ignorant men!"

This was the same old line he'd been spouting all along, but what he said next gave all of us pause.

"Before you arrived, word came from Poonakha ordering the arrest of the Cheeboo Lama, as well as stating that we were to send the rest of you back to the frontier." Here the old gent offered us a crafty grin. "But the order was given verbally. I asked that they put it in writing, but this they would not do, for they are a cowardly lot, unfit to lick the sole of an honest man's boot. Rather they would have me accept the blame, for blame there would certainly be, for the duplicity that they designed." Here the Penlo clapped his hand on Eden' shoulder. "My friend, I am Bhuteau, and you are a *feringhee*, but I do not commit treachery, even if it is against my enemy. So I say go to Poonakha, achieve great things for the good of all our people; but if you ever need assistance, know that you have a friend in Paro."

***

270

"Do you think he was telling the truth?"

Naked but for the blanket covering her waist, Charula lay on her side, with one hand propping her head, the other delicately raking her nails across my chest. One pert breast peeked out at me through her hair, the nipple already swollen.

"About which part?"

"About those people wanting him to arrest your friend."

"The Cheeboo?"

"Mmmmm."

"Yes," I said, "I think he was. I can't see that he had any reason to lie about something like that."

"What about what he said in regard to coming to Eden's aid?"

I hesitated. "I think he *wants* to be truthful. I think that he would help us, if he can."

"*If* he can?"

"The Penlo's in a tight spot," I explained. "He fought on the losing side of their civil war, and is retaining power only through cunning. That sort of thing can fall apart at any moment, so he needs our help against his enemy, the Tongso Penlo. To make Eden warm to that idea, he offers us his help first, hoping that we'll reciprocate in kind."

"And will you?" Her nails trailed down to my ribs, leaving small traces of white that quickly reverted to the colour of my flesh.

"I don't know," I admitted. "I wouldn't trust Eden any further than I can throw him."

"But if such an alliance were beneficial to both sides...?"

"The Penlo's a crafty old codger," I told her. "He knows that his hand may be forced before events unfold. If Eden had even a jot of sense, he'd act at once, before that could ever happen! Dammit all! It's his for the taking: a bloodless war can be won, and a friendly and progressive power set on the Deb Rajah's throne, but he can't bloody see it!"

"*Will* there be war?"

"I don't see how it can be avoided, if Eden refuses the Penlo's help. The fool thinks he's the second coming of Pitt the Elder, and won't deal with anyone else but the power recognized

271

in Calcutta, even if that *power* is nothing more than a sham. He still thinks that he can talk some sense into them. He still thinks that they'll *listen!*"

"Will they?"

"I'm afraid all evidence points to the contrary. Short of putting it in writing, they're doing everything they can to force us to turn back. That hardly seems receptive."

"So if there is to be a war anyway, what difference can it make? Mr. Eden does not have the authority to act as you would wish."

"Authority be damned!" I said, grinding my teeth, but not *completely* from the strength of my conviction. Charula's nails had descended enticingly to my waist…and had taken a maddening notion to dally there. "Leaders must *lead,* regardless of the consequences to their own precious careers! The Crimea was thick with generals who didn't have the stomach to make the right decisions – both theirs *and* ours – and thousands of men died because of it! Oh, I've had a bellyful of their sort, let me tell you!"

I became so aroused in making my point that I grasped her wrist, to cease her distraction, delightful though it was. Her eyes widened, but she didn't struggle to break free. I forced myself to a level of calm.

"If Eden were to act now, far fewer will die than if he plays this madness out to the end. If he supersedes his authority, what of it? Very well, he may be sanctioned by Calcutta, and at the very worst his career might be ruined, but what is that compared to lives?" I shook my head. "But even that's only a vague possibility, because if there's one thing I know about governments it's that they don't punish success, especially if the price isn't high, and it's handed to them on a silver platter."

Having said my piece, I released her wrist, and she immediately resumed her meandering, the vicious minx!

"Perhaps there is truth in what you say, *Bahadur,*" her lips were inches from my ear, and her breath was warm, "but that would be seen as meddling in the affairs of a sovereign state, a thing that you British have been accused of before." Her nails began a lazy meander below my waist.

"And I daresay they would be right," I managed. "It would still be worth it."

But the conviction was gone from my voice, not because I doubted what I was saying, but because she had found what she was looking for at last, and had taken hold.

"Ah!" Her lips were moist and trembling, brushing the very tip of my lobe. "All this must wait until tomorrow. If it is lives that you would save, *Bahadur*, then save mine, for my need is greater; and I pray you, do it now!"

Under the circumstances, it was the only decent course I could take.

Chapter Seventeen

We left Paro early the next day by a steep ascent rising out of the bowl of the valley through a pass that rose to eleven thousand feet. Snow was encountered here, as well as a small fort, and an equally small garrison. The soldiers stared at us with open curiosity as we went by, but offered no hindrance, and we were soon descending the other side, eight miles down a gentle decline, through grass and pine forest, filled with every sort of wildlife you could imagine. Not long after, we came to a village called Pemethong that boasted yet another monastery, although now deserted. We made camp on an open flat, at the end of a day that might have been considered arduous at the beginning of our trek, but which we now thought of as little more than a pleasant stroll.

A good many of the local villagers were unmistakably Bengalis, who, the Cheeboo soon discovered, had been taken in raids many years ago from Cooch Behar, a protectorate principality situated between Assam and Bengal. This caused an initial stir, for it was because of people like these that we had made our journey in the first place, but it soon died when it was discovered that they had lived so long among the Bhuteau that they had become settled here, and now had only an inexact memory of their homeland. It would not have been a kindness to attempt to repatriate them and, no doubt, would have failed at any rate.

Another matter of note occurred while we were encamped here, and was even more immediately pertinent to our mission. We encountered another party of *Zinkaffs* from Poonakha. Among them, still puffed with his own self-importance, was our old friend who had done all the talking at Hah Tampien. Precisely the same scene was played here as well: they had been ordered by the Deb Rajah to see to it that we returned to our own country; then, and *only* then, would they listen to any British concerns. Eden handled it in precisely the same manner as before, replying that he would willingly return if they would say that the Deb Rajah refused to meet with them, but of course this the *Zinkaffs* declined to do, and in fact, ended by agreeing that, if

274

we would not at least return to Paro, we should continue on to Poonakha. But when Eden requested that they precede him there, to explain the situation to the *Durbhar*, they flat out refused, claiming that they must proceed to Paro. More questioning revealed that they had been ordered to levy a fine on the Penlo for allowing us into his territory.

It was yet another cowardly example of Poonakha lacking the political will to obtain their goals, by punishing others for not doing their dirty work for them.

I thought of that wily old man, and wondered if that was a fine that would ever be paid. Pity I never got the chance to see him in his armour; that would have been a sight, and no error.

Shortly after leaving Pemethong, we arrived at the Thimpoo Valley, and took the Buxa Duar road winding alongside the river. Here the travelling was easy, and good time was made. We halted for the night at the village of Chalamfee, situated at the crossroads to Poonakha, and the summer capital of Tassushujung, and we knew that we were getting close.

Throughout the entire encampment, you could feel the excitement in the air, even amongst the bearers. After all the miles and struggle, after all the useless banter and problems overcome, after freezing in the passes and sweltering in the jungles, our destination was finally close at hand. Whatever our future, for good or ill, we were coming to Poonakha.

The next day there was only a short stop at the monastery at Simtoka, where the previous Deb Rajah lived in self-imposed exile. As he was an old friend, the Cheeboo asked for permission to visit him, only to be turned away by his servants. The unfortunate man was powerless to assist them, and indeed he said, that as a former enemy to the current government, he might actually harm our chances of success if it became known that we had communicated with him. The Cheeboo was saddened, but accepted the wisdom of his friend, and move on.

We now passed along a narrow valley with pine forests on either side, gradually climbing to the Dokiew Lah Pass at something over ten thousand feet. Our ascent was no hardship, the incline being so gradual that we were scarcely aware of it until, finally, we reached the top of the pass, and surveyed all that

275

was below us on the other side – the entire Poonakha Valley, with tiny villages, and neat little postage stamp fields, all of varying colours. In the midst of it was the prize: Poonakha itself.

***

We descended the pass, and made camp near a prosperous-looking village by the name of Telagong, inhabited chiefly by monks by the look of them. After all our hardships, and with our goal literally in sight, we were well disposed, but they never even let on that we were there. Whether it had anything to do with their traditions, or whether it was from a desire to be left alone, I didn't know, but they kept their distance with a stoic dignity, and we kept ours, watching them work their fields and orchards from afar – little dabs of orange amongst the lush greenery.

We reached Poonakha during the ides of March (an omen as ever there was). Eden had sent messengers ahead to announce our arrival, and even written the Deb Rajah saying as much, but silence was their only response. In fact, the only communication we received was from one of the guardsmen, when he met us at a fork in the road: one wide and paved, and the other little more than a cart track, veering off to the left. Blandly he declared that we could not take the direct route to the city, but must take this lesser road around the base of the hill, and enter from the back.

Well I was shocked, I don't mind telling you, and I wasn't the only one, either. I heard Austen mutter something under his breath, and saw Lance flush with anger. Simpson barked indignantly, and the Cheeboo actually *frowned*. Even the *sepoys* were grumbling amongst themselves, with dark looks directed at the guardsman, who appeared not to notice.

It was the vilest sort of insult, and the meaning couldn't have been clearer: we were not to be received as equals but as supplicants, and our procession around the city would make sure that all the locals knew it, too. This is where Eden's plans (if, indeed, he had any) began to unravel.

While the rest of us seethed and cursed under our breath, he simply looked attentive, and after the Cheeboo had finished

276

translating, he said, "I understand. Captain Lance, see to it, please."

By the way Lance was chewing at the ends of his moustache, I thought that he came as near as dammit to telling Eden to go to hell (frankly, I thought he couldn't believe what he'd just heard) but after a moment had passed, he straightened in the saddle and snapped a crisp, "Sir!" before rounding on the Sikhs riding in twos behind him. "All right you bloody lot, you heard the gentleman! *Havildar*! Wheel about, order left, two abreast, *if* you please!" The *havildar*, scarcely less annoyed, stood in his stirrups, bellowing orders, and turned the little column by the sheer force of his lungs.

It was hard lines, venting their resentment like that, but the *sowars* didn't take any notice, but obeyed as smartly as if they had been on parade. They seemed to understand where the anger was coming from, and were harbouring plenty of resentment of their own besides. All the while Eden sat his horse like a sack of potatoes, and pretended not to notice.

I thought, "You bloody fool! This is a mistake!" Then I delivered a stern Britannic glare to the yawning guardsman, before turning Maggie's head, and followed as meekly as the rest.

I know what you're thinking: 'Come now, Charlie! First you damn Eden for flouting the natives at the market square in Paro, and now you're damning him again, but this time for doing what he's been told! Can the poor man not do any right in your eyes?' and the answer is no, he couldn't, and he never will. I'll own that I didn't like Eden from the moment I first set eyes on him back in Calcutta, and all the subsequent time spent after that had served to hone a hearty dislike into an especially virulent form of contempt, but that's not the point.

The man's nose for diplomacy was no better than Maggie's, and I'm referring to my horse, you understand, not the chambermaid. I'll allow that the episode at Paro may have had an effect on his decision, but if it did, it had the wrong effect. It does no harm to respect the local customs; in fact it does much good. By and large, people are the same the world over. If you show them that you're willing to get along, and not spit on their idols, with your boot on their neck, chances are you'll get a

277

positive response, it's simple human nature; but if you scratch at their back door, hat in hand, and say, 'Please sir, may I?' they'll treat you with contempt, because that's human nature, too.

Eden didn't know that. In fact all he knew about human nature you could fit on the head of a pin, and have room to spare. He thought that if he knuckled his brow to the *Durbhar* like a good toady, he was showing them how damned willing he was for the talks to go smoothly, forgetting that the *Durbhar* never wanted them in the first place, and would be quite content if they never happened at all. Showing you're willing is one thing, but showing how *much* you're willing is quite another. It can, and will, be used against you.

There's a time and a place to stand, and a time and a place to back down. In Paro the fool insisted upon having his way when it didn't matter, and here in Poonakha he gave in like a lackey when it did. For make no mistake, first impressions count, any schoolboy will tell you as much. Anyone: Lance, Austen, Simpson, even the *havildar* would have told that guardsman, "Toss off, Johnny, we're coming through," because that's the sort of bravado that's won us the Empire, but not our precious Eden. Oh no, not him. He was made of finer stuff than the rest of us, you see.

All those threats he'd made along the way, about returning to Darjeeling if he didn't get what he wanted, had just been exposed as so much balderdash. He would have his talks whatever the cost, and now the *Durbhar* knew it. What Eden didn't realize was that, with that short altercation with the guardsman along the Poonakha road, the talks had already begun, and round one had gone to the Bhuteau.

Round two went to them as well.

We made it to the place allotted for our encampment after a steep descent that was made only after much difficulty. There we waited, biding our time until someone took notice. For one entire day no one did.

On the second day we were visited by more of the Rajah's guard. Their leader strode into Eden's tent without so much as a by-your-leave, leaving his fellows outside. I could see our Sikhs staring across at them, sizing them up in silence, and being sized

278

up in turn. It wasn't difficult to tell what they were thinking: 'One day, you sod. You may have the upper hand now, but there'll come a time when I'll make you eat that smirk.'

Several minutes later Eden came out with the Bhuteau *havildar* by his side. Eden called for Lance and spoke a few words. I saw Lance stiffen as if he'd just been shot, and then he said a few words back. They mustn't have been nice words, for Eden forgot himself to the point of raising his voice.

"Captain Lance! I will have no insubordination, d'you hear! Everything is perfectly in order! Now, I will thank you to do as you're told!"

Lance went very pale, his mouth working silently, and then he was barking for the *havildar*, and another conversation of a similar nature ensued. Then the *havildar* was barking for a *naik*, and the process repeated itself. Finally the *naik* was barking to two *sowars* to follow him, summoning one of the *subudars* among the bearers to come along. Then in a cloud of ill temper, they disappeared in the direction of the baggage, returning minutes later, with two men under close escort.

Simpson growled, "I don't like the look of this, Charlie," and I followed him as he pushed his way through the gathering crowd. When he got to within hailing distance he cried, "Hollo, Chee! What's amiss?"

The Cheeboo looked as morose as ever I'd seen him. "Oh Doctor Simpson, this is most upsetting."

"What is it, man! Come on, out with it!"

The Cheeboo indicated the scowling guardsmen: "These gentlemen have come to take two of our men into custody! Whatever is to be done?"

Just then I spotted Austen emerging from Eden's tent, looking as grim as blazes.

"What's happened," I asked.

He looked at me askance, and took out a cheroot from his breast pocket. Biting off the end, in a clear, sardonic voice he said, "What's happened! Why, my dear Charlie, let me tell you: nothing has happened, nothing in the world…other than the fact that the lunatics have taken over the asylum. Why do you ask?"

"You're being facetious," I told him.

279

Drily he replied, "Really? I hadn't noticed."

"As bad as all that is it?"

He reached out and struck a Lucifer on my belt buckle. The smell of burning sulfur filled my nostrils as he held it to the end of his cigar. A few irritated puffs later, he blew it out and tossed it to the ground. He arched an eyebrow at the Rajah's guardsmen, who were scowling more than ever at the angry crowd gathering around them. "Those chaps have come to take two of our men. In the interest of *entente cordiale* our esteemed leader is allowing them to do so."

"The hell you say!"

"Yes," he agreed. "So it would seem."

This defied all logic. Even Eden couldn't be so daft! Desperate for action, I took a stride toward where the *sowars* were just delivering their wailing charges to the guardsmen, dark scowls being liberally exchanged on both sides.

Austen said, "I say, you won't do anything foolish, will you?"

I stopped and swung around. He looked away, still puffing on that damned cheroot. Airily he said, "Forget that I asked."

By the time I reached the middle of things, both Lance and the *havildar* were shouting themselves hoarse, calling for order, and a *naik* was stamping up and down in front of the ranks, with blood in his eye, brandishing a rope's end, and promising it to the first man that dared step out of line.

But the men were in an ugly mood, and weren't prepared to listen. Already some of the rifles were held at port arms with thumbs taut on the hammers. Meanwhile the miserable subjects of all the unrest, two Bengalis by the look of them, were wailing in terror, beseeching any and all who would listen to set them free.

Unminding, I brushed the *naik* aside, and grasping the nearest guardsman by the lapel of his robe, said, "Release these men!"

Looking back on it now, it was a damned silly thing to do, but a Smithers was ever thus when his duty is clear.

Of course the guardsman hadn't a word of English, but my meaning could not be mistaken. He gaped angrily at me,

280

mouthing something in his own lingo, and it was probably just as well that I couldn't understand him, either. It was an ugly situation, verging on the point of violence.

"Stop that at once! Stop I say!"

I turned to stare, and there was Eden, livid as a wet hen, his bottom lip absolutely trembling.

Once more he said, "Stop it!" and I could have swore that he stomped his foot.

An uneasy silence ensued for several seconds, but was finally broken when I accused him, "This is your doing."

He gave me a stare, virulent with hatred. Then, in a petulant, quivering voice, he cried, "Captain Lance!"

"Sir!"

"You will arrest this man!"

There was a brief pause, followed by a startled, "Yes, sir!" A moment later he was whispering in my ear, with his hand resting on my right forearm. In all the excitement I'd clean forgotten about the Tranter. "Come along, Charlie. There's a good lad."

The situation was as tense as any I'd ever been in, and of course it was my own bloody fault, but what would you? It just wasn't in a Smithers to meekly stand aside and let those ruffians take our poor fellows away.

I still maintained my grip on the guardsman's lapel. He, in turn, looked uncertainly from Lance to myself, all the while maintaining *his* hold on one of the prisoners: a short, wiry chap with a moustache and frightened eyes, wearing nothing but a *dhoti* and a turban. I realized how foolish I must seem, but there was no backing down now.

To Lance I whispered back, "I've no quarrel with you."

To which he replied, "You will have, if you don't let go of that slant-eyed bastard this instant!" I could tell that he meant it, too. The episode had turned everyone that bloody-minded.

Thankfully the day was saved with that ever-familiar bark, and Simpson's voice somewhere behind me. "This is a fine fix, wouldn't you say, Mr. Eden? You allow these johnnies to arrest half of our people, while *you* arrest the other half!"

281

And of course Eden blundered. Caught unprepared at having his authority so challenged, he could only wax indignant, stare down his nose at Simpson, and say, "Don't be ridiculous, doctor! It's hardly half!" making himself a figure of even more ridicule than he already was.

Again that bark. "I bow to your superior arithmetic, sir, but whatever the exact percentage, it appears like a goodly number to me!"

At which I heard Austen stifle a guffaw, but unfortunately, not very well.

Eden heard it, too. He became livid, and stamped his foot a second time. "I will not be made a laughingstock, d'you hear!"

Calmly the doctor replied, "If you are, Mr. Eden, none of us is the culprit." And even the *sepoys* had a titter at that one, but were immediately roared into silence by the *havildar*.

Meanwhile, none of the principals had moved. The Bhuteau still held our man, I still held the guardsman, and Lance still maintained an uncertain grip upon my forearm, obviously wishing he was somewhere else. Clearly one of us had to give way, but who?

"Perhaps an explanation might help?" the doctor suggested cheerily.

I could tell that the proposal took Eden aback. He blinked at the doctor like a discomfited owl. The very idea that he, God's almighty chosen, should explain himself to his people had quite literally never entered his mind. But perhaps I wasn't the only one who had grown to lack confidence in the man. By this time we had all been through a great deal, and much of it had been avoidable, had it not been for his blind stupidity. Although it wouldn't be true to say that mutiny was anywhere on the horizon, a certain exasperation had begun to set in, to the point where Eden's stock had reached an all time low. I think that it was at this point that he first may have realized as much, and saw that he was bound to try to win it back.

Suddenly weary, he gave a nod to Lance. "You may release him, Captain."

282

I felt the pressure disappear from my arm, and at the same time let go of the guardsman's robe. We turned toward Eden, crossed our arms over our chests, and waited.

Eden took us all in, in a long contemplative glance. I daresay he was trying to gauge our mood, which should tell you something. We stared back: some eager, some sullen and angry, and some of us (I'll let you guess who) barking laughter and wildly amused.

Ignoring the doctor, Eden spoke in a clear voice to the assembly as a whole. "Men! Let me assure you that there is not the least cause for alarm!"

Someone shouted, "Then why are these rascals taking our people?"

Eden held up his hands placatingly. "For those of you who don't already know, these men, nay, these *British* subjects, were captured and taken into slavery by rogue elements of the Bhuteau, which the Deb Rajah has assured me have been operating outside of their laws. Since then, these brave souls have managed to escape from their bondage, and made their way to our *protection!*" He emphasized the last word, and gazed 'round all our faces, to be sure that it had sunk in. "These men are *not* under arrest! Do any of you think that I would be so base as to allow such a thing?" He paused again, perhaps to give those of us who did believe he could be so base (or at least boneheaded) a chance to speak up; but of course no one did, so he continued. "The Rajah's guard are here to escort our two comrades to a board of inquiry, to ascertain the guilt of those responsible for their abduction, nothing more. I have been *promised* that they will be returned to us *immediately* thereafter! I have had the strongest assurance from...this fellow." Obviously having forgotten his name, Eden gestured to the guardsman – a tall, evil-looking man, with a spiked helm, a broken nose, and an old sabre scar cutting across his upper lip. Seeing all our eyes upon him, he stood up straight and attempted to look noble and trustworthy, but only succeeded in looking more sinister than ever. Eden continued. "In the interests of justice, and in the interest of cementing the bond of friendship between our two nations, I have given my permission to proceed!"

283

It was all so neat and tidy, but it was also so bloody unheard of that I think it took us all aback. In the disbelieving silence that followed, Eden, the self-righteous little pimp, took it to mean that we had been reassured by the magic of his voice. So he turned to the guardsmen and said, "Right, carry on."

They may not have understood him, but they recognized the gesture well enough, and sensing our hostility (clever lads), lost little time in making off with their charges. It was so pitiful, really; those poor fellows were beseeching us for help, and pleading with Eden not to allow them to be taken and, to our everlasting shame, no one lifted a finger. By the time we had overcome our shock it was too late.

We turned our attention back to Eden, perhaps still half-expecting him to intervene, but he just stood there for a moment, with a self-assured smirk on his face (the one that said he *knew* he was right), and then spun on his heel and, walking briskly past the sentry stationed at the entrance, disappeared back into his tent, leaving us to figure out for ourselves what just happened.

To give him his due, it worked. For no sooner had Eden disappeared than, at a signal from Lance, the *havildar* shrieked, "Parade! Diii-smisssed!" even though, strictly speaking, there hadn't actually *been* a parade, but an impromptu gathering in defense of their own. But at the command the *sepoys* fell out, breaking up into groups of twos and threes, still shaking their heads over the curious ways of the *sahib-log*, and hoping against hope that we knew what we were doing.

As it turned out we didn't. We never set eyes on either of those men again.

I'm sure that there'll be those of you who will say that I'm being too hard on Eden, and I'll readily admit that I'll take a slap at the man every chance I get, because our personal differences would always ensure that our enmity be maintained no matter what the circumstances, but this was a different kettle of fish entirely. If it were merely my dislike that was the issue, I would have (and had done) kept my distance so as not to excite either of our temperaments. But it wasn't personal enmity that was the problem – I can say that with all certainty – it was Eden being an ass, pure and simple. Oh, I know that I had been foolish to

284

intervene, but there had been no one else for those poor wretches, and someone had to. More's the pity that I failed. After thirty years those men's cries haunt me still.

Eden never even tried to help them, or if he did, he didn't try hard enough, not by a damn sight. To him those men were nothing more than pawns, tools to (how did he put it?) '*cement* the bond of friendship between our two nations'. Well he'd done all of that and more. The trouble was, that if you get into bed with a cobra, they might not always react the way that you hope for. I've said it before, and I'll say it again: what he had done was unheard of. Turning over British subjects to foreigners was *simply not done*, regardless of their assurances, which turned out to be nothing more than lies from the beginning. Not only that, but he had turned them over without any of us sent along to insure that they were protected. No, not our Mr. Eden; his head had been too full of his own precious destiny to think of that. And while he planned and schemed for it all to evolve, he never realized that the *Durbhar* had left him at the gate, and taken round two.

***

The next day, as at Paro, the Cheeboo was summoned to the *Durbhar* to get a good telling-off for the aid he had supplied to our mission, even to the point of accusing him of duplicity and seeking his own ends, which was true enough, I suppose, but not in the way that they meant it. The Cheeboo had always wanted peace, and he continued to strive for it regardless of whether or not his struggle was well against the odds. He failed to respond to the threats and accusations, but quietly continued to press his point at every opportunity until, in the end, it was the Bhuteau who gave in, and decided that he would be acceptable as the official translator, after all. When everything was said and done, his behaviour was more British than any we'd fielded thus far. Personally, I thought that it was a great pity that he was a foreigner.

Still, round three to us.

***

The official talks began some days after our arrival, and soon put paid to any idea Eden may have entertained that his policy of appeasement had been a success.

He was told that the *Durbhar* would receive him in a small house just outside the fort, and accordingly he set off with his retinue, which included Simpson and myself.

I won't hold it against you if you're surprised at my being included; I was more surprised than anyone. After all, neither Simpson nor I had exactly endeared ourselves to Eden, especially over the past few days. Simpson I could more readily understand: ever since having removed the tumor from that miller's face back in Tsangbe, his fame had preceded him. Then there was his photography equipment, too, of course. Certainly word of his portraits must have reached here from Paro by now; but I was shocked past the point of amazement when Austen popped by, and asked me to come along.

Naturally I asked him if he was barking mad.

He considered the question seriously. "No," he said, "I don't think so. Why? Should I be?"

"Have you forgotten that Eden was on the verge of arresting me yesterday?"

"Oh that!" he said, waving his hand dismissively. "I shouldn't worry. Our esteemed leader will be too busy to notice you're along."

"But why would you want me anyway? In case you haven't noticed, things have this most amazing habit of going completely wrong everywhere I go."

"Oh posh!" he said, with another wave, "Nothing of the sort!" Then he looked at me, all serious and steely-eyed: "You're our John Bull, Charlie. Mustn't leave *you* behind, what!"

"I beg your pardon?"

"The British lion! The stiff upper lip! St. George in shining armour!" He leaned forward, pointing his finger at my chest, "That's you, Charlie, and all evidence to the contrary, I still believe that you've got a good head on your shoulders, so there!"

"You're daft!"

"Possibly," he conceded. "Got caught cheating in my finals at Cambridge. Sent me down for it, too. That was daft, I suppose. Pater wouldn't have it. Said he'd make a man of me if it was the last thing he did. So I was bundled off to India, and into the army, to remove me from the '*stench of disgrace*' – as he put it – as far away as possible."

In his way, Austen was almost as cracked as Simpson, but I knew a damned fine soldier when I saw one, and had learned to respect his opinion…until now.

So he tried a different tack. "Look, Smithers, I'll level with you. When you first showed up in Darjeeling, out of the blue, anyone could see that you were ex-cavalry, and I said to myself, 'Hello! This one's a likely looking lad!' But you didn't have any official capacity, did you? I could have done a bit of digging, I suppose, but I didn't need to. I know the look of a fighting man, so it was easy to put two and two together, and come up with the right answer."

Warily I asked, "And what answer was that?"

"You're a 'Special', one of Elgin's boys, the crafty old devil! He sends one along from time to time, when he thinks that there's a purpose they might serve. '*No mission too dicey or too dangerous*', that's what they say. Some call it a killer without portfolio."

"Hardly that!" His description was far from comforting.

"No? Ah well, it doesn't matter. The point is that, unless I miss my guess, you're a damned handy fellow to have around when the knives come out."

Even more warily, I allowed, "A Smithers can generally hold his own when he has to."

"Quite so," he replied. "And seeing as how we're about to enter the viper's den, if you'll pardon the mixing of metaphors, it's time that you earned your pay, don't you think?"

"Pay?" I asked.

He laughed and slapped his thigh. "It's like that, is it? Ne'er mind, laddie, think of it as your duty instead!"

That earned him a sharp look, you may be sure. Elgin himself had used almost the exact same words. Austen was right:

the old man really was a crafty devil; I could almost hear him laughing from his grave.

"So anyway, Charlie," Austen said, "I want you to come along."

"You're sure that Eden won't mind?"

He looked mildly surprised. "Didn't Elgin tell you? You're not under Eden's orders. If you were you would never have made it past the outskirts of Calcutta. No, as a 'Special' you report to no one but C & C India, so even if Eden does object, you can just tell him to go whistle."

***

Things began to go wrong almost as soon as we left the compound.

The journey required to reach the little house the *Durbhar* had mentioned was only a short one, thank God, but there was a crowd waiting for us when we emerged, made up of soldiers and bazaar scum, undoubtedly with orders to hinder our progress under the guise of popular discontent. Eden was still stuck on the idea that we could all be jolly good friends, so had neglected to bring an escort of any size, fearing that our hosts might have been *offended*, if you please. No doubt they would have; just our being here seemed to offend them quite enough as it was.

The crowd wasn't in any hurry to make way for us. They just stood their ground, scowling like blazes, as if they were daring us to come on. Eden, who was in the lead, had come to a stop when it was evident that they weren't about to make way, and seemed at a loss as to what should be done. Clearly it would never do for foreigners to see us turn tail back to camp, so there was nothing else for it but for Austen, Lance, Simpson and myself, along with the few *sepoys* that had been brought along as an escort, to come forward and begin to nudge them aside. I got a look at Eden's face as I went by, and saw that he was visibly shaken. Our eyes met, and I'd never seen anyone so torn between gratitude and hatred in my life. Meanwhile we had just begun to make headway again, when the crowd began to throw whatever they could lay their hands on. Sticks, stones, rotten

288

vegetables, and other things even more unspeakable came sailing at us over the crowd-that-was-not-quite-a mob. Some few of us were pelted, but thankfully, not having ever seen, or heard, of cricket, the Bhuteau threw like Frenchmen, and most of the missiles hit their own folk whose shouts of indignation only added to the general confusion.

I can't say how long we suffered this abuse, but it couldn't have been very long before we came to our destination, and the Rajah's guard emerged to form a protective cordon, keeping the riffraff at a distance.

Having run the gauntlet, so to speak, we thought that the worst was over, but no. That was only to be the first part of our ordeal. Waiting for us at the threshold was another one of their bloody *Zinkaffs*, who, with a barely concealed smirk, announced that the *Durbhar* was currently dealing with pressing matters of state, and closed the door on Eden's face without another word.

It was a preposterous situation, and I believe that, honour having been served, our best course of action would have been to return to camp immediately, and come back bristling with cold steel. For I had no doubt that even the few dozen *sepoys* that we had with us would have made short work of that rabble. The Sikhs were regulars from the Punjab, the finest in all of India, and after the insult of the previous day, were spoiling for a fight besides, and by God they weren't the only ones.

A quick glance at my comrades showed that they were livid to a man. Austen was cursing under his breath something terrible, while Lance was worrying his moustache with more savagery than I would have given him credit for. Simpson wasn't saying anything, which was a sure sign, and the Cheeboo looked genuinely unhappy.

Meanwhile Eden, standing with his back to us, so sure that his Great Moment was at hand, only to be thwarted at the last minute (and by a menial at that) said not a word, and outside of a sudden, immense slumping of his shoulders, moved not a muscle. Perhaps it was pure British doggedness that kept him immobile, but I rather think that it was pure indecision. At any rate, of all the arrogance and supreme confidence that had lead him to this point, there was now no sign.

I daresay that he had been severely shocked by the hostility of the crowd, even more so than the rest of us. After all, *we* weren't the Lord's Anointed, and it wasn't *our* destiny to go down in the annals of history as one of the greatest statesmen of all time, but his was, or at least he believed that it was, which amounted to the same thing; and it's my opinion that, just when all of that confidence might have actually been useful, he was becoming riddled with self-doubt.

We stood there for an interminable period, with the sun blazing down, and the crowd beyond the cordon continuing to throw insults, and anything else to hand, and we too proud to give them the time of day. What was worse, the longer we stayed, the harder it would be to turn around and leave, for it would be interpreted (correctly in my opinion) that our leadership was indecisive.

It couldn't go on forever, but of course we had to pretend otherwise. So we continued to stand, with sweat streaming down our sunburnt faces, soaking through the broadcloth on the back of Eden's coat in a long, dark stain. And wouldn't you know, just when I was sure that I couldn't take it any longer, the door to the house opened, and there was that damned *Zinkaff* again, this time to usher us inside.

At first my movements were wooden – my limbs feeling as though they belonged to someone else. So long had we been standing in place that pins and needles began to shoot agonizingly through my muscles, and I had to watch myself to keep from stumbling.

Once inside, we found that the room was darkened by draperies hanging over the windows. After having stood so long in the blazing sun we were all but blind, although blessedly cool. I was able to shuffle along behind the others, more careful than ever not to stumble, and take my place along the nearest wall. I looked around with scant hope, searching for a chair, but was not surprised when I found none.

Eventually my eyes adjusted to the light, and one of the first things that I saw was that room was not overly large, with space for everyone, but not much else. The second thing I noted was that a delegation of Bhuteau were seated on the far side of

290

the room, regarding us with ill-concealed disfavour. So this was the Head Council, the illustrious *Durbhar* we'd been hearing so much about. For the most part I was unimpressed. As my Lord Brampton's man, I had been used to the company of great men in my time, but I didn't see any here.

But then, as I slowly scanned the room, I did notice someone, and suddenly everything leaped into startling clarity.

He was about my own years, with a wispy oriental beard, thin, chiseled features, and a close-cropped skull. His gho was of the finest silk, blazing a deep, dark crimson. But it was his eyes that gripped me: they were dark like a snake's, and the coldest I'd ever seen. No one could ever forget eyes like that. I hadn't seen them since we had exchanged sabre cuts on the hills below Darjeeling, all those months ago.

So this was the great Lord Sangay, erstwhile Nieboo of Sipchoo, newly-minted Jungpen of Poonakha, slighted suitor and would be kidnapper of helpless women…and my mortal enemy.

And as I stared, I gradually realized that he, in turn, was glaring back at me.

Chapter Eighteen

As it turned out the entire *Durbhar* wasn't present, but then they didn't need to be. As far as power was concerned, there were only two men of any importance – the first was the Penlo of Tongso, Lord of the Eastern *Duars*.

In all actuality, he should not have been there at all, as Penlos are not generally included in the *Durbhar*, but he was, and it soon became apparent that everything that the old Paro Penlo had told us was true. Tongso was in control, and the others merely his creatures, there for the benefit of a thin veneer of legitimacy.

Squat and barrel-chested, at a guess I would say that he was approaching sixty, with grey in his beard, and weathered wrinkles around his eyes. Having laid claim to the principal's chair, power and confidence fairly exuded from him, as he treated everyone else in the room as underlings, including ourselves.

The second person of note was the man standing next to him. Possibly ten years junior to the Penlo, with his grey head close-cropped, he was dressed in the style of the Bhuteau, but nonetheless possessed the fine-boned features of an Indian. His mouth was twisted down into a sour frown as he stared at us across the room, and I realized that this must be the Hindustani that the Paro Penlo had referred to, and was the personal adviser to his counterpart from Tongso.

The Cheeboo saw that I had noticed him, and leaning forward, whispered, "He is known as General Nundunum Singh, son of Attaram Singh, and grandson of Runjeet Singh, of who you may have heard."

Indeed I had, as had anyone who had spent more than a fortnight in the subcontinent. Runjeet Singh, the Lion of Lahore, had, in his time, been a valuable ally to the British on the northwestern frontier, where trouble was the order of the day. Ruling the Punjab with an iron fist, he had preserved it as a buffer state between our holdings and the Afghans, who were always looking to have a playful crack at us. He had been a friend, and it saddened me to see his grandson on the opposing side of the room, forever scheming for our downfall; but the

292

aftermath of the recent rebellion was filled with many such stories.

The initial proceedings didn't take long, and with little visible hostility. The Tongso Penlo did most of the talking, suggesting that, as the Cheeboo was recognized by both sides as the official translator, and that as Eden's views were well known to him, he should visit the *Durbhar* daily, where they would also make their views known, and afterward he would return to our camp with his report, and so on.

After he had finished, there was scarcely a pause; then in a subdued voice, Eden said, "Agreed," and that was that.

A few eyebrows were raised, my own included. While none of us had any real idea how diplomacy was conducted, and most everyone trusted the Cheeboo completely, it seemed odd that the talks would proceed with only one principal involved at any given time. Linguistic limitations necessitated using the Cheeboo as a translator, and it was universally recognized that we couldn't do any better, so all was well on that score. But so often the intricacies of meaning are made clearer by a gesture, or a facial expression that could only be determined by sitting down, face to face.

I'm not saying that Eden was wrong, but if it was me I'd have insisted on tagging along. After all that we'd been through to get here, it only seemed natural to want to leave nothing to chance.

I surmised that our experience of just a few hours ago might have still been fresh in his memory: the crowds, the uncertainty, waiting in the sun, all of it. It had shaken him all right, I'd seen it written on his face. Perhaps the thought of being forced to go through all that on a daily basis had been more than he could bear. If it was, I can't say that I blame him, but that doesn't excuse him neither. We were there to do a job, but by allowing the Cheeboo to brave the crowds, day after day, while Eden stayed safe in camp, it struck me that it was a job that was only getting done by half measures.

All in all, I would have to say that round four went to the *Durbhar*. After that it only got worse.

***

Given the reception that we got from the crowd-cum-mob, you'd think that a protest would've been made to the proper authorities, wouldn't you? Well fat chance of that; Eden never said a word, for the extraordinary reason that he didn't want to cause trouble.

One might argue that that's why we were there in the first place: to *cause* trouble. We were there to stir things up, to tell Johnny Bhuteau, "All right, you lot! You're going to get sorted! And until you can prove to us that you can play nice you're going to *stay* sorted, too!" That's what we'd come all those miles, and endured all those hardships to say. We weren't there to make friends, but the fact that we didn't was no fault of Eden's.

I'd had hopes that he would jettison any thoughts of appeasement after that first trying day, but although his conviction had been badly shaken, he arrived at exactly the wrong conclusion, and tried harder than ever.

Ever since we had arrived in Poonakha, the changes in the man had become telling. Oh, he was still as proud as Lucifer, and arrogant as bedamned when it came to dealing out policy to *us*, but he was always meek as a mouse when it came to the *Durbhar*, driving the point home to the locals even further that we came as supplicants, and not as equals. He never really understood the power of public opinion the same way as the Penlo. Eden thought that it didn't matter. The Penlo knew better.

What was needed was a firm hand, because this was what your average Bhuteau most respected. I'm not saying that it was necessary to batter him senseless, but it would be as well if you showed him that you *could*, if you had a mind to. It does wonders for their manners, really.

Of course one of the problems was that the few dozen *sepoys* who had made the trek with us were far too few. The contingent was large enough to guard our baggage and camp, but very little else. All those men that we had been forced to leave behind at Sipchoo and Dhalimkote were coming back to haunt us with a vengeance. Not that Eden would have used them, though. On one of the few times that we did venture out of

294

camp, he *requested* that we be allowed to bring what little escort we were capable of, but it was promptly denied, and that was that.

It was a few days after our initial meeting, while the Cheeboo was busily hammering out the details of the hoped-for agreement, when Eden got it into his head that he must meet with the Deb and Dhurm Rajahs in person. I suppose that he could never quite relinquish the idea that these were the supreme powers in the land, even though the meanest street-sweeper knew that it was the Tongso Penlo calling the shots. Not so our leader. I daresay that he'd found the Penlo's presence perplexing as well as annoying the first time. If he'd wanted to hold talks with a mere Penlo he would have done so while we were in Paro. I believe that he thought he was being clever, and that this was his attempt to circumnavigate the Penlo's influence. If so, he was sadly mistaken.

We'd set off, immediately coming under a barrage of sticks and stones as we had the last time, left sweltering for an hour in a tent that could not have comfortably held half our number, and then finally brought into The Presence: not in the palace, which is what you might have expected, but in another tent out back. Sure enough, there was the Deb Rajah, sitting on a throne, a mere boy of perhaps eighteen years, in all the trappings of his office, and obviously frightened half to death. Beside him stood the Tongso Penlo. The Rajah said not a word while the Penlo stated his (the Rajah's) wishes, which were that, insofar as the proceedings with our mission were concerned, he (the Penlo) would do all the talking for the secular state. After which, nothing would do but that we all parade over to another tent to see the Dhurm Rajah, where the process was repeated (only this time insert 'spiritual' in the place of 'secular'). And with that all of Eden's hopes of being able to deal with someone other than the Penlo were dashed.

Once it was judged that this riveting news had set in, we all trooped off to the *Durbhar* to discuss the progress being made on the treaty. Here even I had high hopes, for in spite of every obstacle imaginable set in the way, the talks had proceeded very well, so well in fact that all had been agreed to, with the

295

exceptions of two minor articles (numbers eight and nine, if you're wondering) where it was suggested that we have a permanent agent in Poonakha, and the appointment of a board encouraging trade.

The Bhuteau ruling class really were the most xenophobic bunch you ever heard of, and they weren't about to have hordes of our merchants traipsing all over the shop, shortchanging the public, and preaching sedition to their peasants. It wasn't anything that we'd pinned any great hopes on in the first place, so Eden was prepared to set them aside. And with that, the last obstacles for signing a treaty had been removed...or so we thought.

Once the formalities had been seen to, and all the articles had been read aloud and agreed upon (among which was the return of all British captives, and our occupation of the Bengal *Duars*, for which we would pay an annuity to the Bhuteau) at the last possible moment, the Tongso Penlo suggested one more article: the return to Bhutan of the Assam *Duars*.

I suppose that we should have seen it coming. After all, the *Duars* bordering on our holdings in Assam fell under the Tongso Penlo's hereditary domain, and it must have irked him more than a little that they were no longer his in fact. The problem was that Lord Auckland (our GG at the time) had had them permanently occupied more than twenty years earlier for precisely the same reason that we were occupying the Western *Duars* today: to put a stop to the constant raids and depredations upon our territory. Even if Eden had been given license to include them in the talks (which he hadn't) it just wasn't on.

I must say I was shocked, and others were as well, but the most shocked of all was Eden. To be faced with this obstacle at the eleventh hour, just when he was on the verge of the success he longed for, must have hit him pretty hard, for anyone could see by the Penlo's overbearing manner that this was not just an idle suggestion. He would have the Assam *Duars* included in the treaty, and that was that.

To give him his due, Eden got up and said that the question of the Assam *Duars* was closed, that as far as he was aware, there hadn't been any official requests in all that time to

296

reopen the subject, that the Raj had been making regular payments to compensate for lost revenues, and besides which the Bengal *Duars* were the only ones he was authorized to discuss. Short of carrying a letter back to Calcutta listing the Penlo's concerns, there was nothing else that he could do.

I'll allow that he said it well. It was bluff John Bull giving his marching orders to the heathen as ever there was. He was severely piqued, of course, and that may have helped, but it was as nice a case of damn-your-eyes, mingled with diplomatic mumbo-jumbo, as I've ever heard; and when you consider that I otherwise loathed the ground he walked on, you may believe every word.

The Penlo didn't like it one little bit, but then I don't suppose that he was used to being slighted. He suddenly became violent, stamping around, back and forth, smashing various items, and throwing others across the floor.

When Eden pointed out that this was hardly helping matters, the Penlo snatched up the treaty and crumbled it in his hands.

"Then we will have war!" he shouted savagely. "You are nobody! You have no authority! We do not *want* the Bengal *Duars*, and as to your government's demands, a *Zinkaff* could have been sent to settle them! Bah!" He spat derisively, "I will have nothing more to do with you! Go!"

Eden was as pale as a ghost, and when he stood up all of us stood with him, expecting to leave at once. Instead, after only the slightest hesitation, ignoring the Penlo, he addressed the *Durbhar* itself.

"I have come to you, in spite of the gravest obstacles, for the sole purpose of securing friendship between our two countries, and I have done everything in my power to bring this about. I see now that it is useless, but I am in no way to blame. Of course it is your right to receive me with hostility, and the consequences of doing so rest with yourselves. I shall return at once to Calcutta and report to the Governor General what has occurred today."

Although he was plainly shaken, he said that rather well, too. Unfortunately no one was paying any attention. They just

297

looked away, or shuffled their papers, pretending not to have heard. Bad form altogether, really. So with the stiffest of bows, Eden said, "Good day to you!" and we left.

It should have ended there, but of course it didn't. Meanwhile I had other things to concern me.

The Jungpen of Poonakha had attended the meeting with the rest of the *Durbhar*, and like the rest, had added little enough to the proceedings. Contrary to the last time, he seemed not to be aware that I was in the room, but busied himself doing this and that, and generally making himself gainfully employed. For my part I didn't at all resent being ignored.

However, shortly after our return to camp, I was having a word with Simpson when an interruption occurred in the form of a tug upon my sleeve. Looking down, I noticed a wizened little man, dressed in a servant's livery that I didn't recognize. Having got my attention, he smiled ingratiatingly, exposing a mouthful of remarkably crooked teeth.

"Pliz!" he said, "You come!"

I looked at him pretty sharp and demanded, "Who the devil are you?"

He just bobbed his head, evidently not understanding a word, and giving my sleeve another tug, again said, "Pliz, mistah!" Then he took a few steps away and turned, beckoning for me to follow, "Pliz!"

I said to the doctor, "What do you think he wants?"

Simpson was clearly intrigued, and barked, "We won't know until we find out, will we?" and set out after him, thus forcing me to follow.

The little gaffer may have been small, but he could move when he wanted to, forcing Simpson and I to break into a trot just to keep up. He led us on a meandering route past the campfires and *sepoy* lines to the edge of our camp closest to the city. Hesitating only briefly to show his pass, he continued on past the guard, and out into the darkness.

Simpson and I came to a halt at the perimeter. He said, "I don't like the look of this, Charlie."

Nor did I. There was no telling what was out there, waiting in the shadows. A Smithers might not be a coward, but he ain't exactly suicidal, neither.

The little man stopped and turned, beckoning.

The doctor called out to him, "Sorry, old chap, but you and your cutthroat friends will have to find someone else!"

Just then a hooded figure stepped out of the shadows next to him, the pale light from our fires glimmering crimson on his robe.

I studied him for a moment, thinking, then asked the doctor, "Are you heeled?"

"Why I should certainly hope so!" quoth he, dragging out an ancient horse pistol, that looked as though it hadn't been cleaned since Inkerman. "But surely you don't mean…"

"Stay here," I told him, "but be prepared, just in case." So saying, I moved cautiously past the perimeter, feeling the reassuring weight of the Tranter on my hip.

When I drew near, Sangay, the Jungpen of Poonakha, pulled back his hood, regarding me with unconcealed dislike, and if you think that venom makes no sound, you're very much mistaken.

"Charlie Smithers," he sneered with an ice-ridden hiss.

Not to be outdone, I replied airily, "Hello, Sangay. What brings you out from under your rock?" Then just for cheek I inquired, "Kidnapped any helpless women lately?" Everything about the man was cold: his voice, his eyes, even his very presence caused me to shiver.

I hadn't thought that he would understand my reply, but to my surprise, I discovered that he spoke English rather well, with very little accent.

For the first time I noticed that his left forearm was swathed in a bandage up to his elbow. He fingered it meaningfully and offered an evil grin, his teeth long, yellow tusks, gleaming dully through his beard. "The lady is far from helpless, Mr. Smithers." Then carelessly he asked, "Perhaps you have become acquainted with her?"

An alarm sounded inside my head, yet I feared it was already too late. "Should I have?"

His laughter was more evil than his grin. "No? Then I wonder why you refer to our first meeting as a *kidnapping.*" But then he waved it away, as if it was of little consequence."It is no matter. Let us just say that Charula Khaur is well worth the effort."

I asked, "Who?" and fancy that I pulled it off so well that he gave me a sharp look, laced with doubt.

Drily he explained, "The lady in question."

I replied, "Ah!" being careful lest my expression gave away too much; but the damage may have been done already. I could have kicked myself for making what I had thought was a harmless little jibe.

"There have been reports from Paro," he said.

"Oh? What kind of reports?"

"From the Penlo's soldiers. It seems that, during your time there, they had waylaid what they had thought was a coolie, only to discover that it was a girl. Is that not remarkable?"

"Hardly," I replied evenly. "Half of our Lepchas are women. What of it?"

"This one was no Lepcha peasant," says he, studying me closely with those cold dark eyes. "The Penlo's soldiers said that she was quite lovely, although," he admitted, "those are not the precise words that they used."

Drily I replied, "They did, did they?"

"Indeed. And they also told me that their sport with her was interrupted by a *feringhee* who answers to your description."

"Come now, Sangay, admit it, all *feringhees* look alike to you people." Still, I didn't like the sound of this. So in order to change the subject, I asked, "How's the arm?"

Those cold, basalt eyes studied me for the longest of moments. Finally, through grinding teeth, he said, "Healing."

I replied, "Oh," and then after a pause, added a rather unsympathetic, "Pity."

My ruse seemed to have worked. I was sure that it was I who occupied the greater part of his attention now.

Fingering the bandage meaningfully, he said, "I have much to repay you for, Mr. Smithers." Then he took a step closer, and

I noticed that he reeked of garlic. "Make no mistake, I always repay my debts."

Uncowed, I replied, "As do I." And offered him a cold smile of my own, "With interest."

Suddenly he cursed and, in a streak of motion, reached for his sword (my God, but he was fast!) and had it halfway out of its scabbard before the ratcheting sound of Simpson cocking his pistol forced him to give pause. He glared as pure a hatred as ever I'd seen.

Angrily he hissed, "Another time, Mr. Smithers!"

Coolly, I looked him up and down. "At your service, Sangay," and turning, walked away.

Simpson met me at the edge of camp, demanding to know what our meeting was all about. I told him. After he'd heard me out, he whistled, long and low.

"Trust you to pick the toughest nut to crack, Charlie. Word is that the Jungpen's a mean bastard, one to be reckoned with. You'd better watch your back."

I didn't think that a touch of bravado would do any harm, so I smiled and winked at him, "I thought that was what you were here for."

***

As I said earlier, our mission in Poonakha should have ended after that last meeting, and indeed, we were in the process of arranging our immediate departure when Fate sent more messengers into camp. This time they were for Eden.

I was giving Austen a hand packing his kit (he was quite useless at that sort of thing, him being a gentleman and all), when he received an urgent summons to Eden's tent. He cocked an eyebrow at me and said that I might as well come along.

We found the Great Man at his writing desk. The Cheeboo and the doctor were there as well. Eden favoured me with a sour look, but otherwise said nothing.

Instead, he passed a sheet of paper to the Cheeboo, saying, "Gentlemen, over the past few hours I have been receiving messages from the *Durbhar*, all of them essentially saying the same thing. As this is written in Hindi, I'll let the Cheeboo Lama have the honours," and motioned for him to begin,

The Cheeboo spent some time fumbling with his reading spectacles and at last was ready:

"Dear Mr. Eden,

"Greetings, sir.

"It has come to our attention that you and your party are preparing to leave us. We entreat you, do not do so, but stay in Poonakha one day further so that we of the Supreme Council will have a chance to air our views.

"Allow us to say, Mr. Eden, that we deplore the most unfortunate proceedings from earlier in the day, and assure you that the Tongso Penlo had no authority to speak as he did. Further the Council approves of the treaty as presented, and pledge to you that we have no aspirations with regard to the duars *currently under occupation by the Government of India, the revenues of which the Tongso Penlo has appropriated in its entirety, and paid the court nothing for the past three years.*

"Indeed, Mr. Eden, the Tongso Penlo has become so corrupted that he is endeavouring to usurp the entire Council, but if you would only stay, we shall resist him, and all may yet be settled amicably.

"Once more, we implore you not to leave, as any such attempt will only end in a disturbance."

The Cheeboo finished and unhooked his spectacles from his ears. "The letter is not signed," he said.

"Nor would they," Eden pointed out, "on the chance that it might fall into the wrong hands." Then, continuing to ignore me, he turned to my companions: "So, gentlemen, what do you think?"

I thought that he asked a shade too brightly, as if he had already made up his mind. Unfortunately, as events unfolded, I was to be proven correct.

All but the Cheeboo were against it, smelling treachery in every line.

"Treachery to what end?" Eden asked. It seemed to me that having been thwarted at the eleventh hour, he viewed these messages as a last minute reprieve.

"It is possible that the Tongso Penlo is trying to buy time," said the Cheeboo, "in order that he might achieve his goal of having the Assam *Duars* included in the articles."

302

Eden turned to the Cheeboo as if he'd just been stabbed in the back. "I thought you were for this," he accused.

"I am for peace, Mr. Eden, and as long as the possibility exists, it should be pursued. All I am doing is pointing out alternate possibilities."

Scarcely mollified, Eden fiddled with a pencil. "Well he can forget about the Assam *Duars*. Even if I wanted to discuss them, I haven't the authority to put them on the table."

"Then there's the question of who this is from," said Austen.

"Why, it's from the *Durbhar*, of course!"

"A few parties, perhaps," said the Cheeboo, "but almost certainly not from the entire *Durbhar*."

Eden's brows suddenly knit. "What on earth do you mean?"

"The Tongso Penlo has already instated many of his own people in the council. For instance the Jungpen of Tassishujung is his son-in-law; and if any of you will recall, it was the Jungpen of Angdu Forung that started their civil war in the first place. He owes a great deal to the Tongso Penlo for intervening when he did."

I spoke up, "Excuse me, sir, but I know of another."

All eyes turned to me, Eden's more sour than ever.

At last, clearly thinking that I didn't possess anything worth mentioning, he invited with a sneer, "Pray share your...*intelligence*, then."

So I told them about Sangay, about our crossing sabres on that day just outside of Darjeeling, which drew a gasp or two. I mentioned further how he wished only ill for the Raj. I told them everything I knew, only leaving out any reference to Charula Khaur.

After they'd heard me out, Austen said, "It fits! I remember him now, from that day at the ambush! The man cloaked in scarlet – and you say that was the Jungpen, Charlie? Well, well! You'll have to watch your back, won't you?"

Drily I replied, "So I've been told."

The Cheeboo said, "It was the Tongso Penlo who appointed Lord Sangay Jungpen of Poonakha. Whichever way the Penlo goes, so goes he."

"Balderdash!" quoth Eden, snapping the pencil, "Nothing of the sort! Just because Lord Sangay owes his appointment to the Penlo doesn't mean that he won't do his duty to his country. And certainly Smithers'…" he paused, searching for a suitably derogatory word, "*intrigue* with him earlier," he sneered out every syllable, "means nothing at all!"

"It means that he's not adverse to raiding our territory," said the doctor with some feeling. "Or abducting our people! You won't find me placing any trust in him anytime soon."

Austen chipped in, "Isn't that why we're here? Expressly for the purpose of stopping people just like him?"

Eden busied himself with carefully rearranging both halves of the pencil on his desk, lining them up in columns of two. I could tell that he was irked because we hadn't told him what he wanted to hear. I could also tell that he wasn't going to let it stop him, neither. Finally, in a clipped tone he said, "Thank you for your opinions, gentlemen. That will be all."

So we all filed out of his tent, Austen stopping just outside the opening, as he pulled out a cheroot. "Well, there's one good thing to come of this, Charlie," he said.

"Oh? And what's that?" I asked, for I was damned if I could see it.

"You won't have to help me with any packing tonight. It looks like we'll be settling in for quite a while." He bit off the end of the cigar and lit it with an ember from a fire. Then tilting back his head, he blew smoke rings into the night air, pausing to admire the perfection of each and every one. Finally he looked at me, without the least trace of humour.

"In fact, we may never leave here at all."

∗∗∗

I arrived at my tent late that night. Charula was already there before me, looking quite fetching in tight sky-blue pyjamas and matching vest embroidered in gold thread. A single pearl was

304

fastened to her forehead, covering her caste mark, and gold filigree earrings depended to her shoulders.

I asked her, "Where on earth do you get all this finery?" But she just smiled, and said that a woman has her ways.

"Do you like it?" She turned slowly, in a complete circle, inviting my admiration.

"Need you ask?" But instead of going to her, I sat heavily on the campstool. It had been a long day, with precious little good to show for it.

"You are tired," she said, kneeling to help me with my boots.

I told her about meeting with Sangay, but she didn't seem put out.

"He does not know that I am here," she said.

"He's heard rumours," and I told her that word had got back to him, about the day she'd been waylaid by the soldiers in Paro.

She still seemed unconcerned. My boot came off with a gentle tug as I unlaced the other. "You will protect me." Then she offered a strange, twisted smile. "My brave *Bahadur*."

"Don't be so sure," I told her, wondering how in the world I had ever allowed it to come to this. But I knew. Of course I knew: she was exquisite.

There came the familiar '*zeep*' of steel. "I still have this." The dagger waved under my nose, and I wondered where she could have got it from. Certainly she wasn't wearing enough to conceal anything even half the size.

"You'd best keep in practice," I told her. "God only knows you might need it."

The knife disappeared as suddenly as it had arrived. "Have no fear on that score, *Bahadur*. I will be ready."

I cupped her face in the palms of my hands. "I could never forgive myself if anything should happen to you."

She smiled. "There is nothing to forgive, for this is my choice."

I allowed, "Well, you certainly went to quite an effort," and she laughed.

305

She took my head and cradled it against her breast. "All that and more, *Bahadur*. All that and more."

It was most pleasant to remain there, and I thought, 'By jove, this is just the ticket when a fellow's down in the dumps.' Presently I reached down and took hold of a nice plump buttock.

She laughed, and protested, "But you are tired!"

"Not anymore."

She gave me a long, speculative look. Then she rose, reaching for my hand. "Come," she said, leading me to the bed.

Much later, as I drifted off into a blissful sleep, my final thoughts weren't about Sangay, or Eden, or even about the Tongso Penlo, either, but rather I was thinking how was it possible that a woman could contort herself so, without ruining her spine?

Chapter Nineteen

Of course Eden chose to stay, as we all knew he would.

"Gentlemen, I was much moved by the Cheeboo Lama's words last night. I, too, want peace, and see it as my duty to remain here for as long as there is the least chance of our success!"

Which was all bollocks, to be sure, but it all amounted to the same thing. Here we were, perched on the very edge of the dragon's lip, and here we would remain until Eden saw fit to tell us otherwise.

Meanwhile the Great Man lost little time in making another blunder.

So convinced had he become that the messages were in earnest, that he decided to throw caution to the wind, and reply without delay. That in itself might not have been so bad, but the tone that he took was.

Too late; far, far too late, he adopted his old pose, saying that as the Tongso Penlo was unwilling to discuss terms, he saw no recourse but to return to Calcutta, where he would report his failure. Obviously he intended no such thing, but was counting on the letter to act as a prod for the *Durbhar* to get off their collective behinds and oust the Tongso Penlo, so that what he percieved as the real talks could begin without delay.

He received nothing in reply that day, but on the next there came a note from the Tongs Penlo, reminding him that there should not be any written correspondence between parties, but that all discussions should take place verbally through the offices of the Cheeboo, which essentially speaking, was correct, but more to the point, he was letting Eden know that he had intercepted his letter and read it. Furthermore he was not amused.

As you might imagine, having been caught out, Eden refused to respond. And yet, against all logic, given that the Tongso Penlo had obviously intercepted his message, he was still counting on support from the *Durbhar*...which, coincidentally, had fallen ominously quiet.

The situation seemed to hang in limbo, until March the twenty-second, a full week after we had arrived. Gladsome tidings came when the council finally broke their silence: all had been settled as Eden wished, and his presence was requested.

None of us, save Eden, gave it much credence. Given that the Penlo had intercepted his letter (with clear evidence that sedition was afoot) the days following would have provided him with ample time to stamp it out. Indeed, the silence emanating from that quarter ever since seemed to confirm it. A correspondence at this late hour virtually screamed subterfuge to everyone else, but when you're reduced to grasping at straws, you take what you can get, and so it was with Eden. He agreed to attend, on the grounds that our mission would not be forced to suffer the presence of either a mob, or the Tongso Penlo. Such assurances were speedily given, and so, with grave misgivings, we set out, our fears soon being confirmed.

The mob was waiting as always, and having improved their aim with the constant practice, we had to step lively to avoid the stones and other missiles that were coming our way. Arriving at the *Durbhar*, we couldn't have been there for more than a minute before an anteroom door opened, and in walked the Penlo, taking his usual seat at the head of the table, with his personal adviser, General Singh, close by his side.

At this point Eden was most discomfited, and you may believe me when I tell you that this was an understatement. As the rest of us had already surmised, something had gone horribly wrong. Still, nothing could be done, but continue as if everything was as it should be...and wait for the sky to fall.

It didn't fall right away. In fact everything seemed to go wonderfully well. The treaty was agreed to, and not a word was said about the Assam *Duars*. The Penlo sat at the head of the table as if nothing in the world was amiss, nodding solemnly as each article was read, and exchanging the odd word with his adviser, but that was all.

Scarcely believing his good fortune, Eden scooped up the treaty and made for camp without delay, on the proviso that he would have four copies made within two days.

Over that time period, Eden and his staff slaved away like navvies, translating the treaty, and making copies of the lists of property and captives to be returned. All the while messages continued to come from the Council urging even greater speed, even to the point of insinuating that he was unnecessarily delaying matters, if you please.

That seemed a bit hard, but Eden could only surmise (and we could only agree) that there were factions within the Council, after all, and that there was a certain window of opportunity to be taken advantage of. Perhaps it was true, or perhaps it was all part of the cat and mouse game the Penlo was playing with us all along. Although we still had our doubts, it was impossible to say with any degree of certainty.

Also, during this time, the Penlo's adviser, General Singh, was a constant visitor to our camp. What he hoped to accomplish, God only knows, but the *havildar* in command made regular reports, saying that the general was spreading sedition and making gifts of money to the men. It seemed shocking bad manners, but Lance only laughed and said, "Let the old bastard spend his money. If there's one thing I know about my lads it's that they won't be adverse to taking his gold, and they won't mind listening to his stories, either, but that's all it'll amount to."

As it turned out he was right. The old man became a great favourite among the *sepoys*, and you could often see them huddled in groups, listening while the general offered his harangue, and the *jawans* grinning and nudging each other, treating the entire affair as if it was the greatest of larks. The *havildar* continued to keep a close watch (the Great Mutiny was still fresh in every mind) but as one *sepoy* put it, "The General sahib is a fine old fellow, who tells us stories that are, perhaps, better suited for children. But we do not mind; it would be rude not to listen after he has given us *annas*."

So the time went, and the end of two days saw the mission once more ensconced at the *Durbhar*, with four copies of the treaty, all present and in order, waiting to be signed.

And of course, exactly as he had the first time, after the reading of the first two articles, the Tongso Penlo interrupted, demanding that the Assam *Duars* be handed over immediately.

Our disappointment was as keen as it could possibly be, like air rushing from a deflated balloon, for it was now clear that the messages from the *Durbhar* had been a farce all along. After twice being on the very verge of success, only to have it taken away at the last possible instant, it was clear to everyone that, if there ever had been a window of opportunity, it was now closed. Still, against all odds, Eden did his best. There were no other options available.

I remember that his face was red with fury. He looked to the Council, no doubt hoping that they would speak up and overrule the Penlo, but with the exceptions of the Penlo's son-in-law, the Jungpen of Angdu Forung, and Sangay, the Jungpen of Poonakha, looking on with evil grins all over their beastly faces, all others pretended not to have heard anything at all, but remained engaged in friendly banter with their neighbours.

Eden tried again. He called upon the room to listen. Then with his voice trembling with the passion born of his vision being dashed to pieces, he briefly outlined what, by now, should have been abundantly clear: he hadn't the authority to discuss the Assam *Duars* even if he wanted to, and he was only here because he had been promised that the question would not arise. Then he went further, pointing out that the treaty had been agreed upon, and that after having relentlessly encouraged him to make haste to have it prepared on time, only to reject it at the last minute, was incomprehensible. He might as well have saved his breath, though, for the laughing and chatter continued, without anyone paying him the least attention.

No one, that is, except the Penlo. Through the services of the Cheeboo, he told Eden, "We have not agreed to the draft treaty," which was as bald-faced a lie as you were ever likely to hear. "You have chosen to come here but lack the authority to discuss all things! Better it were that you had not come here at all!" Then, leaning forward, his voice took on a threatening edge: "But now that you are here, I cannot let you leave until we have settled the only matter that interests me!"

We were saved any further harangue by an adjournment for luncheon, although why we stayed I can't imagine, except that Eden was still concerned about making an impression, as if that might still make a difference! So nothing would do but we should all traipse out to a different tent where food was being served.

It was an open-sided affair, which was unfortunate, as the locals tended to crowd in to ogle the odd-looking foreigners, and to seek any other form of entertainment that they could find. They didn't have long to wait, either, and after that things began to happen quite quickly.

There was no particular seating arrangement, although our people tended to group together, and the *Durbhar* likewise. However, this time the Tongso Penlo chose a seat across from Eden, and as the Cheeboo was close by, continued in his harangue about the Assam *Duars*, to which Eden didn't deign to reply, at which point the Penlo became incensed. Seizing a piece of wet dough from a passing platter, he rubbed it into Eden's face. Apparently this type of thing passes for humour in Bhutan, for the crowd was immensely amused. Not only that, in a bid not to be outdone, the Jungpen of Angdu Forung made a great show of removing from his mouth the food he had been chewing, and offering it to Simpson. Of course Simpson refused, whereupon the Jungpen, feigning a state of rage, threw the disgusting mess in his face. After which, spying the Cheeboo, who was sitting as inoffensively as ever, he seized the watch that was suspended around his neck by a ribbon. Tearing it free, he passed it to one of his fellows in the crowd, where it soon disappeared.

Well, I might be new to the diplomatic, and as a rule I don't like speaking out of turn, but I happened to know that the Cheeboo had received that watch as a present from the Viceroy, so it was high time that someone stood up and took a hand.

However, when I got to my feet Sangay appeared out of nowhere. I suppose he must have singled me out earlier, perhaps even days before, and had been biding his time for this moment to arrive. In his hand was a raw piece of meat, and his meaning couldn't have been clearer.

Well you don't rub raw meat into a Smithers' face and get away with it. As a matter of fact, there are precious few of us who would wait around for that moment to happen, especially when a preemptive action might be more in order.

Rearing back his arm, in his most ice-filled hiss, Sangay cried, "A present from Poonakha, Mr. Smithers!"

"Is that so?" I replied, and punched him in the nose.

Looking back on seventy years of life, there are precious few things that I'm prouder of than that punch – I doubt that the great Nick Ward could have done any better, if I do say so myself. It caught him square on the bridge, and I felt the septum crunch most satisfactorily.

Sangay gave a surprised squawk, while his eyes rolled together, as if trying to focus on where his nose should have been. Then there was a great gush of blood spurting out either side of my knuckles, and he was down like an ox.

I don't know what I expected to follow such a display, but pure silence wasn't it. I looked up, and of course, saw that all eyes were upon me, all registering varying degrees of disbelief. Even Simpson was looking as if I'd just farted in church.

Feeling self-conscious as all get out, I said, "I'm frightfully sorry everyone, my hand seems to have slipped."

Meanwhile, various servants were fluttering around Sangay with fans and smelling salts and whatnot, in an attempt to revive him, so far to no effect. Also, two of the Penlo's guardsmen must have noticed the altercation for they were making their way toward me at speed,

Thinking quickly, I offered a bow to the populace at large: "Gentlemen, I bid you good day," and plunged into the crowd. A half dozen steps further and I'd disappeared altogether.

Well, now I'd gone and done it, hadn't I? Got myself in the stew good and proper? Maybe so, but if there's one thing I can't abide it's a bully, never could, and never will. Present me with the same situation today, and you may be sure that I'll be skinning my knuckles in no time at all.

Right, what next?

Returning to camp seemed like the best plan of attack. Luckily it wasn't too far away, either, it having being decided by the *Durbhar* to conduct that day's business on the same side of the river, close by our encampment.

I daresay that I attracted quite a few stares on the journey; my clothing and features virtually guaranteeing that I'd stick out

312

like a sore thumb. But no one hailed me, or went out of their way to throw a rock, or anything else, in my direction, either, which just goes to show. Left to his own devices, your average Bhuteau would just as soon get on with his life than waste time tormenting some poor bloody foreigner. Proof, if you like, that the hostile crowds we'd been wading through up to this point were as put up an affair as ever there was, and it wasn't difficult to guess who had put them up to it, neither.

Hold on! Some twenty minutes later, just as I arrived at our camp's perimeter, I noticed soldiers of the Penlo's guard taking station, forming a perimeter of their own; but what on earth for? Not on my account, certainly, for I wasn't that big a fish, and word couldn't have been got out so quickly besides. No, this had been preplanned, as sure as little green apples, the treacherous swine! Right then and there, I resolved to make a closer inspection.

Ducking back into the crowd, I began a slow circumnavigation of the camp, noticing as the purple livery of the Tongso Penlo's people gave way to the blue and gold of Angdu Forung, and finally to the green and silver of the Jungpen of Poonakha. This did not bode at all well. It wasn't possible that word of my little dust-up with Sangay had spread so quickly, and yet here they were, as evil a bunch of villains as ever there were, looking damned efficient as they spread out, covering all our main points of entry.

I'd just reached the porters' lines when I froze, noticing that a party of Sangay's fellows had broken through our own perimeter, and by all accounts seemed to be up to no good, and in broad daylight at that.

I thought, 'Of all the bloody cheek!' and scampered across to get a closer look, cursing my luck that I'd had to leave my hardware behind to attend the *Durbhar* (and a fat load of good that had done anyone, too!)

I took up station crouching behind a tent, trying to get a peek at what the rascals were up to. I heard a groan and looking down, noticed one of our Sikhs with his *pugharee* askew, and no doubt a cracked skull beneath. The bounders!

313

Just then two things happened so close together that they might as well have been simultaneous.

Considering that a breech on our perimeter, in combination with an assault on one of HM's soldiers, a serious enough offense, I now determined that the best course of action would be to call out the guard. At the same instant I heard a shriek come from one of the tents along the coolie lines, and saw one of the Jungpen's men come staggering out, holding a hand to his face, with blood oozing through the fingers. But no sooner had he emerged than he was thrust aside and replaced by more of his fellows struggling to get in. By the number involved I knew that quite a struggle was taking place, and even as I watched the tent collapsed around them, followed seconds later by a knife slashing at the canvas from inside. And there! Just for an instant, Charula Khaur's head and shoulders rose through the opening, looking frantically about in search of aid. My heart stopped for a moment when I thought that she saw me, but then she was dragged back into the general melee inside the tent.

I surged to my feet, shouting for the guard, but before I could take a single step, there was a blinding light and a stabbing pain burrowing deep inside my skull.

Desperately I tried to call out her name, but just then, as all those penny novelists love to say, 'there was nothing but darkness'.

***

I came to in the medical tent, with Simpson holding a compress to the back of my neck, and damning me for a Nancy boy at the same instant.

"Wouldn't have done in my time," he muttered "Problem with today's lads is they can't take a little punishment! Why, if we'd had fellows like this at Waterloo we'd all be speaking *Crapaud* by now, *monseurring* everyone in sight! Nothing but Nancy boys, if you ask me!"

See? What did I tell you?

"Steady on," said Austen,"the man's just had his cranium used as a drum. A little Christian charity, if you please."

The doctor barked, "Lucky for you both my hands are occupied, or I'd show you what you could do with your bloody charity!"

And wouldn't you know, that got them both laughing so hard that, at first, they didn't hear my groans when I awoke.

Finally, "Hang on!" quoth the doctor, "Sleeping Beauty's showing some life after all!"

"How long have I been out?" was my immediate query.

Simpson barked, "Days and days, lad!"

I rounded on him. "What?" and his laughter vanished immediately.

For a wonder, knowing better than to continue with his little joke, he said, "The *sepoys* found you down at the bearers' lines, lying next to one of their own, within the minute of your calling out the guard. You were already unconscious, with a nasty great goose egg on the back of your head. Naturally they brought you both here; that might have been twenty minutes ago."

Looking over, I saw the sepoy I'd come across, still dead to the world.

"He'll be fine," Simpson informed me, but I could tell that he was on the verge of asking why I was making such a fuss. His lips had actually begun to form the word, but then I could see that he had finally begun to put two and two together. Sinking heavily upon the table, his hand still on my shoulder, he said, "Oh, dear Lord!"

I thought that Austen would need to be filled in, but when I turned to him, he was already on his feet. "I'll see what I can find out!" he cried, and disappeared through the tent flap without another word.

I looked back at the doctor, but he was studiously looking away.

"He already knew?"

"Mmm?" but rather than continue with the charade, Simpson offered an apologetic smile. "I'm afraid so, old thing. Terribly sorry, but I'm simply awful at keeping secrets – always have been."

"It's all right," I told him.

"It does make a good story, you know."

315

I reminded him, "There are more important things to think about now."

"Quite, old fellow. Quite." He gave my shoulder another reassuring pat before rising to his feet again. "You can be sure that Austen will leave no stone unturned."

While we waited for news, and Simpson nursed my cracked noggin, he was able to fill me in on what had taken place after I had left the *Durbhar* so unceremoniously.

Not much, when all was added up. "The Bhuteau really were pushing it to the limit." He broke off and swore, "If I ever get that Angdu bastard on my operating table, he'll be a sorry little Jungpen, don't you worry! Oh how I wish that I'd punched that big fat gob of his, just like you did!"

"I rather thought that I'd let the old side down again," I said. "Thought it best to make myself scarce."

Simpson winked and said, "Hardly! Those bastards changed their tune right bloody quick when you handed that red-cloaked lovely his teeth for him, didn't they just! Chee had his watch back in no time at all!"

I was glad to hear that, and said so.

"When they saw that you weren't prepared to put up with any more of their shenanigans, they realized that they'd pushed things too far, and sought to make amends." Then his face fell slightly, "Pity about the treaty, though." And then brightened considerably, "But at least Eden's finally ready to admit that there's nothing to gain by remaining here any longer. It's time for us all to go home!"

'Home' for Simpson was Calcutta, but for me the word held a far different meaning. Most times I thought about Yorkshire and Brampton Manor, of milord riding to the hunt with the other toffs, or blowing some poor blighter's backside off for him on the fells, or the simple joy of an English country garden. Aye, that was home…but every so often I still thought of a simple hut, alone under an African sky…

"Home," I said.

The doctor barked, and said, "That's right, old fellow! We'll soon be on our way!"

The prospect was tempting, but before any further discussion could be made, Austen stuck his head inside. His face grim as all get out.

"We've found her!" he said.

***

The Bhuteau cordon remained in place around our camp well into the night, attracting the usual crowd of taunters, stone throwers, and any other heroic figure that thought that the experience might be as amusing as it was lucrative. For aside from the Jungpen's coin for showing up, the riches of our baggage train also beckoned their light-fingered souls.

Given the size and strength of the cordon, it might come as a surprise to some that security was so shockingly lax, and to those people, may I suggest that they never visit Bhutan. I've seen plenty of sharps in my time, and while your average Johnny Bhuteau may lack the craftsmanship of a true Dodger, his dedication to his chosen field is not one jot less, I can assure you. So best stay away, else they'll have you fleeced before you've unpacked your valise.

And it's not that this can all be blamed on a few hopeless incorrigibles neither; it was a national bloody policy. Insofar as that cordon was concerned, you may be sure that the soldiery was in on it as much as the general population. In fact, given another twenty-four hours, I wouldn't be at all surprised if you found that the principals were one and the same, only those in civilian garb would then be in uniform, and vice versa.

The gist of what I would like you to come away with here are two-fold: first, regardless of how it might seem that the Bhuteau cordon was an official screen set up for no better reason than to harass the devil out of us, as well as have a playful go at plundering our lines, it was also part of an elaborate, well-planned operation, setup by none other than Sangay himself, to locate and capture the long-time fugitive of his desire, Charula Khaur. And second: whereas that same cordon might be suspiciously porous when it came to keeping their own folk *out* of our perimeter, it was also amazingly effective when it came to keeping *us* in.

The *havildar* twitched his head slightly to where the Poonakha *Dzong* crouched menacingly on the hill. A castle similar in size and style to the Palace at Paro; in the half-light it looked like a great stone monster, ready to pounce on any unsuspecting passerby that came within reach.

"Yonder lies the fortress," he said, being careful to keep his eyes on us, and not where he was indicating, as if we needed to be told. He had warned us earlier that he had suspected that spies were thick among the Bhuteau cordon, perhaps a few dozen yards away. "Ibrahim Khan and Mir Jafar are already hidden among the outer works." He gestured again, this time to the *sepoy* crouching beside him, "This likely lad here, Ahmad Shah, tells me that this is where they have taken the lady, entering through a postern."

The *havildar* was speaking very seriously, but he had to be a humourist of sorts, for the evil features of Ahmad Shah required a certain suspension of disbelief to regard him as '*likely looking*' in any way, shape, or form. Certainly not that a pockmarked face, or a broken nose were anything to go by; neither were the close-set eyes, or his few remaining teeth; but if Ahmad Shah could show us where they had taken Charula Khaur, he would always remain the likeliest of fellows I'd ever known.

The onset of the evening was promising to be eventful. The crowd (or mob-in-waiting, whichever you choose) had been growing steadily, and the 'innocent' incursions by the 'curious' locals on our camp had been increasing steadily, making the task of the few dozen remaining *jawans* more difficult than ever. Even dragooning the porters into service would be of little help were the Bhuteau to turn ugly. With the exception of a *naik* and half a dozen of his fellows set to guard the horses and supplies, the rest of the Sikhs were positioned along the perimeter, intermingled with the bearers, keeping a close eye on things, while preparing to do their utmost. Lance had ordered them to fix bayonets as a deterrent, but that their rifles should remain empty to avoid any possibility of an accidental discharge. In the purveying mood, with the Bhuteau scowling on one side, and our own fellows

318

tense and grimly determined on the other, a single shot might be all that was needed to bring the cauldron to a boil.

Our bid to rescue Charula Khaur would certainly not make the young captain's life any easier, but he'd insisted we try.

"Our esteemed Mr. Eden is too preoccupied with salvaging his reputation from this shambles to give any thought to what we're up to, so you might as well have a little fun. Besides, after all this nursemaid duty, some honest soldiering will be good for these lads." Then he seemed to contradict himself, insofar as the 'honest' part was concerned. "This line of work would be nuts to most of 'em. Throat-slitters and cutpurse *badmashes*, the best that the Amritsar slums has to offer. Gad! I wish I was going with you!"

In fact, the mission had started on the *jawans'* own volition. Apparently it had been these three men who had found me unconscious, and while others saw to my being taken to Simpson, without waiting for orders, they had commandeered bearers' *poshteens*, and thus disguised, had mingled through the crowd, and set off after the villains who had abducted Charula before they could disappear from sight.

It hadn't been easy in the failing light, through all the twists and turns of the town, the streets gradually rising, but apparently Mir Jafar had been a hillman from Oudh, and what he didn't know about rough tracking in the dark wasn't worth learning. So the trio had been able to arrive at the outskirts of the castle, and watch as the soldiers, dressed in the Jungpen's livery, had disappeared inside with their captive, just as described. Whereupon it was immediately decided that Ahmad Shah should return to camp for reinforcements while the other two kept watch.

Once more I spared a glance at this likely looking fellow. Ahmad Shah's eyes met mine for an instant before sliding away in the direction of the *Dzong*, and there they remained while he stood there with his fellows, grinning with excitement. Earlier I had asked Lance why they had bothered (the woman was nothing to them, after all) and I remembered his reply:

"Aye, they're a curious lot," he'd allowed, regarding his men with a look of amused and exasperated pride, along with a dollop of affection. "Muslims are usually from the tribes along the frontier, where murder and larceny are regarded as just a bit of exercise before breakfast, don't you know. The Hindu are high caste to a man, and could've taught Galahad a thing or two about pride and honour, if they'd ever lower themselves to the task that is, but the Sikh," and here his eyes had wrinkled with a certain kind of warmth I'd only known to be possessed by the finest officers, "the Sikh was learning about soldiering when the other two were still learning their letters, and they're damned good at it, too. My God, they gave us all that we could handle at Chillianwala, and Feresoshah, and a dozen other places I could mention. With the possible exception of the Gurkhas, you won't find a more martial people on the face of the earth." Here he'd looked at me with grave amusement, "And you want to know why? Because it's *fun*, Charlie! Or it's the decent thing to do! Or because they've had a bellyful of those people yonder, and they want to teach them some manners." Then he looked away, smirking beneath his moustache. "Whatever the reason, I'm certain it's most definitely *not* because they'd been noticing a smashing girl making her way through the coolie lines every night for the past three weeks, always over to Smithers sahib's tent, they said it was. Poor devils, and them being curious as kittens, too." Then he'd harrumphed awkwardly (possibly shocked at his own risqué sense of humour) and swatted at an imaginary fly... and missed, apparently. Then, with my ears burning red, he said, "Now be off with you, and leave me to my work!"

That was perhaps thirty minutes earlier, and in the interim a strategy had been hastily formed, ingenious in it's simplicity: Austen and I, and the three *jawans* would evade the cordon, and assault the castle without delay. A lucky break here and there, and it should all be sewn up by breakfast.

Austen said, "Right, Siraj Singh, what's next?"

The *havildar*, whose rank was the equivalent to a sergeant, might have stood on his dignity, and respectfully mentioned that it was an officer's job to formulate a plan, and a sergeant's to carry it out, but he was a grizzled old veteran who, by the look of him, had seen more action than Napier and Wolseley combined, and accepted the challenge as nothing more than his due.

"First you must don the poshteens that my brethren have brought for you, sahib, so that by the grace of Krishna and the setting sun, they will hide your weapons, and you will not be so easily noticed as *feringhees*."

We looked over to where some other *jawans* were holding the sheepskin coats away from sight of the cordon. We ambled over as casually as possible and slipped them on, hoping that no one had noticed.

Siraj Singh gave a terse nod. "Now, see yon gaggle of pox-ridden *badmashes* behind me, the ones filling their pockets with Eden sahib's tableware? Good! Soon they will have a surfeit of their ill-gotten plunder, and will want to return to their own kind, where doubtless they will live like princes on the lavish profits of their cunning…provided that they live to see morning."

That took me aback, let me tell you. The *havildar's* tone never suggested that he might be joking, not even a little, but before it could register completely, I had to listen pretty sharp as he continued. "Go you now, sahibs, and linger near them, and always remember to keep your faces well hidden. Here!" He bent down and, scooping up a quantity of mud in either hand, smeared it liberally in both our faces, as inconspicuously as possible. Satisfied, he continued as calmly as ever, "Make believe that you are likewise searching for loot. When they make to go across, follow close behind, pretending that you are of their number." Possibly just for devilment he added, "Pretend well, sahibs, and you *may* live to tell your grandchildren the tale!" and with that school was out.

With our collars turned well up, Austen and I casually sauntered over to where a trio of enterprising fellows were busying themselves eluding our over-stretched *jawans*, and ignoring the protests of our unarmed coolies, while they meddled their way through our inventory.

I kicked an interrogatory toe against a sack, and made a great show of peering inside, as if I were a looter trying to ascertain the value of the contents. Perhaps predictably, I discovered that it was rice.

It was at that moment that the executive members of the Greater Bhutan Five-Finger Discount Corporation (Poonakha division) made their move, across the few yards of empty ground to their own folk on the other side, their pockets jingling and jangling with booty, and them none too concerned about anyone who might notice, either.

Suddenly inspiration took hold of me. I said to Austen, "Follow my lead," and seizing one of the sacks of rice, took it up and set off after Bhutan's answer to the Merry Men, carrying it clasped in both arms in front of me, thus effectively concealing my face.

From close beside me, Austen hissed in an irritated whisper, "Christ, these things are heavy!"

"Eighty pounds," I whispered back.

"How do you know?"

"That's what's stenciled on the side of the bag." Then to cover what would have to have been an embarrassed silence, I said, "Now be quiet, yonder lie the enemy!" or something equally absurd.

We passed through the guardsmen without molestation, but before I could feel any relief about it, I felt a tug on my sleeve and someone was speaking to me in Bhuteau. By the interrogative tone of his voice, I gathered that he was either asking me, *'Just what the devil do you think you're up to, feringhee pig?'* or *'Good sir, might I enquire as to how much you're asking for yon bag of rice?'* Hoping beyond hope that his meaning was the latter, I said nothing, but replied by simply dropping the sack on the ground and walking away, Austen doing likewise.

It worked rather well. Seeing our booty so abandoned, the local merchants society descended upon it like so many vultures, to the point where we were jostled aside in their frantic efforts to claim salvage rights. But before I could rejoice overmuch, there came another tug on my sleeve, and my hand slid beneath my poshteen to the Tranter.

"Shabash, Huzoor! Shabash!"

I allowed myself a surreptitious peek, and saw that it was only Ahmad Shah, grinning wickedly, and congratulating me on my clever deception. Such folk took bravery with a grain of salt, for it was something that they possessed in abundance themselves, and assumed that it was possessed equally by

322

everyone else; whereas a bit of clever skullduggery was something they could respect. Perhaps, in its way, it was the greatest compliment I've ever received.

No more words were wasted before Ahmad Shah took matters in hand, and led Austen and myself through a labyrinth of the city's unlit streets, all but deserted at this hour. Darkness was descending fast, and once or twice we came to a dead end. Whereupon, with Ahmad Shah cursing under his breath most foully (I *think*, as I hadn't a word of Punjabi, and he no English), we were forced to retrace our steps to where he could find his bearings again. Once we crossed a wooden bridge, and Austen confidently whispered that this must be the Pho Chu River, until we crossed another bridge a little further on, and he claimed that *this* was the Pho Chu, and wondered if the last one hadn't been the Mo Chu after all.

It might have been the Tiber for all I knew, but I kept that to myself, when we rounded a corner and saw the castle a short distance away, surrounded on two sides by low-lying hills lurking in the background, and by the aforementioned rivers on either side. Other than that, I might have been able to tell you which way was up, and which way down, but that was about all. Of north, east, south, or west I'd nary a clue.

However it was fortunate that our little party wasn't depending upon my navigating skills as Ahmad Shah was not similarly hampered, but led us unerringly toward a deeper shadow of irregular shape that turned out to be a pile of rocks. A soft whistle brought us up short, and Ibrahim Khan stepped out of nowhere.

He whispered, "This way, Huzoors." We followed him up a winding path, stepping carefully so as not to twist an ankle. Thankfully, we hadn't gone far when a warning 'hsssst!' stopped us in our tracks. By now my eyes had adjusted to the light, and I could just make out Mir Jafar crouching behind a boulder. Another step and I would have trod upon him.

Here all five of us hunkered down, and I wondered what was to follow. Ibrahim Khan spoke a little English, but Austen's Punjabi was better, and the conversation was crisp amongst them, with much pointing and gesturing besides, not a word of which I could understand.

Being the odd man out, I took the opportunity to study the lay of the land. The castle lurked as nefarious as ever, less than fifty yards from where we lay. The main gateway was battened down for the night, and what looked like a massive wooden stairway had been raised like a drawbridge for good measure. Any plan that involved walking up and knocking on the front door was clearly out of court.

Nothing more was to be done until Austen was finished gathering whatever intelligence was available, so I took out the Tranter, making sure that there was a round in every cylinder before holstering it again. Thirty seconds later I repeated the procedure, telling myself that I mustn't fret.

At last Austen was finished, and saw fit to fill me in.

Indicating the castle, he said, "They tell me that they saw them take her in there. He pointed at what looked to me like a solid wall of stone."

"Right," I said.

"There were half a dozen of the swine. Almost certainly more inside."

"Almost certainly," I agreed. "What's the plan?"

"No idea, old fellow. Neither do the lads," he replied, then suggested, "I was rather hoping that you might have something in mind."

Well I hadn't the foggiest, but before I could tell him as much, there came the squeal of rusty hinges, and a rectangle of light suddenly appeared at the base of the wall as a small postern opened in the general vicinity of where Austen had just indicated. We all looked on as one of the Jungpen's men stepped out of the opening, and began to fumble with the fastenings of his robe.

I said, "That's it," and rose to my feet, considering the Tranter, but drawing my sabre instead.

"Right then, follow me."

324

Chapter Twenty

I was off like a shot, running pell-mell for the castle, without any thought for life or limb, only of the guard as he stood with his back to me, relieving himself against the fortress wall.

So far I was in luck: the ground was even, without any obstacles to send me toppling head over heels, yet soft enough to absorb the sound of my drumming boots, allowing me to close undetected.

Only when I was very close did something – some sound, or vibration – cause him to start and turn. Savagely, I swung the sabre, only at the last instant twisting my wrist so that the flat of the blade connected against the side of his skull. I felt the shock of the blow go up my arm, and heard a sound much like an axe on wood. He sank to the ground with nothing more than what might have been mistaken for a contented sigh.

Turning, I saw that the others were hard on my heels. An urge to rejoice at this unexpected stroke of luck was immediately quelled. Instead, I indicated the unconscious fellow with the point of my sabre, and all I said was, "Bind him!" Then turning quickly, I led the way into the bowels of the castle.

***

The postern opened onto a small room, in the centre of which was a rough-hewn wooden table. On the centre of the table was a crude oil lantern, its chimney grimed black with soot. It's pale light illuminated perhaps a half-dozen chairs of a style similar to the table they surrounded. A guardroom, as one might expect. So far our luck was holding, for it was empty. The man lying outside, bound and unconscious, had been the only one on duty.

On the wall opposite was another door. I crossed the room and inched it open a crack, gritting my teeth to its raucous complaining. I put an eye to the opening, and saw a corridor running past, either end disappearing into darkness. On the far side, a few feet over from ours, was yet another door, this one of stout wooden planks. Beneath its sill was a faint glimmer of light.

325

I could feel the close presence of my comrades gathered behind me, hear the excitement in their breathing, and smell it on their sweat. There was a soft *'tink'* as one of their sabre points came to rest on the stone flags of the floor. Like my Tranter, their sidearms would remain holstered, for this was a night for cold steel.

In one swift motion I swung the door fully open, ignoring the protesting screech of its hinges, and was out in the corridor with my back against the opposite wall, next to this new door, and a warning finger to my lips, pointing to the light flickering below.

Austen stepped forward, holding the lamp from the guardroom high above our heads. Ibrahim Khan and Mir Jafar kept watch on either end of the corridor while I tried the latch. It wouldn't budge.

I motioned for Austen to bring the lamp closer while I bent to examine the lock: a simple iron box containing the mechanism was bolted to the door. A stout metal latch slipped into a wrought iron sleeve, similarly bolted to the jamb.

I wondered what could be done, but could find no answer. I looked at Austen, but his shrug mirrored my own thoughts. In desperation, I thought to insert the point of my sabre between the lock and the jamb, and try to force it, hoping against hope that the bolts might give, even as I knew that the sound might alert whoever was waiting on the other side. Still, something must be done, so I made to try, only to be stopped at the last instant by a hand upon my arm.

I looked over to see Ahmad Shah grinning at me like a satyr…which is a sight that one should always avoid, but doubly so when the only illumination is the ghostly light of a lantern.

It took an effort, but in time I was able to overcome the fright he'd given me to pay attention. Unbuckling his kit belt, he removed what looked like a length of piano wire from a small slit cut into the leather. It was approximately four inches in length, and was twisted into a figure like so: ∫. I should have recognized the device immediately, but owing to the poor light, and peculiarity of our surroundings, it took a moment longer.

In years past, there had been a burglary at Brampton Manor, and various items of silverware had been stolen, some of great value. The local constable had been called in but, unfortunately, had been unable to come up with any clues, other than that the person (or persons) responsible must have possessed a key, as the Silver Room (as we called it) was always locked, and yet the lock had not been tampered with. Naturally the housekeeper, Mrs. Kilns (the only person outside of the Bramptons themselves, who possessed such a key) defied suspicion, as she had been in service for over thirty years, and ran the household in a manner which my old drill sergeant from the 17th might have admired. All remained a mystery until one day old Tomkins spoke of seeing one of the new footman, by the name of Bates, with such a device as I've just described, secreted on his person, and much conjecture had been made as to its purpose. The police constable, familiar with the darker ways of the world, including said device, and how it might be applied, found this to be very suspicious indeed but, unfortunately, could prove nothing. He did, however, include his suspicions in his report to the old earl, who was not overly concerned with the niceties of jurisprudence. The long and the short of it was that Bates was summarily dismissed from service, and if the rumours are true, awoke from a thorough beating (from assailants unknown), with nothing but the clothes on his back, in the hold of a steamer, outward bound for Shanghai.

I stepped aside to allow Ahmad Shah access to the lock. He stepped forward, gesturing for Austen to hold the lantern just so. Whereupon he inserted the device into the rectangular opening. Seconds later, a soft 'click' heralded the bolt sliding back into the cylinder.

The task completed, Ahmad Shah arose with the air of a man who knows the satisfaction of a job well done. Then he grinned and elaborately salaamed, offering me back the lead.

Obviously this door had received some recent attention, for it swung smoothly inward with nary a sound, revealing a stone-flagged landing, and circular stairs spiralling down into the depths below, illuminated, here and there, by lanterns set into sconces along the wall.

Listening carefully, I thought that I could hear voices, but they were too distant to provide any clarity. Asking Austen to station a guard, I hefted the reassuring weight of the sabre, and took one cautious step, and then another, gradually making my way downward, with the remainder of my companions huddled close behind.

Down, down, we went, the temperature growing cooler with every degree of descent. Green encrustations coated the stones on the walls from long years of exposure, and moisture oozed through the crumbling mortar; and still we descended.

After some time had passed, I fancied that the voices grew clearer, but spoke in Bhuteau, leaving me none the wiser. Moments later, we reached the bottom, opening onto an expansive, low-vaulted room, supported by an intricate arrangement of arches.

By now I was able to distinguish the voices as belonging to two men, and as I peered around the butt of the wall where the stairwell ended, I could see them sitting mere yards away, across from one another at a table. They were armed with swords, along with an ancient blunderbuss, generously coated with rust. They seemed bored, as a jailer's lot usually is, and were whiling away the hours with conversation as they waited for their relief. At the far end of the room I noticed a steel reinforced door, with a chain passing through both latch and frame, bound with a simple padlock. On the table, next to the blunderbuss, was a ring of keys.

I turned back to my comrades and, using hand signals, explained the situation and how I intended to proceed. It occurred to me while doing so that they never questioned my authority, not even Austen. During my time in the ranks, I had attained the giddy height of corporal, someone who would have been far beneath his notice, and now, as a gentleman's gentleman, the social separation was scarcely any more equal. Possibly it was a case of my being (presumably) one of Elgin's vaunted 'Specials' that caused his regard, but I rather think it had something to do with the companionship that had grown during the course of our journey. A gentleman he might be, and I nothing but a servant, but I was not *his* servant, nor he my gentleman, and therein was the difference. Out here the foothills of the Himalayas were the great equalizer, where rank was perceived, not by social status, but by ability. That these people believed that I possessed that ability filled me with determination not to disappoint them.

All this I have been able to formulate into words thirty years after the event. At the time, however, it was nothing more than a series of vague emotions in the back of my mind, and was subsequently set aside, as there was still much work to be done. It must be said that Charula Khaur's safety was very much at the forefront of my thoughts. Therefore, with my companions nodding eagerly at the end of my briefing, at the count of three we sprang.

In a trice my sabre was at the throat of one jailer, and Ibrahim's was at the other's. Ignoring their blank, astonished stares, while Ahmad bound their arms with their own belts, I tossed the key ring to Austen. He grabbed it with a deft fielder's hand, and made his way over to the door. Soon the padlock sprang open, and pulling the latch from the chain, he swung it ajar, disappearing inside.

It was strange perhaps, but I felt a twinge of jealousy: that was a moment that should have been mine. Impatiently, I shook it away, and cursed myself for a fool. Let Austen's be the first face that she sees. She would be safe, after all. What could possibly count greater than that?

And then there she was, exiting her cell, leaning heavily against the captain, his arm wrapped protectively around her shoulders.

With her erstwhile jailers safely bound, I sheathed my sabre and rushed over to greet her.

"Charula!"

She gave a cry and tried to run to greet me, but was only able to stumble into my arms.

Alarmed, I asked, "Are you hurt? What have they done to you?"

Bitterly she said. "What men like Lord Sangay always do when their property is stolen, *Bahadur* – they punish the thief."

329

I heard Austen gasp, and looking up from Charula's lovely face, I saw that he was staring at her back. It was only then that I realized that she was still wearing her coolie garb, but underneath a sheet of coarse linen. I looked and saw that it was seeping blood.

Bound as he was, I savagely kicked one of her jailers from his stool, and gently eased her onto it in his stead.

Austen ordered Ibrahim and Ahmad to the top of the stairs should Mir Jafar need assistance. He made to follow them, but stopped short when I removed the sheet.

"I say!"

The back of her coolie blouse had been torn from neck to waist, revealing the livid welts and angry bruises cutting across the smooth coffee colour of her skin.

"He meant to tame me," she said, wincing at my touch. "Those were his words."

"The bounder!" Austen cried, which were strong words for him. I knew several more, but dared not indulge myself with fury. At the moment it was a luxury we couldn't afford.

Austen was the first to gather his wits. "We must be gone!"

Gently I asked her, "Can you walk?"

She nodded, but like one woefully tired. "I believe so, if you will help me."

I wanted nothing more, but although Austen was tall and had the longer reach, I knew that I was the stronger swordsman, and might be needed as such should we run into trouble. I looked at him and said, "Take her."

He blinked at me like the village idiot, so I snapped, "Come on, man! There's not a moment to lose!"

That jolted him, right enough, and he stepped forward while I helped her to rise. She leaned into him, too weak to argue, and, drawing my sabre, I led the way up the stairs.

Our progress was slow, as she found the climb fatiguing. I tried to offer my assistance, but the steps were only wide enough for two. So I tarried as long as I was able, feeling useless in every way, until finally I told them, "Right, come along as best you can. I'll see what's happening up top." With that I charged up the steps, taking two at a time, but still only halfway along when I

330

was brought up short by a sound coming from above: the clash of steel, and I knew that our luck had run out.

***

I heard Ibrahim shout down the stair, "*Huzoor*! Come quickly!" and I was galvanized into action, taking the stairs in leaps and bounds. When my head popped out at the ground floor, there was time for a quick glimpse before I was ducking back down, lively as I could, to prevent my head being taken off at the shoulders. There was a 'swish' as the sword cut the air above me, and then I was up again, this time ready. I was able to catch the next cut on my guard, then parried, giving him the point to the groin.

Leaping up the remaining steps, I seized an instant to take stock. Our fellows were being hard-pressed at the doorway, but for the moment were holding their own. It might have been quite a different story if I'd arrived a few seconds later.

The fellow I'd tangled with was rolling on the ground, loudly bemoaning the loss of his courting tackle. Evidently he'd been able to slip past the *jawans*, and was about to take them in flank, the very moment that I had come along, so he decided to take a swipe at me, instead.

All I could hear was the clash of steel, and the shouts of men coming to grips. Already two of the Jungpen's guardsmen were on the ground, but more were struggling forward to take their place. Mir Jafar was sporting an ugly cut to his temple, and was looking pale, but was still shouting defiance. Ibrahim's *pugharee* had come adrift from an errant cut, but seemed none the worse for wear while, by the sound of it, Ahmad Shah was begging the guardsmen to come on and get their cocoa.

It appeared to be a standoff. The narrow doorway was acting in our defense, allowing only as many of Sangay's men as could be faced by our own at any one time. Even though a fresh replacement stepped in when one went down, they weren't trained by the best in the business, as were our lads.

That was the good news. The other side of the coin was that there were a score or more of the Jungpen's guardsmen

331

standing in the way of our freedom, with more coming on every minute. We were trapped in this one small room without any hope of reinforcement. If we were ever going to get out of here, we would have to fight our way out on our own, and damn soon, too.

Frantic, I went to the stairwell for a peek. Austen was all but carrying Charula with still a few steps to go. I was able to reach down and take hold of her by the underarms, and lift her bodily to the floor. She was only a wisp of a thing, after all.

She moaned just as her legs gave out, but I was able to loop an arm around her waist until Austen caught up. It was painful to see her this way, I don't mind telling you, but for now she would have to hold on as well as she was able. If we were ever to find a way out of here, there would be time for the best of care. Until then, however, it was every man to the pumps; and with that in mind, I forced my attention back to the battle.

Another guardsmen had gone down, and was making a great row of it while being dragged to the rear by his fellows to make room for his replacement. Then Ibrahim lunged, catching his opponent in the shoulder, and the business was repeated.

"Right," I said, drawing the Tranter, "let's see about clearing a path, shall we?"

I walked to the doorway, elbowing my way between Ibrahim and Mir Jafar, leveling the pistol point blank at the nearest Bhuteau face. The poor fellow's eyes widened into tea saucers, and he had the good sense to step back a pace or two. I quickly fanned the Tranter back and forth, first one way, and then the other, and was gratified to see the rest of them take similar heed.

I said to my companions, "Draw your firearms, gentlemen, we've found some work for them, after all." Then I added, just in case any of them had it in mind to start blazing away indiscriminately, "Wait for my command."

Ibrahim interpreted my order to his mates while I risked a look back to see how Austen was doing. Charula looked tired, but was standing mostly on her own. Austen still had one arm around her waist while the other held his Colt.

"Ready?"

He gave me a nod, while Charula, brave lass, managed a smile ever so wan. It was as good as it was going to get.

"Stay abreast", I told them, and this time it was Austen who took on the role of translator. "On my mark, forward!"

Slowly, we stepped out into the corridor with my Tranter, and the *jawans'* horse pistols leveled and ready, hammers at full cock. Without any firearms of their own, the guardsmen were forced to back away, some snarling their defiance, others wide-eyed with fear. It made little difference to me as long as they continued to give ground.

One step. Then two, and then a full half-dozen. We continued to force them back until we had reached the guardroom door. I called out to Austen, "Have one of your men check inside."

Austen snapped a command, and Mir Jafar stumbled to the door. I noted that he was getting weak, and knew that it was only a matter of time before he was out of the fight. He stuck his head inside, and called out something in his lingo.

"It's clear," Austen said.

I nodded Mir Jafar into the room, and called again to Austen, "Now you follow," and felt him brush past me as he helped Charula along.

"Right then, easy does it, lads. Back through the door one at a time, and whatever you do, don't let your guard down."

Ibrahim went first, followed closely by Ahmad. We were close now; once through the door, we could barricade it from the inside, and make good our escape while they whiled away a pleasant evening battering it to pieces.

Naturally, hard on that thought, everything promptly went to hell.

***

I heard the *'twang'* of the bowstring, and immediately felt a sharp pain on my forehead at virtually the same instant, followed by the sound of the arrow careening off the walls as it sped down the corridor. The next thing I knew I was down on the floor, feeling drowsy as all get out, and thinking, 'Damned if that infernal missile didn't strike the same bloody spot where milord's bullet grazed me when all this started!'

Then there was this rather loud chap, with an oddly familiar voice, bringing me back to the present.

Wondering, I looked up to see that Sangay had elbowed his way to the front of the crowd. His nose was grotesquely swollen into a misshapen lump, pushed over to one side of his face, from that earlier acquaintance with my fist. He was exhorting his fellows to get on with it and finish me off. Strange that. He wouldn't have spoken in English, but that's how I remember hearing it. "Now finish him!" he cried, I'm almost certain.

Whatever the case, his men didn't seem to have any difficulty understanding him, for they all lunged toward me at once, like a pack of starving hounds closing for the kill.

It was more my instinct for self-preservation than anything that caused me to react. By the grace of God I could still feel the weight of the Tranter in my hand, and then I was swinging it up and thumbing back the hammer as if my arm wasn't my own, but an extension of my will.

The first man was quite close, screaming like a banshee, with his sword raised high over his head, ready to complete what that unseen archer had started. I felt the Tranter buck in my hand, and he fell away with a shrill scream. After that, all I could see was a solid mass of humanity surging toward me, and the Tranter was bucking again and again for all it was worth, the reports incredibly loud within the close confines of the corridor.

Men went down, but were instantly swallowed by the surge of their comrades as they raced one another to be first in for the kill. I knew I was a goner, but a Smithers doesn't go down without a fight, and I was determined to give them one they'd never forget. I squeezed off one last round, and then heard the hammer fall on an empty cylinder. Imminent death is a wonderful stimulant, and I suddenly found myself roaring defiance and damning them to hell, when the air above my head was suddenly filled with the most frightful din as the *jawans'* heavy pistols came into play, and for that scant window of time, men were falling faster than they could be replaced.

My ears were ringing from the din, and the corridor was filled with the stench of spent powder and blood. I was still shouting at the top of my voice, damning the lot of them, when I felt a hand fist into my collar, and I was being dragged across the threshold into the guardroom.

I heard Charula cry, "*Bahadur!*" but it was Austen's face I saw, looking concerned while he cast a critical eye over the gash on my forehead. Then it was, "Right, up you get!" and he was hauling me to my feet, declaring that I was fresh as a daisy, and sounding too damn much like Simpson for comfort.

Meanwhile, the fighting in the corridor had taken a new turn. Seeing me safe inside, the *jawans* were attempting to slam the door shut in the face of the howling guardsmen, but they weren't having it all their way. They had managed to swing the door shut, but were unable to latch it, and as the pressure outside continued to grow, they were slowly beginning to be pushed back.

My surge of adrenaline had not left; indeed it increased as my mind continued to clarify. I shouted to Austen, "Leave me, you fool! Go help with the door!" He had the good sense to do as he was told, and I was left to fumble fresh rounds into the Tranter.

At first Austen's assistance proved wonderfully effective. He leapt to the narrow opening, inserted his Colt, and squeezed off a few rounds, relieving the pressure for a critical second, and then leapt back again as the *jawans* slammed the door shut.

I seized the heavy wooden table with the intention of heaving it forward as a barricade, but was only halfway there when I heard Sangay cry out on the other side, answered by a bevy of his fellows, and they all rushed forward again, striking the door in unison, like a human battering ram.

The *jawans* were flung aside and the door flew open until it struck the edge of the table, leaving an opening wide enough for our assailants to squeeze through, one man at a time. Austen's Colt accounted for the first one, and the second, and the third before he was empty. In a fury, he flung the heavy weapon into the face of the fourth before drawing his sabre and lunging, spitting his man before he could recover. Whether by misfortune,

335

or by the pressure of the others coming behind, this man fell forward with the blade stuck firmly between his ribs, dragging Austen's arm down with him. With others pressing into the room every second, and no time to do otherwise, he was forced to release his weapon and retreat empty-handed.

The situation was as grim as you ever saw. The door was ajar, with the Bhuteau flooding in every second, and Austen standing defiant, but unarmed. From where I was, straining away, trying to maintain pressure on the table, I was unable to lend assistance. The *jawans* were in an even worse position, being tossed to the corner by that initial great onslaught; they would have to struggle around me first before they would be able to lend a hand. Under the circumstances, when every second counted against us, and the odds for the foe grew ever larger, it would not be enough.

I cried, "Austen!"

His eyes darted over. I slid the Tranter across the table toward him. There wasn't time to register surprise, but he seized it unerringly. Our eyes met for the briefest of seconds, and I motioned with my head, toward where Charula half-stood, half-leaned against the wall. "Save the girl."

That was all that time allowed before Austen was blazing away again. By now a full dozen of the guardsmen had been able to bunch themselves inside, with more crowding in every instant.

Our only saving grace was that the table, partially jamming the door, also bisected the room, keeping them penned in on the right, unable to spread out, and the pressure from behind, coupled by Austen's presence to their front, only served to pack them in tighter than ever, until they were unable to use their sword arms. It couldn't last, of course. Sooner or later it would occur to them to jump the table, or to heave it aside. I had given my sidearm to Austen, whereas my sabre had come adrift somewhere out in the corridor. The table was all that stood between me and certain death.

All this, from the time the Bhuteau had burst in 'til now, had taken a very few seconds. The next few might well finish the business.

By now Ibrahim and Ahmad had been able to regain their feet and take stock. They saw me struggling alone, and came running to lend a hand. Still in the corner, Mir Jafar had been able to rise to his knees but no further, as his wound continued to leech his strength.

Meanwhile Austen continued to blaze away as he slowly retreated, step by step, back toward Charula and the open postern.

The two *jawans* acted in perfect concert, as if they had planned it. As one they leapt to my edge of the table, and hit it full tilt, like two bulls at a gate. Ahmad was slight, and his contribution negligible, but Ibrahim stood a full six feet with a barrel chest to match, and the table jolted against the door, slamming it into the next man struggling to gain entrance, knocking him unconscious, and squeezing his body firmly in place against the jamb, thus denying entrance to those rushing in behind.

Precious little time was wasted wedging chairs against the table to hold it in place, then it was out with their sabres, and seizing the initiative, they leapt to the table's surface to close with our foes.

On the Bhuteau side, I could just make out over the heads of his men, that one of the last to struggle through had been Sangay himself; but instead of taking command of a victorious field, which he no doubt expected, he found himself ignored, and jammed against the wall, his shouts of command lost in the general din.

At first the *jawans'* work could be described as no better than a slaughter; as crammed together as they were, their opponents could only answer back feebly as the Sikhs' blades began to tell. Using the point efficiently, the tally began to mount with every lunge. Soon the air was filled with the screams of their victims, as their blood began to flow freely upon the floor.

It couldn't last, though, for the simple (yet horrible) reason that after so many of their comrades had fallen, the surviving Bhuteau gradually found that they could enjoy the free use of their limbs, and were able to bring their own swords to bear.

337

Gradually they began driving their tiring opponents back across the room.

In the interim, I had not been idle. With my head throbbing like be-damned, I made my way over to where Mir Jafar was still struggling on his knees, weakened from loss of blood. With some effort, I was able to assist him to his feet, and snatching up his sabre, we made our way back to the postern, with his arm draped across my neck, and one or both of us stumbling with every step along the way.

At last we were able to make our way over to where Charula crouched, still leaning against the wall, pale and shaken by the carnage. I took her arm and, with some words of encouragement, was able to guide her through the postern to the comparative peace of the night air. Then I speedily returned to the fray with Mir Jafar's sabre in hand, just in time to meet everyone coming the other way.

We had succeeded in getting this far, but the situation was dire once again. Opposed to an even dozen guardsmen still showing fight (and I had to hand it to them, even after the frightful casualties they'd taken, they remained undaunted, and were determined to see the end of us) one of our men was down, and another (myself) was feeling decidedly off. The two *jawans* were still game, but their pistols were empty. Austen still had my Tranter, but how many rounds were left? Just then, with a tremendous shout, one of the guardsmen rushed forward, with his sword grasped in both hands over his head like an axe, and my question was answered.

Calmly, Austen levelled the pistol and pulled the trigger, but once again the hammer fell on an empty cylinder, leaving him helpless in the face of certain death. Without a moment to lose, I thrust him aside in the nick of time, taking the blow on my blade. But it was delivered with such tremendous force, and weakened as I already was, it drove me to my knees, the shock numbing my arm to the shoulder, and came within a hair of delivering a frightful gash across my face. More by good fortune than good swordsmanship, the guardsman's sword slid off my sabre, passing harmlessly to the side. I struck out in blind desperation, and managed a telling cut across his thigh. His awful cry turned

338

into a scream of pain as he dropped his sabre and tumbled on top of me, forcing me to the ground. Both his hands grasped for my throat, but in desperation, I smashed my hilt into his face, and he fell away senseless.

Now, seeing that our last pistol was empty, and only the two *jawans* effectively guarding the postern, Sangay exhorted his followers onward once more, and with a great shout, they charged, bursting through by sheer force of numbers.

Ibrahim and Ahmad gave ground grudgingly, frantically slashing, left and right. I tried to regain my feet but was bowled over like a tenpin in the rush, and saw Austen go down, grappling with a guardsman, but was up again in less time than you could think it, having wrenched the fellow's sword from his grasp, and was now using it to good effect.

Dazed as I was, I knew that I had to regain my own feet, or the world would soon be one Smithers poorer. It seemed a Herculean task, as my battered and dazed mind kept insisting that I go to sleep, instead; but when I'd made it to my knees and saw Sangay towering over me like a scarlet-clad nemesis, I found the sight wonderfully reviving, and was able to hold him off with the point just long enough to get my legs under me.

Warily we circled, weapons poised, each searching for an opening – Sangay nimble on the balls of his feet, and myself trying my best not to stagger. With his eyes mere slits on that wicked face, the Jungpen growled pure menace. "We meet again, Charlie Smithers!" Then he sniggered an evil laugh, "But this time, I think, will be the last!" So saying he feinted a lunge at my kidneys.

I swung my sabre in a clumsy effort to parry. He was as fast as I remembered, and before I knew it, he darted his point toward my eyes. I was able to knock it aside at the very last instant, but not before he nicked me high on the cheek.

Again he laughed, although his eyes remained cold and hard as stone. "Luck was with you that time, Englishman! It will not be so again!" and he leapt forward, aiming a vicious cut at my head.

I had to give ground, for I could not match his speed. What with the earlier knock on my head back at our camp, followed by the arrow grazing my skull, not to mention being trampled into a bloody pulp, it had already been a trying day. I couldn't hope to best him at swordplay, but fighting wasn't always about speed and dexterity.

He came in high again, hoping to wear me down. I timed it to a nicety, and for a wonder didn't stumble from fatigue, but caught his blade on my guard at the very instant that I launched into him. Sangay may have been the faster of the two of us, but I was the stronger, and I'd taken him by surprise. Then, with our faces mere inches apart, and our crossed blades filling even that meagre space, I raised my foot, and brought it crashing down again, stomping on his toes for all I was worth.

I heard something snap, and he leapt away, howling with pain, almost stumbling when he attempted to put weight on his injured foot. He spat venomous hatred, while his face contorted with pain.

And then the pain gradually transformed into fear.

Murderous bastard, and abuser of women though he might be, he wasn't a fool, and knew that he had reason to be afraid.

Grimly I closed, slashing left and right, pressing him when he hobbled back. He parried as well as he could, but both feet are required for swordplay. His movements were as clumsy as my own had been seconds earlier, and I caught him a fair cut on his sword arm, beneath the shoulder. I swung again and he managed to parry, but made the fatal error of trying to riposte. Out of pure reflex, I slapped his blade aside and ran him through.

He clung to me for a long moment, those dark, merciless eyes now ogling disbelief. Then with blood welling out of the corner of his mouth, his eyes glazed over at last. I stepped aside, allowing his body to tumble to the ground.

However, there was no time to exult. We were still heavily outnumbered, and as I swung around, searching for a new foe, I was able to take stock at a glance.

Austen knelt on the ground beside Charula, with blood trickling down his cheek from a gash along his temple. One arm was wrapped protectively around her shoulders, and the other defiantly presented the point of his sword to the enemy. On the ground behind them, Mir Jafar lay very still.

340

Nearing the end of their strength, Ibrahim and Ahmad, each bleeding from a dozen wounds, stood back to back, circling warily, striving mightily to keep their points raised as they awaited the next onslaught.

Amazingly, none came. The remaining Bhuteau had stepped back and lowered their weapons. Wondering, I thought that it might be because of the death of their leader, but none paid any attention to the corpse at my feet. Instead, all eyes were registering over my shoulder. Chilled with foreboding, I turned to see for myself.

Bhuteau soldiers were everywhere, dozens of them, closing in from the darkness on all sides. I felt my heart sink like a stone, but made ready nonetheless. It's been said that a Smithers doesn't know when he's been beaten.

Onward the soldiers came, looking damned efficient in their helmets and breast plates, too. Some carried lances, others were armed with bows; all looked grim as the very devil.

I moved to be nearer Charula, ready to defend her to my last breath. It was the British thing to do.

With this thought in mind, I looked toward her, I think to capture her face in my memory, and it was here, at this most inopportune of moments, that I was gifted with the 'sight'.

Charula Khaur was looking at me as well, but hers wasn't the face that I saw.

It was Loiyan's face, I swear it. Her beautiful smile, the laughter in her eyes...the love, and in a flash, I wondered how I could ever have mistaken this other girl for her.

I told her, "I'll be with you soon," but her expression never changed, but faded. Seconds later she was gone, leaving me facing the woman who I had done everything in my power to rescue.

I don't know what she saw, but she looked at me with...was it sadness? ... yes, but no. Perhaps it was confusion, or both. When she looked from me to Austen, and then back again, I knew.

Meanwhile the Bhuteau had closed until we were hemmed into a tight circle. I hefted my sabre, and waited; although I must

341

confess that, after what had just taken place, my interest was not what it should have been.

Then an order was snapped and the Bhuteau advance was suddenly arrested. I suppose I must have blinked stupidly at them.

Then one man came forward from the others. By the richness of his clothing, I judged him to be a man of substance. He snapped another command, this one at our erstwhile assailants, and I gaped more foolishly than ever when they dropped their weapons, and were immediately taken under guard.

Our apparent saviour stopped in front of me with his sword still sheathed. Reaching up, he tugged off his helmet and stuck it under his arm, the horsehair plume draping loosely in the still air.

He was an imposing figure. Tall as the rest of his countrymen, he was strongly built, with a face that was roguishly handsome, augmented by a patch over one eye. It struck me that I knew that face, and remembered seeing him sitting at the *Durbhar*, but couldn't remember his name for the life of me.

Calmly, he gestured to our opponents, and said in fairly good English, "They will be sent to the Chinese border, and never see Poonakha again. No tongues will be left to wag about what has happened this night." He gave a slight gesture, "Of course my own people are all chosen men."

"Of course," I replied, without any idea why.

He added, "This entire affair has been most unfortunate," and again I agreed, wondering which particular affair he was referring to. He gestured to Sangay's body at our feet: "It will be put about that the Jungpen had a tragic accident while out for a ride."

I said, "Oh?" and then feeling that something more was required, appended that with, "Good."

He nodded solemnly, then looked up at the stars, as if perceiving in them his next utterance. "There will be war."

I replied, "Yes, I think so," feeling that I was on firmer ground now.

"I would have prevented it if I could, but the Penlo is too strong."

"So I see."

"All he thinks about are his *duars*." He spat derisively, "If he were to get them, the old ways would begin anew. He thinks that he can control you English, but he is wrong."

"Yes, he is."

He looked back up at the stars. "What must you think of us?" When I failed to answer, he allowed a sad smile to crease his lips. "As bad as all that?" Then he laughed, a deep resonance in his chest. "It is no matter. Today the Penlo's star is high, but it will not always remain so. Poonakha and Calcutta will have their war, but then life will continue."

"For those who survive."

He looked solemn for a moment. "Indeed." Then he looked at me again, and I thought I saw pleading in his eyes. "But perhaps then you will see that there are those of us in Bhutan who love our country, and only wish to live in peace with our neighbours."

"I'd like to believe that."

He responded with the fierce force of conviction: "Believe it, Mr. Smithers!" Then he laughed again, and replaced his helmet, signalling that our meeting was at an end. "In the meantime, when you return to Calcutta, you may tell Sir John Lawrence that he has a friend in Poonakha." He turned to go, but then stopped to consider. "And you, as well, Mr. Smithers, you and your friends can thank the good offices of Joom Kulling for your lives!"

He gave me a meaningful stare. It was a name I was intended to remember. I nodded that I understood, and with that he was gone, disappearing into the night like a shadow into darkness, while his men set about clearing the dead, erasing all sights and memories of a night that had never been.

Unhindered, I gathered up our motley crew and, slowly, taking turns carrying Mir Jafar, we managed to limp our way back to camp.

***

I dreamed of Loiyan.

343

It was one of those nonsensical things. There was no rhyme nor reason to any of it, just a senseless pattern that one forgets as soon as he awakes…and interwoven through it all were vignettes of her face, her smile and, God help me, even her smell, and all of it so vivid that it might have been yesterday, and not years, since I last experienced any of these things. Although I can't remember what was said, I know that she spoke to me, joyful as always, and so utterly unfettered that, once again, I found it difficult to believe that I had ever mistaken Charula Khaur for her. Loiyan had a softness about her, a *kindness* I suppose, in a way that this girl could never quite equal. Even there in my dream I wondered how it was that I could have forgotten such things – how I could allow the very essence of her to slip away.

There was one part that I did remember afterward: her face sadly smiling, as she looked up at me and said, "This is a small matter, Chah-lee, but in this world you must taste all that life can give you…but above all, my love, you must *live!*"

And the next thing I knew I was coming to with this vast feeling of loss renewed, a thundering headache, and a stinging sensation in the sole of my foot from where Simpson had driven a pin in the hope of reviving me.

He lost no time in practicing his usual bedside manner, either. My eyes couldn't have much more than fluttered open than he was damning me, in no uncertain terms, for being the most purblind fool that ever was, and angrily demanding to know why I had not sought him out the moment I returned to camp. I had suffered a concussion, sure as blazes, and if it killed me, I shouldn't come crying to *him*, etcetera, etcetera.

It was around this point that his voice became nothing more than an irritation in the background, for my eyes had begun to focus, and I saw Charula Khaur kneeling beside the cot, her face filled with concern, and for the first time I was aware of the cool wet cloth she was holding to my brow.

I interrupted the doctor's tirade, with a voice reduced to a whisper, "But what are you doing here? You've been hurt!"

Simpson wasn't about to allow himself to be thwarted by something so trivial as a private conversation. "She'll live," he

344

said, "a few cuts and bruises, but nothing broken," and continued to tear into me without further pause.

Finally, after he had delivered one last withering broadside for form's sake, he'd packed up his bag and stormed out of the tent to see to Mir Jafar (who, I was relieved to hear, was expected to recover).

The silence was unnaturally loud after he was gone. Charula busied herself by draping a blanket over my knees as though I was the sorriest of invalids. I noticed that, although her movements were brusque, an occasional wince of pain would crease her brow. I protested that such lavish attention was unnecessary, but she wouldn't hear of it, and kept on as if it was the entire point of her existence. Finally I grasped her wrist as gently as I could, wincing only slightly from the throbbing in my skull.

"Charula, look at me."

I had to insist before she complied. Her expression was torn. One instant a deep yearning seemed to possess her, and she would look at me with such intensity that it quite pulled at my heartstrings, but the next a veil would seem to fall over her, and her gaze would slowly slide from my face like a tear down a cheek, to settle upon some object on the floor. Finally, when she realized that escape was no longer possible, she seemed to gather strength, and suddenly she laughed, although it was a sound that carried no mirth.

"At least now I know her name," she said with a touch of bitterness I hadn't heard before, "this other woman of yours." Failing to reply, she mistook my shock for inquiry, and explained, "You spoke of her many times in your sleep," then to erase all doubt she added, "this Loiyan." Here the veil fell once again, and she looked away, her shoulders sagging so abruptly, so completely, that it left an image of utter despair.

As tenderly as I was able I began, "Charula, I..."

But she interrupted. "I knew," she whispered, as if speaking more to herself than to me. "I knew as soon as I heard her name on your lips that there was no use," and here her eyes were so beseeching that I felt them pierce through me. "Oh Bahadur! I had such hopes that you could..." and then she

345

abruptly turned away again, and whispered so softly that I could scarcely hear, and in truth I couldn't say that she intended me to, "love me…"

I fear I was just as quiet when I said, "I can't." But the words were so inadequate. "I'm sorry."

Perhaps it was my pity that braced her, for she suddenly squared her shoulders and, wiping her eyes, asked simply, "This woman, does she still live?"

Once more I felt the old pang, just as I had so many other times before. It felt like a betrayal, but nonetheless I forced myself to say, "No."

Some might have taken this as a sign of hope, a sign that life was meant for the living, but Charula merely bowed her head in surrender, her long black tresses concealing her face.

"I cannot fight a ghost."

There was nothing I could think of to say in reply, but the silence lasted only an instant before she looked up at me again. Her cheeks were streaked with tears, but though her mouth was trembling, she managed a smile.

"But I shall always have my memories."

I returned her smile, resisting the urge to caress her hair. I would have memories of my own.

There remained much more to say; however it appeared that neither of us knew how. In any event, just then there came an interruption in the form of a polite cough just outside the entrance. We had just enough time to rearrange our features into innocent masks, when the tent flap was brushed aside, and Austen stuck his head through the opening. Quickly, he glanced at Charula, and could not help but see, in spite of her smile, how red and swollen were her eyes. Concerned, he looked at me, and asked, "Have I come at a bad time?"

Poor Austen, acting had never been his forte. But as much as I wanted to be alone with Charula, I couldn't bring myself to resent his presence.

"Not at all," I lied. "Come in."

I noticed that he was wearing a clean uniform, and I must admit that it, along with the bandage wrapped around his head, made him look rather dashing. He entered carrying his helmet under his arm. He took another glance at Charula, and then at me, and then back to Charula again. Although the night was cool, his face was flushed as though it was unpleasantly warm.

"I just happened to be close by," he explained, a little too brightly, "and thought I'd stop in to see how you were feeling." I fancy that his smile was genuine, but his eyes were still concerned, darting from Charula to myself, fit to beat the band.

We engaged in small talk for a while, although without making any mention of the previous evening's exercise. I discovered later that this was because he was afraid that he might inadvertently cause Charula to relive the traumatic experience all over again. During that time his eyes came to rest on her more and more. She scarcely returned his attention at all, her mind being otherwise occupied, although she managed a smile whenever she was addressed, but spoke very little in return.

The conversation began to drag, and I could see the misery stamped on the poor fellow's face as plain as day. Eventually, more subdued now, he made his excuses and was preparing to leave, when I was struck by an impulse, and in all honesty couldn't say that it wasn't the 'sight' working its wiles once more.

"Perhaps you would be good enough to escort the lady back to her lodgings," I suggested, sounding more formal than I'd intended.

Both blinked with surprise. I believe that Charula may even have gasped. Then Austen came very close to attention, not even attempting to disguise his pleasure.

"I would be honoured!" he said, suddenly beaming.

Charula frowned, her inflection filled with a different meaning that even Austen must have heard. "But *Bahadur*, the doctor said that I must attend you!"

"Fiddlesticks!" I said, more jauntily than I felt. "I'm as right as rain!" Charula's frown deepened, so I added, "But if it will make you feel better," I turned to Austen, "perhaps you would be good enough to send word for Simson to come visit after he's made his rounds?"

Charula stared at me long and hard, and then, although her eyes were fixed on me, they seemed to turn inward.

Finally, "You are right," and with words heavy with double meaning, she continued, "The hour has grown late, and I am more tired than I had thought." So saying, she rose abruptly, fastened me with one last look, then, with great dignity, turned and left my tent, Austen following, his smile equal parts happy and confused.

If you think that I was cold-hearted you would be wrong. A Smithers may be as human as the next man, but at the end of the day he usually knows what's right. It had taken all of the self-control that I possessed to let her go. My heart felt heavier than it had in a very long time, and I can't say that it didn't break just a little, neither, but right or wrong, the truth of it was that I wasn't ready to give what she most desired. Nor could I say with any certainty that I ever could.

My conversation with Simpson, all those weeks earlier, still echoed in my mind. By ignoring his advice, I had accepted responsibility for my own actions, regardless of the reasons I had pursued them. She wasn't Loiyan, I knew that now, and realized that I must have been more out of my mind than in it, to think that she ever could have been. I couldn't answer as to whether that was healthy of me or not: to continue to look for my beloved in every face that I saw, behind every veil, in every pair of eyes, yearning for the sound of her laughter; but such was my reality, and I had just enough sense to see that, sooner rather than later, it could only make Charula Khaur unhappy.

Moments after, my thoughts were interrupted when Simpson returned with a deck of cards. I don't recall what we played, but it served to while away the evening. I lost more than usual, though, my mind being elsewhere.

Epilogue

The three of us, the Cheeboo, Simpson and I, stood on a small hillock, just outside of Darjeeling. Below, the main road to Dhalimcote meandered to the horizon. A light rain had set in, patting the junipers overhead, forcing Simpson and myself to huddle close to the Cheeboo, who had been the only one with enough wit to think of bringing his umbrella.

A few yards further up the hill, India's new Governor General, Sir John Lawrence, stood beneath a canopy, with that merry bewhiskered old nemesis, Ram Singh, standing attendance at his elbow. Officials and dignitaries were also in attendance, including my master, Lord Brampton, and Amrita Pirāli, who had a genteel hand placed upon my lord's arm. All were focused on the procession below.

Resplendent in their scarlet tunics and pith helmets, the 80th swung along the road in game fashion. The regimental band was thumping away at 'Garryowen', and I could see the confidence in their step as they marched off to war. For after all the diplomacy had finally run itself dry, what everyone had foretold had come to pass.

In truth, it had begun several weeks earlier when two brigades had marched in to occupy the *duars* along the Bengal frontier, but had come marching back quite a bit faster. Joom Kulling had been right after all. When push came to shove, Johnny Bhuteau had proven that he could put aside his differences, and unite against the common foe, and that he could fight. The result was that our generals had been sacked, and reinforcements brought up. Now they were going in again, this time to stay.

Simpson barked. "Better them than me, poor devils!"

The Cheeboo was shocked to the point where he almost frowned. "Oh no, Dr. Simpson! Surely you cannot mean such a thing!"

For once Simpson declined to egg him on. "Ne'er mind, Chee. It's just an Englishman's way of wishing them luck."

While the Cheeboo pondered this in silence, I watched as the vanguard disappeared over a rise to be replaced by a battery

349

of artillery jingling along at the trot, with their Armstrong guns and caissons jouncing behind. Out on the wings, in their dark blue forage jackets and striped *pugharees*, a squadron of cavalry covered the ground at a canter, all businesslike, guarding the flanks of the column by the book. I thought it strange that they were going to fight in places that we had already been.

I had only to close my eyes to see that wonderful alpine country: the lush valleys, snow-filled passes, and raging mountain streams...and the simple folk who had greeted us with so much generosity along the way. Thoughts of it all scarred by the ravages of war tried to intrude, but I pushed them to the back of my mind. No one could say we hadn't tried.

It had been a farce from the beginning, of course, but the effort had to be made for form's sake, and in spite of everything, had come painfully close to succeeding. In the end, it was one man's obstinacy...one man's *greed*, that had killed the initiative. The Tongso Penlo had believed that the Raj didn't intend to fight. It was a fatal error.

Eden had been summoned to the *Durbhar* the day following our episode at Poonakha Castle, and invited to sign the most extraordinary document you ever heard of.

It turned out that the Bhuteau had re-drawn the treaty, if you please, this time with the inclusion of the Assam *Duars*. Eden, of course, replied that he hadn't the authority, and was much abused for his trouble. The Penlo was resolved to have his mountain passes and nothing less.

There followed much to-ing and fro-ing over the next few days. Tantrums were thrown; threats were made and recanted, only to be made over again within the hour. Finally the situation became so intense that Eden was virtually *forced* to sign, and that had been that. It was interesting, however, that, over the course of all the accusations and heated discussion, nothing was mentioned of Lord Sangay's absence, nor was even one word spoken about our rescue of Charula Khaur. It appeared that Joom Kulling had kept his promise.

We left Poonakha a few days later, arriving at Paro on the thirty-first of March, 1864. The Penlo, that old worthy, once again proved a staunch friend and ally, and I began to feel that

350

the ordeal was finally coming to an end. Indeed, we arrived at Darjeeling less than two weeks later, after a relatively uneventful journey.

Throughout all that time, Charula Khaur honoured my wishes, maintaining her distance, while her nocturnal visits became a thing of the past. Once or twice, when his duty allowed, I spied Austen walking alongside her, leading his horse by the bridle – Charula maintaining a distant silence, and Austen seemingly content just to be near her. What others thought of the dashing young captain paying such close attention to what appeared to be a common coolie no one said, but we were homeward bound now, and spirits were on the rise. Simpson and the Cheeboo tended to visit me more often, but they, too, kept their thoughts to themselves.

For myself, I wished them both good fortune. Austen's future lay in India, and whereas a native wife might curtail many military careers, I had my doubts that the son of a nobleman, with a world of influence at his command, would allow such petty prejudice to stand in his way.

Upon arriving in Darjeeling, I was met by none other than Lord Brampton himself, with Madam Pirâli at his side, looking as beautiful as ever, and spreading the sunshine of her presence in a way that had my lord grimacing more shockingly than ever, as his frequent attempts at smiling seemed not to have gained much ground.

The reunion with my master was most gratifying, I must say. He greeted me like the proverbial son, and plied me with questions about my adventure, while insisting on my joining him in a toast to its conclusion. Although he claimed that the reason for their coming was to partake of the beneficial air, it was Amrita who confirmed otherwise.

"Lord Brampton has missed you, Charlie," she told me when we were alone together. "Indeed, he has been quite anxious for your safety ever since you left."

"It's good of you to say so, ma'am."

"Not a bit of it!" she scoffed. "He dragged me away from Calcutta in order that we might be here to greet you upon your return!" She didn't smile, but her eyes were a-twinkle when she

351

added, "Not only that, but he had the temerity to insist on using my supposed frail femininity as an excuse to come!"

We regarded one another. The period of my absence seemed to have changed her; she had grown more...*comfortable*, I suppose. This was confirmed with her very next breath.

"But all that is by the by," she said airily extending her hand, and I wondered if she desired that I kiss it. When I didn't catch on, she twiddled her fingers and frowned, "You must congratulate me, Charlie!" and then I saw what must have been the world's biggest diamond on her finger, barring only the fabled *Koh-I-Noor*. So I ended up with my lips covering her knuckles after all.

"My very warmest congratulations, ma'am!"

"Thank you," she said, admiring her splayed fingers for a moment. Still looking at the diamond, she continued, "Lord Brampton has made me very happy, and it is my most ardent intention to return the favour."

"You already have, ma'am."

She regarded me quite seriously. "Thank you, Charlie," and just for the moment the nervous young girl returned. "You do believe me, don't you?"

I thought that my reply called for solemn formality. "Indeed I do, madam."

Her relief was evident. In one quick exhalation she said, "Charlie, I do want us to become good friends!"

I smiled, "We will, ma'am, I'm sure of it."

Since then the better part of a year had come and gone, and my premonition held true. A more devoted friend to my lord (or, for that matter, myself) I could not hope to find. Amrita Pirāli continued to shed her radiance upon us lesser folk until she was admired by one and all. Even some of the more backbiting wives from the garrison, who were more prone to gossip than most, and had nothing good to say about anyone (including the Governor General), could find little fault in my mistress, the colour of her skin notwithstanding. Amidst much celebration, she and my lord were married in St. Andrews in mid-October. A few weeks later war was declared, and the world once again became a serious place.

Ever since the mission's return to British territory, there was never any doubt as to what the result would be, and the buildup of troops had begun shortly after the government received Mr. Eden's report in July. Finding themselves without a written agreement, an unprotected border, and a diplomat who had been much abused in the bargain, the government had no other option. An assault on two fronts, from Bengal and Assam, was subsequently launched, and as had been my experience with the Bhuteau, once they realized they were faced with a stalwart adversary, they had melted away without any serious conflict. The *duars* had been occupied, and victory declared…but, alas, prematurely.

Whether it was the Tongso Penlo's doing, or his Hindustani adviser, General Singh, the populace of Bhutan was soon mobilized against the invader. Our people, caught unaware, and vastly outnumbered, saw that their positions were untenable and, deciding that discretion was the better part of valour, chose to retreat. But today they were going in again, with more men, greater determination, and a newfound respect for their adversary. As I said earlier, this time they were going in to stay. In the diplomatic wrangling that was sure to follow, I had little doubt that Joom Kulling's name would figure largely, and that he would profit by it in the bargain.

The 11th Rajputs were marching past now, looking smart in their blue turbans and red jackets, when I saw the Governor General turn his head slightly, and Ram Singh lean attentively forward. A moment later Ram detached himself from The Presence, and came walking down the slope to where the three of us were huddled beneath the remains of the Cheeboo's well-travelled and tattered umbrella.

"This is very interesting," said the Cheeboo. "Whatever could it mean?"

Bark! "Well I'll lay odds he's not coming to see you or me, Chee!" Simpson gave his head a twitch in my general direction, "I'll warrant it's our young *beau sabreur* he'll want!"

I dismissed this as just more of the doctor's usual nonsense, but this time his assumption proved correct.

Ram Singh came to a stop in front of our happy trio, his own umbrella significantly more pristine than the Cheeboo's. He nodded a perfunctory greeting to the doctor, for this was the first time we'd had a chance to meet again since Calcutta, as the GG's party had arrived only the previous day. He offered his hand to the Cheeboo. "I have not had the opportunity to thank you, sir, for the services you have rendered on behalf of my country. Please allow me to do so now."

The Cheeboo hesitated, but then accepted his hand. "On behalf of your country and my own," he said, "I only wish that my poor services had been more fruitful."

"Indeed," Ram grimly replied, "war is an unfortunate business."

Bark! "To hear you two talk, you'd think this was the Great Mutiny all over again!" scoffed the doctor. "Call this a war? Just a duel of manoeuvres is all!"

The old Sikh turned a weary eye his way. "And yet the Bhuteau forced us to retreat, Doctor."

"Aye, they did that," Simpson allowed, "and a disgraceful bit of blundering it was, too. Mulcaster lost our guns running from Dewangiri through sheer ignorance, without a single set-piece battle having been fought along the way!"

"And thank heaven for it. Our forces were heavily outnumbered," Ram reminded him. "General Mulcaster took the best course of action not to fight."

To which the doctor retorted, "Aye, and Johnny Bhuteau chose the best course of action not to fight when we first went in, because he knows that, given anywhere close to equal numbers, we'd have the measure of him!"

Then Simpson voiced everyone's fears when he said, "The question is, now that our numbers are closer to being equal, will the Bhuteau make a stand?" And then he ventured to answer the question himself: "I'll wager that he won't!"

As it turned out, he was both right, and wrong. In the weeks to come, for the most part the Bhuteau chose to withdraw from the field rather than come to grips. On the few occasions when they didn't withdraw, the superiority of our arms and discipline came into play, and they were swept away with little

354

difficulty. Faced with the inevitable, the Tongso Penlo sued for peace, and the war was effectively over.

"I pray you are right, Doctor," Ram replied, and before Simpson could get in another word, he turned to me.

"Sir John would like a word, if you please, Charlie."

Well you don't often say no to the Viceroy of all India, and Ram's umbrella offered greater shelter from the elements than the Cheeboo's besides, so I didn't hesitate to comply.

"And I would like a word also, my friend," Ram said when we were alone. He linked a companionable arm through mine, and we sauntered along as if we were the best of chums. I'm not sure if we ever were though, really. He was the finest chap to while away the hours and to raise a glass with, but beneath his jovial face full of whiskers, he was a crafty old beggar, who had been the mastermind behind my traipsing off with Eden in the first place, and I didn't trust him above half.

Ram produced his pocket flask, and used it to indicate the cluster of gentry beneath the canopy. "It would appear that I was wrong about our new Lady Brampton," he admitted with a disarming smile. "My wife's third cousin's number two son had nothing suspicious to report while you were gone. On the contrary, he said that the lady behaved quite the way a woman who has been smitten might be expected to behave." Raising the flask he said, "To the happy couple!" and took a hearty mouthful before offering it to me.

I partook somewhat more modestly, and said, "So you admit that people can be exactly as they seem?"

He considered the question before angling his head noncommittally to the left, and then back to the right. "Perhaps," he allowed, although he managed to say it in such a way as to discourage me from believing that he actually meant it, "but my experience has taught me to expect otherwise. Let us just say that I found the lady to be the exception to the rule." Offhand, he added, "She certainly has made a difference to your master."

"Aye," I agreed, "I've never seen him so happy."

He regarded me from the corner of his eye, "I would imagine that makes life simpler for you, hey?"

I observed him suspiciously. "So what if it does?"

He threw his head back and laughed, great gales straight from the belly, and I could hear the drops patting on my homburg as the umbrella momentarily swayed out of control. "Now who is seeing ghosts behind every shadow, Charlie!"

I would have retorted, but we had neared the canopy where the toffs were waving their toppers majestically to the passing troops. We were now in the domain where it was best not to speak unless spoken to.

However, one last item did occur to me, so I whispered, "A favour."

His face was a congenial mask as he studied me. "If I can."

"Before I took my leave of Lord Elgin, he spoke of my journey through Africa. I haven't mentioned that time to a soul since I returned to England, so I'm curious as to who informed him."

"Ah yes!" He smiled at the memory. Ram had been fond of Elgin, but then they were two of a kind: crafty as foxes the both of 'em. He studied me for a moment, then made up his mind. "I suppose that it is no matter now," he said with a half-smile. "You are hardly likely to blab it about the country." When I didn't reply, he shrugged and said, "Very well. Perhaps you remember visiting the Pasha during your stay in Khartoum?"

"Of course," but then I stopped and stared at him. "Do you mean to tell me that that decent old geezer was…"

"No one so exalted, I'm afraid. Perhaps you remember his personal physician?"

I had to close my eyes to recall, because at the time, I was usually raving with delirium, unsure of what was, or wasn't, real.

"A short little cherub of a fellow," I ventured, "with a kindly face and spectacles?"

Ram nodded, "As accurate a description of Sa'id as any, I suppose." He looked at me with some meaning, "His full name is Mohamed Sa'id Smith, a product of an alliance between his Egyptian mother and a certain RSM Bertram Smith, a member of His Britannic Majesty's Expeditionary Force during the Napoleon's campaign in the Middle East."

I felt my eyes widen, "You mean…"

356

"Occasionally Sa'id's reports include items that are considered newsworthy: for instance the appearance of a lone Englishman in a canoe, evidently having approached Khartoum from upriver on the Nile. He said that this poor unfortunate was more dead than alive, riddled with malaria, and dysentery – raving about Maasai warriors, Arab slavers, and the existence of a vast lake on the African interior."

In a voice not much more than a whisper I replied, "*Ukerewe.*"

"Yes, I believe you are correct. A full year before John Speke was able to confirm it, in fact."

"You already *knew?*" Somewhere in the conversation both of us had dropped the pretense of not knowing that Ram Singh was privy to the most sensitive information throughout the Empire.

"It was thought best not to make mention of it," he explained. "The notoriety you would receive was contrary to the interests of…certain circles."

"A man of his hands," I recited from my conversation with Elgin, the better part of a year earlier, "capable of living in rough country."

"Precisely so, Charlie. A person of that nature quite naturally draws the attention of those dedicated to service to the Empire."

I stopped, stock still, unaware that Ram Singh had continued on a few paces before turning, and that I no longer enjoyed the presence of his umbrella.

"How long had you been planning this?" I demanded.

Unabashed, Ram replied, "When our people in England sent us the sailing manifest for the *Carnatic* the day it steamed out of Newcastle. Nothing specific, but we thought that you might come in useful. However, when it was decided to send Mr. Eden to Poonakha, your name was at the top of the list."

I hadn't properly absorbed this information before I very nearly exploded, "Well I wasn't much bloody help though, was I!"

Several heads turned. One with a monocle looked me up and down suspiciously, as if I had just come unstuck from the

357

bottom of his shoe. Amrita offered me a quizzical smile, while Lord Brampton, quite properly, frowned his disapproval. Ram Singh was about to reply, but Sir Lawrence prevented it when he turned and saw me. Affably he said, "Ah! So this is the man, is he?"

Ram's flask disappeared as if by magic, as he gravely replied, "It is, Sir John."

The Viceroy smiled, and beckoned me closer, "Well, let's have a look at him!"

I approached with some hesitation, for although I had become used to being in the midst of the great and powerful as my master's servant, I had yet to become conditioned to being seen by them, let alone under their scrutiny. However, I couldn't help studying Sir John in turn. Tall and thin for starters, his face was serious and clean-shaven, but for a wealth of side-whiskers running down to his jaw. It was also weathered to a dark bronze – a sure sign of an old India hand.

Below, a squadron of lancers trotted past. Behind them the road was empty. This wing of our renewed invasion was at last underway. I wished them a silent Godspeed.

Sir John heaved a sigh, "Well that's that, then," and ushered me aside with a word to Ram Singh, "Lend us your umbrella, will you?" I hurried to accept it from him, and held it over both our heads as he led me out from under the canopy, while I wondered what on earth this could entail.

He opened by saying, "Official functions are necessary, I suppose, and the lads seem to enjoy it, but they can be the most confounded nuisance at times." Once we were safely out of earshot from those remaining under the canopy, he continued, "I wanted to speak with you in private, but I understand Lord Brampton will be returning to England soon, and I might not get the chance." I confirmed that we were indeed leaving that very afternoon, and he nodded and said, "Quite so," before adding, "I couldn't help but overhear the last part of your conversation with my servant."

I managed to stammer, "Terribly sorry, sir. It won't happen again."

He waved this away with an impatient "tacht!" that sounded so much like my mother. "What I mean is that I believe that I can guess what prompted you to say such a thing, and I can assure you that you're quite wrong. From what I've been told you provided an exemplary service. Why," he continued, looking serious as all bedamned, "not only that, you saved one of Her Majesty's subjects from a life worse than death."

I recalled lunging for the Tranter that day when the coolies were flogged, and any number of other follies I'd very nearly committed, only to be saved from myself through the good offices of my friends, and replied, "Hardly exemplary, sir."

Sir John didn't reply directly, but it was as though he was reading my mind. "Eden filed a complaint against you, did you know?"

"No, sir, but I can't say that I'm surprised."

"Indeed!" he barked a gruff laugh that sounded ever so much like the doctor. "Well, I told him to go to blazes, and then I told him that your set-to that night in the Poonakha *Dzong* was the only episode during the entire mission that redeemed at least a shred of British honour!" Then he hurried on to say, "Mustn't mention it, of course. Can't be going around telling everyone that one of our Specials damn near started a war before our fellows in the diplomatic could make a proper balls up of things. Officially it never happened."

To this I wholeheartedly agreed. The less said about that night the better but, mystified, I told him, "Sir, I did not act alone," but was ignored.

Instead he offered me a sidelong glance, and damned if he didn't wink! "Not to worry, though, a word will be whispered in the proper ear."

Still none the wiser, I managed to stammer, "I'm afraid that I don't understand, sir."

He gave me a knowing look and grinned. "Come now, Charlie, admit it! This sort of work agrees with you, doesn't it?"

Well, I was surprised at that, I don't mind telling you, as well as feeling proper stung! As stiffly as I was able, I retorted, "Sir, when he has to, a Smithers can hold his own as well as the next man, but that's not to say that he goes looking for trouble. I was only doing my duty."

I thought that he might be angered by such a heated response, but instead he nodded triumphantly, and said, "My point exactly. You're the perfect man for the job."

I was so astounded that I forgot to mention his honorific. "Job! *What* job?"

Sir John placed a hand on my arm and admonished, "I must caution you to lower your voice, Charlie! We don't need the entire world knowing, now do we?"

We both looked around as surreptitiously as possible. Several pairs of eyes were upon us, curious that a servant should be speaking in private with the most powerful man in India. Lord Brampton looked on indulgently, and perhaps even with a certain amount of pride. I wondered who had been talking to him, and what had been said?

Only slightly quelled, I hissed, "To blazes with what the whole world knows! It's what I *don't* know that worries me! Now, Sir John, perhaps you'd be good enough to explain?"

Irritatingly enough, in answer to my question, Sir John asked another. "Do you believe in the Empire, Charlie?"

It was difficult to answer that without a snort of derision, so I gave him one. "Of course I do! I'm British, aren't I?"

He nodded soberly, "Yes, but do you believe in what we're trying to accomplish?"

More carefully, I replied, "I've seen enough greed and folly to last me a lifetime, but, at bottom, I believe that we try to do what's best."

"And all this," he gestured to where the disappearing column was marching off to war, "what do you think of it? I won't ask about folly, because we both know there's been an abundance of that, but what about greed?"

Puzzled, I replied, "Nothing like that, sir. It seems to me that we bent over backwards trying to do what's right. All we stand to gain are the mountain passes, so we can be left to live in peace."

He seemed pleased. "Precisely so." Then he got down to it, "Look here, Smithers, HMG wants you to continue on."

I stared at him as if he'd just said something lewd. "You must be mad!"

The corners of his eyes crinkled, which was the equivalent to peels of laughter from anyone else. "Hardly that, I think. The world's a nasty place, Charlie, and we control a great deal of it. If we're to make a difference for the better, we're going to need people like you." Then he said something that sounded amazingly close to what my guv'nor had told me when I was just a lad. "Most of what needs doing will have to be done in secret, so there'll be precious little glory in it for you, and I don't believe that the pay is very generous, but," and here he looked me full in the face, "all we ask is that you do your duty."

I was stung, you may be sure, and retorted, "Sir, my duty is at my Lord Brampton's side!"

For the first time during our conversation he looked genuinely surprised. After taking a moment to collect himself, he seemed about to say something more, but the obstinate set of my chin must have caused him to reconsider. Instead he gave a little shrug, and ended with, "To be sure, it was just a thought," and offered me his hand. I took it, and gave it a cautious shake. "I wish you a pleasant voyage."

Taking this as a dismissal, I turned to go, but he called me back. "There is one other thing."

"Oh?" I replied, "And what might that be, sir?"

"We have evidence that Lord Sanjay had been plotting to descend upon our mission, and murder everyone in it. So you see, Charlie, your contribution was invaluable, and for that you have the thanks of Her Majesty's Government."

I stared at him hard, looking for the lie, but couldn't see it. Besides, it fit. That cold-hearted bastard was more than capable of the deed.

"Well that was fortunate then, wasn't it, sir?"

"Indeed," he said. "Goodbye."

The gathering under the canopy was breaking up when I turned away, deep in thought. Simpson and the Cheeboo had already decamped ahead of me, and Lord Brampton was escorting his wife to where our brougham awaited to the rear, in the partial shelter of some trees. I was hastening to precede them, when I chanced to look upon the road one last time, and saw that it was no longer empty.

An officer, resplendent in his scarlet coat and blancoed helmet, sat astride a magnificent roan that I knew to be Austen's. He was leaning from the saddle, speaking to a native lady standing at his stirrup. I would have recognized her at any distance.

Austen was leaving with the column. As part of the headquarters staff, he no doubt had been delayed tying up loose ends. Now he was saying his farewells. Even as I watched, transfixed, he leaned even lower, and circled Charula's waist with his arm, and pulled her to his lips.

Embarrassed, I looked away as quickly as I was able…only to be drawn back to the scene again. The kiss was long and lingering, with both of Charula's arms encircling Austen's neck. Had there been any other witnesses, it would no doubt have been deemed as an unseemly display of affection, but there was only myself, and though I felt a tremendous pang of yearning, it was intermingled with a curious sort of contentment.

At last the moment passed, and Austen touched his peak to her before cantering off to catch up with his comrades. Charula watched him go until he was lost over the rise. Then she turned and began to climb the gentle slope of the hill, an open parasol over her shoulder. It was here that she chanced to look up, and saw me looking down at her. Although the distance was still considerable, she stopped dead in her tracks.

She couldn't see my smile, nor what I hoped were raindrops streaming down my face, but she raised a solemn hand in silent recognition all the same.

"Coming, Smithers?" Lord Brampton's voice cut across my thoughts like dawn's first light upon a dream. "We must make all haste to get Lady Brampton out of this interminable weather!" At the same time I could hear Amrita protesting that she was not made of paper, and that she would come to no harm from a small bit of rain.

I continued to stare down the slope at the little figure, still standing, awaiting my response. What had she said? We would always have our memories – yes, that was it.

I raised my own hand, "Coming, My lord!" and turned away.

At last we were going home.

The End

Afterword

Through the course of researching this book, one question continued to play over and over in my mind: why did the Bhuteau behave as they did toward the British mission? After all, Britain was by far and away the preeminent power in the region, with a reputation for not thinking twice about annexing entire countries, rightly or wrongly deserved (I suspect that it was a bit of both), so you'd think that Bhutan would have been the quietest, most peaceful of neighbours, and done their level best to keep under the Raj's radar, but they didn't even try. Throw in the fact that they had no national army to speak of, but only various bands of men-at-arms owing their allegiance to whichever Nieboo, Jungpen, or Penlo they happened to be serving under, with little or no sense of discipline, and *absolutely* no modern weapons; had I been the Deb Rajah at the time, I would have been bending over backwards to make certain that Eden's journey was as comfy as could be. No, forget that, *I* would have been the one hot-footing it all the way to Calcutta, and not t'other way around, bringing captives and concessions in humble hand, and hoping against hope that Lord Elgin would decide that I was basically a harmless fellow before sending me on my way. But that didn't happen either.

From what I came to understand, their belligerence could stem from only two things: patriotism or ignorance, or possibly both, and you might want to throw a bit of xenophobia in there, also. Even today Bhutan is largely a closed country, and that's not solely due to the natural barriers along its borders, either, but a desire to maintain a way of life that is unique in the world. Might it not be logical to speculate that the same set of ideals existed then as well?

There is an abundance of evidence to suggest that the culture of Bhutan was vastly different from any other that the British ever encountered, and that can only have come about by their desire to keep alien influence outside their borders. Even had Eden been wildly exaggerating, few things could have startled a very staid and proper English mind more than their first meeting with the Jungpen of Dhalimcote, which happened

364

as I recorded it, as did virtually every other similar instance in the book, including the insults offered to the British delegation in Poonakha.

As well as these occasions, several of the characters were real, too: Elgin and Lawrence are a matter of record, as well as Eden. But so too were Doctor Simpson and the Cheeboo Lama, along with Captains Austen and Lance (I would never have chosen the name 'Lance' for a fictitious character in a million years!), not to mention Eden's man, Power, and the commissariat sergeant, whose life Charlie saved at Dhalimcote, but as I said earlier in the Preface, their personalities were all my invention, some derived on a whim, while others by their actions. Here I am specifically referring to Eden.

I may have wronged the man, but I don't think that the evidence supports that. As Lord Auckland's son, Eden had every reason to be ambitious, as well as to believe himself to be infallible. Trying to live up to the family name, as well as gaining the respect of his esteemed father, may have been a driving force behind his pushing on to Poonakha when all evidence indicated that he was not welcome there. Several times along the way, there was ample reason to abandon the mission as, indeed, Colonel Durand, the Foreign Secretary, said as much in a letter to the Colonial Office: shortage of food, deserting bearers, and the belligerence of the Bhuteau nobility themselves, each with more than one occurrence, required a man with only the wildest of optimism to think that anything could be gained from continuing. It seems that Eden was such a man, as he appears to be the only one to be surprised when the mission failed.

Given this setting, war was virtually unavoidable: a limited invasion to take control of the Western Duars, as had been done previously on the Assam frontier; the public safety, as well as British prestige could hardly afford otherwise. It is to the credit of both sides that this was achieved without the horrendous loss of life that was typical of the time.

CW Lovatt

Bibliography

Henry, Yule and Burnell, A. C. *Hobson-Jobson: An Anglo Indian Dictionary.* Ware, Hertfordshire: Wordsworth Editions Limited, 2008.

Ricard, Matthieu. *Bhutan: The Land of Serenity.* London: Thames & Hudson Limited, 2008

MacGregor, Charles Metcalfe. *A Military Report on the Country of Bhutan, containing all the information of military importance which has been collected up to date, 12th July, 1866.* British Library, Historical Print Editions, 1873

Rennie, David Field. *Bhotan: and the Story of The Dooar War.* Varanasi, India: Pilgrims Publishing, 2009

Eden, Ashley. *Political Missions to Bootan.* Varanasi, India: Pilgrims Publishing, 2005

Wild, Antony.*Remains of the Raj: The British Legacy in India.* London: Harper Collins, 2001

Biography

CW Lovatt, is the award-winning author of numerous short stories, as well as the best-selling novel, *The Adventures of Charlie Smithers*, the critically acclaimed *Josiah Stubb: The Siege of Louisbourg*, and also co-author of *Wild Wolf's Twisted Tails* (pun very much intended). He lives in Canada, and is the self-appointed Writer-in-Residence of Carroll, Manitoba (population +/- 20). *Adventures in India* is the second book in the *Charlie Smithers* collection.

Lightning Source UK Ltd.
Milton Keynes UK
UKHW012007021222
413123UK00001B/19

9 781907 954417